THE GIRL IN ROOM 105

Get in touch with Chetan Bhagat and access content created by him here:

Instagram

X

Facebook

YouTube

Threads

LinkedIn

Spotify

Moj

Website

CHETAN BHAGAT

THE GIRL IN ROOM 105

an unlove story

HarperCollins *Publishers* India

First published in 2018

This edition published in India by HarperCollins *Publishers* 2022
HarperCollins *Publishers* India, Cyber City,
Building 10-A, Gurugram, Haryana – 122002, India
www.harpercollins.co.in

2 4 6 8 10 9 7 5 3 1

P-ISBN: 978-93-5629-096-9
E-ISBN: 978-93-5629-108-9

Printed and bound at
Nutech Print Services Pvt. Ltd.

FSC
www.fsc.org
MIX
Paper | Supporting responsible forestry
FSC® C195953

This book is printed on FSC® certified paper
which ensures responsible forest management.

*

HarperCollins *Publishers*, Macken House, 39/40 Mayor Street Upper, Dublin 1, D01 C9W8, Ireland

To those who never give up
And
To those who, like me, find it hard to unlove

Acknowledgements and A Note to Readers

Hi all,

Thank you!

In times of Instagram, Facebook and YouTube, you definitely deserve thanks for picking up a book, and especially for picking up my book!

No book is one person's effort alone. For this one, too, I have many to thank:

My readers, who continue to support and motivate me with their love. It keeps me going, makes me come out of my lows, and think up new stories to tell you.

Shinie Antony, my editor, friend, first reader of all my books—thanks for your invaluable help.

Those who gave valuable feedback on the manuscript. (Alphabetically) Aamir Jaipuri, Anusha Bhagat, Bhakti Bhat, Kushaan Parikh, Mansi Ishaan Shah, Michelle Shetty, Prateek Dhawan, Virali Panchamia and Zitin Dhawan—thank you for all your help and suggestions.

Mohit Suri, Vikrant Massey, Kashmira Irani, Sankalp Sadanah, Anshul Uppal and Siddharth Atha for their friendship and help in supporting the book.

The editors at HarperCollins India for all their efforts to make the book better.

To the entire marketing, sales and production teams at HarperCollins India for working so hard on the book.

To all the online delivery boys and girls who put the book in my readers' hands.

My critics. You help me improve and keep me humble. I am not perfect. Neither am I always right. I will work harder and get better. And those who don't always agree with me, I respect your opinions as well. All I would say is, our differences aside, let's work to make people read more. It's important.

My family—a pillar of support in my life. My mother Rekha Bhagat, my wife Anusha Bhagat, and children, Shyam and Ishaan. Thank you all for being there.

We celebrate love. But sometimes, we must unlove too.

With that, it's time to meet the girl in room 105.

Prologue

On board IndiGo flight 6E766 HYD-DEL

'Fasten your seatbelts, please. We are passing through turbulence,' the flight attendant announced.

Eyes shut, I fumbled to find the belt. I couldn't.

'Fasten your seatbelt, sir,' the flight attendant personally reminded me. She looked at me like I was one of those dumb passengers who couldn't follow simple instructions.

'Sorry, sorry,' I said. Where was the other end of my belt, anyway? My head hurt from a lack of sleep.

I had spent the whole day in Hyderabad at an education conference and was on the last midnight flight back to Delhi.

Damn, where the hell was my buckle?

'You are sitting on your belt,' the person next to me said.

'Oh, stupid me!' I said, finally clicking my belt shut. My eyes still refused to open.

'Tough flight, isn't it?' he said.

'Tell me about it,' I said. 'I need a coffee.'

'No service at the moment—because of the turbulence,' he said. 'Going for an event?'

'Returning from one,' I said, somewhat surprised. How did he know?

'Sorry, I saw your boarding pass. Chetan Bhagat. The author, right?'

'Right now a zombie.'

He laughed.

'Hi, I am Keshav Rajpurohit.'

An awkward side-by-side handshake followed.

We passed through angry clouds. They didn't like this hard metal object disturbing them. The aircraft rattled like a pebble in a tin. I clutched the armrests, a futile search for stability at thirty-eight thousand feet.

'Nasty, eh?' Keshav said.

I breathed deeply through my mouth and shook my head. Relax, it's going to be okay, I told myself.

'Isn't it amazing? We are in this big metal box floating in the sky. We have absolutely no control over the weather. A strong gust of wind could rip this plane apart,' he said in a calm voice.

'That's comforting, Keshav,' I said.

He laughed again.

Half an hour later, the weather had calmed down. The flight attendants resumed cabin service. I ordered two cups of coffee for myself.

'Would you like one, too?' I said.

'No coffee. Do you have plain milk?' he said to the flight attendant.

'No, sir. Just tea, coffee and soft drinks,' the flight attendant said.

Where did he think he was? A dairy farm? And how old was he? Twelve?

'Tea, then,' he said, 'with extra milk sachets.'

I gulped down my first cup of coffee. I felt like a phone with low battery that had finally met a charger. I rebooted, at least for a few minutes. I noticed the nightsky outside, the stars sprayed across it.

'You look better now,' Keshav commented.

I turned at an angle to look at him properly.

A handsome face with striking eyes, deep and brown. They looked like they had seen more life than a man his age, which I guessed was around mid-twenties. Even in the dark, his eyeballs gleamed.

'I am addicted to this stuff,' I said, pointing to the cup. 'Not good.'

'Worse things to be addicted to,' Keshav said.

'Cigarettes? Alcohol?' I said.

'Even worse.'

'Drugs?' I whispered.

'Even worse.'

'What?' I said.

'Love.' This time he whispered.

I laughed so hard, coffee spilled out of my nose.

'Deep,' I said, and patted the back of his hand on the armrest. 'That's deep, buddy. I guess coffee isn't so bad then.'

He ran a hand through his hair—which he wore short, in a military crew-cut—and touched the gold stud that glinted in his left ear.

'What do you do for a living, Keshav?' I said.

'I teach.'

'Oh, nice. What do you... '

'I am from your college.'

'Really?'

'IIT Delhi. Class of 2013.'

'You just reminded me how old I am,' I said. Both of us laughed.

'Actually, I might have a story for you,' he said.

'Oh no, not again,' I blurted out, and then kicked myself mentally for being so blunt. Exhaustion had made me forget my manners.

'I'm sorry. I didn't mean to be rude,' I said.

'It's fine,' he said and rubbed his hands together. 'Wrong of me to presume you would want to listen to it. I'm sure people come up to you all the time.'

'Sometimes they do. But I didn't have to be obnoxious. Sorry.'

'It's okay,' he said. He stared at the seat in front of him.

'I'm tired. Mind if I rest?' I said. He didn't respond.

I shut my eyes. I wanted to sleep, but couldn't. The overdose of caffeine and guilt prevented me from dozing off.

I opened my eyes after twenty minutes. Keshav was still staring at the seat in front of him.

'Maybe I can hear your story in short,' I said.

'Don't feel obligated,' he said, still looking in front.

Of course, I feel obligated, dude. Especially if you sulk and don't make eye contact.

'Listen,' I said, 'here's the thing. You said addicted to love. So, it's probably a love story. I am tired of love stories. Really, another Chetan Bhagat love story? Such a cliché now. I want to write

something else. Not just about two people pining away. Who does that these days, anyway? Nowadays, people don't fall in love. They swipe left and right…'

'It's not a love story,' he said, interrupting my blabber.

'Really?' I said, one eyebrow up. 'And can you please look at me when you talk?'

He turned to face me.

'It is about an ex-lover. But it is not a love story,' he said.

'Ex-lover? You guys broke up?'

'Yes.'

'Let me guess. She broke up. And you still loved her? Wanted to get back?'

'Yeah,' he said, his lips tight.

'And did you?'

He shook his head.

'I couldn't,' he said.

'Why?'

'Leave it. You don't have to listen to me.'

'I am just asking.'

'I am tired. Mind if I rest?' he said. He leaned back on his seat and down came his eyelids. He actually went off to sleep. Damn, you never do that to a writer. You don't make him take late flights, pump him up with coffee, start telling a story, and then snooze off at a cliffhanger.

I had to shake him by his shoulder.

'What?' he said, startled.

'What happened between you and her?'

'Who? Me and Zara?'

'Is that her name? Zara? Zara what?'

'Zara Lone,' he said.

'So, tell me what happened.'

Keshav started to laugh.

'What?' I said, surprised.

'For that I have to tell you the full story, Chetan.'

'So, tell me. Maybe I will write it too.'

'You don't have to. As I told you, this is not really a love story. You can always write another cute boy–cute girl romance. Half or quarter girlfriend types.'

I ignored his sarcasm.

'Just tell me the story. I want to know what happened between you and Zara Lone,' I said.

Chapter 1

Six months ago

'Stop, my bhai, stop,' Saurabh said, snatching away my whisky glass.

'I am not drunk,' I said. We were in a corner of the drawing room, near the makeshift bar. The rest of the coaching class faculty had gathered around Arora sir. They would never miss a chance to suck up to him.

We had come to the Malviya Nagar house of Chandan Arora, owner of Chandan Classes, and our boss.

'You swore on me you wouldn't have more than two drinks,' Saurabh said.

I smiled at him.

'But did I quantify the size of the drinks? How much whisky per drink? Half a bottle?' My words slurred. I was finding it hard to balance myself.

'You need fresh air. Let's go to the balcony,' Saurabh said.

'I need fresh whisky,' I said.

Saurabh dragged me to the balcony by my arm. When had this fatso become so strong?

'It is freezing here,' I said, shivering. I rubbed my hands together to keep myself warm.

'You can't drink so much, bhai.'

'It's New Year's Eve. You know what that does to me.'

'It's history. Four years ago. It's going to be 2018.'

'Feels like four seconds ago,' I said.

I took out a cigarette packet, which Saurabh promptly grabbed and hid in his pocket. I pulled out my phone. I opened the contact details of my next intoxicant, Zara.

'What did she say that night?' I said, staring at Zara's WhatsApp profile picture. 'We are done, that's what she said. What did she mean *done*? How can she say *we*? I am not done.'

'Leave the phone alone, bhai. You may accidentally call her,' Saurabh said. He lunged for my phone. I dodged to avoid him.

'Look at her,' I said, turning the screen towards Saurabh. She had put up a selfie as her DP—pouting, hand on waist, the black sari a dramatic contrast to her fair, almost pink, face.

She didn't always have her picture as her DP. Often, she would put up quotes. The 'let life not hold you back' kinds, statements that sound profound but actually mean nothing.

Her WhatsApp display picture was the only connect I had left with her. It was how I knew what was happening in her life.

'Who wears black saris? She doesn't look that great,' Saurabh said. He always did his best to help me get over her. I love Saurabh—my best friend, colleague, and fellow-misfit in this crazy drive called life. He's from Jaipur, not far from my hometown of Alwar. His father works as a junior engineer in the PWD. Like me, he too didn't get placed after campus. Both of us worked our asses off at Chandan Classes, even as we hoped to get out of there ASAP.

'It's Zara. She always looks great,' I put it plainly.

Saurabh shrugged.

'That's part of the tragedy.'

'You think I am mad about her because of her looks?'

'I think you should shut your phone.'

'More than three years, dude. Three crazy, crazy years.'

'I know, bhai. If you promise not to drink anymore, we can go back in. It is cold here.'

'What do you know?'

'That you dated Zara for three years. Want dinner?'

'Screw dinner. More than three. Three years, two months and three weeks to be precise.'

'You told me. Rendezvous 2010 to New Year's Eve 2014.'

'Yes, Rendezvous. That's when we met. Did I tell you how we met?' I said. My feet were finding it harder to find the floor. Saurabh held me tight to prevent me from falling.

'Yes, you have told me. Fifty times,' Saurabh muttered.

'There was a debating competition. She was in the finals.'

'Bhai, you have told this story a zillion times,' he said. I didn't care. He could hear it a zillion times plus one.

Chapter 2

A little over seven years ago

Clash of the Titans, debate finals
Rendezvous Fest, IIT Delhi
October 2010

She stood on the left podium. Her upright posture made her look taller than her five feet three inches. She wore a white salwar kameez, and a fuchsia dupatta with silver piping. I should have focused on her debating skills rather than her attire. However, even her debate opponent paused for a few seconds to take in Zara's stunning, model-like looks.

The Seminar Hall stage had a banner with the debate topic: Should public display of religion be banned?

Zara Lone was debating against Inder Das, the reigning champion from Hindu College. Both had reached the finals of Clash of the Titans.

The packed hall was waiting for the duo to make their final rebuttals.

Inder, with his loose kurta, curly hair and rimless glasses, looked like he had walked out of a Bengali art film, one of those where everyone waits for five seconds before the next dialogue.

'Last I heard, we are a free country,' Inder said. 'Our Preamble uses the word "secular". The state will not discriminate or meddle in the profession of any religion. Article 25 through to 28 in our Constitution guarantees freedom of religion.'

Damn, people know the articles of the Constitution? I didn't even know the Constitution had something called articles. I had no view on either side of the debate. I only wanted Zara to win. I wanted to see her smile.

Zara raised her hand to object. However, she had to wait her turn as Inder wouldn't stop.

'Article 25 says, and I quote,' Inder said and paused, fumbling through his notes.

When people say 'I quote' and pause, they come across as scary-level intellectuals. Let's face it, nobody wants to mess with the 'I quote' types.

Inder spoke again, or rather quoted.

'All persons are equally entitled to freedom of conscience and the right to freely profess, practise, and propagate religion.' He paused again for us to digest that. 'Miss Zara Lone, you are arguing not only against our culture, but also against the Constitution. You not only want to take away our Diwali celebrations, you want to break the law, too.'

He finished his speech and tossed his notes aside in disgust; I could smell his pomposity from where I sat. Inder shook his head, as if to say, *Why are we even debating this*?

The crowd broke into applause. I had a sinking feeling. Would Zara lose?

All eyes turned to Zara. She waited for the applause to die down before she spoke.

'My opponent seems to have a good knowledge of the Constitution. I compliment him for that,' Zara said. Inder smiled.

'However, ladies and gentlemen, we are here to discuss the right thing to do, not just quote Constitution clauses we can Google in two seconds.'

The audience sat up straight. This petite fireball was not going to give up so easily.

She continued, 'The Constitution is the foundation of our republic, but it can be changed. Have we not made Constitutional amendments?'

Zero decibel silence in the hall.

'So the issue here is not what is written, but what *needs* to be written,' she said.

'Yes, superb! Shabash,' I blurted out aloud. My voice echoed in the silent hall. Damn, I had thought more people would applaud. The entire audience, including Zara Lone, looked at me.

'Thank you.' She smiled at me. 'But save it for later.'

The five hundred-odd audience burst into laughter. The serious vibe thawed a little, even as I went stiff. I wanted a power cut, absolute darkness and complete invisibility so I could run out of the hall. Zara went back to her argument.

'My friend only quoted Article 25 partially. Article 25 does say that all persons are equally entitled to freedom of conscience and the right to freely profess, practise, and propagate religion, but it also says, "subject to public order, morality and health". How did my esteemed opponent miss out on that?'

'So, if it bothers others,' Inder said, interrupting Zara, 'as a Muslim, would you stop the azaan from being called on loudspeakers five times a day?'

'Yes, I would.'

The audience let out a collective gasp. A Muslim girl saying this on stage had everyone's attention. Unfazed, Zara continued. 'You can still pray five times a day. Maybe have an app to remind you on your phone. Listen to the prayers on headphones. But don't impose them on the whole neighbourhood. And I would appreciate it if you didn't say things like "as a Muslim". I am not here as a Muslim, I am here as a finalist in the Clash of the Titans debate competition.'

The applause was deafening. A few minutes later, one of the faculty members from the judging panel went up to the podium to announce the results.

'The debates were excellent today. However, to argue for restricting displays of religion is difficult all over the world, let alone India. You had the harder side, Miss Zara, and you defended it with logic and poise. Hence, the winner for this year is Miss Zara Lone.'

A standing ovation followed. Zara came to accept the trophy. I clapped like a maniac. A fellow hostel-mate egged me to whistle. Did I tell you I had the loudest whistle in IIT Delhi? I put my right thumb to my index finger in an 'O' shape and brought it to my mouth.

Tweeeet! My whistle, loud and shrill, suited a football stadium more than a debating contest. Many intellectual types turned to me again, wondering why such a crass person had been allowed in here.

My whistle caught Zara's attention. She looked at me, trophy in hand, and smiled. I pulled out my fingers from my mouth.

'Dude, easy. She is your girlfriend or what?' a guy next to me said.

No, she isn't, but she will be, I wanted to say. After all, the universe had already decided it.

I stepped out of the hall and walked towards the food stalls.

'Thanks for the cheering.' I froze on hearing her voice.

'Zara?' I said, turning around.

'Yeah. Nice college. Are you from here?'

'Yes. How about you?' I said.

'Delhi College of Engineering. Missed IIT by a few marks. Not smart enough.'

'You demolished him in there. You are definitely smarter than me.'

We walked out on to the main road, which was dotted with food kiosks due to the festival.

❖

'As you guys walked, Zara asked if you were hungry. You guys ate together. Exchanged phone numbers…' Saurabh said, breaking my story narration.

'What? How do you know this?' I said. A waiter saw us out on the balcony. He came to us with a tray of drinks. Despite Saurabh's attempts to stop me, I picked up a glass of whisky.

'Arrey, bhai, please. You ordered a plain dosa. She ordered a parantha. The parantha wasn't good. You gave her your dosa. The rest is history. Let's go in. I am turning to ice here.'

He hugged himself. I took a big sip of whisky. It went down my throat like a little ball of fire.

'Have a drink,' I said, 'it will make you feel less cold.'

'Not really. Alcohol actually leads to heat loss. It is heat coming out that makes your skin feel warm.'

'Golu, seriously, stop the JEE chemistry. It's New Year's Eve,' I said. I brought the glass close to his mouth. He looked at me once, then with great reluctance took a sip.

'Good job, my Golu,' I said. 'So you know about the dosa too? You want to know about our next meeting? The first real date?'

'Please, no, bhai. Let's hang out with the other staff inside. They already think we are antisocial.'

'Screw them. We freaking hate this job,' I said. 'How do you expect us to socialise?'

'Let's talk to them a little bit.'

'In a minute. I just need to make a call.'

I pulled out my phone. I opened Zara's contact. Saurabh saw her picture.

'No, bhai, no.' He reached for my phone. I ran ahead of him as he clumsily and unsuccessfully chased me.

'Bhai, my kasam. You are not calling her.'

'It's New Year. I can't even wish her?'

'Bhai, no!' he said as I shushed him.

'Shh. It's ringing,' I said. I used my left hand to keep Saurabh at a distance and my right hand to hold the phone to my ear.

One ring. Two rings. Five rings. Seven rings.

'Hello?' I said as I heard a voice. 'Hello, Zara. Don't hang up, okay?'

'The person you have dialled cannot be reached. Please try again later.' It was the Airtel lady, the emotionless bitch. If only she knew how important this call was to me.

'Couldn't get through? Good. Leave it,' Saurabh said.

I dialled again. Same seven rings. Same cold Airtel bitch.

'Stop it, bhai. She will see all those missed calls and freak out.'

'I don't care,' I said. Once you have already faced the humiliation of giving the other person multiple missed calls, it doesn't matter if it is two or three. Or seven. Or ten.

That is why I dialled her a tenth time. And this time it wasn't the Airtel lady.

'Hello.' I heard Zara's voice. Her one word alone made me feel better than any whisky in the world could.

'Hey, Zara,' I said, clearing my throat and stretching the 'hey' longer than necessary. Saurabh let out a sigh of disappointment. I stepped away from him.

'Yes, Keshav,' she said in measured tones. She sounded cold. Colder than the Airtel lady.

I wondered what to say next. 'I have been trying to call you,' I managed to say.

'I know. And you should realise that if someone doesn't pick up the phone ten times, then maybe they can't talk.'

'Nine times. Not ten. Anyway, are you busy?' I said. 'I can call later.' I needed an excuse to call her again and hear her voice another time. I heard music in the background. She was at a party too. Maybe in the black sari. I wondered if her idiot loser boyfriend was with her.

'What is it, Keshav? Why have you called me?' she said.

I stepped to a corner of the balcony. Saurabh did not follow but kept an eye on me from a distance.

'I just wanted to say happy new year. Why are you interrogating me like this?' I said.

'Hold on a second,' she said, as her attention shifted from me to someone else at the party. 'Hi,' I heard her say, 'you look lovely too.'

'Zara, are you there?' I said, when I didn't hear anything for a long while.

'There are just too many people here. Anyway. You know what we decided, right?'

'To be together forever and ever?' I said. Damn, why did I have to say that?

'What?'

'Didn't we, when we went on our trip? New Year in Goa.'

'That was a long time ago, Keshav.'

'Six years ago, 2011 New Year's Eve,' I said. When the heart breaks, the part of the brain that stores data on past dates works perfectly.

'I meant when we broke up. We decided to not be in touch. Something you don't follow. It's been years since we broke up now.'

'Okay, so kill me. Kill me because I called to wish you. Kill me because New Year's Eve makes me remember you. Or kill me because it is the anniversary of the day we first made love.'

'Keshav, stop it.'

'Stop what? Thinking about you? I wish I could,' I screamed. 'I so freaking wish I could.'

Saurabh came running to me. He gestured to check what the matter was. I shook my head. He motioned for me to put the call on speaker. I complied.

'Are you drunk?' Zara said in her soft, almost caring voice.

'How does it fucking matter? Drunk or not, I miss you, Zara. What are you doing with that loser Raghu?'

'Stop calling him names, Keshav. And I have to go.'

Saurabh sliced his hand in the cold Delhi air, indicating I end the call. Of course, I ignored his sane advice.

'Oh, so protective of your Raghooooo,' I said, mocking his name. 'Maggu Raghu. That's what they called him in hostel. You know that? Mag-gu Rag-hu.'

'I don't have to take this, Keshav,' Zara said, 'I am going to hang up. Don't call me back.'

'So touchy for that freaking nerd. That nerd who loves his fuck-all dotcom company more than anything else. He can never love you like I do.'

'That fuck-all dotcom company is one of India's hottest startups—and Raghu created it. Do you know its valuation? Why am I even telling you this?' Zara said, her voice irritated.

'So that is why you went to him. For his money,' I said.

'I went to him because I wanted to belong. I wanted a family. And you were running scared. Instead of manning up, you abused my folks.'

'And what did your folks do?'

'You have tried this before. It won't work. You can't provoke me. Now, bye. Don't call me again or I will have to block you.'

'Block me? Are you bloody threatening to block me—'

I had to stop mid-sentence because she had ended the call.

'Anyway, even I have to go,' I said to nobody on the phone.

'She's cut the call, bhai,' Saurabh said. Fine, she hung up on me. Why pretend she didn't?

I looked at Saurabh. I expected a slap. He came forward and hugged me. The whisky, rejection and his hug added up. I began to cry loudly.

'Bloody bitch. "I will have to block you"—I love her every minute and this is what she says to me,' I said between sobs.

'Bhai, you have to leave this girl. It's been too long,' Saurabh said.

'I am so over her,' I said. The biggest lie of the freaking millennium.

'Good. Shall we go in?'

'Wait. I have to call her once more. I have to tell her I am over her.'

'No, bhai, no...'

Before Saurabh could react, I had dialled her number again. The phone rang. I expected her to cut the call. However, someone picked up.

'Yes?' a male voice said on the other end. Damn, it was the lover of the century, Raghu.

'Oh,' I said, 'happy new year.'

'Listen, Keshav, I want to be civil, but I have to tell you to stop bothering Zara.'

Fucker, who was he? Her dad? Her watchman? And 'I want to be civil', who talks like that? What the hell does that even mean?

'I am not bothering her,' I said, trying not to slur.

'I think you are. And you do this regularly.'

'I don't.'

'It has happened many times in my presence. Please stop. I am requesting you,' Raghu said, his voice poised and calm. He probably only had coconut water to drink on New Year's Eve.

'See, bro,' I said, trying to figure out what to say next, the whisky making it difficult for me to structure a logical, decent sentence. All I really wanted to say was, 'Fuck off, Zara is mine'. However, even in my drunken state, I knew that wasn't the best idea.

'Just cut the call,' I heard Zara's voice over his. Bitch. Bitch to the power of five.

'Yes, Keshav?' Raghu said, his voice patient.

'See, bro,' I repeated. 'Can I speak to Zara?'

'She doesn't want to speak to you.'

'How do you know? Give her the phone.'

'She just told me. Now can you let us be in peace? Happy new year. Bye.'

'Listen, Raghu,' I said, my voice dropping.

'What?'

'Listen, Raghu, I will come and …' I said things I don't want to repeat here. Mostly because I don't remember them. I think it involved me doing unmentionable things to Raghu's mother, sister and probably grandmother. I said all this in explicit Hindi, using words that would make even the truck drivers of Rajasthan blush.

'And I will take a danda and …' I said as Saurabh took the phone from me. He cut the call and kept my phone in his pocket.

'What chutiapa are you doing?' Saurabh yelled at me, something he never does. I looked away from him as I realised what I had done.

'You were cursing Zara,' he said.

'Nope. Only Raghu,' I said.

'Have you lost all shame?' Saurabh said.

'I just wanted to speak to Zara. Asshole picked up.'

'Because she doesn't want to talk to you,' Saurabh said.

'I am fucking never ever calling her again.'

Saurabh shook his head and smiled sadly.

'I mean it.'

'Why are you obsessed with this girl?'

'May I have my phone back?' I said softly.

Saurabh patted his pocket.

'I am keeping it. And I will smash your phone to the floor if you don't come in. Right now.'

❖

We came back into Chandan's drawing room. Kamal sir, chemistry teacher in Chandan Classes, walked up to us.

'Happy new year ji. Another year, another JEE. Another round of students ji,' he said and laughed at his own joke.

I touched my glass to his.

'Where were the two of you? Arora ji was asking,' he said.

'Sorry, we wanted some air,' Saurabh said.

'And now some whisky,' I winked. 'Kamal ji, will you get me a drink?'

'Sure,' he said. 'I will be right back.'

Saurabh glared at me after Kamal left.

'Stop,' he said.

'Last drink. Can I have my phone back?'

'Never. That wasn't cool, Keshav. How you shouted outside.'

'Golu ji. When you scold me, you look too cute. Your round face becomes red like a tomato ji,' I said.

'Stop it,' he said.

I moved towards him.

'Happy new year ji. Another year, another JEE,' I said and tickled his paunch.

'I said stop it.'

I dipped my hand into his trouser pocket to get my phone back.

'Never,' he said, as he laughed and tried to push my hand away.

'You have become even more fat, Golu,' I said, feeling his belly. 'You love your mithai, no?'

'Better than loving what you can never have,' Saurabh said, shoving my arm away.

Chapter 3

'Come in. The great Rajpurohit sir,' Chandan Arora said. His voice came out muffled because his mouth was full.

The entire room reeked of pan masala, which had its epicentre at Chandan's thick lips. He chewed gutkha as he waved towards a seat. I sat down and waited while he finished chewing the various substances in his mouth. I stared at the pictures on the wall behind him. In some photographs he posed with past successful students, along with their IIT admission letters. A framed, fake and photoshopped certificate said, in bold letters, 'Chandan sir, the ultimate king of JEE chemistry', something an ex-student had made for him. In another picture, a sunglasses-wearing Chandan stood with arms folded on top of the main multi-storey building at IIT Delhi. It signified his conquering of the IIT entrance exam system. Chandan never made it to IIT himself. He used to be a chemistry professor at Venkateswara College in Delhi University. Ten years ago, he started taking JEE chemistry tuitions in the garage of his Malviya Nagar house. Business grew and finally became Chandan Classes. He now rented a three-storey house in Malviya Nagar, in the same lane as his own home. Fifteen full-time faculty members worked for him. Seven of them were IITians, a fact he never stopped gloating over. 'Yes, I never did IIT. Now look, IITians work for me,' was what he said to parents of new students who were worried about Mr Arora's credentials. Sometimes he would pull me out of class for display.

'Look at him. IIT Delhi 2013 batch. Now works for me,' he would say, emphasising the 'me'. Once, I remember him saying, 'Does he look like there's anything special about him? See, if he can get into IIT, your child can too.'

Splat! The sound of a mouthful of spit and gutkha being emptied into a dustbin brought me back to the present.

'So, Rajpurohit sir, how are your classes going?'

Apart from being an IITian zoo exhibit, I taught mathematics at Chandan Classes. And today Chandan Arora had summoned me to discuss my work.

'Good, Chandan sir,' I said with a fake smile. 'We just finished the calculus module.'

He slid a file towards me.

'Rajpurohit ji,' he said, 'this is the feedback from your students. Some say you discouraged them from trying for IIT.'

'No, sir.'

He shut the file.

'Then why are they saying this?'

'Sir, those must be the weak students. They rank last in every mock-test. They have no aptitude for science. Parents are pushing them. I don't think they should be wasting their time trying for IIT.'

Chandan leaned back. His comfortable leather chair creaked under his heavy frame.

'We are not a career guidance centre, Rajpurohit ji.'

'But they say they don't even want to do IIT. Their parents made them join here.'

'So who are we to interfere in family matters? Our job is to take classes.'

'Sir, but—' I said, before he interrupted me again.

'And, I also note you have not brought in new students.'

'Sir, I am busy taking classes.'

'You have to do marketing too. Meet new visitors when they come to the centre. Convince them to join. You never do that.'

I hated it. I despised meeting parents, especially parents of kids who would never make it. The JEE exam had a selection rate of less than 2 per cent. Hence, most who try for IIT fail. Of course, when you are selling coaching classes, that is not what you say. You make them dream—that their son or daughter will get into IIT.

'Rajpurohit ji, sorry to say, but you need to be more of a go-getter.'

Sure, I wasn't that. Whatever the hell go-getter means.

'I will try, sir,' I said. I swore to myself that I would update my résumé and LinkedIn profile again. I deserved a better job. Damn, I deserved a better life.

❖

'What happened? The gutkha-chewing asshole said something?' Saurabh said. We sat on the tiny floor rug in the tiny living room of our tiny two-bedroom flat. I poured out two large pegs of Blenders Pride. I had promised Saurabh I wouldn't drink for a month post the New Year's Eve debacle. I hadn't. In fact, it had been more than a week since that one-month embargo had passed.

'Forget it.' I handed him a drink.

'Something is the matter. You haven't opened a bottle for a long time. Is it the Kashmiri girl again?'

'Zara? No.'

'I don't like taking her name. You sure?' Saurabh said.

I shook my head. He wasn't wrong to ask. Zara was always on my mind. All it took was for me to see a DTC public bus on a route we used to take together. I would spend the rest of the day thinking about her. Or I'd see a girl in a chikankari salwar kameez—something Zara liked to wear—and five more hours would be wasted. It felt like my brain had rewired itself; all neural passages led to Zara. I noticed the ice in my whisky glass, which relates to snow. Snow happens in Kashmir, hence Zara. I could see our coffee table made of wood. Wood comes from trees. Zara liked nature, including trees. There, my brain could lead from anything to Zara.

And yet, I wasn't drinking because of Zara today.

I took a big sip as Saurabh remained silent. Men know when not to probe. I finished my first glass and poured a second drink for both of us. I gave the glass to him.

'I'll join you, as long as you keep it under limits,' Saurabh said.

'I need it tonight.'

'You can tell me what the matter is. If you want to.'

'I hate my job.'

'Me too. Tell me something new.' He sniggered.

'We can't be stuck in Chandan Classes forever. We went to IIT, for God's sake.'

'You did, bhai. I am a simple NIT-wallah from Nagpur.'

'You are no less though. Why are we stuck in this idiot's coaching centre?'

'That asshole Chandan said something?'

'Yeah. But there's more.'

'What?'

'I blew two interviews.'

'Which interviews?' Saurabh sat up straight.

'Okay, I am sorry. I applied to a few companies. I saw the ads on LinkedIn.'

'You never told me!'

'Sorry, I meant to. I thought, let something happen. Out of ten places, only two called me for interviews. Both sent a rejection on the same day.'

'Who?'

'Infosys. And Flow Tech, a small software company in Gurgaon. I thought I did alright. Bloody hell, man. Body shop sending Indian programmers to Dubai. They didn't give me a job.'

I finished my drink bottoms up.

'Screw them,' Saurabh said after a pause.

'They asked me why I joined a coaching centre after IIT.'

'There is a stigma. Coaching classes on our résumé. Like we suddenly become unfit for corporates,' Saurabh said.

'Updated your LinkedIn?'

'Nothing to update.'

I opened Saurabh's LinkedIn profile on my phone.

'At least put up a good picture. You look like a child-molester,' I said.

'Show me,' Saurabh said and took the phone. 'And you look like a member of a dance troupe. Why is your earring visible? You think that helps get a job?'

I took the phone back and looked at my picture.

'It's my Rajasthani culture.'

'No tech company wants a guy with jewellery.'

I kept my phone on the table.

'We suck. We can't even put up a nice profile picture.'

'Sir, that is why I tell you, start eating gutkha. Enjoy Chandan Classes and your meaningless life.'

I glared at Saurabh.

'Sorry, sorry. Yes. We won't give up.'

Saurabh switched on the TV and changed the channel to the news. The prime-time story was about police lathi-charging girls at the Banaras Hindu University campus. The girls' fault? They were protesting because they didn't want to be molested.

'Are they serious? That's the UP police. Hitting girls during a silent, non-violent protest?' Saurabh said.

Zara liked to attend protests too, my brain flashed a thought. My neural circuit was at it again.

I lapsed back in time, to several years ago, when we had an activist-date.

Chapter 4

Seven years ago

'How is going for a protest at Jantar Mantar a date?' I said. We came out of the Barakhamba Road metro station in Connaught Place and walked towards Parliament Street.

She tied her hair up in a bun. With a hairpin in her mouth, she said, 'Thanks for joining me. It means a lot.'

'What is the protest about exactly?' I said. She had told me on the phone that it had something to do with Kashmir. With great effort I had gathered the courage to call and ask her out after Rendezvous. She had teased me, asking if I was actually asking her out on a date. I gambled with a 'yes'. I told her we could go wherever she wanted. Well, she chose a protest.

'The Indian Army is committing atrocities on civilians in Kashmir. We are gathering to protest against that.'

Like most people around me, I had little idea about the Kashmir issue. I knew Pakistan wanted it, India would never give it up and some people in Kashmir didn't want to be with either country. It mattered little to me. This was just a chance to bunk classes and spend the day with Zara Lone, the most beautiful, smart and articulate woman in the world.

We reached Jantar Mantar. Around fifty students sat outside the monument. They held placards.

'Stop Innocent Killings in Kashmir.'

'Pellet Guns Blind Protestors. Stop Using Them.'

'Indian Army, Stop Atrocities on Kashmiris.'

Zara walked ahead of me. She went up to a small group of protesters. They stood up to hug her. She introduced me to them.

'Afsana, Zaheer and Karim,' Zara said, 'meet my friend Keshav.'

I shook hands with them. Now, I am not communal or racist or anything. However, let me just say this, the current situation was a little different from what I was used to. Back in my hometown, Alwar, we don't really mix with people of other religions. My mother might have fainted seeing me in a crowd of Muslims. My father's friend circle is almost entirely from the RSS. Hence, we don't really know many Muslims anyway.

'Razaq, Salim, Ismail,' Zara introduced me to some of the others. I shook hands and smiled. I noticed their somewhat surprised expression when they heard my name, or when they noticed my earring. One of them gave me a choice of placards to hold. I took the relatively safe 'Peace in the Valley' sign. I clasped my banner in my arms as all of us sat down on the ground. Zara looked at me and smiled.

'What?' I said.

'Thanks. For coming and supporting me.'

Yes, I was supporting her. To be with her. But was I supporting the protest? I don't know.

'What exactly is going on, anyway?' I said.

'Last week, the Indian Army fired pellet guns to disperse protestors in Kashmir. One protestor may turn blind.'

'That's terrible,' I said, shocked.

'Yes, this needs to stop. Kashmir needs peace.'

'But why did the Army shoot pellet guns?'

'Because that's what they do,' Ismail said. He stood up along with his friends and walked away to shout slogans. Zara spoke to me when nobody was around.

'It's not that simple, actually,' she said. 'The protestors threw stones at the Army.'

'Why?' I said, confused.

'Because they don't like the Indian Army.'

'But why?'

'The Army has to find terrorists in Kashmir. Terrorists go mix with civilians. Sometimes, in hunting terrorists, civilians get harassed or hurt. So they hate the Indian Army.'

'What else is the Army supposed to do?'

'Not hurt innocent people for sure. Why are they firing pellet guns?'

'What would you do if someone threw rocks at you?'

'You don't understand,' Zara said, 'it's complicated, this Kashmir thing.'

I really didn't understand. I could have argued with Zara, but a) I didn't know much about the issue, b) Zara was a professional debater, and most importantly c) I wanted to have a real chance with her and not blow it over some stupid politics.

'You are absolutely right. Maybe you can tell me more about Kashmir. If we meet again,' I said.

'We will,' she said and squeezed my hand. A touch initiated by her is good, I told myself.

As the slogans became louder, Zara leaned over and whispered in my ear. 'Listen, I simply want peace. Violence is never good on either side. I love India. I love Kashmir.'

I nodded and smiled at her.

'Kashmir needs progress. That's why I want to finish my studies and teach there. Education will bring peace. Nothing else.'

'You want to do a peaceful dinner later?' I said.

She laughed. I took it as a yes.

Three months later

'Did we have to wake up at five o'clock? I am so hung-over. How far is this place?' I said, trying to catch my breath.

'Shh, see that Dona Paula statue on top of the rocks? We are going there. Ten more minutes,' Zara said.

I carefully placed one foot in front of the other on the black rocks as we walked towards the point where Zara wanted to see the first sunrise of the year.

'We came to Goa to chill. Is it even legal to wake up so early here?' I said.

Zara laughed.

'Seriously, we had such an amazing night,' I said, 'and what is this now? A punishment?'

We had come to Goa for our first holiday, and to celebrate New Year's Eve together. Zara and I had made love the night before, and I had hoped to cuddle in bed all day and tell her how much I loved her. Of course, it is hard to profess undying love to someone who sets a 4 a.m. alarm.

'It will be worth it, mister,' Zara said, walking ten steps ahead of me.

Dona Paula is located along the sea near Panjim in Goa. The rocky terrain lies close to where the Zuari and Mandovi rivers meet the Arabian Sea. It took us forty-five minutes from our hotel to reach the white statue of a couple made famous by several movies.

We sat on top of a large rock, the sky still dark.

'We are facing west. The sun rises in the east,' I said.

'I know,' Zara said. 'Still, it is the new year. When daylight breaks, I want to witness it with you, holding your hand.'

She entwined my fingers with hers as we stared at the empty dark sky and the sea. I thought about last night, probably the best night of my life so far.

There was a hint of pink in the sky.

'Happy new year, my love,' Zara said, taking my hand to her lips.

'My love, happy new year,' I said. We kissed, and didn't stop till the entire sky was lit up

I looked at her face. Would I ever get used to so much beauty?

'Why do you love me?'

'What?' Zara said and laughed. 'Are we fishing?'

'Seriously, why? You are beautiful, intelligent, fun and articulate. You can get anyone. Why me?'

'Well, I think you are handsome.'

'I am serious, Zara.' I didn't want to be humoured out of this. Zara exhaled as she spoke after a pause.

'Well, it's hard to find a man who can acknowledge a woman's intelligence and be genuinely okay with it.'

'What?'

'I am serious. And I like your innocent politics.'

'But I don't like politics.'

'I know. You are not left-wing or right-wing or this ideology or that. And yet you are naturally a good person. Not sexist, not communal, not biased. Just a nice guy.'

I nodded and smiled.

'But the real reason is the earring.'

'What?'

'For some strange reason I find it really hot. Come here you.' Zara reached out for me again and the Dona Paula statue, I swear, winked at me.

❖

'Bhai, where are you?' Saurabh snapped his fingers in front of my eyes. I looked at the TV screen, even though my mind had just played a Jantar Mantar video from the past.

'Huh?' I said. 'I am here only. What did you say again?'

'I said this country has gone mad. Listen to the college VC. He is saying we can't take every girl's complaint seriously.'

'Idiot,' I said, my mind still in Dona Paula.

'Lost in thoughts of her.' Saurabh rolled his eyes. 'I can tell from your face.'

I am always thinking of her, I wanted to say.

'It's just the whisky.'

'Not just the whisky. I know the date today, bhai,' Saurabh said and leaned back on the sofa.

'What date?' I said.

I opened my phone to check. Thursday, February the 8th. In a few hours, it would be February 9th, Zara's birthday.

'Oh yes, of course. Wow, I actually didn't think about that today,' I said.

'That's a first,' Saurabh said. 'Congrats. You are feeling like shit. But at least for other reasons.'

'I did remember it two days ago though,' I said. She turns twenty-seven. I kept my glass down, pressed the sides of my head with both palms, trying to squeeze her out of my thoughts. I didn't want to remember her. How we spent her past birthdays together. How I climbed up the mango tree and entered her hostel room through her window; I did this while balancing a cake and flowers in my hand. How we spent the rest of the night in bed, legs entwined, imagining a life together. Or at least I did.

'Sorry, I shouldn't have brought her up. I didn't realise it wasn't on your mind,' Saurabh said.

I shook my head, still squeezing my temples.

'It's okay. I can handle this.'

'Just don't call her. Remember last time?'

My hands left my head, they had to carry whisky to my mouth.

'I am not calling her, ever. I can't be humiliated anymore,' I said. A part of me was dying to see her DP on WhatsApp. Maybe she had a new one for her birthday. The one last week had a selfie of her and Raghu, arms draped around each other. I just hoped she had changed that picture. Hell, I didn't want to hope for anything. I wasn't going to look.

Saurabh nodded slowly, not believing what I had just said.

'Take my phone away if you want,' I said.

'No, bhai. I trust you,' Saurabh said. 'In fact, to celebrate this new strength of yours, let's have one more drink.'

He refilled our glasses. The Blenders Pride bottle had reached the halfway mark. I checked the time. It was eleven-thirty. Fine, I could do this.

I could just enjoy drinks with my friend on a Thursday night and not call her. Even on her birthday. I had felt this control for the first time in years. The last four birthdays of hers since our breakup, I had called her first thing at midnight. Of course, she didn't answer the phone three out of the four times. The one year she did pick up, she said she had family around and couldn't talk. I told her I had only called to wish her. All she said was a lame, cold thank you. One shows more warmth before ending a wrong number call. Is it that easy for some people to move on? To go from one person to the next, like switching TV channels? Sure, the breakup was partly my fault. But could she get over me so easily? Why was I not over her, then? Like there was a defect in my head. It just wouldn't let go. And why was I thinking of her again? I checked the time, it was midnight. My body tightened, as it prepared to fight an impulse. The impulse to pick up the phone and call her. To tell her I still loved her, and to give me one more chance, please, please.

I tried to bring my focus back to the present moment. My drink was over. There was no more ice on the table. It gave me something to do. I went to the kitchen, took out ice from the freezer. I returned and made another drink. Ten past twelve. Wow, I had made it. Thankfully, Saurabh came up with a new topic.

'That Chandan is having an affair.'

'No! Who would sleep with him?' I said.

'That secretary of his.'

'Sheela aunty?' I grinned. 'Are you serious? She is, like, fifty years old. And, what, a hundred kilos?'

'Good enough for our man. The bigger the better,' Saurabh said and laughed.

'Sheela aunty and Chandan! That is one gross visual.'

'Nobody asked you to imagine them,' Saurabh said.

We began to giggle. I had known Sheela aunty since I had joined Chandan Classes. She often shared her tiffin with me. Last I heard, her married son's wife was going to have a child.

'She gave me bhindi yesterday,' I said. 'That's how I imagine her. The woman with the tastiest lunch. Now you are telling me, wait, gross—how do you know?'

'I went to give her the weekly attendance report. Her phone was lying open next to her. Chandan had sent her WhatsApp messages.'

'What messages?'

'Those kiss emojis. And a few of the red lips.'

'Maybe the idiot doesn't know what those emojis mean.'

'"Sheela ji, you are too beautiful", he had said next.'

'What!' I said. 'No way! He could have just...'

'Next was, "Sheela ji. Can't wait for tonight",' Saurabh said. 'I saw it, bhai. Sideways, but I saw it.'

'Wow. Where do they do it?'

'Where else? Haven't you seen the sofa in his office?'

'Yuck. I have sat on that sofa so many times.'

'Hope they wipe it afterwards,' Saurabh said.

'Shut up,' I said. 'I will never sit in that office again.'

'You think he makes Sheela wipe the mess afterwards? Because, well, she *is* his secretary.'

The alcohol made everything seem extra-funny. Saurabh and I went hysterical with laughter. The little scandal in our boring workplace had added a spark to our super-dull life. Saurabh laughed so hard he slid off our slippery fake-leather sofa. He said he wondered if Chandan spat out the gutkha before they kissed. This time I laughed so much I, too, slid to the floor, holding my stomach.

'Bhai, look,' Saurabh said, and shook the almost empty Blenders Pride bottle.

'Okay. We had too much. What time is it?'

'It's almost two, bhai.'

'Wow. We discussed Sexy Sheela and Stud Chandan for so long?'

'They are probably doing it in the coaching centre right now,' Saurabh said.

'Shall we go check? Imagine if we walk in. We will say we just came to pick up some notes.'

'Let's go,' Saurabh said. The coaching centre was a five-minute walk from our house. Somehow, in our intoxicated and confident state, we felt a sting on Chandan was an amazing idea.

'Yeah, let's,' I said.

My phone beeped. I had a message. After a few seconds, it beeped a few more times.

'Who is messaging me so late?'

'Must be some phone company message. Buy more data and shit,' he said and put his head sleepily on my shoulder.

'Why the hell do they message so late?' My eyes began to droop shut.

The phone beeped again.

'Damn you!' I picked up the phone.

I cracked open my right eye to look at my locked home-screen:

5 new WhatsApp messages from Zara Lone

I shook my head in disbelief. Was I that drunk? I rubbed my eyes and read it again. I had read it right. I shook my shoulder to wake up Saurabh.

'Golu, get up,' I said. 'See this.'

'What? I don't freaking want their extra 5 GB, bhai. Let me sleep.'

'Saurabh, see the screen.'

Saurabh groaned as he lifted his head.

'Zara messaged you?'

'Yeah.'

'Did you message her first?'

'No, I swear. I am drunk, but I didn't. We were talking about Chandan and Sheela. I haven't touched my phone.'

'Oh,' he said and fell silent.

'Should I open it?'

Saurabh picked up a Bisleri water bottle from the table. He drank with big, loud, annoying and slow glugs.

'Tell me, Golu,' I said.

'Of course, bhai,' Saurabh said, wiping his mouth. 'What kind of a question is that? You won't check your own phone?'

I opened my WhatsApp and saw her messages.

'So you don't even wish me anymore?' said the first. The rest followed.

'It's my birthday. I hope you remember.'

'Just was surprised you didn't wish me.'

'Anyway. Don't know why I was thinking of you.'

'I guess you are busy.'

She had a new display picture. It was a solo black and white selfie. She looked as stunning as ever. I saw her chat status was 'online'.

'Golu, what is this?'

Saurabh read the messages.

'Either she has realised your value or she just misses the attention,' Saurabh said.

'Should I reply?' I said.

'I don't know.' Saurabh yawned. 'I am sleepy.'

'This is important, Golu. I need your clear thinking. I am too involved and too drunk.'

'Wait,' Saurabh said. 'Let's wash our faces. Come back to our senses.'

We struggled to reach the bathroom. We splashed our faces with chilled water.

'Are you there?' She sent another text. She must have seen the double blue ticks after I had read her messages.

'Golu, what do I reply?' I said.

'Whatever. Just have a normal conversation.'

So bloody insightful.

'Yes,' I replied.

She didn't respond for a few seconds. I saw the 'typing…' message, which went and came back as she corrected herself.

'I miss you,' she said.

A tremble ran through me. Saurabh saw the message. I

stepped away from him. I wanted his advice, but I didn't want him to see all my private conversations.

'Wow,' I texted, 'really?'

'Yes. Life is quite incomplete without you.'

I heard a retching sound. Saurabh had puked on the coffee table. Some ambience for a romantic chat.

'Sorry,' Saurabh said, 'I will clean it up.' He went to the kitchen. I turned back to my phone.

'You serious, Zara? You know what that means to me.'

'I do. I tried to be tough and cut you off. It doesn't work. I miss you.'

'What about Raghu?'

Saurabh wiped the table with a washcloth.

'Everything okay?' he said.

I raised a thumbs-up to him.

'Raghu's a nice guy. Very nice. But he's not the one,' Zara replied.

I choked up as I read her message. Yes, I still had a chance. Thank you, God.

'I miss you too. So much,' I replied.

'Yeah, right. That is why you forgot my birthday.' She added an upset emoji.

'I didn't, baby. I had to control myself to not wish you. Don't be upset.'

'I am kidding,' she said, along with her favourite laughter with tears emoji.

'Lol. Can I call to wish you?'

'Why call? You are not going to wish me in person?'

I kept my phone aside. I folded my hands up to the sky. Divine intervention had just taken place. She herself wanted to see me.

'Of course, I do. When? In the morning?'

'How about now?'

I checked the time.

'What? It's almost 3. Where are you?'

'In my room. Himadri.'

'You are in the hostel? On your birthday? Didn't go home?'

'Will go tomorrow. There's a party. Family mostly.'

'Where's Raghu?'

'Hyderabad.'

'Oh. You want to step out? Can you?'

'It's difficult to leave the hostel at this time. But you can come. If you want to.'

'How?'

'Oh. Someone's forgotten. How they'd climb trees to come wish me.'

'Ha ha. That was years ago.'

'I miss those days.'

'Me too.'

'I guess you can't do all that now. You have passed out of college.'

'What?'

'It's okay. You don't have to come.'

'I can. I will come. Now?'

'It's too late and cold. Risky too. You aren't a student anymore.'

'Is your room still 105? Facing the mango tree?'

'It's okay, K. We will meet later.'

She had called me K after years. I even missed her abbreviations.

'Just tell me your room number, Zara.'

'Of course, it is still 105. I love my room. Why?'

'Nothing. See you in half an hour.'

She sent a grin smiley back. She knew me enough; I'd never give up a challenge or a chance to meet her.

I kept the phone in my pocket. Saurabh lay flat on the sofa.

'Wake up, we have to go,' I yelled into his ear as I shook his shoulder.

Chapter 5

'This is insane. Completely insane,' Saurabh kept chanting. His teeth chattered as he sat pillion on my bike.

'Ready?' I said, putting on my helmet.

'It's freezing.'

'Zip up your jacket.'

'It's late. We are so drunk. Why do we have to go now?'

'It's Zara, Golu. She herself invited me. On her birthday.'

'Meet her in the morning. I am sleepy, bhai.' He rested his head on my back.

I kick-started the bike. The vibrations of my Enfield woke him up.

'You are not even a student anymore. How will you get into the campus?' Saurabh said. His voice vibrated along with the bike.

'I have my old ID.'

We left the compound of my house and headed out towards the Outer Ring Road to reach the IIT main gate, a ten-minute drive.

'Slower, bhai,' Saurabh said. He held my shoulders tight. 'My stomach doesn't feel so good.'

'Don't puke on me, okay? Tell me to stop if you need to.'

'Slow down, anyway. There could be cops.'

Saurabh was right. We had so much whisky inside us, the cops' breathalyser would probably blow up.

A police checkpost came up ahead, two hundred yards before the IIT main gate. A cop signalled us to slow down.

'Damn, we are dead,' Saurabh said.

'Wait,' I said. I slowed down the bike, as if to comply with the policeman. I brought the bike to a halt a few steps from him. However, I did not shut the ignition. Two other cops walked towards me. In a second, I put the bike into first gear and zoomed off. I could hear the cops scream from behind.

'What the hell was that?' Saurabh said and turned around. 'They have a bike too. They will chase us.'

'Take out my ID. It's in my jacket pocket. Quick.'

As Saurabh fumbled and pulled out my old IIT student card, I reached the gate.

'Keshav Rajpurohit, Kumaon hostel,' I said, with the same confidence as when I was a student. I didn't remove my helmet.

'ID?' the security guard said.

Saurabh flashed my old ID. He hid the 'valid until' date with his finger. It is amazing how even under alcohol's influence, the brain knows how to cover its ass from authorities.

The IIT security guard let us in.

I tore into the campus. I took the road towards the institute building on the way to Himadri hostel.

'Are the cops coming?' I said.

Saurabh looked back.

'No. They stopped outside the main gate.'

'They never come inside campus,' I said and grinned.

The cops were familiar with IIT students, who often took their bikes for a spin outside at weird hours. For the most part, they left them alone.

'Terrible idea, anyway. Now the cops have your bike number.'

'They won't care.'

'How do you plan to get inside Himadri?' Saurabh said.

'Like I used to. Mango tree.'

'Seriously, bhai? You are not a student anymore. You won't just get into trouble with the profs. You will go to jail.'

'Relax.'

I parked the bike fifty meters away from Himadri. The main entrance of the girls' hostel had twenty-four-hour security. A patrolling jeep also took rounds every hour to check if the guard had dozed off. The mango tree at the back was the only way I could get in.

Room 105 was the corner room on the first floor of Himadri.

It was somewhat cut off from the other rooms, and was where Zara had been staying from the time she joined IIT five years ago. It had a big window with a lush green mango tree outside.

Fortunately for Zara, when she had joined IIT as a PhD student, the much-in-demand room had become available. We used to call 105 'our little home', as this was where we met most of the time.

I never took Zara to my hostel. Forget the rules, which did not allow girls, I was also aware of how female-deprived the boys there were. Walking in with a Zara and locking the door of your room—that would just rub salt in their wounds.

Of course, I was not allowed into Himadri as well, which was a strictly girls-only hostel. However, if you were reasonably agile, the tree outside room 105 had uses apart from yielding delicious mangoes every year. At least one night a week I would climb it. Once at first floor height, I would jump across through the window of 105 and I'd leave before daylight. Nobody ever found out that Zara had a male visitor. The whole system worked beautifully. Of course, until we broke up.

Saurabh and I walked towards the back of Himadri to reach the mango tree. I removed my jacket.

'So this is how you used to—' Saurabh started, but I interrupted him.

'Shh ... low volume, please.'

'Where is her room?' Saurabh whispered.

I pointed at her window.

'What if you fall?'

'Done it a dozen times.' I waved my hand airily.

'With Blenders Pride in your blood?'

'Relax, I am fine.' I twisted my body side to side as warm-up. I clasped the trunk with my hands and lifted one leg up to the first branch. I had done this so many times, my movements were reflexive. Once up on the tree, I looked down at Saurabh. We whispered to each other.

'You wait here. If anyone comes, cough,' I said.

'How will that help?'

'That's true. It won't. Okay, if anyone comes this way, distract them. Give them some reason why you are here.'

'What? What is a coaching class tutor doing at a girls' hostel at quarter past three in the morning?'

'I don't know,' I said, brushing leaves off my face.

'Bhai, you haven't thought this through.'

'It's fine. Nobody will come,' I said and looked up. I climbed a few more inches and looked down at Saurabh again.

'Damn. Big problem,' I said. Saurabh's face dropped.

'What?' Saurabh said.

'I didn't get her a gift.'

'Seriously, bhai, that's your big problem?'

'I'm meeting her after years. On her birthday. With no gift.'

'Send her an Amazon voucher later. Now please go up. Just get it over with.'

'No gift, no cake, damn,' I mumbled, pulling myself up with my arms. I noticed that my fitness levels had dropped. I guess teaching maths at Chandan Classes didn't keep me as fit as when I was the volleyball captain at IIT Delhi. I reached Zara's window. She had kept it slightly ajar for me, just like she used to.

I stretched out my hand to push the window wide open so I could enter. The room lights were switched off. Maybe she had gone back to sleep. Or maybe she was pretending to have done so in order to enhance my surprise. Zara had a bit of crazy in her, just as I did. At least she used to. Maybe that is why we connected in the first place.

The branches had grown since I last climbed them. Instead of jumping into the room as before, I simply hooked one leg over the windowsill. I held the window frame with my hands and pulled the rest of my body in.

'Happy birthday to you,' I sang softly as I shut the window. I tiptoed into the room, my eyes adjusting to the darkness. I only heard the mild hum of the convection heater in response.

'Happy birthday, dear Zara,' I continued to sing, standing near her bed. She's the one who had invited me. However, I couldn't presume she'd be okay with me sliding under her sheets and hugging her like old times. No, I couldn't just cuddle her. We weren't together anymore, I reminded myself.

But she did say she missed me, a voice in my head said. I took out my phone and switched on the torch. The white LED light lit up wherever I pointed it. I saw Zara in bed, fast asleep. The quilt almost covered her face.

'Zara,' I said, my voice soft. I did not want to startle her.

'It's Keshav. I am here,' I whispered again.

She didn't react. I found the bedside lamp's switch with the help of the phone flashlight. Watery light filled the room. Zara lay in bed, covered in her white quilt with pretty pink flowers printed all over it.

'Hey, birthday girl,' I said. 'It's me, I'm here to wish you.'

No reaction. Okay, nice acting, very cute, I thought. I looked around her room. She had a bundle of white paper sheets, probably study material, on her bedside table. Her iPhone lay on top of the study material, and was connected to a charger. Like always, Zara had Johnson's Baby Lotion next to her. She applied it on her face and body every night, and always smelt like a baby.

'Hey, Johnson's baby,' I said, 'wake up.'

I placed my hand on her shoulder, over her quilt, and shook her gently. She didn't move.

Had she been drinking, too? Maybe those were drunk messages, I thought. Is that what made her call me to her room? She sounded pretty articulate though.

Was she acting? Was it her way of making me wait? Or maybe even making me get into bed with her, without actually asking?

My mind grappled with the alternatives. It was so hard to be a guy and choose what action to take with a girl sometimes. A part of me wanted to be bold and go for it.

Slide into bed with her, kiss her happy birthday, that voice said.

Okay, maybe not on the lips but on the forehead. Forehead kisses are fine, right? another voice said.

No. Don't ruin it. She's called you over. Let her decide the pace, a counter-voice, total killjoy, said.

With reluctance, I chose restraint. But acting or not, I had to wake her up.

I shook Zara's shoulder again, this time with more force. She didn't budge. I pulled the quilt away from her face. She lay there still, as if in deep sleep.

'Okay, Zara, enough jokes. I came to wish you in person. Happy birthday.'

She didn't react.

'Are you going to wake up?' I said.

No answer.

'Zara, I know what will work. I will slip into bed with you. That will make you wake up.' My breath caught on a laugh.

She still didn't respond, so I bent to push her a bit, to make space for me. It felt heavy.

'Zara,' I said, this time my voice loud. 'Are you okay?'

I touched her forehead. It felt ice-cold. My heart pounded hard. Something was wrong. I pulled the quilt down further from her face. Her neck had dark red marks on it.

'Zara, baby,' I said. I touched her cheeks, eyes and ears in quick succession. Everything felt cold.

'Wake up,' I said, I don't know to whom in particular. I switched on the main light in the room. The light from the bright hundred-watt-bulb made me scrunch my eyes at first. However, it also let me see Zara clearly, lying absolutely still.

'Zara,' I called out loud. I brought my fingers close to her nostrils. I felt nothing. I had seen in movies how they check someone's pulse. I lifted up Zara's thin, cold wrist. No pulse. I tried checking it a few more times. Nothing.

Zara was ... dead?

I felt nauseous. I needed air. I stood up and pulled the

window wide open. I looked down. Under the moonlight, I could make out Saurabh. He stood there, shifting his weight from one leg to the other. He noticed me at the window and waved to check what was going on. He pointed a finger down, suggesting I come back. I couldn't respond. I tried to throw up but couldn't. Confused, Saurabh threw up both his hands in exasperation.

I turned back into the room. No, my Zara couldn't have died. This was a bad dream. I stood still and stared at her body, hoping she would wake up.

The phone vibrating in my pocket jolted me. I picked up Saurabh's call. He spoke in a naughty, teasing voice.

'Bhai, what's going on? You went back in. Getting lucky? Should I stay or leave?'

'Saurabh,' I said and stopped.

'Yes?'

'Saurabh, come up.'

'What?'

'Just come up.'

'Why are you calling me to your girlfriend's, or ex-girlfriend's, room?'

'I beg you, Saurabh, come up,' I said, close to tears. He sensed something was wrong.

'Will Zara be fine if I come up?'

'Come,' I said and hung up. I went to the window again. I pointed the phone flashlight at the tree trunk to help him.

He looked around nervously and lifted a leg to climb. The mango tree creaked. They are designed for monkeys, after all, not overweight, ninety-kilo humans.

'Careful. Now put the left foot on the next stump,' I whispered as he reached closer. Fortunately, nobody heard the commotion on the tree this late at night.

He placed his leg across the window. I pulled him in.

'What's going on, bhai?' he said.

I shut the window and bolted it from inside.

He saw her lying in bed.

'She's sleeping?' he whispered. 'You haven't woken her up yet?'

'She's dead,' I said.

Saurabh jumped back a step.

'What?' he screamed.

'Keep it quiet. It's a girls' hostel. Male voices should not be heard here.'

'Screw the male voice, bhai. What the hell are you talking about?' Saurabh said, his volume rising higher, along with his blood pressure.

I grabbed him by the neck and covered his mouth with my hand. He groaned.

'Please, keep quiet,' I said. 'You are freaking me out. Quiet, understood?'

Saurabh nodded, my hand still on his mouth. I released my grip.

Saurabh coughed as he spoke again, this time in normal volume.

'Are you sure?' Saurabh said. 'Maybe she isn't well.'

'She's gone. Her body feels like ice. She isn't breathing. Look at her face,' I said.

He noticed the red marks around her neck.

'How did she die?' he whispered.

'How the hell do I know? This is how I found her.'

'But she just messaged you,' Saurabh said, pacing up and down the room.

'Yeah,' I said. I opened my phone again. Yes, this wasn't a dream. I had her messages. She missed me and wanted me to wish her in person. I sat down on Zara's study chair. I examined her face, as calm as a sleeping baby's. The love of my life had died. But the shock of it all meant I couldn't feel any pain.

'What do we do?' Saurabh said.

'No clue,' I said, 'but sit down, please. You pacing is making me nervous.'

'I am so scared,' Saurabh said. I felt fear too. But I couldn't have a meltdown like him. Someone had to think.

'I have never seen a dead body before,' Saurabh said, as if I hung out with corpses all the time. 'Bhai, do something.'

'Shut up, Saurabh. I am thinking what to do. Do you have any ideas?'

'No, bhai. We should have never come here. We were happy at the booze party in our apartment. I said before itself that it is a terrible idea…'

He continued to rant, jamming my thoughts. I wanted to slap him, but couldn't. Yes, he had tried to stop me from coming to her room, so I let him vent for five minutes. After that, more out of exhaustion than anything else, he sat on the wooden easy chair in the room.

'We have to inform someone,' I said. 'We have no choice.'

'How?' Saurabh said. 'What do we say we are doing here? In a girls' hostel room. At this time in the morning. With the occupant dead.'

'So what do we do? Run away?'

'Maybe. It's still dark. Let's leave the same way we came and vanish.'

I considered the idea. We sneak out, go back home, and pretend this never happened. However, something didn't seem right about that option.

'How did she die?' I said.

'What?'

'How did Zara die? She was alive an hour ago. Healthy.'

'I don't care, bhai. Right now, we need to get out. Fast.'

'She wasn't sick.'

'Yeah, so?'

'Someone killed her,' I said.

Saurabh sprang up from his seat.

'What?' he said. 'We are at a murder scene? Let's leave, bhai. Now.'

He went to the window.

'We can't leave like this, Golu. Sit down, please. Let's think this through.'

With heavy steps he went back to the easy chair.

'Why stay? So people eventually find us? And assume we did it?' he said.

'If we run away, they will definitely think we did it.'

'How will they even know we came here?' Saurabh said, wiping sweat off his face. 'It's still dark outside. Let's go.'

'You don't understand. This is big. A PhD student murdered in an IIT hostel. Not only the insti, but the entire police and media will be all over this one.'

'So?' Saurabh clasped the armrests of the easy chair tight.

'So they will dig.'

'Anyone could have done it. There are over a thousand students on the campus alone.'

'But the main-gate guard might remember us. And, of course, the policemen at the checkpost might remember my bike too. And that we went into the campus.'

'So what? We came for a ride at night.'

'And they will search for fingerprints in the room. Mine are on the window. On the bed. Even on her face.'

'Fingerprints?' echoed Saurabh, his face white.

'Your prints are on the easy chair now,' I said. He immediately released his grip on the armrests.

'Bhai, what is going on? Some Crime Patrol shit?' he said and stood up. 'Can't we wipe everything and leave? I really want to leave.'

'We can't, Golu.'

'Our lives will be ruined.'

'No, Golu. If we wipe fingerprints and flee, then we are ruined.'

'So what do we do?'

'We stay and say the truth.'

'That we drank a bottle of whisky, chose to ride drunk, dodged a cop, showed an invalid ID to the institute guard and climbed up into the girls' hostel late at night. Are you insane, bhai?'

'Those are bad things, yes. But that doesn't make us murderers.'

'Murderers?' Saurabh squeaked. 'How can you even say that word? We haven't done anything.'

'I know. That's why we need to stay. Now, who do we call first?'

I took out my phone.

'Are you sure, bhai? You are not exactly having the best ideas today.'

'If you want to leave, Saurabh, you can,' I said. He didn't have to be a part of this mess.

'I didn't say that, bhai.'

'I mean it. Whatever happens, there is going to be some trouble. You don't have to be here.'

'Didn't we decide at our booze party that whatever we do, we do together?' he said. I looked at him. In some ways, having a best friend is way more important than having a lover.

'I love you, man,' I said.

'Me too, bhai. Who are you calling?'

'Her parents, her boyfriend or the police. These are the choices.'

'Should we just walk down? We can find the watchman and tell him everything. Let him make the calls.'

I let out a huge breath. He did make sense.

'Not a bad idea. But,' I paused.

'But what?'

'But if we don't call these people ourselves, they will find out we were here and never stop suspecting us. Let's call them first and then go to the watchman.'

'I have never called the police in my life,' Saurabh said.

'Same here. I'll call the police last.'

'Parents?'

'That will be hard too. Let me call that Raghu first.'

'You have his number?'

'Yeah,' I said.

He had called me a few times before, to tell me to stay away from Zara. I had saved his contact, to have some way of reaching Zara in case she blocked me. I checked the time. It was 3:36. I dialled his number. The phone rang. Nobody picked up. Eventually, I heard a service message in Telugu, perhaps telling me that the person could not be reached. I tried again. No response.

'Seems to be sleeping,' I said.

'Call her dad,' Saurabh said.

I dialled Safdar Lone's number. What would I say to him, I wondered. Hi, uncle, sorry to bother you. It's me, Keshav. Remember you said to stay away from your daughter? Well, I am in her room. Oh, and by the way, she is dead.

'Yes?' Safdar said, his voice sleepy and angry at the same time.

'Uncle, it's me. Keshav.'

'I know. Have you seen the time?'

'3:38, uncle.'

'What do you want?' he said.

'Uncle, Zara ...'

'What?'

'Mr Lone, Zara ...'

'You need to forget about Zara. I thought I made this clear years ago. Are you drunk again?'

I *was* drunk, sort of. Most of my high had vanished though.

'Uncle, please listen to me, it's important,' I said, trying to collect my thoughts.

'What?'

I couldn't break the news.

'Can you please come to Zara's hostel? Now.'

'What? Why?'

'Please. It's important. Come right now. I am here.'

'Wha…'

I cut the call. I don't know why, but speaking to her father made everything more real. Zara had died. Gone. No, I couldn't go to pieces. Not right now. I had more calls to make.

'Police,' I said out loud, 'what's their number?'

'100?' Saurabh said.

'That's the general number. Should we call the local police station?'

'You mean the same guys who just chased us?' Saurabh said.

'Shut up,' I said. I Googled the Hauz Khas police station number on my phone and called them.

Someone picked up after five rings.

'Hauz Khas police,' a tired voice said on the other side.

'We are calling to report a crime,' I said.

Saurabh looked at me with a worried expression.

'Where are you calling from?'

'IIT Delhi. Himadri hostel. Room 105,' I said.

'Nature of crime?' the voice said in a monotonous tone.

'Murder. Of a student.'

I heard something drop at the other end.

'Who is speaking?' the voice said, now alert.

'This is Keshav Rajpurohit. I will be waiting here for you. At the entrance of Himadri hostel, IIT Delhi.'

'Who's the victim and what's your relationship?'

'Zara Lone. I am her friend and an ex-student.'

'Please stay there. We are sending a team,' the voice said briskly.

I ended the call. Saurabh and I looked at each other.

'Let's wait downstairs?' Saurabh said. He just wanted to be out of the room, and away from the dead body.

'Yeah,' I said. I stood up and opened the door to the dark and empty corridor outside. Saurabh walked out of the room. I remained inside.

'What? Let's go,' Saurabh said.

'Wait. Just one minute,' I said, turning back. I walked up to her bed. I leaned forward and kissed her forehead. A teardrop fell on her cold face.

'Happy birthday, Zara. I love you.'

Zara remained still.

'Bhai,' Saurabh said and knocked on the door, 'let's go.'

'Coming,' I said. I straightened up, looked at her one more time, and then left the room.

Chapter 6

We went down the steps to the main entrance of Himadri. Seeing us emerge from the hostel, the watchman jumped up from his chair looking stupefied.

'Stop. Who are you?' he said.

'Watchman sahib,' I said, 'we want to talk to you.'

'What are you doing inside the girls' hostel?' he said.

'Listen to us, watchman sahib,' I said, 'someone has died.'

'What?' he said, his mouth open.

Before I could say more, I heard police sirens. The Hauz Khas police was more efficient than I had expected. A Delhi Police Maruti Gypsy entered the hostel compound. An IIT Delhi security patrol car followed it. Three cops stepped out of the Gypsy. One of them wore a police cap and his uniform had epaulettes. Seemingly the senior-most in the group, he walked up to us. I read his name tag: Vikas Rana. Two constables and four IIT Delhi security officers walked behind him. The watchman almost collapsed.

'Who is Keshav Rajpurohit?' Inspector Rana said in a rough baritone.

'I am Keshav, sir,' I said, extending a hand. He ignored it.

'You called us?'

'Yes, sir,' I said. 'I found my friend, Zara Lone, dead. Room number 105.'

The security officers looked at me, shocked.

'Who are you?' one of the security officers said. 'A student?'

'Ex-student,' I said. '2013 batch. Kumaon hostel.'

'2013?' said the same security officer. 'What are you doing here now?'

'I came to visit her,' I said and added, 'It's her birthday.'

'But how can you come into the girls' hostel?' His voice got louder.

'Can we not waste time and examine the body, please?' Inspector Rana said.

❖

A constable used a handkerchief to open the door of Zara's room.

'Careful,' Inspector Rana said, 'there could be fingerprints.'

Saurabh and I looked at each other. The only fingerprints they might find on the door handle would be ours.

The police entered the room. Zara, or Zara's body, lay there, quilt removed and the room lights on.

'Don't touch anything,' Inspector Rana warned.

We already have, inspector, I wanted to say. One of the constables took pictures of the body, on his phone. He said something about the official photographer not being available at such an odd hour.

Inspector Rana walked up to the bed. He examined Zara's neck.

'Not a suicide. Someone strangled her.'

A gust of cold air from the open door accompanied his words. Everyone fell silent until one of the security officers spoke again.

'How did this happen, Laxman?' he said, addressing the watchman. Watchman Laxman folded his hands.

'No idea, sahib.'

'Did you see anyone come in?' the security officer barked at him.

'Nobody. I was on duty throughout.'

'Did you sleep off or leave your post?' the security patrol officer shouted, to reclaim his authority and show the police he meant business too.

Watchman Laxman shook his head. His body seemed to shrink, and not because of the cold.

'Tell me, honestly. You know I can check CCTV footage of the entrance,' the patrol officer said.

The patrol officer had to deflect blame too. For, despite all his patrolling and supervision, someone had come in and murdered a student.

'No, sahib, I was on duty. Awake,' Laxman said.

'So how did two-two men get inside the hostel then?' the security officer said, pointing at Saurabh and me. Laxman had nothing to say. The patrol officer slapped him. I guess he had to display his toughness to the police.

'Stop it,' Inspector Rana said. 'Don't do our job.'

'Sorry, sir,' the patrol officer said. He looked ashamed at being shouted at in front of his juniors. Perhaps he had wanted to be an investigating officer in the police too. People want to grow up and become cops. Nobody dreams about guarding an engineering college full of nerds.

'You couldn't prevent the crime, now at least let us investigate it,' Inspector Rana said.

The patrol officer hung his head low.

'Sorry, sir.'

Inspector Rana ignored him. He walked around the room, saw Zara's phone. He disconnected the charger and lifted the handset with a handkerchief. He passed it to a constable who put it in a plastic bag. He checked the documents on her desk. He couldn't make any sense of the quant equations related to big data model simulation, Zara's PhD topic. He dropped the papers back on the desk and walked up to the window. It was bolted shut.

'The window is closed, the murderer entered from the door,' he said.

Despite not wanting to get into trouble, I had to speak up.

'Sir, the window was open,' I said. 'That is how Saurabh and I came in. We closed it when we went down to inform the watchman.'

The inspector turned towards me.

'Who are you really? And this fat guy? How and why are you here?'

'Sir, I can explain everything,' I said.

Over the next few minutes, I told everyone how Saurabh and I had ended up here.

'And so I asked Saurabh to come up. And we decided to call the police,' I finished my story.

I looked at everyone's faces. No one appeared convinced. The patrol officer seemed most offended, less at the murder, more at my audacity.

'You climbed into the IIT girls' hostel? An outsider? Who do you think you are?'

'Sorry, sir,' I said, 'it was a mistake. But...'

Inspector Rana walked up real close to me, eyes inches from mine. After staring at me for what seemed liked an eternity, he turned to Saurabh.

'Is your friend telling the truth?'

Saurabh spoke like Ranbir Kapoor in the film *Jagga Jasoos*.

'Ye ... ye ... yes, sir.'

'So why is your voice shaking?' Inspector Rana said.

'Ju ... ju ... just like that, sir.'

'Are you sure you guys didn't kill her?' Rana said. I felt the ground beneath me shift a little. Were we suspects?

'No, sir,' I blurted out, 'I swear on my mother.'

The inspector's eyes bored into mine.

'Maadarchod, every murderer will swear on his mother if it helps him get away.'

'No, sir, but...' I said, shocked by his language.

'Shut up,' he said. He turned to the constable. 'Bring them to the police station.'

'Sir, you—' But Inspector Rana interrupted me.

'Take the watchman's statement too. Get the entrance CCTV footage. Anyone informed her parents?'

'I did, sir. Her father is coming,' I said.

Saurabh tugged at my hand, suggesting I keep my mouth shut.

One of the constables marked the area and took more

pictures while Saurabh and I stood silently in a corner. The patrol officer stepped out to call the IIT director as the cops rummaged around her room.

'What's happening here? Where's Zara?' Safdar Lone's voice startled everyone in the room.

❖

Police stations in India are a good way to time travel. If you want to see Indian life in the Seventies, with no computers and tons of brown paper files, a police station is a good place to visit. Of course, the Hauz Khas station had a bit of modernity too. They had two computers, both with fat CRT monitors. They ran on Windows software from the Nineties. At nine in the morning, the station was jam-packed with people, as if the police were distributing free 10 GB data cards. Lack of sleep and last night's alcohol had already given me a headache. The cacophony in the station made the pain worse.

Saurabh and I sat separately, as we had been told. They didn't want us to talk and concoct a fake story. As if we couldn't WhatsApp each other from across the room, if we wanted to do that.

I waited for several hours. Inspector Rana finally called me into his office, a ramshackle room in which the desk and two chairs barely fit.

I sat down in front of him and yawned. He continued to read a file, one eye still on me.

'Sleepy?

'A little,' I said.

'Go wash your face.'

'It's fine.'

He threw me a stern glance.

'Do as I say,' he said. I complied. I splashed filthy water from a filthy tap in a filthy bathroom on my face. I returned to his office and sat down again, my eyes open extra wide.

'I had to make you wait outside. The other option was lockup.

I am sure you didn't want to spend the night there.'

I imagined myself behind bars, and my parents finding out. They would yell at me more than any cop would. No, not that option.

'No, sir. Outside is fine.'

'Though behind bars is where you belong, if you actually killed her.'

'I did not, sir. Honest.'

'I need more than that to be sure.'

'I love her, sir. More than you'll ever know. Zara is ... was ... my world. Why would I kill her?'

'Because you couldn't get her?'

'No, sir, I did. She messaged me herself.'

I passed my phone to him. He read my last WhatsApp chat with Zara.

'Ask anyone in my batch. They will tell you what it would mean to me if Zara herself wanted to get back with me,' I said.

The inspector scrolled through the chat a few times. I continued to talk.

'I called the police, sir. I called her father. I even tried to call her boyfriend.'

'Wait. Boyfriend?' he interrupted me.

'Yes, Raghu. He didn't pick up. It was late. He lives in Hyderabad.'

'Give me his number.'

'It's on my phone, Raghu Venkatesh.'

The inspector noted down Raghu's contact details. A constable came to his door.

'The father took Zara Lone's body home,' the constable said.

'What the hell! How so soon?' Inspector Rana looked put off.

'Father is a big shot. Maybe used his connections,' the constable said.

'Where do her parents live?'

'Westend Greens. Near the Shiv statue on the Delhi border,' the constable said.

'Rich girl,' the inspector scoffed. 'Speak to them about a post-mortem, please.'

'I checked. Father declined. Too disturbed,' the constable said. 'Sir, you know these Muslim people. Their religion doesn't permit cutting up dead bodies. We put too much pressure, there will only be more drama.'

'How will we solve the case if they don't let us do an autopsy?' Inspector Rana screamed.

The other man didn't answer. He took that as a cue to leave.

Rana turned to me after the constable had left the room.

'You loved her. Why are you not sad?' Rana said.

'I don't know, sir,' I said. 'I know she is gone but I cannot believe it, cannot accept it. It is like I will wake up soon and...'

'It has happened. Zara Lone is dead. And you may have killed her. Found on the crime scene. Smelling of alcohol.'

'No, sir, it's not like that.'

'Former lover unable to get over her. She called you. You forced yourself on her. She declined. You couldn't take it.'

'I didn't,' I roared. Then in a more sober voice, 'I mean. I didn't. I just went to wish her happy birthday.'

The stress finally made me cave in. Tears spilled from my eyes. I began to cry. Zara had died. I would never see her again. I wouldn't hear her voice. I couldn't message her or see her status, scraps I had lived on for the last few years. Worse, the police thought I had killed her. They could make me spend the rest of my already miserable life in jail. I folded my hands.

'I haven't done it, Rana sir. I could never do it.'

'So who did it? And stop crying. What a baby.'

'I don't know.' I composed myself.

The inspector picked up the intercom. Another constable came in.

'Any luck with the girl's phone?'

'It's a locked iPhone, sir. We don't know the passcode.'

'It has touch ID, right? The thumb one?'

'Yes, sir.'

'So use the dead girl's hand to open it.'

The constable scratched his head. 'When the phone is switched on the first time, you have to enter the numeric passcode, sir.'

'Did some idiot in the station switch the phone off?'

'No, no, sir. It seems like the phone was switched off, kept for charging, and switched back on.'

'So we can't unlock the phone?'

'No, sir. It is a six-digit code. It will lock forever after ten failed tries.'

'These stupid phone companies. Call the service provider. Get call logs.'

'Already done, sir.'

'Did anyone call the girl's phone today? It rings, right?'

'Two missed calls, sir. From a contact called Raghu Cutie Pie.'

'I will call him right away. You check the location of Raghu Cutie Pie last night from the cell tower.'

'Sure, sir,' the constable said.

The inspector turned to me.

'Wait outside, Keshav,' he said. 'I can hold off on an FIR for a while, but you can't leave the station.'

'I won't, sir, I promise.'

'Sleep on the floor outside. Find a corner.'

'I can rest on the chair. But, sir, one thing.'

'What?'

'You are calling Raghu. May I stay and listen to this call?'

'Why?'

'I don't know. Just curious.'

'Oh, you are a detective now?'

'I found the body. I knew her. Of course, I am curious. Plus, maybe I can help you.'

The inspector shrugged; he didn't care. He dialled Raghu's number and put the call on speaker.

'Hello, good morning,' a lady answered. Her voice had a Telugu accent.

'Hello, is Mr Raghu Venkatesh there?' Rana said.

'Wait, one minute aan, doctor is inspecting him. I pass phone to him. Who is calling, please?'

'I am Inspector Vikas Rana this side. Who's speaking?'

'Nurse Janie, sir. I looking after Raghu sir here.'

'Where?'

'Apollo Hospital, sir. Wait aan, I give phone to him.'

We heard her speak in Telugu to someone. After a few seconds Raghu came on the line.

'Hello?' Raghu said.

'Hello, Mr Raghu, Inspector Vikas Rana from Hauz Khas police station speaking. Can you talk?'

'Yes, sir.'

'Have you heard the news?'

'What news, sir?'

'Do you know Zara Lone? A friend of yours.'

'My fiancée, sir,' Raghu said.

'Oh. I am sorry, Mr Raghu. We found Zara's body in her room. She's no more.'

The phone went silent.

'Mr Raghu?' Rana said.

'What?' Raghu said after a few seconds.

'Your friend, or fiancée. She was found dead in her room. We think she was murdered.'

'Are you serious? Who is this? Did you send those men too?' Raghu said, fear in his voice.

'Which men? This is the police. We have her phone. You gave her two missed calls today. One at 8:14 in the morning, and the other at 8:32.'

We heard a fumbling sound as Raghu checked his phone. He spoke again.

'I can't ... sorry, I can't believe this.'

'Her parents have her body. You can call them.'

'Yes, I will, right now,' Raghu said. 'This is not ... I can't ... sorry, I am unable to talk.'

'I understand. This has been a shock to you.'

'It's Zara's birthday today,' he said, his breathing audible over the phone. 'Our wedding is in two months.'

The word 'wedding' made my chest hurt. I looked away from the inspector.

'Sorry, Mr Raghu. We can't bring her back. But we will do our best to find out who did it.'

'Why would anyone want to hurt Zara?' Raghu said.

'Do you know anyone who might?'

'Some people attacked me three days ago. I thought it was a local gang extorting money.'

'Really? Who? When?' the inspector said. He took out a notebook to write it all down.

'Three goons. Late at night. Right outside my office in Cyber City. They came on bikes and hit me with hockey sticks. Broke the windows of my car. I managed to scream, otherwise they would have hurt me more.'

'Are you injured?'

'A head wound. And a fracture in my arm.'

The inspector took down notes furiously.

'Is that why you are in hospital?'

'Yeah. I am in Apollo. I planned to be there for her birthday ... and ...' he paused. We heard sobs on the phone. Raghu, my biggest enemy in life, was crying. Yet I didn't feel good about it. The inspector let Raghu cry for a while before he spoke again.

'I can see you are disturbed. I will hang up now but we may have to talk later. Take care.'

The inspector ended the call.

The cop who had come earlier was back.

'Sir, phone records will come tomorrow. However, they confirmed Mr Raghu's cell tower location in Hyderabad last night.'

'Yeah, he is admitted in a hospital there,' Rana said and turned to me. 'Are you going to sit in my office like a jamaai all day? Go, wait outside.'

'Of course, sir,' I said, and stood up to leave the room.

Chapter 7

Click! Flash! Click! Click! The flashes, the camera clicks and the loud journalists screaming for my attention disoriented me. At noon on the day of Zara's death, reporters from every publication and TV channel in Delhi had descended on the Hauz Khas police station. Around thirty journalists had crowded the station entrance. Through bits and pieces, they tried to figure out what had happened. Inspector Rana refused to talk to anyone. No constable would dare to speak to the media without permission either. Around noon, when I stepped out of the police station to get something to eat, reporters bombarded me.

'Are you Keshav Rajpurohit?' said one.

I gave a brief nod. The reporters went into a frenzy. They jostled with each other to shove their mikes closest to my face.

'Did you find the dead body?' said another.

'Did you break into the girls' hostel?' yet another wanted to know.

'Are you her ex-boyfriend?' came one more question.

Dazed, I didn't know what to say and whom to speak to first.

'Please, let me go,' I said. 'I haven't done anything. I don't know anything.'

I don't know why I had to say that. It only fanned the flames further. The questions became louder and more intrusive.

'Are you saying you might be considered a suspect?'

'No,' I said, 'nothing like that. When did I say that?'

'Were you still having physical relations with Zara Lone?' said one reporter, who was wearing thick-lensed glasses. I wanted to sock his spectacled face. I had to control myself. If I hit a journalist in a police station it wouldn't help my case. I gritted my teeth.

'I need to step out, let me go,' I said.

'Did you murder Zara Lone, Mr Keshav Rajpurohit?' the spectacled reporter asked next.

'No!' I screamed. Unable to move ahead, I turned around and ran back into the police station. I could stay hungry. I just didn't want to be eaten alive.

I went up to Saurabh, ignoring the inspector's instructions to stay away. He was snoozing on a wooden bench. My brain had officially stopped functioning. It didn't feel sorrow, fear or even tiredness. I couldn't sleep like Saurabh. I saw a TV perched on a dusty shelf, high on the wall opposite me. It was running a particular news channel. After a few ads, the channel flashed the 'Breaking News' sign.

'Kashmiri Muslim girl murdered in IIT Delhi hostel'.

A reporter stood in front of the IIT gate, right next to the security checkpost where I had shown my outdated ID card.

I could see a dozen other reporters parked outside the gate as well; the director must have denied entry to the media. Only shots of the IIT Delhi sign on the main gate were being shown.

The volume was very low, so I walked up close to the TV to listen. One finger in his ear, the reporter spoke to the anchor, Arijit, in the studio.

'Arijit, so far what we know is the victim is Zara Lone, a PhD student at IIT Delhi. She was found murdered in her room, number 105 at Himadri hostel, around three in the morning. It seems her ex-boyfriend, who is also an ex-IIT Delhi student, broke into her room to wish her on her birthday, which was today, and found her dead.'

'Wait a minute,' Anchor Arijit said, pen in hand. 'Did you just say her ex-boyfriend broke into her room?'

'Yes, Arijit. His name is Keshav Rajpurohit. He graduated around five years ago. Zara Lone and he were in a relationship then. Incidentally, Zara finished her graduation from Delhi College of Engineering and then joined IIT Delhi for a PhD programme, so she remained on campus. However, Keshav and Zara's relationship, sources tell us, was over a while ago.'

I was famous. I was being talked about on TV, but not like

one of those IIT guys who open billion-dollar startups, become CEOs or launch political parties. My claim to fame was breaking into girls' hostels.

'But can you elaborate on breaking into the room?' Arijit said. 'Boys are not allowed in IIT girls' hostels?'

'Well, yes, IIT Delhi has a strict policy of not allowing men into girls' rooms. So Keshav came in through the window by climbing a mango tree. Unfortunately, we were not allowed into the campus, so we can't show you the mango tree.'

Of course, it was unfortunate. The country could not see the mango tree. Or the mangoes that grew on it.

'Go on.' Arijit shook his head, so bothered by it all that his neck was coming loose.

'So he climbed into the room to wish her and found her dead. Then he informed the police and her parents. That's his version.'

'Exactly, that is *his* version. Now, what are the police doing?'

'I think it is too soon. But Keshav is at the Hauz Khas police station. He seems to be in a daze, or maybe even angry, we have some visuals.'

Suddenly, I was on screen, looking every inch a psycho.

'No!' I was screaming. They played my 'no' on loop five times, like they do in TV serials.

'I must add,' the reporter said, 'we are hearing that Keshav Rajpurohit is from Rajasthan, and his father, Naman Rajpurohit, is a senior RSS member there. It's a politically connected family.'

What? Why is that a *must add*? I touched my earring. Why did my parents have to come into this? I checked my pockets. I couldn't find my phone. I had left it on the chair I had been sitting on in the police station. Fortunately, I found it in the same place I had left it. I guess nobody would steal from a police station. I had ten missed calls from home. Four from Chandan Arora. Two from Sexy Sheela, who must have called me on behalf of Chandan. Before I could call them back, I heard my name on TV again.

'So have the police arrested Keshav Rajpurohit? Or are his political connections helping him?' Arijit said.

What the hell, I thought. Why should I be arrested? And what political connections had I used here? I didn't want my father to ever find out about this. The reporter continued to speak.

'No, Arijit, no arrests so far. Keshav is cooperating with the police or being detained, we don't know yet. According to the police, they are looking at several angles. They will try to talk to other hostel-mates soon.'

'But why haven't they arrested the ex-boyfriend? Or anyone?' Arijit said, incensed.

Because I freaking didn't do anything! Ten minutes since the story had broken on TV, and this guy wanted someone arrested. Thankfully, what the reporter said to this was even spicier than Arijit's ex-boyfriend theory.

'See, Arijit, we are also hearing, though there is no way to confirm it, that there could be a terrorism angle here. You see, Zara Lone was Kashmiri, and a Muslim.'

Of course, being a Kashmiri Muslim is definitely a *you see* kind of situation. It puts you on the terrorism radar immediately. Within seconds, to my relief, Arijit had forgotten me.

'A Kashmiri Muslim girl. Killed under mysterious circumstances. Is this part of a deeper conspiracy?' Arijit questioned no one in particular.

'We don't know that yet, Arijit,' the reporter said humbly.

Arijit didn't appreciate this kind of a non-committal answer. He leaned forward, even closer to the camera. 'Ladies and gentleman, we have a big story here, and your channel has been the first to show it.'

That was a lie. I had seen thirty reporters at the police station itself. Everyone had covered the story at the same time.

'The big question, before we go into the break, ladies and gentleman, is this,' Arijit said, speaking each word with deliberation, like his own life depended on this case. 'Has terror reached India's elite institutes?'

An ad for Patanjali toothpaste, made from herbs used by rishis two thousand years ago, replaced the murder story. In the ad, rishis meditated peacefully, thinking of toothpaste formulations perhaps. In contrast to the anchor of the news show they sponsored, Patanjali's toothpaste models had an immensely calm air. The ad ended with Baba Ramdev's picture. I have never been happier to see Baba Ramdev's grin. I just didn't want the channel to go back to Zara.

Of course, nobody cared about what I wanted. Within minutes, Arijit was back, this time with something he called 'an esteemed' panel. Six people—socialites, ex-cops, somebody who ran a think-tank on Kashmir and a retired IIT professor—occupied six little windows on the TV screen. How do news channels do this? How do they line up so many jobless people from different areas of expertise so fast?

Arijit had his own window, double the size of the others. He opened the discussion. 'The question is this, my esteemed panel, has extremism reached our elite shores? Could there be a terror angle here? And does this case also show that nobody is safe in Delhi?'

'I don't know about the terror part,' the Kashmiri think-tank guy started to say before the socialite lady with a bindi the size of a ten-rupee coin out-shouted him.

'Forget terror! My question is, Arijit, what is the institute security doing? What are the Delhi Police doing? Hauz Khas is a posh area. If that is not safe, what is? Is this a national capital or a crime capital?'

'Exactly! If even the rich are not safe, what are the police doing?' Arijit said.

The ex-cop said something about at least giving the police a chance to investigate. The socialite lady shut him up. The ex-IIT professor never spoke a word.

'Come, Rana sir has called you,' a constable came up to me and shook me by my shoulder.

❖

'Your parents called. They are trying to reach you,' Rana said. His voice seemed calmer than before.

'Sorry, I had kept my phone away,' I said. Anyway, I wanted to avoid them as much as possible.

'They are on their way from Alwar. Should be here in a few hours.'

'Damn,' I said.

'What?'

'Nothing.'

'Call your friend here as well. Let's talk.'

I went out and woke up Saurabh. Both of us went back to Inspector Rana's office.

'This case is big. National news,' Rana said.

'I know, sir,' I said.

'What? How?'

'I saw on TV. The reporters,' I said.

'For your own sake, stay away from the reporters.'

'I didn't speak to them, sir. They crowded around me when I went out to eat. I ran right back in.'

'Have you eaten anything since morning?'

Saurabh shook his head vigorously. Inspector Rana asked a peon to get us snacks. He came back with two cups of tea and aloo pakoras. The inspector ordered us to eat. I took slow bites as he spoke again.

'Your father spoke to me. He is, what, RSS pradhan sevak in Rajasthan?'

'One of the state pranth pracharaks.'

'Yeah. He also spoke to the south Delhi MP. Hauz Khas comes in the south Delhi area.'

I now knew the reason for Rana's new tone, not to mention

the tea and snacks. The only way to make power behave in India is, well, more power.

'I won't go easy on you because of your political contacts. If at all, I will be more strict,' he said, as if reading my mind.

'Of course, sir. But we really are innocent,' Saurabh said, his first words since morning.

'Innocence alone can set you free,' the inspector said. 'The case is on TV. If media says police went soft due to the accused's connections, I am in trouble.'

Was I the accused? No, I wasn't, right?

'Sir? Accused?' I said, bewildered.

'I mean *if* you were the accused. Circumstantial evidence is there. But, luckily, we have some more information now that could help you.'

'What?' both Saurabh and I spoke in unison, adding belatedly, 'sir.'

'According to the campus register, you entered the campus on your Enfield bike at 3:14. It means the earliest you could be in Zara's room is 3:20.'

'Yes, sir. That's when I reached. My bike is still parked on campus.'

'And you called her parents at 3:38 and the police at 3:40. The police arrived at 3:52 and we saw the body at 3:54.'

'Right, sir,' I said. I didn't understand why he was mentioning so many different timings.

'So, let's say you arrived at 3:20 and killed her, say, by 3:35.'

'I didn't, sir.'

'Shut up and listen.'

'Yes, sir.'

'So, say, you killed her at 3:35. I saw the body at 3:54. Well, I am no post-mortem expert, but I have seen enough bodies in my life. That body didn't look like it had died twenty minutes ago. It felt a lot more stiff and cold.'

I heaved a sigh of relief.

'I know, sir. She was dead when I reached. Cold to touch.'

'Well, an autopsy would have helped us more. Her parents didn't allow it.' Rana laced his fingers together.

'Why?' I said.

'Religious reasons? Who the hell knows? They say they want to give her a proper burial. In autopsy, we do cut up the body. But we also stitch it back, but the parents won't listen.'

Saurabh and I kept quiet. The inspector spoke again.

'Anyway, I have sent a coroner. Hopefully, they allow him to do an external examination. He may have something to report.'

He opened his notes.

'There's no injury other than strangulation marks on the neck. No sexual assault or rape as far as we could make out.'

It was amazing he could talk about dead bodies and sexual assault like we discussed trigonometry and algebra at the coaching centre. 'We have taken statements from some of her hostel-mates. Was it a holiday on campus?'

'Could be. A week-long mid-term break. We used to have one in February,' I said.

'Yeah, not too many people in the hostel. In her wing, only three other girls were present. The rest have gone home.'

'Right, sir,' Saurabh said.

'There's CCTV footage from the hostel entrance. We are going through it. We have asked for Zara's phone records. We checked the fiancé's cell tower location already. We even spoke to him. I haven't slept all night. Aren't we doing our best?' the inspector said. One minute I was an accused. The next, I was expected to behave like a supportive spouse.

'Yes, you are, sir,' I said, 'doing your best.'

'So why are they flashing "Clueless Delhi Police" on TV?' He pounded both his fists on the table. 'What are we supposed to do? Go into everyone's home every night so nothing bad ever happens? How can we prevent crime? We can only solve it, right?'

'Right,' I said, mainly because that's what I thought he wanted to hear.

'And it takes time. There's no app to solve a murder, is there?'

'Not yet,' Saurabh said. Damn you Saurabh, did you have to say that, I cursed inwardly. The inspector looked at Saurabh, who stared at the floor.

'No, sir,' I said.

'They want us to arrest someone. Right now. If I arrest no one, we are lazy. If I arrest all the people I suspect, I am confused and brutal. What am I supposed to do, for heaven's sake?'

I really tried to think about what he could do besides not yelling. 'I don't know, sir,' I said, 'maybe ignore the news.'

'I can ignore it. But the netas don't. And my seniors report to the netas. And those seniors come after me.'

Inspector Rana's phone rang, interrupting his rant. I supposed that, even though you did get to beat up people and that could be fun, it wasn't easy to be a police officer after all.

'Yes. Okay,' Rana said on the phone and paused. 'Good. You sure? You saw the full footage? What time? 2:02 to 2:41 a.m. Okay, good.'

The inspector stepped away from us. He took a few notes while still on the phone. He came back to us after the call.

'So, I was talking about speaking to your father earlier. I respect him. A gentleman. He never tried to threaten or use influence.'

'Right, sir. He would never do that.' Especially for a useless son like me, I wanted to add, but didn't.

'And I do want to give him good news when he arrives.'

'Which is?'

'That you are not the main suspect.'

Main suspect? I didn't want to be even a non-main suspect.

'Right, sir,' I said, wondering how long it would be before my parents arrived.

'The watchman was away from his post. 2:02 to 2:41 a.m. Confirmed from CCTV footage.'

'Oh,' I said, 'so someone entered the hostel then?'

'Could be. But there's more,' Inspector Rana said, a glint in his eye.

'What?' Saurabh said.

'Zara Lone had a big fight with this same watchman, Laxman Reddy, one month ago. She slapped him in the lobby. In front of several girls.'

'Really? Why?' I said.

'That I don't know. But we will find out. See, I told you we are good.'

'Yes, sir. Just out of curiosity, who told you about the fight?' I said.

The inspector picked up his notes.

'Ruchika Gill, fourth-year student at Himadri hostel. Room 109. Another girl, Subhadra Pande, room 203, also confirms this. My sub-inspector just finished talking to them. My team is working hard on the case. And we have probably solved it. The stupid media will never highlight this.'

I remained quiet. The inspector stood up.

'Biren,' he shouted. A constable came running in.

'Huzoor,' he said.

'Is that Laxman Reddy here?'

'Ji, huzoor. He is sleeping on a chair outside.'

'Slap him twice to wake him up. Send him in.'

'Ji, huzoor,' he said and left, overjoyed at the idea of officially getting a chance to use his authority on someone.

The inspector turned to us

'Wait outside. Sorry. You still can't leave.'

Saurabh and I stood up. As we walked out of the room, we saw Laxman walk in, spine bent, hands folded.

The sound of loud slaps reached us as Rana welcomed Laxman into his office.

Chapter 8

'Keshav. Keshav beta,' I heard my mother's voice as I woke up. I looked around to orient myself. Despite the noisy police station, I had finally fallen asleep on a bench. The clock in front of me showed four o'clock.

'Maa,' I said and rubbed my eyes. 'When did you arrive?'

'Just now. What happened? Why are you here?' she said.

'Where's papa?' I said.

'There.' She pointed towards Inspector Rana's office. My father stepped out of Inspector Rana's room just then and walked over to me.

'We called you ten times. You didn't even call us back once,' he said.

'Sorry, papa,' I said, 'I just…'

Before I could finish my sentence, I broke down. My father, unaffected, wiped his face with a handkerchief. My mother hugged me to her. Nothing had ever felt better in my entire life. I wanted to be in my childhood room and have her put me to bed.

'Why are you creating a scene in the police station?' my father said.

'Sorry, papa,' I said, extricating myself from my mother's arms. I wiped my tears. Others in the police station threw me sympathetic glances, perhaps thinking I was about to go to jail for a long time.

'What were you up to? We thought you were taking tuitions while looking for a job.'

It wasn't the right time to correct my father and tell him that I *did* have a job. I worked as faculty at a coaching institute, which sounds way better than 'taking tuitions'.

'I didn't do anything wrong, papa, I swear on you and maa.'

'You broke into a girls' hostel. Drunk. All our friends and relatives know this. The whole country knows this.'

'I mean, I didn't kill anyone, papa. I didn't hurt anyone.'

'Big favour you did. Thank you, son. Thank you for not being a murderer.'

'That's not what I meant, papa.' I started to cry again. 'I swear I didn't know this would go so wrong.'

'That Muslim girl,' my father said in a savage tone. 'She spelt trouble from day one. I told you years ago. I thought you ended it.'

'Yes, we had.'

'Then? You lost your brain again? Going back to her! Wasn't the shame you caused me last time enough?'

'You are shouting, Rajpurohit ji,' maa said. 'Please let's discuss this later. Can we leave? Come, beta, let's go home.'

'I can't leave,' I said. 'Inspector told me I can't leave.'

'He agreed. I had to beg him,' my father said.

'Why did you have to beg?' I said. 'They know I didn't do anything.'

'They can still keep you. You and your friend better thank him before we go.' My father pointed to the inspector's room.

❖

'So,' the inspector said, spinning his mobile phone on his table, 'you are lucky.'

Saurabh and I nodded. We had resolved to keep our mouths shut.

'The watchman. We have enough against him to make an arrest.'

Saurabh nodded again. The inspector continued.

'The media will be satisfied now, hopefully. Arrest within twenty-four hours. Not bad, no?'

I kept nodding.

'You can go now. But there are some conditions. Agreed?'

We kept quiet.

'Agreed or not?' he shouted.

I guess like those websites that make you click on 'agree' without reading the terms, we had to do the same here.

'Of course, sir. We agree to all conditions,' I said. I just wanted to leave.

'So, here they are. One, you will not leave Delhi. In fact, Keshav, you will come and report to me every day.

'Two, no media. I don't care how much they pester you. You do not talk to the media.'

'Yes, sir,' I said.

'Three, if I need anything else, you help me. I don't know how IIT works, so if I need to, I will come to you.'

'Yes, sir,' I said.

'Good. I think the case will be closed soon. We will have the killer behind bars.' Inspector Rana stood up. We took our cue and stood up as well.

'We can go now, sir?' Saurabh sounded disbelieving.

'Unless you like staying in jail,' Inspector Rana laughed, probably for the first time all day, or week, or year or in his entire career.

Saurabh dashed out of the inspector's room. Before I left, I gathered courage enough to ask the inspector one question.

'Excuse me, sir, did you find out more about the watchman? Why did Zara slap him? How do you know he killed her?'

'Go home. You will find out in the news.' He winked at me.

Chapter 9

'Hey, Keshav.' Raghu tapped my shoulder from behind. It was the day of Zara's funeral.

After leaving the police station, I had recounted everything to my parents. I had to even explain everything to Chandan Arora, who had been calling me continuously. 'I am with you,' he had said, gutkha in mouth, when he spoke to me on the phone. 'You can say to media that you work for a reputed coaching class company. Chandan Classes. We are going national, you know.' I had to tell him I couldn't talk to the media, let alone use this as a PR opportunity to promote his classes.

Saurabh and I had come to the Muslim graveyard in Chattarpur, near Zara's house.

'Hi, Raghu. When did you arrive?' I said, turning towards him.

He had his left arm in a cast. His forehead and the back of his neck had bruises. He wore a white kurta pyjama. He removed his black-framed spectacles and rubbed his eyes.

'Yesterday evening. So, you saw her?' he said in a soft voice.

I nodded.

'Tell me everything. Please,' Raghu said, 'I don't want to be in the dark.'

Somehow, after Zara's death, I didn't feel as much animosity towards him. I wondered if he knew about the messages Zara had sent to me before her death. Maybe I should tell him, I thought. I had already shared them with the police, who would probably tell him eventually. I wanted to rub it in his face that Zara wanted to get back with me. Scolding myself for thinking such shallow thoughts, I recounted the night of Zara's death to him in as much detail as possible. However, I toned down the exact messages she had sent me.

'We reconnected, I went to wish her. That's all,' I said as I finished the story.

He nodded, his gaze down.

'It's terrible,' I said into the awkward silence.

He bit his lip and looked into my eyes for a long time. No words, just this level look.

Did he think I had done it?

'I went to her room because...' I began to say again.

'I know. I went to the police station last night. I found out about your chat with her.'

'She messaged me first,' I said defensively.

'How does it matter now?' he said. 'We lost her. Forever. Because of this godforsaken city. I had told her to move much earlier.'

I looked away. Zara's father came up to us then, wanting to speak to Raghu in private. He and Raghu walked away from me.

Saurabh and I went to the grave. Zara's body lay wrapped in a white shroud. I had an absurd feeling that she was waiting for me to come closer and talk to her, and that when I did so she would wake up and smile that beautiful smile, a smile that would make everything alright again.

A few elderly Muslim men nearby were praying aloud in Arabic. Safdar came to stand close by, his face grim, hands clasped. Even though Muslim funerals usually don't have women present, Zara's stepmother, Zainab, stood behind him a bit further away, along with some relatives.

Zara's father took a handful of mud and placed it under Zara's head. I saw Zara's stepbrother, Sikander, who I knew was in his early twenties but looked way younger due to his baby face. I had only seen Sikander in some old family pictures. Zara's father, originally from Srinagar, became a widower when Zara was three years old. When Zara turned five, he married a widow called Farzana, in Srinagar. Farzana had lost her first husband to militancy in Kashmir. Sikander was her son from that marriage. Hence, Zara and Sikander grew up together as step-siblings in Kashmir. Eight years later, Safdar and Farzana got divorced, after

Safdar discovered that her family had militant roots; Safdar hated fundamentalists. They separated, each taking their biological child with them as they went their own ways. Safdar moved his business to Delhi, and Zara shifted with him. In Delhi, Zara's father married his accountant, Zainab. Sikander, meanwhile, stayed back and grew up with his mother, Farzana, in Srinagar.

Sikander stood near Zara's body, fingers interlinked. He picked up a ball of mud and placed it under Zara's chin. He sobbed as he performed the ritual.

Zara and Sikander had remained close after their parents' separation, even though Safdar discouraged the contact. Sikander, from what Zara had told me, was a poor student. She used to help him with his lessons and ensure he passed his exams. When Zara left Kashmir, his grades slipped and he never made it past class five.

'I just hope Sikander is fine. He is a baby,' Zara often said to me.

I noticed Prof. Saxena, Zara's PhD guide from IIT Delhi. He had come to the funeral along with his wife. Prof. Saxena was also the dean of student affairs at IIT. He went up to Safdar and they spoke to each other for a few minutes.

As Prof. Saxena stepped away, Zara's father called Raghu and handed a fistful of mud to him. Obviously only close male relatives performed this ritual and, I guess, Safdar saw Raghu as part of the family. A maulvi recited Arabic verses as Raghu placed the earth in his hand under Zara's shoulders. My resentment against Raghu came rushing back. Why did he get to be with her at the end? Why was I watching this from a distance, like an imposter? Why was no one calling me to pay my respects?

The maulvi's prayers filled the air as Zara's male relatives lowered her body into the grave. People ahead of me covered my view, so that I had to elbow my way to the front. I whispered to her for the last time.

'Forgive me, Zara, for not fighting for us.'

'What, bhai?' Saurabh said, as he heard me mumble.

'Nothing,' I said, my head averted to shield my wet eyes from him.

'Shall we go?' Saurabh said. 'I don't think they want us here.'

'Let me offer my condolences to her father and then we can leave.'

As they covered Zara's body with more earth, Safdar spoke to a tall man in his thirties. The man stood with his back very straight, and had the typical Kashmiri apple-cheeked complexion. I went to them and waited politely for them to finish their conversation.

'Thank you again, Faiz. You left duty and came all the way,' Safdar said.

'What are you saying, uncle? This is family. What happened is just tragic,' Faiz said.

Safdar nodded and embraced Faiz before the latter finally left. Then Safdar noticed me.

'Did you have to come here?'

'I just wanted to offer my condolences,' I said.

'You were there. In her room. And now you have the guts to offer sympathy?' he thundered.

'Uncle, I loved your daughter. How can you even think…'

He put up his hand to stop me.

'I told you to leave her alone. Why didn't you?'

'I loved her.'

'That is why you let your family humiliate her?'

'I can't control them. Even you didn't support us, uncle.'

'I gave you an option,' he said. 'And I am giving you one now.'

'What?'

'Just leave. Khuda Hafiz.'

❖

I reached Alwar in the afternoon. I had taken Inspector Rana's permission to go home for a day. I wanted my parents around, lest I had an emotional breakdown. My mother sensed my pain and prepared all my favourite Rajasthani dishes. Over gatte ki subzi and hot phulkas topped with desi ghee, I watched the afternoon news.

'Breaking News: Watchman arrested for the murder of IIT Delhi girl.'

Anchor Arijit gave the details.

'Himadri hostel watchman Laxman Reddy has been arrested for the murder of Zara Lone, a Kashmiri PhD student in IIT Delhi.'

The visuals showed a dazed Laxman being escorted into a police van. Arijit continued, 'Sources say Laxman Reddy would often stare at the girls sitting outside in the Himadri hostel garden and make them feel uncomfortable. In fact, about a month ago, he tried to shoot an upskirt video of a student while she sat on her scooter. Zara Lone confronted Laxman and they had an argument. Zara Lone had slapped Laxman in full public view at the time.'

My mother walked into the living room with more phulkas. She picked up the remote and switched the TV off.

'You have come to get away from this case,' she said.

'Maa, what are you doing?' I said. I pulled the remote out of her hand. 'They are giving new information.'

'She's dead. Whatever information they give, that Muslim girl is not coming back. Thank God.'

'Maa,' I shouted, 'stop it. She died less than a week ago.'

'She caused enough trouble when alive. Please don't let her affect you now that she is gone.'

'Enough, maa,' I said. I took a phulka from the plate in her hand.

'What happened with your job search?'

'I am trying, maa. Had interviews. Let's see.'

I didn't have to see, they had rejected me already.

After my mother left the room in a huff I switched on the

TV again. Arijit was speaking to a reporter.

'So what else are we hearing?' Arijit said. The reporter spoke into his mike.

'We are at the Hauz Khas police station. Laxman Reddy is now in police custody. The Delhi Police claims they have solved the case in record time. They have ample evidence to convict the watchman. In fact, the assistant commissioner said that it is high time the media accepted that they were wrong in harshly judging the Delhi Police, which has in fact done a fantastic job in this case.'

'Well, self-congratulations apart, how does the Delhi Police know for sure it is the watchman?' Arijit said.

'The CCTV footage shows the watchman missing from his post for forty minutes. He had voyeuristic tendencies. Zara Lone, who had slapped him, had also filed a complaint against him. The police said Laxman Reddy comes from a village two hours from Hyderabad, in Telangana. A few days ago, Zara Lone's fiancé and internet entrepreneur Raghu Venkatesh, who lives in Hyderabad, was violently attacked by local goons. This incident could be connected to Laxman as well. Mr Raghu evaded death, but suffered significant injuries and was admitted in the Apollo Hospital. Back to you, Arijit.'

The camera shifted to Arijit in his window next to seven other tiny windows with one panellist each.

Arijit made the opening remarks to start the debate.

'So, here we are. A case of a serial stalker and voyeur who was allowed to remain a watchman in a prestigious institute like IIT. On our panel today we discuss: shouldn't the IIT authorities take responsibility for not acting on a complaint against a watchman for weeks? Did IIT kill Zara Lone?'

A few panellists immediately began to speak, cutting each other out. I couldn't understand one sentence, and the loud noise was hurting my ears. I picked up the remote and switched off the TV, restoring silence in the room.

'Thank God you shut that subzi-mandi debate,' my mother said from the kitchen.

❖

I tossed and turned in bed for an hour. I could not sleep. But I wasn't thinking about Zara and crying like I had been doing every night; tonight my mind was on something else. Did Laxman Reddy actually kill Zara? The question kept ringing in my head. Yes, he had a motive. Zara had slapped him in public. There was circumstantial evidence too. He left his seat that night. He could well have done it.

And yet, something didn't add up. I couldn't specify the reason, but I had a strange feeling in my gut. As Delhi police declared victory and the media created noisy panels to discuss security, something didn't feel right.

I called Saurabh.

'Sleeping?' I said as he picked the call.

'No, bhai. Watching videos.'

'What kind of videos?' I said and smirked.

'Shut up, bhai. YouTube.'

'Yeah, right. How's Chandan Classes?'

'As screwed as ever. Gutkha man asked about you.'

'Am back tomorrow. To join you in your misery.'

'Take your time. I will handle it here. Are you feeling okay?'

'Okay is still quite far. Cried less than three hours today. So that is an improvement.'

'It will get better.'

'Hope so. But something else is playing on my mind too.'

'What?'

'You saw the news?'

'They arrested Laxman Reddy. Creep used to make upskirt videos of IIT girls. What is upskirt, bhai?'

'If a girl is wearing a skirt, trying to take a video of under that skirt.'

'How sick and stupid is that?'

'I know.'

'Glad they got him.'

'Yeah. He's sick, Golu. But did he kill Zara?'

'What? You heard, right? Missing from his post. Zara slapping him. Complaints.'

'Yeah, but…' I hesitated. 'I don't know. Something doesn't seem right…'

'You are just disturbed, bhai. In shock. I suggest you spend some more time at home. And please stop watching TV.'

Chapter 10

'What do you think? Delhi Police isn't so bad, eh?' Rana winked at us, keeping his teacup back on the table. By now he felt a bit more like a person than just a police officer. I had begun to think of him as 'Rana' rather than 'Inspector Rana'. Saurabh and I were in his office; we had come for our daily check-in.

'Amazing, sir, to find the murderer in two days,' Saurabh said, buttering him up for no particular reason.

I had not touched my tea. 'Have your tea.' Rana turned to me.

'Sir, are you sure it is the watchman?' I said.

Rana raised an eyebrow. He turned to Saurabh and laughed.

'Motive. CCTV evidence. He's from Telangana. Sent those goons to hurt Zara's fiancé. It is an open-and-shut case.'

'Is it?' I said.

Saurabh kicked my foot, urging me to shut up. He wanted the daily check-ins to stop, so he was going to agree with whatever Rana said.

However, I had to ask. 'Why would Laxman hurt Raghu?'

'Because Raghu had confronted Laxman too. It is he who encouraged Zara to file a complaint.'

'You spoke to Raghu?' I said.

'You think we are idiots? Of course we will speak to the fiancé.'

'Oh, okay,' I said. 'I am sorry.'

'He came to the police station, confirmed Zara's fight with the watchman,' the inspector said, irritated. 'Anyway, you guys, get out.'

'Sir?' Saurabh said, as he stood up.

'Yeah?' Rana said.

'Do we have to still come every day? You have the killer now.'

'Hmmm ...' Rana leaned back in his seat. 'You are right. But I still need to know your friend is there if I need him.'

'Of course, I am here, sir. I live five kilometres away. I teach at Chandan Classes every day,' I said.

'Okay. Only Keshav needs to meet me. Once a week. Or when I call you. Saurabh, you don't have to come anymore. Happy?'

Saurabh's face lit up with joy, like a prisoner released after three decades in jail.

'I am available anytime, sir. I just have one request,' I said.

'What?' Rana said.

'Can I speak to the watchman once? Only if you are okay with it?'

'What?' Saurabh gave me a dirty look. We were literally getting a get-out-of-jail pass. Why did I have to finger anyone?

Rana laughed, came over to me and slapped my back.

'What the hell is wrong with you? Who are you? Detective? Jasoos?' Rana said.

'I am just a tuition teacher, sir. If you let me talk to him just once, sir...'

The inspector sighed and went back to his seat.

'Come tomorrow late night. Can't have anyone see this.'

'Thank you, sir,' I said.

'Whatever you do, don't botch up my case,' he said, draining his cup.

❖

I had never been inside a police lockup before. The Hauz Khas station has four of them, these little rooms to keep prisoners in before they move to proper jails or obtain bail. A constable opened Laxman's cell for me and stood outside.

It felt strange inside the lockup. What if someone locked the cell with me in it?

Laxman squatted on the floor. I saw fear in his eyes as I approached him. His body trembled and face turned to the side as if expecting a blow, a default whenever anyone met him in the police station, I guess.

I wore jeans and a blue-and-white check shirt. I neither looked like a new prisoner, nor a cop. I stood in front of him, as he eyed me with fear. The constable outside watched us for a minute, but soon lost interest. He opened his phone to watch a pirated version of *Tiger Zinda Hai.*

'I am Keshav,' I said. He looked surprised. 'You saw me that day.'

I knelt down on the floor to his level.

'I am Zara's friend,' I said. 'I mean, I was.'

His face blanched. I knew Zara. I would definitely hit him now, he was probably thinking. He lifted up his folded hands.

'Sahib, I didn't do anything. I promise I did not kill Zara madam.' His voice broke and he began to wail. The constable tapped the iron bars with his bamboo stick.

'Keep quiet,' the constable said, eyes on Katrina Kaif as she sang on his phone.

'Control yourself, Laxman,' I said soothingly. 'I have come to help you.'

Laxman looked at me with distrust.

'You need to tell me what happened,' I said.

'I don't know, sahib. I sit at the main hostel entrance. I can't keep track of what is happening in each room. I swear on my children I didn't do anything.'

I put a finger to my lips, pointing to the constable.

'Zara madam had slapped me. But it was my mistake only.'

'You were making a video of a student?'

'Yes, yes. Big mistake.' He shook his head violently.

'You had a fight with Zara?'

'I got angry, I threatened her. But what can I do in reality? I am a poor watchman. I won't just go kill her.'

'Then who did?' I said.

'I don't know, sahib.'

'Why were you not at your post?'

His eyes fell from mine. 'I went to the bathroom.'

'For forty minutes?'

He kept looking down.

'You better answer, Laxman. If you don't, you are here for life.'

I lifted his chin with my hand.

'Reddy, if you hurt my Zara, before they punish you, I will kill you.'

'I didn't, sahib. I didn't kill Zara madam.'

'From 2:02 to 2:41, where were you?'

He gestured for me to come closer and whispered something in my ear.

'What?' I pulled back from him.

'Yes, sahib. That's the reason.'

'How?'

'On my smartphone, sahib.'

'Where is the phone?' I said.

'At home. Gave it to my wife when she came to visit. Sahib, I didn't do anything, sahib. Killer coming from window...'

'What?'

'The killer coming from window, sahib. Because window was open when you went in.'

'Yes.'

'If I had to kill, why would I need to go from window? I can walk up to the room. Pretend there is parcel delivery.'

'Yes, you can enter through the door. But you could still kill her, bolt the door from the inside, and exit from the window, so nobody suspects you,' I said.

He fell at my feet.

'I didn't, sahib, I swear on my little daughter.'

❖

We walked through the lanes of Shahpur Jat and reached the main road. We had just collected Laxman's phone from his house.

'Sorry, what do I have to do with this phone?' Saurabh said.

'You said you won the hackathon at NIT. Is it true?'

'Of course. Bhai, I've even hacked Tinder to give me a premium account without paying for it.'

'Great. I need you to hack Laxman's phone.'

I hailed an auto rickshaw. The driver first grumbled at how short the ride to Malviya Nagar was. Saurabh gave him a lecture on how app-based taxis would soon decimate auto rickshaws if drivers kept up this attitude. Shocked by the unwanted sermon, the auto driver agreed.

'Hack this phone? Why?' Saurabh said when we had sat down in the auto rickshaw.

'Laxman told me he sneaked into the guest toilet at Himadri that night when he left his post. Because it gets Wi-Fi.'

'Why did he need Wi-Fi in the toilet?'

'One guess,' I said. 'You went to engineering college, right?'

'Oh, of course,' Saurabh said.

'I need you to check if he's lying.'

'To see if he actually went to porn sites at that precise time?'

'Yes, and from that location. Can you?'

'Easy. This is hardly a hack. I just need the browser history files on the phone. It will have all the time stamps and sites visited. And if we can go to Himadri and connect to their Wi-Fi network, I can double-check if this phone's IP address is actually connected to—' Saurabh was saying when I interrupted him.

'Dude, if I knew all this, I would be a real engineer and have a real job. Talk in simple terms please.'

Saurabh looked at me, surprised.

'Take me to Himadri. Get me on their Wi-Fi network,' he said.

❖

'Excuse me,' I said. 'I really need to call a cab, and my phone is out of data. Can I have the Wi-Fi password here?'

I stood in the Himadri hostel garden carrying six fat books of physics, chemistry and maths in my arms. I wore thick glasses and had not shaved for three days. I also wore an ill-fitting shirt, old rubber sandals and polyester pants. In other words, I resembled a typical IIT research scholar.

Saurabh stood across the road, in front of the hostel, within Wi-Fi range.

The girl had just arrived at the hostel in her Activa and had parked it next to me. She looked me up and down when I asked for the Wi-Fi password.

'Student?' she said.

'Yes. PhD. Vindhyachal hostel.'

'Himadri2018G,' she said. 'H and G capital letters.'

'Thank you,' I said. As I walked away from her, I typed a WhatsApp message to Saurabh.

'Got it. Himadri2018G.

He replied after a minute.

'Connected. Now downloading IP history and DNS sites.'

'Talk in English,' I replied.

'Nothing. Downloaded everything I need. Let's go home. I am hungry. You better cook tonight,' Saurabh messaged back.

❖

'Youporn.com,' Saurabh said. '*Hot desi bhabhi has fun with stud devar*. That's from 2:10 to 2:14.'

'What?' I said. We sat at our dining table eating French fries, the only dish I could whip up at short notice for ever-hungry Lord Saurabh. Saurabh had his laptop open, with Laxman's phone tethered to it.

'That's what his phone's browser history says. You want me to go through your phone?' Saurabh said.

'Very funny. What's next?' I said.

'*Neighbour does big-busted eager Mallu aunty*. Shall we have a look at eager aunty too?'

'Wait, so he was actually watching porn?'

'Sure he was. Look at this: *Sardar honeymoon couple leaked video*. Wait, how can they be sure it is an actual honeymoon video?'

Laxman had not lied. He was literally jerking off when away from his seat.

'*Jaipur college-girl shows* ...' Saurabh was still listing the sites out. 'Bhai, one thing is for sure, he only likes desi porn. He skipped international videos. Kind of patriotic, no?'

'Shut up. When does his party end?'

'Around 2:29 a.m.,' Saurabh said.

'Enough time for him to walk back and reach his post at 2:40.'

'And wash up before, I hope,' Saurabh said.

'Stop it. Open the IP address logs on the Himadri network.'

'We can. But don't you want to watch *Hot Tamil couple enjoy in Indian train*? I am curious. Maybe IRCTC can sponsor this one.'

'Golu, this is not a joke. This is about someone's life.'

'Okay, fine,' he said. He switched from the browser history to the IP addresses file.

'These are the IP addresses, or unique identifiers of all devices that logged into the Himadri Wi-Fi network,' Saurabh said. He scanned the excel file for a few seconds.

'Yes, Laxman's phone was connected to the network. Confirmed,' Saurabh said.

'Show me,' I said.

He showed me a table with IP addresses on his laptop screen.

'This is real proof. Laxman is innocent,' I said.

'Yes, sick as it is, he didn't kill anyone at that time.'

'Thank you, Golu,' I said and ruffled his hair. 'I will take this to Rana.'

'Welcome, bhai. But can I ask one thing?'

'Sure.'

'Why are you getting involved in this? We are free now. Why bother? Let the police do their job.'

'But, see, they botched up. Laxman didn't do it.'

'Let Laxman fight it out. Or let the police eventually figure it out. Zara is gone, bhai. Let her go from your mind too.'

'I know, I should. If only I could,' I said with a sigh. Saurabh saw my distraught face. He gently placed an arm around my shoulder.

'I guess, somehow, I still want to stay connected to her,' I said. 'I want to find out who did it. Who took Zara away from me just when she wanted to come back?'

'I will print this out. We can take this to Rana tomorrow.'

'Thanks.'

'It's okay, bhai. Just don't sport that Devdas look, please. Nobody is allowed to make that sad face while eating French fries.'

❖

'Hmmm...' went Rana, tapping the bridge of his nose with an index finger and inspecting the printouts we gave him.

'Browser history, huh?' he said. He scrunched his eyes to read the metrics on the page.

Saurabh stood up and moved over to the inspector's side.

'See, sir, these are the IP addresses. And on this next page are the time stamps and sites visited on Laxman's phone.'

Rana scratched his three-day-old salt-and-pepper stubble.

He grunted. 'Sit down, sit down.'

Saurabh went back to his seat. The inspector placed the sheets down on the table. I expected him to scream out 'superb' or 'good job' or something like that. Instead, he cracked his fingers one at a time.

'This means Laxman is innocent, sir,' I said, wondering if Rana had not understood what this meant. 'He was in the bathroom, masturbating and watching porn.'

'So who killed Zara then?' Rana said.

That's your job to find out, I wanted to say. Instead, I shrugged.

'If Laxman didn't do it, then won't the suspicion be back on you?' Rana said.

'What?' I said.

The inspector smirked and tilted his head. He slid the sheets back towards me.

'Take this back. You never gave this to me,' he said.

'What do you mean?' I said.

'You like coffee?'

'Excuse me?'

'Let me treat you to expensive coffee,' Rana said and stood up.

❖

'Give me good coffee. But not too bitter,' Rana told the barista at Starbucks in Hauz Khas Village.

'A latte, sir?' the barista said, somewhat unnerved by Rana's uniform.

'Plain hot milk,' I said. Saurabh ordered two chocolate muffins.

The inspector took out his wallet. The cashier at the café looked aghast at the preposterous idea of a policeman paying and quickly declined. The inspector smiled and put his wallet back in his pocket.

We collected our beverages and took a seat near the window.

'So this is where young people, what do they say, hang out?' Rana said, adding three sugar sachets to his coffee. 'Two hundred rupees for coffee. Daylight robbery.'

I wondered if not paying at an establishment counted as daylight robbery too.

'I agree, sir,' Saurabh said, servile as per norm.

'Anyway, I brought both of you here because I wanted to have a frank talk. I hope I can trust you.' Rana gave us a level look.

'Of course, sir,' I said.

'Where do you work, Keshav?'

'I told you, Chandan Classes.'

'How much do you get? In hand.'

I looked at him, surprised. Saurabh politely looked in the other direction.

'Around 45,000 rupees a month,' I said.

'See, even you make more than I do. I get, after all deductions, 42,000 rupees a month.'

I guess he hadn't counted the unlimited free Starbucks lattes in his package. I wondered what to say in response. Like, did he not know the pay scales before he took up this job? I chose to keep silent.

'I have fifteen years of experience,' Rana continued. 'You started what? Four-five years ago? Is it fair?'

I shook my head, feeling guilty. I felt personally responsible for the central government's compensation policies. I wanted to tell him I had to listen to a gutkha-chewing, obnoxious boss all day. I would happily trade places with Rana. Take a little pay-cut and get the power to slap people around and demand free coffee? I am up for it.

Saurabh showed us his pinkie finger and excused himself to use the toilet. Rana continued.

'I worked hard my entire tenure. Excellent annual reports. Yet, my promotion is stuck for the last five years. They won't make me assistant commissioner of police.'

I nodded, sipping my milk. What did this have to do with Laxman's browser history?

'Meanwhile, some idiot from some IIT will mug up and clear the IPS exam. They will make him my boss and give him a rank above me.'

I wondered if I was the idiot from IIT he was referring to. Actually, no. I was the IITian who couldn't clear the IPS exam, which made me an even bigger idiot.

'It's not a fair system. Colonial hangover,' I said.

'What?'

'From the British time. They made the civil services.'

'Yeah, stupid goras. I am one of the rare, honest inspectors in the force, and they treat me like this.'

I guess free beverages didn't count as being dishonest, compared to the opportunities a corrupt inspector in Delhi Police could get. The coffee was just a tiny perk.

I wondered how to make Rana feel better. I guess when someone feels their life sucks, it's always good to tell them how your life sucks even more.

'I am from IIT, sir. I never managed a job from campus. One of those rare IITians who graduated without an offer.'

'Why?'

'Poor grades. Messed up the few interviews I had. Had a breakup. Was disturbed in that phase of life.'

'Ah. That is why Chandan Classes?'

I nodded. I didn't tell him it was also because I wanted to remain in Delhi, as close to the IIT campus as possible. Zara still resided there, and staying nearby was the only way I could ever get a chance for a reunion.

The inspector smirked.

'You like your job?' he said.

'Hate it,' I said.

'Really?'

'On some days I feel I would prefer to be in jail than show up for work.'

The inspector laughed.

'Guess we are in the same boat then,' he said, feeling more bonded to me than ever, because of our stagnant careers. Saurabh had by now returned from the washroom. He picked up a newspaper and opened the jobs and classifieds page. The inspector's phone rang. He took the call.

'Yes, Sharma sir,' Rana said and stood up, as if Sharma sir could see him. 'Ji, Sharma sir. Of course, sir, no sir, we have the watchman and a solid case. Yes, sir, we will file the chargesheet soon, sir. No sir, you don't have to call again, sir. Okay, sir.'

When he ended the call, I said, 'You will release Laxman, right? He is a creep, but he didn't murder Zara.'

'Ah, see, now that's why I wanted to talk to you here. You never know who may hear us at the police station.'

'What?' I said.

Saurabh looked up from his newspaper to listen as well.

'This high-profile, media-covered case is my best shot at a promotion. There is a provision for out-of-turn promotion. My seniors may recommend me because of this case.'

'That's good, sir,' I said.

'Yeah. But only if I solve the case. Which, in their eyes, I have.'

'With Laxman as the killer?'

'Yes, even the media stories have died down,' he said. He picked up the main section of the newspaper and opened the city pages.

'See, nothing today. My seniors, the media and public at large believe that Laxman did it. Case closed in their heads.'

'Except for the fact that he didn't,' I said, my voice a bit too firm for Rana's comfort.

'Is he your brother?' Rana said, his voice loud.

'No, sir,' I said, 'but he's innocent.'

'So I release him? And the media starts another drama?'

'Drama?'

'Yeah. Police caught an innocent man because he was from a poorer class. Police still can't catch killer. Delhi Police is useless. More and more nonsense. And who will be held responsible for this botch-up? Inspector Rana. You think anyone will promote me then?'

I wanted to tell him that an innocent man could not spend his life in jail to enable his promotion. Of course, I didn't.

'Sir, won't Laxman have to be proven guilty in court?'

'Yes.'

'So eventually this will come out. He will confess what he was up to. His lawyers might get the same data.'

The inspector laughed. He took a tissue and wiped his latte moustache. Saurabh glared at me. He didn't want any more confrontations with the police.

'What is so funny?' I said to the inspector.

'This is not a movie. It's real life. What kind of lawyer do you think Laxman will get?'

'Doesn't the government give poor people one?'

'Exactly. And how much will they care about a watchman? Laxman will be lucky if his lawyer shows up at a hearing.'

'But still. He didn't do it. And there's proof. It will come out eventually.'

'Fine. Maybe it will. In three years. By then Inspector Rana will be ACP Rana. Away from this police chowki nonsense. Laxman can be out then.'

'Sir, but...'

'All this detective nonsense you are doing has to stop. I saved you. Now stop making my life difficult.'

Saved me? The fact that I didn't kill anyone might have also played a role in ensuring my freedom, I wanted to snap back at him.

'Sir, I don't want to disturb your life. I just want to find out who is the killer. And for that, we need a proper investigation. Not lock up an innocent man and close the case.'

The inspector looked at Saurabh and me in quick succession, then shrugged and finished his cooled latte.

'What if the media gets this evidence about the watchman's innocence?' I said.

The inspector kept his cup down.

'Are you threatening me?'

'No,' I said. 'But what I am saying could happen.'

'You bastards. A week ago both of you were begging me to let you go. And you are ordering me around now? Telling me I don't know how to do an investigation.'

'No, sir,' I said. 'I am just saying let's find out who did it. I will help you.'

'How will you help me? You are a tutor at Chandan Classes,' Rana said.

Saurabh pressed my arm, telling me to not respond.

'Sir, can I say something?' Saurabh said.

'What do you want to say now?' the inspector said, his voice annoyed. 'He is teaching me investigation? Does your idiot friend know what we have to face? That dean of student affairs insulted me the day before.'

'Who?' Saurabh said.

'That Prof. Saxena. Chutiya said I have no business roaming around campus. He tells this to me, the police. Wants me to get all the permissions. Threatens to call the HRD ministry. Bloody, you want me to investigate? Tell that stupid dean to not insult me.'

'You met Prof. Saxena?' I said.

'Yes. If the college doesn't care, screw this case.'

'Prof. Saxena was also Zara's PhD guide,' I said.

'So, why is he stopping us? Giving some bullshit policy like no media or police on campus,' he said.

'I don't know, sir,' I said.

'Listen, tutor,' Rana said, looking at me sharply. 'You think I didn't know the watchman didn't do it?'

'You know?' I said, shocked.

'I have investigated criminals for fifteen years. I can tell from their eyes. He's a tharki, but no murderer. Your data only proved my hunch right.'

I was nonplussed. 'So why did you arrest him?'

'Because I don't have the killer! And everyone wants closure. TV anchors, people, social media, activists and my seniors.'

Inspector Rana stood up jerkily.

'Listen, I may have free coffee, which is overpriced anyway. I also want my promotion because I deserve it. But I am not an evil man. I will still try to find out who did it. But until then Laxman stays in.'

'Understood, sir,' Saurabh said, scared by the inspector's towering presence.

'Get me the killer. I promise I will release Laxman that day. Even if it means I have to change my stance.'

'Sir.' I, too, stood up. 'What can we do to help?'

'Ideally, stay away,' Rana said.

'We can, sir,' Saurabh said, nudging me with his elbow. He was also standing now.

'Anything, sir?' I said.

'Help me navigate IIT. Is there a way you can access the campus?'

'Yes. I am an alumnus,' I said.

Saurabh turned to me.

'Bhai, inspector sir is telling us to stay away.'

'He is an aashiq,' Rana laughed. 'How will he stay away?'

Chapter 11

'Mock-test in mathematics. This Sunday at 10 a.m.,' I announced in my class at the end of my session. Most of the two dozen-odd students groaned. I ignored their passive protest and left the classroom.

In the corridor, I checked my phone. I had two missed calls from Raghu. He had also sent me a message.

'Leaving Delhi soon. Can we meet once?'

Before I could respond, the smell of Chandan Arora's gutkha reached me.

'No checking phones during work hours. I have told you before,' Chandan said from behind me.

'Sorry, sir,' I said, mentally picturing smashing my phone on his bald head.

❖

'Thanks for coming,' Raghu said.

'No issues. How come you wanted to meet up?' I said.

We had come to Social in Hauz Khas and were at a table facing the Hauz Khas Lake. He wore a black sweater, which matched his thick spectacle frames. He had a cast on his left arm. In his right hand, he held an iPhone X. It had released three months ago and cost more than a lakh rupees.

'I want to understand what happened,' Raghu said.

'I told you the sequence of events at the funeral.'

Raghu looked at me, unconvinced.

'What? Why are you looking at me like that?'

'You know, Keshav, you have bothered and insulted me in the past. A lot.'

'What do you want? An apology?' I said.

The waiter brought us two cups of masala tea. Raghu responded after the server left.

'No. What would an apology do now?' he said. He took a sip of his tea and continued, 'And I don't care about the insults. I am not a confrontational guy. All I ever wanted from you was for you to leave Zara alone.'

I shot up from my chair.

'And I didn't. I couldn't get over her. Yeah, fine. Sorry. May I leave now?' I said.

'Sit down, please, Keshav. I said I don't want an apology,' Raghu said.

'What *do* you want, Raghu?' I said, sitting back. 'And it was Zara who wanted to come back this time.'

'Calm down, please. I don't like it when you use such an aggressive tone,' Raghu said.

Because you are a scared fuddu, I wanted to say but kept quiet.

'The first thing I want is this,' Raghu said, pointing to his cast. 'This has to stop. I am not a violent person. I just wanted to live a simple life with Zara.'

'Hey,' I said. 'Are you suggesting I am behind this? I sent people to hurt you?'

'No accusations. While I would like to know what happened, my parents don't even want me involved. Please, I beg you, don't hurt me or my family. My father and mother are really scared.'

'I didn't do anything, Raghu,' I said. 'Why would I?'

'I'm not saying you did. *If* you did have something to do with this, please stop. I want peace.'

'Raghu, I have called you names and made fun of you. But why would I hurt you? Zara and you dated for over three years. Did I do anything?'

'I will kill that fuddu, you said to Zara once.'

'I said that in anger. When drunk. Please, Raghu, I haven't done anything. Anyway, they arrested the watchman.'

He became quiet. He still looked unconvinced.

'Raghu, you don't trust me, I get that. But I swear, I didn't hurt anyone. Not Zara, not you, alright?' I said.

He gave a brief nod and looked down at the table, lost in thought. Then he spoke softly, so softly I had to strain my ears to hear him.

'She was my world. The miracle of my life.'

I could have told him this myself, I thought, but he was still speaking in that slow-motion voice of his.

'I had a new investor from Silicon Valley lined up. I have always wanted to move there, but Zara didn't agree. She didn't want to drop her PhD midway.'

'She wanted to go back and teach in Kashmir, right?' I said. That is what she used to tell me during 'our' days.

'Yeah. But I finally convinced her and we decided to spend a few years in the US and then do something in Kashmir later. She was to get her PhD in a few months and we were to go to San Francisco. I had even shortlisted apartments in Mountain View. But now...'

His voice choked and he dropped his face into his palms. The sound of his whimpers was unmistakable. Others in the restaurant started throwing us curious looks. He cried without any inhibitions. Afraid of being mistaken for a kidnapper, I stuffed tissues into his hand.

'Thank you,' he said, wiping his face with the paper napkin.

'I didn't do anything. Do you believe me? Look into my eyes and talk, Raghu.'

'I do,' he said, finally making eye contact.

'Good,' I said. 'I bear no grudges. Not anymore.'

'Sorry, my parents are in a panic. They have hired twenty-four-hour security. They feel nervous when I leave for office. We are all so scared.'

'I can imagine. But I have no interest in you ... except...' I paused.

'Except what?'

'I want your help.'

'What kind of help?'

'In finding out who killed Zara. I am helping the police.'

'You are? Didn't the police say the watchman did it?'

'He may not have.'

'Actually, even I was surprised when they said it was Laxman.'

'You were?'

'Yes. I have met that watchman. He didn't have that murderer look. But the police said so on TV.'

'The police sometimes say or do things to shut the media up.'

'So, who killed Zara? I want to know too.'

'That's what I need your help in finding out.'

'I want to work on this with you. My parents want me to cut off completely from all this. But let's do this.'

'No, Raghu, I don't want to work with you,' I said, interrupting him. 'I only want you to help me. You knew her and her world well.'

Raghu looked at me, startled. I kept a firm expression. He sighed.

'Whatever you need,' he said.

'Okay,' I said. I took out my notebook. 'I have some questions.'

'Sure.'

'Firstly, why did it surprise you when you heard the watchman did it?'

'It seemed unlikely. Sure, Zara complained about Laxman. However, he had begged her for mercy many times after that. Once even in front of me, when I visited Zara on campus.'

'So what did Zara do?'

'She softened. She didn't withdraw her complaint, but delayed follow-up. He had told her about his little daughter and that he was the sole earning member in his family.'

'Anything else that makes you feel it is not him?'

'The people who came to beat me up.'

'What about them?'

'They didn't seem to be from a village like Laxman. From

their clothes and accent, they appeared to be city-dwellers. I told this to the police. I don't think they really listened.'

I looked up from my notebook.

'What exactly happened to you that day?'

'I finished work late. Came out of my office building. While I was waiting for my driver, four guys came and started beating me up. I thought they wanted my phone or wallet. They didn't. Just wanted to hurt me.'

'For how long?'

'Until Gopal, my driver, arrived with the car. They threw stones at the car, smashing the windows. Then they ran away. Gopal stepped out and found me lying on the street, bleeding.'

'And he took you to the hospital?'

'He took me home first. My parents took me to Apollo Hospital. Doctors there told me I had a fracture in my left arm and a concussion. They admitted me to keep me under observation.'

'You told Zara about this?'

'Of course. I messaged her from the car itself. She wanted to come down to Hyderabad. But that horrible Saxena didn't let her go.'

'Prof. Saxena? Her guide?'

'Yes, he said he had a deadline on a paper and needed her help. She couldn't leave.'

'Didn't she protest? Knowing Zara, she wouldn't have listened.'

'Yes, she wanted to come anyway. But I stopped her. Her final thesis approval was three months away. Why upset Saxena at this time?'

A waiter hovered over us, expecting us to order something else apart from tea.

'One egg bhurji and pao,' I said. 'And for you Raghu?'

'What do you have in veg? Something light?' he said to the waiter.

He settled for a vegetarian club sandwich, one of the most boring dishes ever.

'Were you in touch with Zara from the hospital?'

'All the time.'

'What did she talk about, if you don't mind?'

'Usual stuff. She checked on my health. I told her I missed her. We spoke about our marriage function plans. Our move to the Bay Area.'

'Was all this done on chat?'

'Some WhatsApp chats, some calls. Would you like to see my phone?'

He extended his iPhone towards me.

'No, I don't think that's right. Did she say anything about being in danger?'

'No.'

'Was she upset with someone?'

'Only Saxena. I will tell you exactly what she said about him,' he said and scrolled through his WhatsApp chats.

'I hate him. I just simply hate him,' Raghu read from the phone and looked at me.

'Anything else?'

'You see for yourself,' he said, handing the phone to me. I hesitated for a second before I took it. I went through his chats with Zara.

I scrolled up to the day Raghu was attacked. He had sent a picture of his bleeding arm to Zara. She had reacted in shock, and had called him. I saw chats in which they discussed who could have done it, but could not figure it out. The subsequent day, the chats had a lot of 'how is my baby' and 'baby misses you' kind of stuff. He had sent a selfie of himself on a hospital bed. She had sent kisses and love back, and a promise to be in Hyderabad as soon as possible.

The next day, Zara had sent Raghu a message calling Prof. Saxena an 'asshole'. Raghu had replied, 'Don't piss him off. Just twelve weeks and you never have to see him again.'

On the night before Zara's birthday, Raghu had sent a selfie with a message on his arm's cast: 'The pain of being away from you on your birthday is way more than any physical pain I feel.'

'I wish I could be there with you,' Zara had replied.

When you have been with someone, you never imagine they can be intimate with someone else. I wished I didn't have to see this. I took a deep breath to remain calm. I scrolled down further.

Raghu had sent a message at midnight sharp.

'It's midnight. Not supposed to be up so late in the hospital, but happy birthday, baby! You are the love of my life! Wish I was with you. I love you.'

'Thank you. I love you too, so much,' Zara had replied.

Raghu had replied with a hug and kiss emoji.

A couple of hours later, Raghu had sent another message: 'Hey, birthday baby, good morning'. Half an hour later, he had sent another one.

'How's my birthday girl doing? Still sleeping? Called you twice.'

However, these last two messages did not have two blue ticks on Raghu's phone. Of course, they had remained unread.

I returned his phone to him.

'I am sorry,' I said.

He nodded.

'I loved her so much.'

I didn't want to hear any more about Raghu and Zara's romance. I decided to change the topic.

'Was there anyone Zara truly hated or disliked? Apart from Saxena?' I said.

'You knew Zara. Such a positive person. Saw the best in everyone.'

That is why I was with her, buddy, I wanted to tell him.

'Nobody?'

'Just Saxena. She hated him. I do too.'

'Why? Because he didn't give her leave?'

'No, much more than that. He intentionally delayed her

thesis for over a year. And I think I can tell you now, he made a pass at her.'

'What? A pass?'

'He propositioned her. To approve her thesis sooner.'

'Dean Saxena? Seriously?' I said. 'He's like forty-five years old.'

'Forty-eight, actually. Zara put up with him for years. Stuck on because he controlled her final PhD thesis approval.'

'I can't believe it. Prof. Saxena taught us when we were in college, remember? Such a workaholic.'

'People have a different side to them when they have power over someone.'

'It's shocking. Zara never reported it?'

'It's not easy taking on your PhD guide. Throwing away years of work. Giving up your career maybe. She sent me an email in frustration once.'

'Email?'

'Yeah, a year ago. Wait.'

He fumbled with his phone for a few seconds.

'Check your email,' Raghu said.

I read the email Zara had written to Raghu. As I went through the contents, my mouth fell open.

'Sick. What a bastard,' I said.

'I felt the same at the time,' Raghu said. 'If Zara's career wasn't at risk, I would have personally reported him.'

'Anything else you would like me to know?' I said.

'Yeah, you know about Sikander, right?'

'Zara's stepbrother? Saw him at the funeral.'

'Yes, he hangs out with shady people in Kashmir. Zara was always telling him to take up a proper job.'

'What shady people?'

'She wouldn't tell me. You know how she was, you couldn't push her to tell you things. Especially her family matters; "off-limits" is what she used to say.'

'So how do you know?'

'I heard her scold Sikander on the phone a few times. Something about taking the right path. She would avoid talking or meeting him in front of me though.'

'Fine, thanks,' I said.

'Anything else?'

I shook my head. Raghu stood up to leave.

'You have my number. Please keep me updated if you can.'

'I will try.'

'Thanks. And let me know if you need anything,' Raghu said. The waiter arrived with the bill and Raghu settled it with his black Centurion American Express card.

'Would you like anything else, sir?' the waiter said to me after Raghu left.

'Three large whiskies, neat,' I said. I sat alone, drinking, with only Zara's memories for company.

Chapter 12

Four years ago

'Milk cake?' Zara said.

'Yeah. That's what Alwar is famous for. You have to try it.'

After a three-hour drive, we had covered the 150-kilometre distance from Delhi to Alwar. Zara sat next to me in the cab's backseat, looking out of the window with great interest.

'What's that? A big fort?' She pointed ahead.

'That's my house,' I said.

'Really?'

'I wish,' I laughed. 'It is the Bala Qila or Alwar Fort, built in the fifteenth century by the king at that time.'

'It's beautiful! I hope you will show me around the city.'

'We have not come here for tourism. If your in-laws are here you can visit anytime.'

'In-laws?' She gave a happy giggle. 'Keshav, I know I tease you about this, but what you are doing is so cute.'

'What?'

'Making this effort. To make me a part of your family.'

'You already are. But you remember what I told you? About how to act with my parents?'

'No.'

'What?' I said, exasperated.

'Kidding. I do remember. But I am also going to be myself. If they have to like me, they better like the real me, not someone I pretend to be.'

'Zara, come on. These are parents. Some drama we have to do.'

'Oh, so I shouldn't wear my hot pants to sleep at night?'

'Zara, are you crazy?' I was aghast.

'Ha ha, relax. Don't over-manage this. I am amazing with parents. They will love me, wait and see.'

'Their son does, too much.' I moved close to her.

'Don't even try,' she said, pointing to the driver.

❖

Zara adjusted her blue and white dupatta as she read the nameplate outside my parents' bungalow.

Sh. Naman Rajpurohit, Advocate

Mahanagar Karyavah, RSS

'You informed your parents about my coming, right?' Zara said, sounding just a little bit nervous.

'Of course,' I said, only partially truthful as I rang the bell.

I had told my parents I was bringing a friend along for the weekend. However, only my mother knew it was a girl. Even to her, I hadn't mentioned Zara's name. I didn't want her prejudiced even before meeting her. Nor had I told my mother we were dating. 'A friend of mine wants to see Alwar,' is all I had said to her over the phone. My mother did express surprise over my friend being a girl. 'Yeah, she is doing her PhD at IIT,' I had said, trying to sound as casual as possible. Indian parents find it easier to accept an inter-gender friendship when it is linked to academics.

I knew my parents would love Zara once they met her. I would then tell them about our decision to be together for life.

'Sorry, I was in the kitchen,' my mother said as she opened the door.

'Namaste, aunty,' said Zara, putting her palms together delicately. The bangles on her wrists clinked and caught the light.

'She's so beautiful,' my mother said.

Zara smiled demurely.

'Maa, this is Zara,' I said, but I don't think my mother heard me.

'Come inside. It's so hot,' she was saying to Zara.

❖

'Lunch will be ready soon,' my mother said, bustling away to the kitchen, leaving Zara and me in the living room.

Zara sat on a sofa, her eyes scanning the walls, filled with Rajasthani paintings and framed pictures. She saw a few photos of my father with political bigwigs.

'Is that the PM?' she said.

'Yeah, he was a CM then, though.'

'Wow, your father seems connected.'

'Senior member of the RSS. As senior as married men can go, frankly.'

'Meaning?' she said, surprised.

'Top positions in the RSS are usually only given to bachelors.'

'Wonder why. Maybe it is a way to choose the wise ones. If you are truly smart, you remain a bachelor,' Zara said and laughed.

She walked up to the wall to take a closer look at the pictures. I imagined her in this house after we were married. We would sit in the lawns. She would chat with my mother and father. Maybe a baby or two would arrive on the scene. I wondered what to name them. How about a name from both sides, like Kabir?

I looked at Zara; she looked so vulnerable in this large room, with her hands clasped behind her back like a little girl. And I felt happy that she was here, finally, in my home.

'You were a cute kid.' She peered at a black-and-white photo of me playing in a park.

'Thank you.'

'What happened later?'

'Shut up,' I said. She laughed again.

'Sorry, sorry,' my mother said as she re-entered the living room. She dabbed at the sweat on her face with her sari pallu. 'Are you hungry?'

'No, maa. Sit down and let me introduce you both properly,' I said.

'Yes, beta,' my mother said, looking at me fondly. She

perched on the sofa, patting the seat next to her, and Zara came and sat with her.

'Maa, this is Zara, my friend from Delhi. Zara, this is my mother. I am her only son, she is my only mother.'

Zara folded her hands again and smiled.

'Zara as in…?' my mother said. 'What's your full name?'

'Zara Lone, aunty.'

'Oh,' my mother said and fell silent. Then she spoke in a rush, to compensate for her discomfort.

'You are beautiful, beta, are you a model?'

Zara's eyebrows went up a little even as she smiled.

'Maa, come on,' I intervened. 'She got PhD admission at IIT straight after B.Tech. Very few people get that.'

'Sorry, I meant it as a compliment.'

Zara said, 'You have a beautiful home. I love all the pictures on the wall.'

'Thank you, beta. Look, how well-mannered she is,' maa said to me.

'What? And I am not?' I said.

'Boys don't know how to talk. I always wished I had a daughter,' my mother said. She then turned to Zara. 'Where are Lones from?' In India, people have to know where you come from. Only then they feel comfortable enough to talk to you.

'I am from Kashmir, aunty. Srinagar. Moved to Delhi more than ten years ago.'

'Kashmiri? Oh,' maa said. She stretched out the 'oh', as if I had brought a Martian home.

'It's in India only, maa,' I said, my tone sarcastic.

'I know. See, boys don't know how to talk.' She gave Zara a conspiratorial look.

Then to me, she said, 'Have you shown your guest her room?'

She was referring to Zara as 'your guest', not 'your friend' or even 'Zara'. Not the best start.

'I'll do it,' I said.

'Good,' maa said and turned to Zara. 'You want to see Alwar today or tomorrow?'

'Whenever Keshav says we can go.'

Maa looked at me, surprised by the 'we' in 'we can go'.

'Only a few places in Alwar to see. Anyway, let's eat lunch. Zara, hope you don't mind, it's pure vegetarian.'

'Not at all, aunty. I love vegetarian food.'

'I thought you people like non-vegetarian.'

When parents address your girlfriend as 'you people', it is definitely not a good sign.

❖

'The Rajasthan CM is visiting Alwar next week. I have invited him for a stop at home,' my father said. He removed his socks and placed them inside his shoes. He had come home at eight in the evening. Zara was in the guestroom, taking a shower before dinner. My mother was doing an evening aarti in the puja room. I felt she was singing her bhajans very loudly today, perhaps to re-emphasise her identity to Zara. This passive-aggressive stealth communication mothers do with their sons' girlfriends is a refined and deadly art form.

My father and I sat in the living room. I hoped he would ask me something about my guest. However, he had only one thing on his mind.

'Can you stay back next week? It's the CM. Will be good for you to meet him, no?'

'I have work in Delhi, papa,' I said.

'What work? It's not like you have a real job.'

I wanted to tell him I had a boss ten times worse than those found at 'real' jobs.

'I have classes, papa. Students will be waiting.'

'The CM of Rajasthan visits your home. You want to do tuitions?'

'It's what I do.'

'Are you going to apply for a proper job? In companies?'

'Yes, papa. I took what I could get for now.'

'If only you had done better in college. It's hard to explain to friends why my son couldn't get proper placement after IIT.'

I trained my gaze down. We had discussed this a dozen times before. 'We have our Agrasen ji. He's pranth pracharak in Rajasthan. He owns a marble factory. He will give you a job if I ask him.'

'I don't want to work in some family-owned marble factory in Rajasthan, papa.'

'Why? At least you will be a real engineer. Better than giving tuitions.'

'It should be a multinational. At least a top Indian company. Otherwise, what is the difference?'

He shook his head in disappointment. He stood up and began to twist his upper body side to side, to crack his spine. I said, 'Let me know the exact time the CM is coming. I'll come down for a few hours if I can.'

'Oh, you are bigger than the CM now? You will come down once you know the CM's exact time?' Papa sat back on the sofa.

'I just meant instead of staying the whole week.'

Zara opened the door of her room. My father heard the sound.

'Someone is upstairs?' he said.

'Yeah, papa. I told you I am coming this weekend with a friend.'

'Did you? Staying here?'

'Yeah. Just for the weekend. Wanted to see Alwar.'

Zara came out of her room and took the steps down to the living room. She wore a simple lemon-yellow salwar kameez. With her damp hair and bare face she looked more beautiful than ever. When my father saw her, his jaw dropped. He whispered to me, 'This is your friend?'

'Yeah. She's doing PhD at IIT.'

'But...' Before papa could say more, Zara had reached us.

'Namaste, uncle,' Zara said. Papa stood up, more in shock than out of respect.

My father folded his hands. No words came out of his mouth. Why do so many Indian men get tongue-tied in front of women?

Zara had listened to me. She wore a full-sleeved kameez, which covered her wrists and most of her neck. I had given her strict instructions not to show any skin. She said I made my parents sound like the Taliban. She didn't get it. Parents need one measly reason to hate their child's choice. Strike one, doesn't dress conservatively enough, game over.

'Papa, this is Zara. Zara, my father,' I said.

My father gave the briefest nod. He sat back down. The three of us sat in the living room, which had become so silent the clock's ticking sounded like a hammer being struck on the wall. My father, who had been lecturing me in full flow a few seconds ago, had zero words to say right now.

'Zara is doing her PhD at IIT Delhi,' I said, 'in big data networking. Computer science.'

My father nodded and smiled, but his vocal cords remained on strike. Zara initiated some conversation.

'You are a lawyer, uncle?'

'Hmmm...' my father gave an unhelpful grunt in response.

'You have your own practice?' Zara said.

'Used to. Now full-time Sangh,' my father said. Wow, finally the man had spoken.

'Sangh?' Zara said.

'RSS. You know RSS?'

'Yes, Rashtriya Swayamsevak Sangh.'

'Where are you from?' my father said, the must-ask question for all Indian elders. Maybe parents should just insist on address-proof or a copy of the Aadhaar card when they meet their child's friend for the first time.

'I live in Delhi. But Kashmiri, originally.'

'Oh,' my father said. 'What's your full name?'

My father feels it is totally normal to have a conversation that sounds like a cross-examination.

'Zara Lone, uncle,' she said.

My father absorbed her last name with the help of a long, deep breath. Yes, she's a Muslim, papa, relax. They don't bite, I wanted to say.

'I have to talk to his mother,' my father said, and stood up. He went to the puja room. The bhajans stopped. I heard incomprehensible voices that suggested a serious discussion.

'Everything okay?' Zara said to me.

'Yeah, why?' I smiled extra-bright. 'Nice salwar kameez, by the way.'

❖

I sat at the dining table having tea with my parents the next evening. Zara was out on her own, shopping in the street market in Alwar.

'Your father wants to know why you have brought this girl home,' my mother said. I turned to my father. I wanted to know why he had to route what he wanted to know from me through my mother.

'Papa, she wanted to see Alwar. And I thought she will get to meet you too.'

'Why do we have to meet her?' my father said.

'It's nothing, right?' my mother said. 'I told your father. She is just a friend who wanted to see Alwar. You offered your home as it is safer. So many crimes against women these days.'

'Yeah, but ...'

'But what?' my father said.

'She is a good friend, papa.'

'Good friend? Who has girls as good friends?' my father said. Normal people, I wanted to answer but didn't.

'You bring a Kashmiri Muslim girl home and we can't even ask questions?'

'Why are you getting angry?' my mother tried to pacify her husband. 'IIT has students from everywhere. She seems like a decent girl. She will see Alwar and leave. Why are you getting worked up, Rajpurohit ji?'

'Your son brings a Muslim girl home and you are not concerned?' my father said. I couldn't tell exactly what my crime was. That I had brought a *girl* home or a *Muslim* home? Maybe both.

'Why, beta? Is there anything to worry?' my mother said in her most soothing voice.

Worry? Zara and I together counted as a 'worry', I guess.

'Maa, didn't you say she was beautiful?' I said.

'Yeah, so?' my mother said. My father gave her a dirty look; how dare she call a non-Hindu beautiful?

'She's intelligent too. She's doing a PhD from IIT. On big data networking. Cutting-edge stuff.'

'Big data what? Like data package?' my mother said, genuinely confused. I need not have mentioned Zara's thesis topic, I guess.

'She's passionate about social causes. She's not materialistic. Wants to do something for Kashmir once she finishes her studies. She is respectful—' I said before my mother interrupted me.

'That's good. But why are you telling us all this?'

Both my parents were by now staring at me with horror. I took a deep breath.

'I like her, maa,' I said.

'What?' my mother said, as if I had admitted to necrophilia or something.

'I like Zara. She likes me too. We want to be together.'

'See,' my father screamed. He stood up from the dining table. 'I am your father. Not an idiot. I could sense it the moment I saw her.'

'Together? You want to marry that Muslim girl?' my mother said, finding her voice again.

'I want to be with Zara, maa, who happens to be a Muslim. And five feet three inches tall. And fair like Snow White in the fairy tale. How do all these stupid superficial attributes matter?'

'Being Muslim doesn't matter?' my mother said, her eyes and mouth making three round Os on her face.

My father retorted with the same clichéd line millions of Indian husbands use to palm off responsibility. 'Go, love your son some more. First he graduates last in class. Then he can't get a job. And now he wants a Muslim girl. Tell me this is not because you have spoilt him.'

My mother reached me in a flash and whacked the back of my head. She hadn't done this to me in fifteen years.

'Ouch.' I rubbed the back of my head. A Rajput mother's whack can really hurt.

'Have you lost your mind? You want to marry a Muslim girl?' she said, as if I had just requested for seed money to start an online cocaine shop.

'*Kashmiri* Muslim,' my father added, to rub it in that Zara was somehow worse than just a plain vanilla Muslim.

'Papa, she's an educated girl from a good family in Delhi.'

'It's people like her who threw Hindus out of Kashmir,' my father said.

'What? Zara has a blog to promote peace and unity in Kashmir,' I said. 'What are you even talking about, papa?'

'Blaw ... what?' my father said.

'Blog. She writes on the internet about Kashmir and the need for peace there. Talk to her and listen to her views.'

'I am not speaking to these Kashmiri Muslims about Kashmir. Just tell me when she is leaving our house,' my father said. He walked up to the sofa and sat down in a huff. He sulked as he switched on the TV. A news channel came on. To make things worse, the prime-time debate was about stone-pelters attacking the Indian Army in Kashmir.

'Look at them, ungrateful people. Our Army keeps them safe. They throw stones at our jawans and shield terrorists.'

I stomped across and stood in front of the TV. 'I don't know the Kashmir issue too well. But I am sure it is not as simple as people just being ungrateful,' I said.

'You refuse to see sense.'

'Papa, Zara and I love each other. This is not about some stupid politics.'

'Love?' my mother screamed from across the hall. 'Your papa is right. You should get your brain checked.'

'Move away from the TV,' my father said in a gruff tone.

'No, papa, talk to me. Tell me what is wrong with Zara, apart from her religion?'

'I don't want to talk about this. Please send her back.'

'If Zara was a Rajasthani Rajput, you would be fine, no?'

'Don't talk back to your father, or I will give you one more slap,' my mother hissed.

I turned to plead with my mother.

'Maa, please look beyond her religion.'

'How? Will anyone in our khandaan look beyond it? Tell me honestly, at the wedding, what will people be talking about?'

'Is that it? Gossip at the wedding ceremony?'

My father made a tch-tch sound.

'It's not just that,' my mother said. 'The problem is you do not care about your father. And that is what hurts him.'

Maybe I just imagined it, but I heard a sniffle from my father. When parents decide to do a full-frontal emotional assault, nothing is off-limits. Crying dads and slapping moms are a routine part of how Indian kids are hammered into shape and manipulated to give up on things they really want.

'How is this about papa?' I said.

'He's in the RSS,' my mother said. 'Already his rise is limited because he is married. But they are still considering him for a more senior position.'

'So?' I said, confused.

'Now you will bring home this Muslim girl. What will people say?'

'How is it connected? Isn't RSS just a social organisation? To promote Indian nationalism? That's what they say all the time.'

'See, I told you. He doesn't care,' my father said. 'He will marry a terrorist, I tell you.'

'Terrorist?' I shouted. 'She's an IIT student.'

'Shut up,' my mother said. 'Enough is enough. I got fooled. You ask her to leave tonight itself.'

'Tonight?' I said.

'Yes,' my mother said.

'It's not even safe to drive back to Delhi at night,' I said.

'Your father can arrange an RSS worker to accompany her. Can you, Rajpurohit ji?'

My father nodded.

'And you stay away from her.'

'But maa ...'

'Or stay away from us,' my father said.

'Maa, this is not fair.' I turned to my mother.

'I will burn myself if you marry her,' my mother said. 'Call a worker, Rajpurohit ji.'

The doorbell interrupted our conversation. My father stood up and opened the door.

'Milk cake, anyone?' Zara's cheerful voice filled the room.

❖

'One more hour,' I said, checking Google Maps on my phone. 'And you should be in Himadri.'

Suketu, one of the RSS workers in Alwar, was driving us in his Honda City to Delhi that night. Rajpal, an adolescent volunteer, sat in front with Suketu. Zara and I were in the back.

'What is this sudden job interview that came up?' said Zara, slightly breathless from all the hurry.

'It is OLX, you know the second-hand goods website?' I said, making things up as I spoke. I had just seen an OLX ad banner a few kilometres back.

'What's the job?'

'Coding, what else?'

'Oh. And they wanted to interview you on a Sunday?'

'Yeah, tomorrow morning. Their CEO is in town or something.'

'Bhaiya, I bought a second-hand mobile phone on OLX,' Rajpal piped up. 'Works pretty good.'

Okay, so these morons in front were listening to our every word.

'Which brand?' Suketu said.

'Redmi,' Rajpal said. 'Keshav bhaiya, if you get a job at OLX, tell us about the best deals first.'

'Sure,' I said.

'Sunday? The CEO is meeting you?' Zara said. 'For a coder job.'

'I don't know, Zara. Why are you interrogating me?'

'It's just a bit strange. This was my weekend to meet your parents as your girlfriend.'

'You did meet them.'

'Weren't you going to talk about us?'

'Can we discuss this later?' I pointed to the people in front. She ignored my signal.

'Did they not like me?'

'Are you mad? Didn't you hear my mother? She called you beautiful.'

'Doesn't necessarily mean likeable.'

'They liked you. Of course, they liked you. You want to stop for dinner at the border dhabas? Suketu bhaiya, let's make a quick stop.'

❖

'You are acting weird,' Zara said as we walked to a jute charpoy in the dhaba.

We had stopped at Rangeen Dhabha, one of the last open-air eating places before the urban chaos of Delhi took over. Suketu and Rajpal went to use the toilet, allowing us a moment of privacy.

'Zara, I was thinking. Why don't we go through your parents first?'

'But I thought we decided to start with your folks.'

'Yeah, but we could do it the other way too,' I said, and flipped over the laminated menu. 'You want to try gobi paranthas?'

'Did you chicken out?' she said in a lowered tone.

'I am not chickening out, okay?' I said, my voice loud.

'Yeah, bhaiya, don't eat chicken here. Not safe.' Rajpal had returned from the washroom.

Chapter 13

'Stop being so self-conscious,' Zara said as we reached Westend Greens, a super-upscale farmhouse-only neighbourhood located along the Delhi–Gurgaon border. We had taken an Ola; the mobile app made taking a cab to anywhere easy. The IITian-founded Indian company was already valued in billions. Why couldn't I think of an idea one-thousandth of this level? Why couldn't I even get a proper job? Or make a proper tie knot?

'This tie has a life of its own,' I grumbled.

'The suit was unnecessary. You are only meeting my family. It's not an interview.'

'They see me in a suit, they believe I am a professional. Otherwise, the moment I mention IIT tuitions, it is over.'

'It's not tuitions. You are faculty in a cutting-edge test preparation centre,' Zara said.

When Zara put it like that, my career didn't seem as horrible. That is why I loved her. She saw the best in everything, including the pretty ordinary me.

A watchman opened the gate as our Wagon R entered her mansion.

'This is your house? And you still live in a tiny hostel room?' I said, as I noticed a garden the size of a volleyball court in front of her half-acre bungalow.

'I love my room. 105 is my life.'

'You can have a good life here too.'

'It's much better to be on campus. Commuting is a pain. Okay, final checks, mister. Ties, belts, shoelaces and nerves? All good?' Zara pinched my nose. Have I mentioned that? She was always pinching my nose. Most annoying.

❖

'Can I serve you some more gosht?' Safdar said in his thunderous voice. We were seated for lunch on chairs that resembled the thrones in mythological TV serials. Safdar was at the head of the eighteen-seater dining table.

He was wearing a black bandhgala, with two gold bracelets and a Rolex watch on his left wrist. His French beard was dyed black. His wife, sitting to my left, had said little so far. Her pink silk salwar-kameez, dupatta half covering her head, and her diamond and jade necklace, which probably cost as much as one of the small apartments they keep advertising on the Dwarka–Gurgaon Expressway, spelt upper-crust. Her hair looked naturally black; I figured she was no more than a decade older than Zara.

'No, sir, I am quite full,' I said. Even though I didn't eat much meat, I had made an effort to do so today. I had to fit into Zara's family.

'So, Zara tells me you and she have a lot of dosti,' Safdar said, eating his biryani with an ornate fork and knife.

Unlike idiot me, Zara had already spoken to her parents and prepared them in advance. Hence, unlike the electric shock I had given my mother and father, Zara's parents seemed calm. At least they hadn't threatened suicide yet. 'We sort of, kinda like each other,' is what she had told them. Unfortunately, for native Hindi speakers like my parents, there was no equivalent word for 'sort of' or 'kinda'. I don't think my father was a sort of, kinda guy anyway.

'Sir,' I said as I cleared my throat to speak.

'You don't have to call me sir.'

'Can I call you uncle? Or Mr Lone?'

'Uncle is fine. So tell me about your dosti.'

'We have known each other for almost three years. We met on campus.'

'And our daughter never told us. What do you think, Zainab? Zara joined PhD in IIT for her dost?' Mr Lone said and laughed. Zainab only responded with a half smile.

'Uncle, I graduated from IIT within a year after Zara joined.'

'I am joking. Anyway, what do you do now?'

I got a sinking feeling. In a small voice, I said, 'I am faculty at a test prep company.'

'Test prep, as in?'

'It's pretty hi-tech, dad. They are working on apps to do test preparation. Keshav is part of it,' Zara said.

Zara had made it all up. The only hi-tech thing Chandan Arora probably ever did was to order his gutkha online.

'Like an education startup?' Safdar said.

'Huh, yeah, uncle,' I said. 'It's bricks and mortar at present, but we are going to go online.'

'Good. I think of investing in internet companies sometimes too,' Safdar said. 'People care much more about Apple phones today than apple orchards.'

Everyone laughed. I liked Zara's dad. At least he made an effort to have a proper conversation.

'I heard you are one of the top fruit exporters from Kashmir,' I said.

'God has been kind.'

Zara brought us back to the main topic.

'So, as I told you, dad, Keshav and I like each other.'

'I can see that,' Safdar said.

'We need your blessings,' Zara said.

'Oh,' Safdar said, surprised. 'Zainab, see these app-making kids of today. How they ask their parents directly.'

'You know, dad, I am always frank with you.'

Safdar laughed.

'Of course. So what do you want me to do? Meet his parents?'

'No,' I burst out.

'What?' Zara looked at me surprised.

'Sorry, Zara, I should have told you. But, uncle, my parents are not supportive of this. I'm sure you can guess why.'

'When did this happen?' Zara said. I continued to look straight at her father.

'Uncle, I love your daughter very much. I will do anything to make her happy. Please bless us. My parents won't. But we need at least one side to be with us.'

'But, Keshav…' Zara said and then lapsed into silence.

Safdar let out a huge breath.

'Well, parents are important. I must say, even I wasn't too happy when Zara said she wants to be with you.'

'Because I am a Hindu?'

'Yes, but I am not that old-fashioned.'

Relief made me stammer. 'Th … thank you, uncle.'

He nodded his acknowledgement. 'Yeah, so anyway, we can take care of that,' he said.

After lunch, we moved to the garden. Zara's father and I sat on a swing. Zara played with their dog Ruby, a German Shepherd who wanted to snooze in the sun more than run after Zara. Zainab had retired for a nap.

Zara came up to us panting and sat on the swing as well. Safdar spoke to me again.

'So, tell me, what is the situation with your parents?'

'Yes, even I want to know, Keshav,' Zara said.

I told them, censoring all the anti-Muslim comments, about the conversation I had had with my family in Alwar.

'Ah, so that is why we left Alwar early,' Zara said.

'You went to Alwar?' Safdar said.

'Casual visit. Well, until I was kicked out.'

'Nobody was kicked out,' I said. It is hard to hear negative things about your parents, even when they are against you.

'So they hate Muslims?' Safdar laughed.

I looked at him, surprised.

'No. They have a few Muslim friends. But to have their only son marry a Muslim—that's too much for them.'

'You want to see a person's true prejudices? Ask if they will marry their children into a community,' Safdar smiled.

'They are nice people. Trust me, they are just scared. They love me. They will come around. Just, right now it is difficult.'

'What do you suggest?' Zara said.

'We get married. Then I convince them. They have little choice then,' I said.

'You want me to let Zara marry you without meeting your parents?' Safdar said.

'You can meet them if you want to. It will only make things worse.'

Safdar sat back.

'If you ask me, you guys should end this,' Safdar said.

'We can't,' Zara and I said at the same time.

Safdar looked at Zara and me.

'Please help us, uncle,' I said.

He stood up and paced around the swing twice.

'Say something, dad,' Zara said.

'It will have to be our way. We can do a nikaah.'

'Whatever,' I said.

'We can give you the shahada in a ceremony before or even during the nikaah.'

'Shahada?' I said, hearing the word for the first time.

Safdar turned to Zara.

'Your dost doesn't know? Yet he loves a Muslim girl.'

'Dad, what is this shahada business? I don't think we need to…'

'Of course we need to,' her father broke in. 'His parents will disown him. Let's do things properly from our side.'

'But what is shahada?'

'An oath,' Safdar said.

'Dad, please. This is all too old-fashioned.'

'Old-fashioned?' Safdar's nose went up an inch. 'How dare you call it old-fashioned? You have any tameez left, or not?'

Zara shrugged and sat on the grass with Ruby.

'Sorry, uncle, I am fine with any tradition. I just didn't know,' I said.

'This girl is mad,' Safdar said. 'Extra-modern for no reason.'

'But what is this oath, uncle? Shah-what?'

'Shahada. It's simple. Just a couple of lines.' He raised his palms and murmured something in Arabic, 'lā ilāha illā llāh muhammadun rasūlu llāh. There is no god but God. Muhammad is the messenger of God. To make you one of us.'

'Us?'

'A nikaah can't happen unless both bride and groom are Muslims. You have to convert,' Safdar said.

Maybe I was giddy from the swing, but I swear I felt the ground move beneath me.

'Would you like some tea? We have wonderful Kashmiri kahwah,' Safdar was saying, as if the kahwah came free with the conversion.

❖

'Trust me, I didn't expect this turn of events,' Zara said, cupping my face.

I took her hands in mine and kissed the inside of a wrist.

'I can't convert, Zara. Please understand. I love your religion, but I can't convert. My parents will kill themselves.'

'So don't.'

'How do we marry?' I said.

'Under the Special Marriage Act. The Indian Constitution allows it. People from any two faiths can go to court and marry. No religion, no caste drama. Just the way it should be.'

'We do a court marriage?'

'Yeah, if you can't convert.'

'And your parents will also not come?'

'Forget come. I will get disowned too. And my dad will also send thugs from his warehouse to beat us up. So filmi, no?' Zara raised her eyebrows comically.

'I am serious, Zara. We can't be parent-less on both sides. That's not a good start.'

'So convince your parents.'

'Can't.'

'Convert.'

'Can't.'

'So we have to give them up for the sake of our love.'

'Zara, what are you even saying?'

'Nothing.'

Zara freed herself from my arms.

'I am trying my best, Zara.'

'Is this your best? I don't think so. I don't see you telling your parents, "This is my girl and that's that".'

'They are my parents, Zara.'

'That they will always be. But the way we are going…' She stopped mid-sentence.

'What?'

'Nothing. Good night.'

❖

My phone rang in the staffroom. I picked it up.

'It's Safdar. Can we talk?'

'Keshav!' came Chandan's loud call. 'Come to my office.' His fat stomach reached the staffroom before he did. I covered the phone with my hand.

'Chandan sir, I am on an important call. Give me five minutes?'

'Important call? What? Being interviewed by other coaching centres?' he said, one eyebrow raised.

'Sir, family,' I said, moving away from Chandan. 'Yes, uncle, how are you?'

Safdar came straight to the point. 'Zara says you are not comfortable converting to Islam.'

'No, sir, I mean, I would, sir, but my parents won't be able to take it.'

'So forget Zara. Stop meeting her.'

'But, uncle…'

'Stop means stop. I opened my heart to you. You betrayed us.'

'Betrayed?'

'Your parents threw my daughter out when she came as a guest. I welcomed you into the family. But you don't want to respect our wishes.'

'Uncle, it's about one's religion…'

'Enough,' he said, interrupting me. 'You went to PVR with Zara yesterday?'

'Yes, sir,' I said, wondering how he knew.

'And she came to your apartment afterwards?'

'Zara told you?' I said.

'No. I have people who track you. And if need be they will hurt you.'

'Hurt?'

'You are just a kafir. Taking advantage of my precious daughter. Leave her alone, or it won't be good.'

'Are you threatening me, uncle?' I said, just to be clear.

'I don't threaten. I display kindness, and when betrayed, I take action. For my family's honour, if necessary, I will draw blood.'

The word 'blood' sent shivers down my spine. Chandan Arora walked into the staffroom again and shook my shoulder.

'If your loving family call is over, let's talk work?'

❖

'That wasn't cool, Keshav,' Zara said.

'I know,' I said, taking a bite of the falafel kebabs in her friend Sanam's kitchen.

We were at a New Year's Eve party at Sanam's aunt's house.

Even though Zara and I hadn't officially broken up, our relationship was beginning to resemble a war zone. We rarely met. When we did meet, we didn't talk anymore, we argued. Somehow we ended up at the same topic—we have no future. I didn't want to convert or disown our parents. Zara couldn't believe I wouldn't fight for us.

At the party, I had told Zara I wanted to talk to her alone. Sanam's kitchen was the only quiet place we could find in the entire house.

'You drunk-dialling me every week is bad enough, but how could you call my dad?' Zara said.

'I didn't realise it. I searched for Lone on my phone and ended up dialling his number.'

'And since he picked up, you felt it was okay to yell and abuse?'

I avoided eye contact with her. I looked at all the party food kept in aluminium foil trays near the stove. Three days ago, too many drinks and an accidental call had meant Safdar Lone heard some wonderful abuses from his almost-had-been Rajasthani son-in-law. I had screwed up, and had no excuses. Still, I remained stupidly defiant.

She continued to stare at me. I smirked. Yes, I could smirk at Zara then. I didn't know how much this girl meant to me. Or that I would be pining for her years later.

However, at that time, stupid me couldn't care less.

'Your dad deserved it,' I said.

'What?'

'Didn't he threaten me and tell me to stop meeting you? I told you he called me at work.'

'Did I stop meeting you? Did I, Keshav?'

'No,' I said sheepishly.

'Didn't I give you enough chances to think about what to do?'

'Yes, but you have started avoiding me now'

'Because you have no answers for us. It's better we stay away from each other then.'

'Just like that?'

'Not *just like that*. It's hard. Super hard. Keshav Rajpurohit, I left that scholarship from MIT for you. Joined IIT just to be close to you. You think it is *just like that* for me?'

'Oh, so now I am supposed to feel guilty? Give up my parents and God because you gave up a scholarship?'

'I don't like your tone, Keshav.'

'I don't care.'

'Fine, then. I will go hang out with my friends. You are the one who pulled me aside.'

'Go wherever.'

'I am leaving. Keshav, I know it sounds kiddish. But can we, like, officially break up?'

'What?'

'We kind of have already. But, like, let's be clear. From now on, no contact.'

'Zara? Are you mad?' I said.

'I was mad. I'm coming to my senses now.'

'I got drunk and called your dad. Big deal. What do you want me to do? Say sorry? I will.'

Zara shook her head.

'It's not just that. It's more. Anyway, no point going over it again. We are done. Bye.'

'Zara,' I called after her, but she had already left the kitchen to join her friends. At least on that day, I had too much pride and ego to go after her. And, yes, she was right. I didn't have answers. Just as I had no measure of how desperately I wanted to be with this girl.

❖

Someone was shaking me by my shoulder.

'I am never coming to pick you up like that again,' Saurabh said, continuing to shake my shoulder, switching off the past videos playing in my mind.

'Huh? Oh, Golu. You are here. You are my jaan, Golu.' I ruffled his hair as I came back to my senses and the present moment.

Apparently, I had had a bill for ten whiskies at Social, which Saurabh had paid for last night. One of the waiters had used my phone to dial his number when I passed out at my table.

'I saw their conversations. Between Zara and Raghu. Full-on love,' I said, as if that justified my alcoholic meltdown.

'They were dating. Of course, they will have such conversations. When will you stop this Zara business?'

'What will I stop? God only stopped it. I didn't convert. That's why he punished me. Took her away. Right when she wanted to get back.'

I felt like crying again. Saurabh noticed and spoke again.

'Shut up. Take a shower. Teach your class. Move on,' Saurabh said, a rare strictness in his voice.

'Did you know, Prof. Saxena made an indecent proposal to Zara?'

'Your IIT dean?'

'Yeah, Zara's guide. I have an email in which Zara says everything he did. I have to meet that bastard,' I said.

I stood up and walked to the bathroom.

'No meeting anyone,' Saurabh screamed from behind. 'Focus on work.'

'I will finish my classes first, Golu. Relax,' I said, splashing water from the tap on my face.

Chapter 14

'Laxman, you will get out. It just won't happen so soon,' I said.

I had come to meet Laxman in Tihar Jail, in west Delhi. An undertrial, he was allowed to see visitors during designated hours.

'Sahib, my wife is alone. There is no income,' Laxman said.

'I am sorry, Laxman,' I said. 'Help me, and I will help you.'

We sat in the meeting area, a dingy room with several rickety chairs.

'What can I do for you?' Laxman said.

'I want to know who used to come to meet Zara at the hostel.'

'Her parents, not much though. Once in two months.'

'And?'

'Raghu sahib. Once a month he would visit Delhi. He would come to pick her up and Zara madam would leave for a few days.'

I sucked in my breath sharply.

'And?'

'Prof. Saxena, sometimes.'

'When?'

'It will all be in the visitor's book. I think he came around three times last month.'

'Did you hear them talk?'

The watchman shook his head.

'He would go to the common room. Zara madam would come there. Sahib, when will I be able to go back home?'

❖

'Yes, what can I do for you?' Prof. Saxena said. He sat at his desk, face partially hidden by piles of files, books and a super-computer with a gigantic CPU, probably used to make big data models.

'I am Keshav Rajpurohit, sir. Alumnus from here. Graduated five years ago.'

Prof. Saxena had thin grey hair on his head that looked like it hadn't met a comb since he had graduated. His paunch remained hidden under his desk. He did not look up from his computer.

'I am not looking for assistants right now.'

Students lined up to work with Prof. Saxena, in the hope of a recommendation when they later applied to US universities. A nice reco letter from him could help research students earn a full fellowship at an MIT or Stanford.

'I don't want to be your assistant,' I said.

'So, why are you here?' he said, eyes still on the monitor.

'I want to talk about Zara Lone.'

'What?' he said, looking at me for the first time.

'She did her PhD under you, right?'

He stared at me.

'I am sorry. Who are you again?' he said.

'Keshav Rajpurohit. Batch of 2013.'

'And how are you related to Zara Lone?'

'She was a close friend.'

'Really? Close friend?' Prof. Saxena said. 'You are her ex-boyfriend, aren't you? My other students told me you were the reason she gave up a wonderful scholarship at MIT.'

He leaned forward in his chair, forearms on the table.

'Yes, sir,' I said, clearing my throat. 'The point is, I found her body. When I went to wish her on her birthday.'

'You are the boy who broke into the girls' hostel?'

I nodded.

'She had a fiancé, right? I've met him, he's PGM from here. Raghu Venkatesh.'

PGM referred to President's Gold Medal, given to the topper of the batch. Of course, Maggu Raghu had scored straight 10 GPAs—grade point average—in all semesters, ensuring the 'nerd of the batch' medal belonged to him and nobody else.

'Raghu is from my batch as well.'

'Doing really well. Sequoia Capital funded his artificial intelligence company. Many Silicon Valley companies want to invest. A true IIT Delhi success story.'

Unlike me, a true IIT Delhi failure story.

'I am aware. Sir, do you know anything that could help solve the murder of Zara Lone?'

'What?' His chair creaked as he sat up straight. 'The watchman did it. We all saw the news. Terrible.'

'The watchman didn't do it, sir.'

'Really?'

'Yes, sir, a hundred per cent sure he didn't.'

'Who are you? The police?'

'No, sir.'

'First that inspector, what's his name, Rana bothered me. Wanted to send his team all over campus. Thankfully, he became quiet since they got the watchman.'

'Why didn't you allow the police to come to campus and investigate?'

'This is a place where people study, not some criminal interrogation zone. I told him to get lost. And I am sorry, but you are wasting my time too.'

'I am helping the police, sir. Since they are not allowed here. I just have a few questions for you.'

'What nonsense. You may be allowed on campus as an alumnus, but you can't go snooping around. I can bar you from entry.'

'No, you won't,' I said, in a calm but firm voice.

My sudden defiance startled him.

'Is this how you talk to your teachers? Please leave.'

'Is it true that you propositioned Zara?'

'What?' the professor said, his face turning white. Even though he kept up a defiant posture, his lips trembled.

'You delayed her thesis. Asked her to sleep with you.'

'That's nonsense. I am going to call security and have you thrown out.'

He picked up the intercom in his room.

'Don't make that mistake. I can say what I am saying to the media as well,' I said.

'Like they will believe you. The person who breaks into women's hostels!' he scoffed, still on the phone. 'Hello, security? Send some people to my office please. Yes, unwanted person.'

Acting as if I no longer existed, he went back to work on his computer.

I opened email on my phone and after a couple of moments, said, 'Check your inbox.'

'Why?' Prof Saxena said even as he clicked his computer's mouse. He opened the email that I had forwarded to him. His mouth fell open as he read it.

To: Raghu

From: Zara

Hey Love,

How are you? So far away from me in Hyderabad. Today is one of those days I really, really wish you were here. I tried calling you. Your secretary told me you are in meetings all day with people who have come from San Jose. Well, good luck with that. Hope they go well. Call when you can? I really need to talk. I have already told you about the creepy feeling I get from Prof. Saxena. You also know how many times he has asked me out for coffee. What I haven't told you are a few more things he has done. I thought they were inadvertent or harmless, but it has happened too often now. For instance, he often comes up behind me and touches my hair when I am working on the computer. Two days ago, he put his arm around my shoulder when I showed him a printout. When I wriggled away, he said, 'Why don't we get closer? Intimacy always helps people connect.'

Raghu, I felt so creeped out, I wanted to jump out of his office window. I don't know why I didn't tell you about it right then. I guess I thought it was a one-off. But today, he did it again! I went to show him an Excel sheet on my laptop, and he kissed my right cheek and said I looked like a Kashmiri rose!!! Then I am not sure, but I think he pulled my hand towards his ... oh gosh maybe he didn't mean to, but Raghu, it was gross! I wanna quit, but how? What do I do? I am so confused. Call me soon.

XOXO

Z

'This is utter lies,' Prof. Saxena said, his voice quivering.

'It's an email from your research scholar who has been murdered. The PGM fiancé is witness,' I said.

'I don't know what you are talking about.'

'Hostel registers show you visited her eight times in the last three months. I don't think you have ever visited any other student in their hostel.'

Someone knocked on Prof. Saxena's door.

'Sir, you wanted us to come?' the institute security officer said as he walked in.

Two other guards stood behind him.

'Actually,' Prof. Saxena said, 'we are fine. You can leave.'

The security officers gave us confused, irritated looks and left.

'What do you want?' Prof. Saxena said to me.

'Before we get into that, we all know what you want.'

'What?'

'Padma Vibhushan. You might even get it soon.'

'Because I am the best in my field. I could have gone to any university in the world. I chose to stay in India.'

'How noble of you,' I said. 'But imagine the news: Prof. Saxena harassed his PhD student. They will give you a special Padma then?'

He put his head in his hands. It is amazing how amiable people become when the power balance shifts against them.

'What do you want? Really?' Prof. Saxena said.

'I am only trying to solve Zara's murder.'

'Okay. So what? You think I did it?'

'I didn't say that. But did you? Did you, you bastard?'

It felt strange to talk to a faculty member like this, yet oddly satisfying.

'What? I didn't kill anybody. What are you saying?'

I stood up. I leaned forward and grabbed his shirt collar.

I said, not very coherently, 'You creep. Zara wanted to come back to me. You troubled her. Harassed her. And I don't know what else. Now you sit here like an innocent geeky professor.'

To make up for my inarticulate speech, I slapped Saxena hard across his face. I held on to him, wanting to slap him again and again. However, he began to whine.

'Please leave,' Prof. Saxena said. 'Don't hurt me.'

'Did you kill her?'

'No. Please let me go.'

I released my grip and sat back. He put a hand on his heart.

'I have never hurt a fly in my life. Why would I kill her?'

'Maybe you thought she would reveal the truth about you once she had her PhD degree, something you couldn't delay anymore. Maybe you got scared, went up to her room and killed her.'

'No, I swear on my kids, no,' he said. He pinched his throat like an eight-year-old.

I stood up.

'If you did, better admit it. Or else, I will come back with the police.'

He shook his head, and still pinching his throat, he said, 'I swear, I didn't do it.'

'I'll see you soon, asshole,' I said. I slammed the office door behind me and left.

❖

'The dean?' Saurabh said, walking on the treadmill at the lowest speed possible. I had finally convinced him to come to the gym with me.

'Can you believe it?' I said. 'That bastard dean. You read the email, right?'

'I did. I have two things to say,' Saurabh said.

'What?' I said, and increased the speed of his treadmill to four kilometres per hour.

'Slower, bhai.'

'It's fine. Your heart rate should go up. You weighed yourself? How much was it?'

'Ninety-five point five.'

'That's too much, Saurabh.'

'I am working on it. One day I will have a six-pack like you. Actually, I do have one. It's just hidden under some tissue.'

'That tissue is called fat. And it is not some tissue, it is a lot of it. Anyway, now say the two things you had to say.'

'Fine. One, what my brain says, and the other, what my heart says.'

'What?'

'Brain says, I really wish you would stop pursuing this. Even Rana said, "Ideally, stay away".'

'Screw the brain. What does the heart say?'

'The heart says,' Saurabh said and stopped the treadmill. 'Wait, my heart is actually racing too fast.'

'You just started.'

'I know, just pacing myself. Anyway, bhai, my heart says, this is so freaking interesting and intriguing. Really? The dean of students at IIT Delhi, top quant prof in the world, might have murdered a student?'

'He swore on his kids, but he's a smartass. He could be acting.'

I lifted a ten-kilo dumbbell and handed it to Saurabh. Saurabh found it too heavy and went to replace it with a two-kilo one.

I shook my head.

'Bhai, my body is tender. You can't push it so much, so fast. Anyway, what will you do next about the dean?' Saurabh said.

'I will meet his wife. Try to find out if he wasn't home that night.'

'She will tell you?'

'I don't know. I have no other way to find out.'

'Hmmm ...' Saurabh started doing bicep curls with a weight that a toddler could pick up. Both of us looked at each other in the gym mirror.

'I want you to come,' I said.

'Me?' Saurabh said, surprised.

'Yeah. Observe everything. Ask any questions if you like, and later give me your view.'

'You want me to come? For something my brain says you should stay away from?' Saurabh laughed.

'Yes.' I grinned.

'Why do you think I would do that?'

'Because between you and me, it is all about the heart. I love you,' I said. I sent a flying kiss through the mirror and winked at him.

'Oh dear. Profs or students, you IITians are all creeps,' he said, finishing his set.

❖

'Prof. Saxena is not at home,' said the lady who opened the door.

'Mrs Parminder Saxena?' I said.

'Yes?' Mrs Saxena said. She adjusted the dupatta over her nightie, Delhi's official housewife dress.

I took out my alumni card.

'I am Keshav Rajpurohit. Ex-student here. This is my friend Saurabh. May we come in? It is you we want to talk to.'

'Me?'

'This is regarding Zara Lone. Prof. Saxena's student who died.'

Prof. Saxena's wife looked left and right, and then gestured us in.

Chapter 15

Over a cup of tea, I told Mrs Saxena what I knew about the case so far, leaving out Saxena's antics towards Zara for the time being.

'And that is why we are here. To talk to everyone who knew Zara. Until we find the real killer, the police won't let the innocent watchman go,' I said.

'But why talk to me?' said Mrs Saxena in a bewildered way. 'I hardly met her. Maybe once or twice when I visited Prof. Saxena in office. She seemed like a nice girl.'

'Was Prof. Saxena friendly with his students?' Saurabh said.

Mrs Saxena looked taken aback.

'Not particularly. He's so lost in his work. He's not a friendly person in general. A bit grumpy always, if you ask me,' Mrs Saxena said.

'Did he ever go meet his PhD students in their hostels?'

'Never. He's the dean and their guide, why would he?' Mrs Saxena said, somewhat offended by my question.

'Mrs Saxena, sir went to meet Zara eight times in her hostel in the last three months,' Saurabh said.

'What?'

'It's in the hostel register,' I said. 'I am sorry to tell you this, Mrs Saxena, but I think sir had an extra interest in Zara.'

'Extra?' she said, confused. At forty, Mrs Saxena had probably led a shielded campus life. Her idea of a controversy or scandal would be if the maid skipped work two days in a row.

'He wanted a relationship with Zara,' I said calmly. 'He propositioned her several times.'

'What?' Mrs Saxena gasped. The whistle of a pressure cooker in the kitchen disrupted our conversation.

'Black daal in the pressure cooker?' Saurabh said, sniffing in the direction of the kitchen. I glared at him.

Mrs Saxena exploded. 'Are you insane? My husband? One of the world's best researchers in his field?'

Then the cooker whistled again.

Saurabh jumped up from the sofa.

'I'll go turn the gas off, Mrs Saxena,' he said. 'Two whistles are enough for black daal, right?'

She nodded grimly.

'I am sorry to be the one to tell you, Mrs Saxena,' I said smoothly.

'This is hundred per cent nonsense. Hundred and one per cent. Is there any proof?' she said.

'If the news made you uncomfortable, the proof will make you even more so.'

'What is the proof?'

I held out my phone to her. She read the email quickly and returned my phone. Saurabh came back from the kitchen. All of us sat in awkward silence for a few seconds.

'I am not here to spoil your marriage,' I said.

'Too late for that,' she said. She picked up her phone and called her husband.

'Come home,' Mrs Saxena said when he answered. 'No, right now. I said come home now. I don't care about the senate meeting. You come home now, Vineet.'

She turned to me.

'What do you want?' she said.

'Your help. In finding out the truth,' I said.

'What truth? You have proof. You have ruined my life already.'

I wanted to tell her that it was the professor who had ruined things, not me. However, I decided to stick to the agenda.

'Your husband might have killed Zara Lone.'

'What? Vineet? What is wrong with you guys? My husband was trying to have an affair? Is a murderer?'

'Please be calm, Mrs Saxena,' Saurabh said, 'and listen to Keshav.'

'Ma'am, he had a clear motive. Zara could have exposed him

once she received her PhD degree. He had the opportunity. He lives on campus. He could have stepped out from home at night and walked to Himadri. He could enter Zara's room through the window, kill her and leave. Before anybody found out, he could have been back in his bed,' I said.

'You mean our bed?' Mrs Saxena said.

'Yes, ma'am.'

'It is Vineet we are talking about. He went to IIT and Stanford. You really think he could do such a thing?' Mrs Saxena said.

'Did you really think your husband could be sexually harassing a PhD student?' Saurabh said. Mrs Saxena fell silent.

'Ma'am, this may be too much for you. But we need to know the truth,' I said.

'What?'

'Did your husband leave home that night?' I said.

Before she could answer, the doorbell rang. Mrs Saxena got up and opened the door. Prof. Saxena walked in almost in slow motion as he had a slight limp in his left leg.

'What the...' he screamed when he saw Saurabh and me in his house. 'What the hell are you doing here? How dare you come to my house?'

Mrs Saxena went up to Prof. Saxena. Before he could react, she hit him across his ear.

'Pammi!' Prof. Saxena said, hand on ear.

Mrs Saxena deposited two more slaps in response. Hell hath no fury like a Punjabi woman scorned.

'They are lying, Pammi,' Prof. Saxena said, almost in tears.

'I know they are not,' Mrs Saxena said.

Saurabh and I stood up to leave.

'We just had a few more questions for Mrs Saxena. We can come back later,' I said politely.

'No, wait,' Mrs Saxena said, 'ask me now. Vineet should be here.'

We sat down again. Prof. Saxena continued to stand, hand on ear.

'Mrs Saxena, where was your husband on the night of February 8th?'

'What does a stupid wife like me know? He could have left for an hour while I was asleep.'

'No, Pammi. I didn't.'

'I gave up my career in California for you, Vineet, you slimeball. I was a senior consultant. All for your desh bhakti and research obsession. And this is what you do to me?'

'Pammi, nothing happened!'

'Because *she* didn't let anything happen!' Mrs Saxena said shrewdly, taking a step towards him with her hand raised.

Prof. Saxena took a step back. 'Please don't hit me.'

'I will ruin you. You bloody creep.' She turned to me. 'What do I have to do? Should I sign a document saying my husband was missing that night?'

'No,' Prof. Saxena screamed and fell at his wife's feet.

'That would do it, right? Enough proof to put him away for life?' Mrs Saxena said.

I shrugged. I had no idea.

'Whatever you give us we will submit to the police,' I said.

Prof. Saxena continued to kneel on the floor.

'I beg you. Yes, I liked her. She was beautiful and smart. I became weak. But nothing happened. And I swear on you, I didn't kill her.'

'So, who did?' I said, even as his wife shrieked, 'Not on me. Don't swear on me, you dirty man.'

'I don't know.'

'Boys, go to the police,' Mrs Saxena said furiously.

'Did anyone see me go to the hostel that night? Or leave my home?'

'I will say I did,' Mrs Saxena said.

'Ma'am, you are angry now. We want to know the truth

more than anything else,' I said. 'Can you please think in a calm manner and let us—'

Mrs Saxena interrupted me.

'How can I be calm? I left a two hundred thousand dollar-a-year job for this idiot. All for his "principles".'

I stood up to leave.

'We will give you some privacy. Let's go, Saurabh.'

'Sure, and ma'am, just one more thing,' Saurabh said at the door.

'What?' Mrs Saxena said.

'Don't leave the pressure cooker closed. The black daal will get overcooked.'

❖

'Dean Saxena?' Rana said, almost choking on his extra-hot, full-cream eight per cent-fat milk and hundred per cent-free latte at the Hauz Khas Starbucks. Saurabh and I sat across from him.

Inspector Rana put his cup down. He gave out a loud, Raavan-like laugh.

'Yes,' I said, in a steady voice. 'And you will agree there is enough evidence.'

'Yes,' Rana said and continued to laugh.

'So, why are you laughing, sir,' Saurabh said, still a bit afraid whenever he spoke to Rana.

'I'm not laughing at you. The whole situation is so funny. That ass was being so righteous. Not letting me come to campus. Turns out he's just a tharki prof,' Rana said and laughed again.

I stared at my cup of milk and waited for the inspector to finish giggling. He spoke again.

'From the watchman to the dean of IIT. Wow, just look at the class jump. The media will have so much fun with this.'

'So, we arrest him now?' I said. 'How does it work?'

'Not so simple. We definitely need the wife's testimony that her husband was out that night. Otherwise, I am not sure.'

'Not sure?'

'It's a masala media story, definitely. But releasing the watchman to arrest the dean? If we get this wrong, Delhi Police will be lynched.'

'So you won't arrest him?'

'Get me the wife's testimony,' Rana said. He checked his watch. 'I have to go. I have to get a haircut.'

We saw Inspector Rana to his Gypsy.

'What about Zara's email?' I said.

'Only shows the prof was a pervert. I can't book him for murder for that.'

I nodded. The inspector patted my back.

'Not bad though. Good work.'

❖

'Maggi? Again? The maid has cooked gobi aloo and chapatis.'

'I am bored of the maid's food,' I said.

We stood in the tiny kitchen of our apartment. I stir-fried peas, carrot and capsicum in a kadhai. I added garam masala to the vegetables and tossed them around with a ladle. On the other burner, I boiled three packets of Maggi noodles. Saurabh saw the quantity in the vessel and added two more packets.

I served out my improvised, value-added Maggi noodles in two bowls.

We moved to the dining table and ate our one-dish dinner.

'So, Mrs Saxena declined, eh?' Saurabh said, slurping a long noodle into his mouth.

'Yeah. She had said it in anger. Later on, she must have reflected. Her husband might be a jerk, but she doesn't want him in jail for murder.'

'So no wife testimony.'

'Yes,' I said and refilled my bowl. 'If we have to get the prof, we need more solid evidence.'

'The noodles are superb, by the way,' Saurabh said.

'Thanks.' I blinked. 'You think Saxena could have done it?'

'If Zara could destroy his life's work, yes,' Saurabh said.

'He didn't show up in the CCTV footage of the hostel entrance. The only other way to come up is the mango tree,' I said.

'Yeah,' Saurabh said, 'and since the window was open, it means Zara opened it.'

'Yeah, she could have. She thinks, this idiot pervert has come up the tree to wish me. Fine, a few more weeks and I am free. She opens the window.'

'Then?' Saurabh said.

'He enters. Kills her. Leaves. Back in bed. Cuddles up to his Pammi. End of story. Yeah? Totally adds up, right?' I said.

Saurabh thought for a few seconds and then shook his head.

'What?'

'No. Not possible,' Saurabh said.

'What's not possible?'

'Limp. He has a limp,' Saurabh said.

'What?'

'Did you see, he walked in so slowly into his house. Didn't he have a slight limp?'

'Did he get hurt recently?'

'Not sure. Open your laptop,' Saurabh said.

We searched YouTube videos of Prof. Saxena. Most of them were mega-boring talks at engineering conferences that could also double up as videos to cure insomnia. In one, from a few months back, we could see him walking up to the stage.

'It wasn't just that day. He has a proper limp,' I said.

Saurabh kept quiet as he browsed through a few more videos.

'He couldn't have climbed the mango tree,' I said after a few minutes.

'Yeah,' Saurabh said. 'It was so tough for me. If one of your legs isn't okay, impossible.'

'It's not Saxena,' I said and slammed the laptop shut. 'I better tell Rana.'

I stepped away to call the inspector. Saurabh waited till I ended the call and came back to the dining table.

'What did he say?'

'That we are idiots. We would have made him look so bad if he had arrested the dean.'

'True. Anything else?'

'Just that. And a few affectionate Delhi abuses,' I said.

Chapter 16

I asked Prof. Saxena to meet me in Deer Park just outside the campus. This time he agreed immediately. He wore a blue IIT Delhi tracksuit with white stripes. He walked one step at a time, raising his left leg with effort at each step.

'Prof. Saxena, I know you didn't kill her.'

He looked at me, surprised.

'What?' he said.

'Your limp saved you. You can't climb a tree.'

'I told you I didn't do it.'

'Prof. Saxena, neither did the watchman.'

'He didn't?'

I told him about the browser history on Laxman's phone.

'Our country is strange. Keeping an innocent man locked up,' Saxena said.

I nodded. 'Sir, the question still remains, who did it?'

'How would I know?'

'You knew her for years. You must have some theory.'

'Have you met Zara's family?' Prof Saxena said.

'Yeah. Her father and stepmother.'

'Her stepbrother?'

'Sikander? No. I heard about him a lot though. And I saw him at the funeral.'

'Listen, I could be accused of being communal when I say this, but, I don't get a comfortable feeling about Zara's father or her stepbrother. I find them shady.'

'Why?

'There could be violent fundamentalists in her family. Those who eliminate people at will.'

'You mean terror groups?'

'Well, now that you say it, yes.'

'Zara was far away from all that. You are basing this on something?'

'We were in the big data server room once when I heard her talk on the phone to her stepbrother. She mentioned guns.'

'Guns?'

'Something like, "Guns are not the answer, Sikander".'

'That could be a general statement.'

'Trust me, it didn't sound generic. Her stepbrother seemed to be part of some group. Zara wanted him out of it. More details I honestly don't know. I felt scared, so I never discussed it with her.'

We walked out of the park. The professor went up to his car and took the driver's seat.

'Anything else?' I said.

The professor spoke after a pause.

'Pammi said something after the funeral.'

'What?'

'The parents didn't look as sad as you would expect. Not just the stepmother, but even her father. That happens, though. People can be in shock.'

'Thanks, sir,' I said. 'That's helpful.'

The professor turned on the ignition of his car.

'It's amazing. You are trying to catch her murderer even though she wasn't with you anymore.'

I smiled. 'Now I can see why she gave up her scholarship for you,' he said. His next words were almost lost under the noise of the car's engine. 'Ah, young love.'

❖

'I don't know what he meant,' I said, sipping cold soda. 'He just said that he finds the family shady.'

Rana and I were on the terrace of Raasta, a bar in Hauz Khas Village. I had offered to buy Rana drinks, to compensate for the Saxena fiasco. Not that the inspector had to pay at any Hauz Khas bar anyway. He ordered a large rum and coke. I stuck to soda.

'Shady? Like what? Cousins marrying uncles types?' Rana said.

'No, no,' I said, 'what are you saying? Saxena felt the family had connections to terror organisations.'

'These bloody Kashmiris! Anything is possible.'

'Zara was not a terrorist,' I said. 'She took me to peace rallies.'

'All surface bullshit. Inside, all violent,' Rana said. He turned to his left to check out a table where three girls had just arrived. One of them, around twenty years old, was wearing a short red dress.

'She doesn't feel cold?' Rana said, in a tone you only hear from Delhi men. I brought him back to the topic.

'Zara's father has a successful business. He left Kashmir because of the strife.'

The inspector ignored what I said and continued to talk about the girls at the next table.

'These girls don't feel scared coming out dressed like this? Then they blame the police if someone squeezes their ass,' he said, eyes still on the girl in the red dress.

I kept quiet until he had had his fill of leching at them. Finally, he turned to me and grinned.

'Sorry, what were you saying?' he said.

'I don't think Zara's father is associated with any terror group.'

'How can you say that? He could have sympathy for them. Pay them money.'

'His previous wife Farzana did have fundamentalists in her family. He hated all that. That's mainly why he divorced her.'

'Hmmm …' Rana said. 'Anyway if this is a terrorism case, it is out of our hands. The Anti-Terrorism Squad will get involved. A far more senior officer will handle it. Not a chutiya like me.'

I didn't know whether to nod, and thereby affirm that he was a chutiya. Or say, no way any other officer can handle it better than you, sir, and come across as a chutiya myself. I decided to sip my soda instead.

'Drop it,' the inspector said, squinting his eyes. 'If there are terror groups involved, they will kill you. Not worth it.'

'So, we never find out who killed Zara?' I said too loudly. The three girls at the other table turned to look at us on hearing the word 'killed'.

'Maybe it is just a simple honour killing. None of this terror business,' Rana said, shaking his glass so the ice cubes would mix with the drink better.

'Honour killing? Zara's father killed her?' I said, shocked.

'Or had her killed. It does happen. I have seen cases.'

'Why?'

'She liked to fuck Hindu boys, no?' Rana said.

My ears rang. All I wanted to do was take his face apart. To rip out the mouth that had uttered those words. It took all my strength to sit still. Bad idea, I told myself, to hit a policeman.

'Her parents liked Raghu. He was ready to convert too.'

'That Madrasi would become Muslim? Just to be with her?' Rana said, as if Raghu had agreed to a sex-change operation.

'Zara's father had asked me to do the same.'

'And you said no?' Rana said.

I nodded.

He slapped my back. 'That is my brave Rajput boy. No girl is worth leaving your God. Well done.'

'I couldn't. My parents would have committed suicide.'

'Of course. How dare they ask anyone to change their religion? I told you, they are strange.'

'The point, Rana sir, is this. They didn't hate Raghu, or Zara having a Hindu boyfriend. They actually liked Raghu for his success.'

'They liked that Madrasi because of his willingness to become Muslim.'

'Well, yes, that too. I don't see any grounds for honour killing.'

'You never know. Maybe the old man wanted her to marry someone else, a khandaani Muslim. Did you see, that old man didn't cry one bit at the funeral?'

'That's what Mrs Saxena said too.'

'That tharki dean's wife?' Rana said.

'Yeah, Saxena told me,' I said. 'Also, now that you mention this angle, Safdar had threatened me in the past.'

'When?' The inspector's eyes lit up. 'See, you didn't tell me this.'

'When I said I can't convert. He wanted me to leave Zara. He told me he can hurt me or have me killed.'

'He's just a goonda living in a farmhouse. The tharki dean is right. They are shady people.'

As I processed Rana's words, the inspector turned towards the three girls again. 'That one in the red dress. She wants it real bad tonight.'

❖

'What makes you think you can investigate my daughter's murder?' Safdar said. His voice thundered through his giant porch. Saurabh and I had gone to visit him on a Sunday morning. I told him the story so far, until the point where we found Laxman and Saxena innocent.

'All this garbage about her PhD guide. What was the need for you to fish around?'

'Aren't you shocked, uncle? That her guide harassed her. Aren't you angry?' I said.

'I am angry with you. You won't leave my daughter alone even when she is dead.'

'I just want to find out who killed her.'

'Who are you? The police? Her family? Who?'

I kept quiet.

'You and Zara had no rishta,' Safdar said through gritted teeth. 'Now get out of my house. And my dead daughter's life.'

Safdar stood up, a signal for us to leave.

'Uncle, don't be agitated. It will only make things worse,' Saurabh spoke for the first time, his voice steady.

'Worse?' Safdar said. 'What can get worse? I have already lost my daughter.'

'What could be worse, uncle, is people talking about an honour-killing angle here,' Saurabh said plainly. Cute how he still called him uncle, all respectful even when accusing him of murder.

'What?' Safdar said, blinking. 'What is wrong with your dimaag? Who is this mental friend of yours?'

'He's my best friend. And he's not mental. He's quite smart. Please sit down,' I said.

Saurabh smiled. Safdar sat down again.

'Uncle, why did you say no to Zara's autopsy?' I said.

'What? And let all those haramis cut up my little girl's body? Do you even know what they do during an autopsy?' Safdar said.

'They find out what happened,' I said.

'What do they find out? More masala for the news channels?'

Saurabh and I didn't respond. 'Did you see when she died how they feasted on the news. Nobody cared about Zara or her family's feelings. What else did you want? For them to discuss if she was raped or not?'

'She wasn't raped,' I said. 'Nothing like that happened. I saw the body first.'

'What if some lunatic TV anchor made it up? Do you know what the family goes through?'

If Safdar was hiding something, he was doing a good job of it.

'Uncle, I am only asking this because the question may come up. Where were you that night?' I said.

Safdar looked at me and spoke after a pause.

'At home. Preparing for her birthday party.'

'You have witnesses?' Saurabh said.

'The entire staff of the farmhouse.'

'They are your staff. On your payroll.'

'Ask anyone. Separately. They will all tell you the same thing. Wait a minute, are you actually accusing me?'

'Some people might. Honour killings do happen,' I said.

'What nonsense,' he scoffed.

'I didn't see you distraught or in tears. At the funeral. Or any other time.'

'I am not an emotionally expressive person in public. My little girl ... her room is still there, just as she left it. I step in and I cry alone. Don't you dare say I don't feel pain.'

'Maybe you do. But if—'

'What "if-if" you are doing? I didn't do anything. I am not the kind of a person who can hurt anyone, forget killing my only daughter.'

'You threatened to kill me,' I said.

Safdar locked eyes with me. We continued to stare at each other for a few seconds before he spoke again.

'You think you can just accuse me of killing my own daughter? And people will believe it?'

'So is that it? You didn't do it because I can't prove it?' I said.

'Can you prove it?'

'Let's go, Saurabh.'

I stood up to leave. Saurabh followed me to the garden. We passed the swing, where Zara's father had told me to take the shahada. I almost expected Zara to be there, running behind Ruby. I walked fast as I didn't want to cry.

'Stop,' Safdar's voice came from behind us. I turned around. I expected to see film-style ruffians waiting to thrash us at their master's command. However, Safdar was standing there alone.

'Come in,' he said.

Saurabh and I froze. I wondered if he would take us to a dungeon and feed us to hungry crocodiles he kept in a secret pond.

'Follow me. Let's talk in my study,' he said.

❖

Safdar's study, like the rest of his house, had a nawabi opulence. Expensive silk carpets from Kashmir adorned the wooden floor.

One side of the room had a giant teak study table and oversized leather chairs. A black leather sofa set occupied the other end. Bookshelves with hundreds of books covered an entire wall. Safdar, Saurabh and I sat on the sofas.

'How much do you know about Sikander?' Safdar said to me.

'Zara liked him a lot,' I said. 'She was always nostalgic about growing up with him in Srinagar. She said he was a simple boy, too innocent.'

Safdar gave a sneering smile at my last word.

'And? What else?' he said.

'You discouraged Zara from keeping in touch with him.'

Safdar sighed.

'I did discourage her. Because Sikander is a member of T-e-J,' Safdar said.

'What's that?' I said.

'Tehreek-e-Jihad. A separatist group in Kashmir.'

'Separatist, as in?' Saurabh said. 'Like actual terrorists?'

'Depends on who you ask,' Safdar said, rubbing his hand on his thigh.

'I don't understand,' Saurabh said.

'The Indian government thinks T-e-J is a terror group. T-e-J and its supporters think they are working to liberate Kashmir.'

'Liberate it from what?' I said.

'From India,' Safdar said.

'And do what? Make their own country?'

'Well, T-e-J wants Kashmir to join Pakistan. Some other groups in Kashmir want independence. There are so many of them, more than twenty maybe.'

'Twenty? Why so many?' Saurabh said.

'It's usually because leaders of one organisation fight over power. They break away and make their own group.'

'Power is more important than being united for their cause?' Saurabh said.

'Of course. Who cares about Kashmiris, anyway? You think

if twenty organisations truly cared about Kashmir, the valley would be in this state?'

While understanding Kashmir was interesting, I had to get back to the topic.

'Uncle, sorry, but how is all this connected to Zara?'

'I fear,' Safdar said, 'Zara became involved with T-e-J too, because of Sikander. Something happened. And so they...'

Safdar stopped mid-sentence and sighed again.

'You should have told the police this. So they could find out what really happened,' I said.

'And have them label my daughter a terrorist?'

'Zara could not have been a terrorist. She was a smart, rational person who believed in debates and activism. She hated violence,' I said.

'How will you convince anyone of that? Her own stepbrother is part of a terrorist organisation. She went to Pakistan. It's apparently there on social media. Enough for those media vultures.'

'Pakistan?' Saurabh said.

I remembered Zara's Instagram posts from last year. She had visited a literature festival and posted pictures from there.

'You mean her trip to the Karachi Literature Festival?' I said.

I opened Instagram on my phone. She had posted three pictures from the litfest a year ago. The first picture was a selfie as she sat in the audience at a Fatima Bhutto session. The second showed the entrance of the litfest, with the 'Karachi Literature Festival' sign. The third showed her in a silhouette, at Clifton beach at sunset. Her long hair was blowing in the wind. The dim light hid most of her face. I remembered how I had called her after seeing this picture, begging her to take me back.

I forced myself back to the present moment.

'You mean this trip?' I said.

Safdar took my phone as I continued. 'Zara used to attend

literature festivals all the time. She went to the one in Kasauli, Bangalore and Kolkata too. In fact, I went to the one in Jaipur with her five years ago.'

'I have not seen these,' Safdar said, his voice soft. He gently touched the pictures on the screen to make them larger. 'How did you get them?'

'She posted them on Instagram. For all to see,' I said.

Safdar wiped his tears.

'I miss my girl. So much,' he said.

Unlike at the funeral, Safdar seemed vulnerable and weak.

'So, help us. In finding out who did this to Zara,' I said.

He shook his head.

'You don't understand. We are Muslims. People start with a doubt. Even both of you. You felt I could have killed my daughter.'

Saurabh and I looked at each other.

'Everyone is a suspect, uncle. Until we find out who did it,' I said.

'If the police link Tehreek with Zara's killing, she will be branded a terrorist. And me too. A rich Muslim businessman has to be a terrorist sympathiser, right?'

'Are you?' I said, my face expressionless.

He looked at me, surprised.

'Have you lost your mind? I absolutely hate these extremists. They have ruined my state. Their actions taint all the good Muslims in the country. They killed my daughter. Forget giving them money, I will pay to get all of them killed,' he said, his voice filled with anger.

Saurabh and I remained quiet. Safdar spoke after composing himself.

'What can I do, anyway, for you or anyone else to stop suspecting me? It's not like I know anything. They did what they did.'

'Uncle, you mentioned that Zara's room is still as it used to be,' I said.

'Yeah.'

'If it is okay, we would like to search it,' I said.

❖

Zara's room in her father's house had more square footage than our entire Malviya Nagar apartment. It had a four-poster teak bed in the centre, with an elaborate blue embroidered silk bedspread, and several framed pictures on an enamelled sideboard. The antique furniture in the room made it resemble Rajasthan's top heritage hotels. Apart from lighter curtains, her room had not changed much since I had last visited several years ago. The intricate carpet, with a pattern of zinnia flowers woven into it, was still there.

'We clean her room every day,' Safdar said. 'She still lives here.'

I scanned the framed pictures. Most were from holidays with her family. One was of her and Raghu, holding hands at India Gate. I saw one of Zara as a child. She was standing next to her father, a little boy and a woman in a traditional Kashmiri kaftan.

'Is that Sikander?' I said.

'Yeah. And that's my ex-wife, Farzana,' Safdar said. 'It's the only picture from the past that I allowed in this house.'

I noticed the six antique closets. Zara kept her clothes and other belongings here.

'Uncle, is it okay if we open these?' I said.

Safdar nodded. Saurabh and I divided three cupboards each between us. I opened the first closet. They held Zara's clothes. I recognised a red and white floral print salwar kameez that I had gifted to her on our first anniversary as a couple. I felt like a trespasser as I fumbled through a box of accessories, comprising necklaces, earrings and hair clips.

'What do you expect to find?' said Safdar, only mildly curious.

'I don't know,' I said, as I moved to the second cupboard. 'Never done this before.'

The second cupboard held her undergarments. I shut it and moved to the third, which had handbags and shoes.

'Anything?' I said to Saurabh.

'Just clothes, clothes and more clothes,' Saurabh said. Zara had four cupboards full of clothes.

Forty-five minutes later, we had rifled through all her closets apart from the one with the lingerie.

'You checked that?' Saurabh said, pointing to that cupboard.

'Nah. I don't think we should,' I said.

Saurabh glanced sideways at Zara's father. Safdar was checking his phone, bored with our pointless exercise.

'Uncle, excuse me,' Saurabh said. He pointed to the second cupboard. 'Can we check this one?'

'Do whatever. If I stop you, you will doubt me. Shameless you are, going through my dead daughter's stuff,' Safdar said, still busy with his phone.

'Sorry, uncle. We just...' Saurabh said before I shushed him.

I opened the second closet again. It had boxes made of canvas kept on various shelves. The boxes were filled with bras and lace underwear. Saurabh lifted a few garments from a box.

'We don't have to go through this,' I said.

'Fine,' he said, placing the contents back in. I pushed one of the boxes back into the cupboard. It hit something hard at the back of the shelf.

'What's that?' I extended my arm deep inside. I touched a keypad. 'There's a safe,' I said.

'Pull it out,' Saurabh said.

Safdar noticed.

'What happened?'

'Uncle, there's this little Godrej safe,' Saurabh said. He tried to pull out the iron box from the cupboard. He couldn't. Safdar walked up to us.

'I remember this. She bought it online. She said she wanted to keep some jewellery and money.'

'It's bolted to the back,' Saurabh said.

'Yeah, of course. I got it done,' Safdar said.

'Do you know the keypad code, uncle?' I said.

Safdar shook his head.

'There must be keys,' Saurabh said.

'I don't have them,' Safdar said.

We searched the entire room for an hour but couldn't find the keys either.

'We will have to break it open,' Saurabh said.

'How?' Safdar said.

'It's just a small safe. Any hardware guy with a metal cutter can do it,' Saurabh said.

❖

Clang! The front plate of the safe fell out as the fabricator shut his welding torch. He took his thousand bucks for the five-minute job and left.

I emptied out the contents of the safe and placed them in the middle of Zara's bed. Safdar, Saurabh and I sat around them.

I then picked up the items one at a time. The first was a passport.

'That's Zara's passport,' Safdar said.

'Should I make a list?' Saurabh said, taking out his phone.

'Sure,' I said.

I dictated the contents as Saurabh noted everything down on his phone.

'Money in various currencies. Indian rupees, around twenty thousand. US dollars, nine hundred. Pakistani currency, ten thousand rupees.'

Safdar's phone rang.

'It's from my godown. I need to take this call. Do what you have to. I am in my study,' Safdar said and left the room.

I turned to Saurabh after Safdar left.

'He seems genuine, right? Or do you think he is faking it?' I said.

'Can't say. He didn't stop us from searching though.'

'Fine. Let's keep going. Velvet pouch. Let me see what is inside. Earrings,' I said as I shook out the contents.

'Gold earrings with diamonds and other inlaid precious stones. Old, traditional types,' I said.

'Look expensive,' Saurabh said as he noted the details.

I went through the remaining contents of the safe.

'A brown paper bag,' I said. I turned the bag upside down. Several items fell out.

'Wow, condoms,' Saurabh and I said in unison.

'And what is this?' Saurabh said. He lifted up three, white, rectangular paper boxes, the size of a chocolate bar.

'Prega News', it said on top of the boxes.

'These are pregnancy kits,' I said.

'Oh, yes. I have seen Kareena Kapoor advertise these. Do they help you get pregnant?'

'No silly. They tell you if you are. Why does Zara have these?' I said.

Saurabh shrugged.

Each box had a small sticker on it. The sticker had a barcode and text that read, 'PregKit. INR 50'.

'Well, she was in a relationship,' I said, answering my own question. 'Engaged, too.'

I swallowed the lump in my throat and picked up the next item.

'An Oppo phone box,' I said, opening the box. It had a cell phone in it.

'Switch it on,' Saurabh said.

It took a minute for the phone to boot up. The phone connected to a network, indicating it had a SIM card. No numeric lock.

'Zara's phone?' Saurabh said.

'Not her main phone for sure. She had an iPhone.'

'What number is this?' Saurabh said.

To find out, I dialled myself. My phone rang.

'It's funny. The number starts with +92,' I said, checking my phone.

'Bhai, that's a Pakistan number. It's a Pak SIM.'

I threw the phone aside. There's something about Pakistan that makes you jump in fear.

'She had a Pak SIM?' I said. 'Let's note down the number.'

'Anything in the phone? Contacts? Pictures?' Saurabh said.

I opened the phone. It only had three contacts. They were 'S', 'I' and 'W'.

I went to the picture library.

'There are some pictures from the Karachi litfest,' I said, going through the images. 'Wait. Here's one of Zara and Sikander, a selfie.'

'Show me,' Saurabh said. 'He's holding a machine gun!'

They were sitting on the floor of what looked like a hotel room; Sikander was holding the gun in his arms.

'Damn,' I said. 'He is totally a terrorist.'

'They are smiling. Zara too,' Saurabh said. I was in a tizzy. Was Zara part of them? The Tehreek-e-whatever they called themselves?

The room in which the picture was taken had a window. I couldn't see much apart from a lot of wires, advertisement hoardings and some ad banners.

'Is this also taken in Pakistan?' Saurabh said.

I zoomed in closer to the picture. The resolution dropped, but I could make out a couple of Devanagri words on the hoardings.

'Hindi ads outside. They are in India,' I said.

I kept the phone aside and moved to the next item.

'A business card,' I said. 'In Urdu? Or is this Arabic?'

Saurabh shook his head as he noted down the details. He had no idea.

'A small plastic pouch with white powder,' I said.

'Talcum powder?' he said.

'Why would she keep talcum powder in a safe? Want to taste it?' I said.

'Are you crazy? Could be cyanide or something. You never know with these terrorists.'

'Zara wasn't a terrorist,' I almost said, but why did Zara Lone, who I thought of as the perfect woman, have these things in her safe?

'A brass capsule. Whoa, is this a bullet?' I said.

Saurabh lifted up the tiny piece of lethal metal.

'Yeah,' Saurabh said. 'What else?'

'Some coins from Pakistan.'

'Fine, let's take photos.'

Saurabh used his phone to take several pictures of each item we had found in the safe.

'This is not the Zara I knew,' I said.

'Bhai, with women, you can never tell what is going on,' he said, zooming in on the bullet.

Safdar finished his call and came back to Zara's room.

'Ya khuda,' he said, when he noticed the pregnancy kits and the bullet. 'What is all this?'

'We should ask you. It's in your house,' Saurabh said.

Safdar picked up the phone and saw the picture of Zara and Sikander with the machine gun.

'I swear upon Allah, I didn't know about any of this,' he said.

He picked up the white packet. 'What is this?'

'No idea,' I said. 'By the way, can you read this?' I handed him the business card.

'Hashim Abdullah, Commander. Tehreek-e-Jihad,' Safdar said.

'Anything else?' I said.

'No. No phone number or address.'

I collected all the items and placed them in my backpack.

'We have to take all of this with us,' I said.

Safdar thought for a second and then nodded.

'You loved her,' Safdar said as I stood up to leave.

It was not a question, but I still answered. 'Yes.'

'She loved you a lot too, Keshav.'

'Did she?'

'She badly wanted to be part of a family. She thought she would get that with you. But when your parents didn't like her, it broke her.'

I stayed silent. Did he not know this was a raw nerve?

'She fought with me for a year because I had insisted on your conversion. She lost you. Cut off from me. That is when she became close to Sikander again.'

'Maybe. I tried to reconnect but she kept avoiding me,' I mumbled.

'Because even though she loved you, you couldn't give her what she craved—a stable family. Neither could I. My three marriages kept things ... unstable. She lost her mother, then Sikander and then you. My poor girl went through so much alone.'

'I am sorry, uncle,' I said gently. 'No need to tell me all this.'

Safdar pointed to my backpack.

'If this goes to the police or media, it is all over. Zara, the girl you say you loved, will be labelled a terrorist forever.'

'I won't go to anyone yet. Because, if this comes out, the killer or killers will get alerted,' I said.

'Bhai, are you serious? You are still interested in chasing the killer?' Saurabh said, speaking after a long time.

'Why not?' I said.

'Because if terrorists are involved, they will blow our brains out too,' Saurabh said. He climbed off the bed.

'Can we talk about this later?' I said to Saurabh.

'There's nothing to talk. I am going home,' Saurabh said and walked out of Zara's bedroom.

'Your friend is right. These people are dangerous. Painful as it is, it may be better to accept they killed Zara and just move on,' Safdar said.

I zipped up my backpack and slipped it onto my back. I stood up to leave.

'I have a problem in life, uncle. I have always found it hard to "just move on".'

Chapter 17

'Still angry? Eat something at least,' I said. Saurabh and I were in the staffroom of Chandan Classes at lunch. He had not spoken to me for three days. Our home resembled a silent operation theatre. Like quiet surgeons, we went about our daily lives without talking to each other. I tried all kinds of temptations—whisky, rasgullas, high-definition porn—to get his attention. However, he refused to say a word. He didn't even shout, curse or break things. No, when Saurabh is upset, he sulks.

Two other faculty members were eating their lunch in the staffroom, sitting a few chairs away from us.

'I ordered fresh chole bhature. Have one at least,' I said. The intoxicating aroma of fried dough and spicy chole hit Saurabh's nose, but he battled every instinct and ignored the food. He continued to read his five-inch thick *Organic Chemistry* textbook, which was heavy enough for bicep curls in the gym. He continued to stare at the hexagonal structure of the benzene molecule for no particular reason.

'I am not going to put us in danger. Come on, aren't you keen to find the killer too?'

'Not if the killers use machine guns as a selfie prop,' Saurabh said.

'Ah, at last the man speaks. Don't tell me you are not curious?'

'Bhai, it is not about being curious. It is about not wanting a dozen bullets pumped into my ass. You are going to investigate a terrorist organisation? People who kill people for fun?'

'I have no interest in their organisation. I only want to know what happened to Zara.'

'Why?' Saurabh said, his voice loud enough for the two faculty members to turn and look at us.

'Speak softly,' I said.

'Get lost,' he said. 'I am not going to talk only.'

'I need closure, Golu. I never had that with Zara. Even when she broke up, she cut off contact all of a sudden. Now when she wanted to get back she is gone forever, with so many questions unanswered. I never got closure.'

'Sorry, this closure-closure you keep doing. What exactly is closure, bhai?'

'Forget it.'

'I've never had a girlfriend, so I neither know nor have to deal with all this. Good only.'

'You said you would help me. Heart-head, remember?'

'Bhai, you better use your head. Or they will cut off your head. This isn't just about seeing the dean's wife in a nightie. This is Taarikh-e-Jumma.'

'Tehreek-e-Jihad,' I said and smiled.

'Whatever. Just hand over all the contents from the safe to Rana. Leave it up to him.'

'Like he will do anything. He is happy to let Laxman rot in jail.'

'That's Laxman's bad luck, and the country's misfortune that this is how we solve cases. Nothing to do with us.'

'I understand. How about this—we do eventually go to the police, but investigate a bit more ourselves. Safely.'

'How?'

'I will tell you. Can you please eat the chole bhature first?' I said. 'Look, this bhatura is so fluffy.'

I shunted the plate of food towards him. Saurabh looked at the plate like he had found his missing child after several years.

'I didn't even have breakfast,' Saurabh said.

'Why?'

'To show you I am upset,' Saurabh said, and tore into a bhatura. He ate like a caveman, ripping the ten-inch long puffed fried bread to shreds in seconds.

'Never take your anger out on food,' I said.

'What kind of investigation will tuition masters like us do, anyway?' Saurabh said, grabbing the second bhatura before he had finished the first.

'There's nothing big I plan to do. I just want to talk to Sikander. He's Zara's family, after all.'

'The stepbrother? The one who probably carries around an AK-47 like a phone powerbank?'

'Let's just talk to him on the phone first.'

'Hell, no, bhai. Once they know your phone number, they will come after you.'

'We will call from that Pak SIM. I am sure the contact "S" is him.'

'Bhai,' Saurabh said and paused.

'What?'

Saurabh raised his hand, asking me to wait. Five seconds later, he let out a loud burp. The two teachers looked at us in disgust.

'Charming,' I said.

'Whatever. I was saying, bhai, you can give him a call, but for the record, I told you before, you are taking panga for no reason.'

❖

We sat on the bed in my room, a quilt wrapped around each of us.

'How do you know "S" is him?' Saurabh said.

'We will find out,' I said. I dialled the number. With every ring, my heart beat a bit faster. Nobody answered the call.

Ten rings later, I cut the call and shook my head.

'Dead end?' Saurabh said.

'Yeah. No answer.'

'And with that, the Zara Lone investigation ends. Goodnight,' Saurabh said. He lay down flat in the bed and covered himself with the quilt.

'I will try one more time,' I said. I dialled the number again. No response.

'Keep trying. Nobody will pick up,' he said, head under the

quilt. 'Bhai, different topic—did you try Tinder like I told you to? Apparently, you get laid for free.'

I ignored him and kept my phone aside.

'Go to your room and sleep, Saurabh,' I said.

'No, bhai. After all this talk of terrorists, I am not sleeping alone.'

'Golu, look at your size. How can you be scared to sleep alone?'

Saurabh didn't answer as he pretended to fall asleep.

I switched off the bedside lamp, lay down next to him and stared at the dark outline of the static ceiling fan above me. Thoughts flooded my head. Did I really not know Zara? Had I been pining for and idealising a girl who was somebody else? Or did she change after our breakup? Did my parents' insults turn her into a fundamentalist? Why would Sikander hurt her, especially when she loved him so much?

A few minutes later, guilt flooded through me. I thought about what Safdar had said, about how I didn't see Zara's deep need for a stable family, and how my family's lack of acceptance might have hurt her. Confused and lost, I tried to grapple with all the what-might-have-happeneds.

The phone's loud ring interrupted my thoughts.

'Fuck. The Pakistani phone is ringing,' Saurabh said. He sprang out from under the quilt and ran around the room, as if someone had thrown a bucket of cockroaches on the bed.

'What do we do, bhai?' he said.

'Relax. He's only calling back.'

'On a Pakistani phone,' he screamed, as if Pakistani phones could explode and kill you the moment you picked them up. I put a finger on my lips, signalling Saurabh to remain quiet.

I took the call.

'As-salaam-alaikum,' a man said on the other side.

'Hello,' I said. 'I mean, as-salaam-alaikum. Sorry, wa-alaikum-salaam.'

The man on the other end went quiet.

'Is it Sikander?' I said.

'Kaun, janaab?' he said.

'You have called Zara's phone, right?'

'Who is speaking? Where did you get this phone?' he said.

'I am Zara's friend.'

'What's your name?'

'Keshav,' I said.

Saurabh raised both his eyebrows when I mentioned my name. I had to place my hand on his mouth so he wouldn't shout.

'Shh, I have to tell him, or else he won't talk,' I whispered to Saurabh and went back to the call.

'I am Keshav. Zara's friend. Is it Sikander? We met you at the funeral.'

'Did we?'

Okay, so it was Sikander.

'You remember me, right? Zara's Rajasthani friend.'

'Aapa mentioned you.'

'She did?' I said, wondering what Zara had told him about me.

'How did you get this phone?'

'Sikander bhai, can we meet?'

I pressed Saurabh's mouth shut with my hand again because he had opened it to protest against the word 'meet'.

'Why?' Sikander said.

'I had some questions regarding Zara's death.'

'What about it? The killer is in jail.'

'The watchman didn't do it.'

'I don't know anything about it.'

'Let's just meet once.'

'No,' he said, and cut the call. I released my hand from Saurabh's mouth.

Saurabh stared at me with eyes wide open.

'What?' I said.

'You want to meet a terrorist?'

'He's part of Zara's family. Anyway, he won't meet or talk.'

'Good. I want us to reach a dead end. So you stop this murder-case obsession.'

'And do what instead? Teach bored students how to crack an impossible entrance exam?'

'It's our job, bhai.'

I picked up the Oppo phone and dialled Sikander's number again. He picked up after three attempts.

'I said I don't want to meet. Don't ever call me again,' Sikander said.

'My other option is to give everything I found at Zara's house to the police,' I said.

Sikander became silent. Saurabh waved his hands in the air to demand urgent attention. I muted the phone.

'What now?' I said to Saurabh.

'You are threatening him? A terrorist?' Saurabh said, panic in his voice.

'Relax,' I said, and went back to the call.

'Are you there, Sikander?'

'Yes,' he said.

'Sikander, I have no interest in going to the police and I have no interest in whatever work you do. I am talking to everyone in Zara's life only to find out who killed her.'

'You think I would kill my aapa? Someone who meant so much to me?'

'I never said that. I just want to meet you. We met her father too.'

'We? Who else is there with you?'

'Only my best friend, Saurabh.'

'Please, not my name,' Saurabh said loud and clear, so I had to shut his mouth with my hand again.

❖

Paharganj would make a great setting for a video game. Navigating the streets while remaining unhurt could be the challenge. Saurabh and I dodged auto rickshaws, cycle rickshaws, cows, donkeys, motorbikes, hawkers and thousands of pedestrians as we made our way through the narrow by-lanes. We finally reached our designated meeting place, the Nemchand Pakoda Shop located between the Qadam Sharif shrine and the Shiv Mandir, an unintentionally secular location.

Sikander, in a light grey pathani suit, was already in the shop. He had grown a stubble, perhaps to make himself appear more grown-up and to hide his rosy baby face. His legs bounced up and down as he looked from side to side, scanning every customer in the shop.

He hadn't noticed us yet.

'Bhai, we can still leave,' Saurabh said. 'He could have a gun inside his kurta. He might kill us.'

'Why would he do that?'

'For anything that pisses him off. Like if we don't leave enough chutney for his pakoras. Anything.'

'Chutney?'

'We are going to eat pakoras here, right? This place is famous for them.'

'I am going in,' I said, shaking my head.

'I am here, what do you want to talk about?' Sikander said, as soon as I walked up to him.

'Before we begin, should we order some food?' I said.

Food would keep Saurabh busy and make him feel less scared. We ordered half a kilo of mixed pakoras, along with three cups of sweet masala tea.

The waiter brought our order in minutes: a sampler of gobi, aloo, onion, chili and palak pakoras, all spicy and double fried. There can't be a tastier or unhealthier way of eating vegetables than pakoras.

Sikander didn't touch the food. Saurabh picked up one of each kind.

'You aren't eating?' Saurabh said to Sikander. 'Try some.'

When Saurabh is scared of someone, he begins to suck up to that person.

'We need your help. We are trying to solve Zara's case,' I said.

'*He* is. I am just tagging along,' Saurabh said, as he bit into a green chili pakora.

'How can I help?' Sikander said.

'Weren't you close to her?' I said.

'Aapa was like a second mother to me.'

'Did someone from Tehreek-e-Jihad kill her?'

Sikander stood up at the mention of his organisation. Saurabh turned and hid his face in my shoulder.

'I need to leave,' Sikander said.

'Why?' I said. 'We just met. Sit down. Please, just five minutes.'

Sikander looked unconvinced but sat back down. I moved a cup of tea towards him. He shook his head stiffly.

'Who told you about Tehreek?' Sikander said. 'I thought you had no interest other than aapa.'

'I don't. When did you last speak to Zara?'

'Three days before she died. She called me.'

'What did you guys talk about?'

'None of your business. Brother and sister talk.'

'Stepbrother, right?' Saurabh said, a hot gobi pakora in his mouth. Sikander glared at him.

'Step-siblings can be really close too,' Sikander said.

'Of course,' Saurabh said, in his typical sucking-up tone. 'Try something, Sikander bhai, the chili pakora is too good.'

Sikander ignored Saurabh and turned to me.

'Aapa just said she hadn't seen me for a while. And that … I should look for a proper job.'

'What work do you do otherwise?' I said. 'If you don't mind telling me.'

'Just odd jobs. Sometimes in Delhi, sometimes in Srinagar.'

'What kind of odd jobs?'

'Loading trucks. Helping Kashmiri merchants move stuff all across the country. That kind of thing.'

'Don't get upset, but are you connected to Tehreek-e-Jihad?' I said.

'I don't want to answer that. Why do you care?'

'All I want to know is if Zara was connected to Tehreek. Tell me that at least, Sikander.'

'Not at all.'

'So then ...' I began, but Sikander stood up again.

'What?' I said. 'Why are you standing?'

He didn't answer. Instead, he took out a revolver.

Saurabh's mouth fell open. Even though Sikander had not told us to, Saurabh raised both his hands up in reflex, a result of watching too many movies. One of his hands held an onion pakora.

'Sikander bhai, we are just talking. What is the need ...' I said, keeping my tone as calm as possible.

'Shut up, harami. Enough is enough. I know aapa and your relationship ended long back. What is this jasoosi you are doing now?'

He pointed the gun at my face. I felt like I was having a cardiac arrest. I spread my palms in a conciliatory way.

'I am sorry I upset you. I only want to talk.'

'I am leaving. Don't follow me, understand?'

The waiters, customers and the shop-owner froze in their respective positions as Sikander walked out of the shop. He reached the lane outside and shoved the gun back in his kurta pocket. Within seconds he vanished into the Paharganj crowd.

'He's gone,' I said to Saurabh. 'You can bring your hands down.'

'Uhh ouu unn ...' Saurabh said, hands still up.

'Finish what's in your mouth.'

Saurabh swallowed and spoke again.

'What the fuck!' Saurabh screamed. 'I have parents. Fuck, fuck, Keshav, I am never coming with you again. We take tuitions, we are not James Bond's nephews.'

'We are fine. He's the coward who ran away.'

'Screw him. You said, come we will just have pakoras. He would have turned us into pakoras.'

I signalled to the shop-owner for the bill.

'It's okay, sahib. Consider it free,' the shop-owner said, holding his breath until we left.

Chapter 18

A week after the pakora fiasco, we sat in our living room, watching a reality show on TV. Little girls in makeup danced to item songs. Saurabh's eyes were glued to the season finale. I surfed on my phone in between watching the programme.

'Give me your phone,' Saurabh said. I ignored him.

'Why do you watch this? I find such shows disturbing,' I said, eyes still on my phone.

'I will tell you what is disturbing,' Saurabh said, snatching my phone.

'What the hell, Golu?'

'What were you doing on the phone?'

'Er, nothing. Checking if my LinkedIn profile was up to date.'

'There's nothing to update. We still have the same lousy résumé.'

'I thought maybe a new picture.'

'Bullshit. Why do you have the Twitter screen on your phone?'

A little girl began to gyrate to '*Munni badnaam hui*' on TV. The judges and the audience cheered her on with thunderous applause.

'How is this shit legal?' I said, ignoring Saurabh's question.

'Answer me, bhai.'

'Just,' I said, 'keeping updated. Current affairs.'

'I can see here. You searched Tehreek-e-Jihad on Twitter.'

'Did I?'

Saurabh switched off the TV. He came and sat on the coffee table to face me. The coffee table creaked as it bore a weight far beyond its capacity.

'Bhai, I am super-serious,' Saurabh said, staring into my eyes like he was trying to hypnotise me.

I looked down.

'You saw that psycho's gun. You will never touch this case again.'

'I was just fooling around on my phone.'

'Searching for terrorist organisations is fooling around?'

'I became curious. See, we already know this. Sikander is part of Tehreek. He ran away when I asked him about Zara and Tehreek.'

Saurabh put a finger on his lips.

'Shh. Bhai, I said listen to me. You. Are. Going. Mad.'

'What?' I said.

'Some shit happened. Terrorists killed Zara. End of story. You will never think about this again. Ever. No more theories. No more analysis. Just wipe it from your head.'

'How?' I said. 'There's nothing else I can seem to think about. Nothing else I find meaningful in life, or give a fuck about.'

'Getting a new job?

I shook my head.

'I do need a new job. But I don't give a fuck about it really.'

'How about finding a new girl?'

'Not in that frame of mind. One girl gave me enough pain.'

'Tinder, bhai, pain-free love. Do you know, I had two matches on Tinder.'

'You did? What happened?'

'Nothing. They unmatched me when we chatted.'

'What? Why?'

'They said they valued honesty. I said fine. They asked me what I am looking for. I told them.'

'What did you tell them?'

'I said sex. Or anything physical. Even a hand job is okay,' Saurabh said with a straight face.

'What?' I said. 'You said what?'

'I told you. I was honest.'

I burst out laughing.

'And then?' I said.

'They deleted me. Bitches. Honesty, my ass.'

'Come here my "anything physical" darling,' I said, trying to bear-hug him.

'Get off me. And be serious,' Saurabh said.

'I am serious,' I said, while I continued to laugh. 'But seriously, "even a hand job is okay"? You actually said that?'

'I will move out. Choose between the case and me,' Saurabh said.

'What?' I said. Laughter evaporated from my face.

Neither one of us spoke for a minute.

Saurabh stood up from the table. 'I got my answer. I will leave this weekend,' he said.

'What senti drama are you doing?' I said. I pulled his hand to make him sit down again.

'What?' he said and turned to me.

'Screw the case. I have already lost a lot. I can't lose you.'

'Really, bhai? You will do that for me?'

'Don't fish now. Switch the TV back on. I want to see if that *Munni badnaam* girl wins.'

❖

'Enrolment has crashed. Unacceptable,' Chandan said.

The smell of paan masala, cheap cologne and general obnoxiousness filled the room. Chandan had read an article in *The Economic Times* about the importance of weekly management meetings in corporates. He loved the idea, ignoring the fact that Chandan Classes was a dictatorship and not a corporate. We now had to report on Saturday mornings at eight o'clock, two hours before classes started. Chandan wore formal suits for these meetings. He looked like a south Indian movie villain's sidekick who had dressed up for his daughter's wedding.

Everyone from the faculty to the peons to Sexy Sheela hated the idea of these early morning meetings.

'Superb move, sir,' Brij Chaubey, a chemistry teacher, had said at the first meeting.

'We have really become professional,' said Mohan, or pulley-sir, a physics teacher famous in Delhi for teaching one topic, pulleys, better than anyone else.

Sucking up to Chandan Arora was an art form. Literally for Sexy Sheela, and figuratively for the other faculty; they were far better at it than us. However, all the fake praise failed to lift Chandan's mood today.

'Look at the student numbers. Dropped to 376 from 402 a quarter ago,' he said. When he made the 'r' sound in 'dropped', a tiny speck of paan masala escaped his mouth and landed on top of my wrist. Saurabh saw it and made a disgusted expression. He passed a tissue to me to express his sympathy.

'Mr Saurabh Maheshwari,' Chandan Arora said.

'Yes, sir,' Saurabh said, sitting up straight.

'Please pay attention,' Chandan said.

'I am paying, sir.'

'What do you teach?'

'I beg your pardon, sir?'

'What subject?'

'Chemistry. You hired me for that, sir.'

'Tell me all the Gas Laws,' Chandan said.

The eight faculty members present and Sexy Sheela gave each other awkward glances.

'Are you serious, Chandan sir?'

'Yes. I want to know if my own people know their stuff or not.'

'Boyle's law, Charles's law, Graham's law of diffusion, Avogadro's law and Dalton's law of partial pressure. You want me to explain each of them, sir?' Saurabh said.

'No need,' Chandan grunted. 'But explain why enrolment is down. It has to be the quality of teaching.'

Nobody said a word in response.

'I am cutting everyone's salaries, ten, no twenty per cent this month,' Chandan said.

'What?' I blurted out. Everyone looked at me shocked, as if I had told Hitler to his face that he had a funny moustache.

'Don't you understand? Business drops, your salary drops,' Chandan said.

'You never increased our salary when enrolment rose,' I mumbled, not loud enough for him to hear though.

'What did you say?' Chandan said.

'Nothing. Sir, other coaching classes have opened. There are also online apps now to prepare for JEE.'

While we prepared children to face cut-throat competition, our own business wasn't immune to it.

'Are you selling Chandan Classes? Are you telling students to bring their friends? That's the best way to get new students,' Chandan said.

'We are faculty, sir. It doesn't look dignified ...' Saurabh said.

'What dignity? This is dhanda, behenchod. You understand?'

Sexy Sheela blushed at Chandan's use of Delhi's official greeting. Maybe I imagined it, but I think seeing this alpha male side of her lover turned her on a little.

Saurabh looked at me. I tried to telepathically tell him to stay calm.

Chandan continued, 'And stop calling yourself faculty. This is not a university issuing degrees or diplomas. This is a coaching centre. We teach students to clear an exam. And we make money from it.'

Everyone around the table hung their heads low.

'Get out, everyone! This time it is a pay-cut. If the numbers don't improve next quarter, I will fire people. Every faculty member must get ten new students in every quarter. It's a must. Mr Gas Laws, you especially, understand?'

'Yes, sir,' Saurabh said.

❖

'I hate him!' Saurabh whispered fiercely to me in the corridor. 'Can you get that jihadi Sikander to kill this guy?'

I laughed.

'I wish I could. But that chapter is closed. I chose my brother,' I said, ruffling his hair.

❖

'She responded?' Saurabh said.

'Yeah. In fact, she wrote to me first,' I said. I stared at my phone, still trying to make sense of the Tinder app, where I had found a match.

'You are lucky, bhai. What's her name?'

'Sonia,' I said.

We lay in bed at home on a Saturday night. Saurabh had given me a Tinder tutorial, teaching me how to swipe and talk to the matches.

'Is this how people find love these days?' I said. I thought about meeting Zara at Rendezvous. What would happen today? Would she have swiped left or right on my picture?

'Courtship is dead, bhai. Whatever you want, say and get it fast,' Saurabh said.

'She just messaged, "Hey what's up",' I said.

'That's good. She has initiated. Message her,' Saurabh said.

I replied with a 'Hi'.

'So you wanna meet?' she replied.

'You have lucked out, bhai. She wants to meet so soon,' Saurabh said when he saw my phone.

'Shall I say yes?' I said.

'Of course. You have a date.'

I replied with a 'sure'.

I waited for the new love of my life to reply. She answered after five minutes.

'One hour 5k. Includes BJ and one shot straight.'

I turned the screen towards Saurabh.

'What?' Saurabh said and read the message. 'Oh, professional. Sorry, bhai. Unmatch her. She sounds like trouble.'

I unmatched Sonia and our love story ended within six

minutes. I switched off the lights. Saurabh still wanted to sleep in my room.

'I am tired. Goodnight,' I said to Saurabh in the darkness.

'Sure, goodnight, bhai. But one thing?'

'What?'

'You think that Sonia would have bargained?'

❖

I sat alone in the classroom, checking test papers after class. Saurabh came in and shut the door,

'What's the matter?' I said.

'Chandan gave me a warning,' Saurabh said.

'Warning?' I said, looking up from an answer-sheet.

'I didn't get any new students. He cautioned me that I would lose my job if I don't bring in new students next month.'

'I haven't brought in any either. In fact, I convinced one to leave,' I said.

'You did?'

'He wanted to study fashion. How can a person like that clear the JEE?'

'Bhai, Chandan will kill you.'

'Don't worry,' I said. 'That student had paid the entire year's fee. Non-refundable. Chandan won't lose money. But at least the student will not waste a year here.'

Biswas, the peon at Chandan Classes, came into the classroom carrying a tray filled with cups of tea. We picked up one each.

'Biswas, will you get some biscuits?'

'Chandan sir said no more biscuits,' Biswas said.

'What? Why?' I said.

'Cost-cutting or something. Kya maloom what he says,' Biswas said and left the room.

We sipped our tea in silence, wondering how many days we had before Chandan fired us. I resumed correcting the students' answer-sheets. Saurabh spoke after a few minutes.

'Bhai, I never wanted to become an engineer. I became one because my parents wanted me to. Serves me right for doing something I didn't believe in or felt passionate about.'

I made a face without looking up from the answer-sheet in my hand.

'Can I say something?' Saurabh said. 'Don't get too excited.'

'What?' I said.

'I miss the case.'

'Zara's case?' I looked up at Saurabh.

'Yeah, it made me feel alive. Like we were doing something that mattered. We had a purpose.'

'Really?'

'Like when I hacked Laxman's phone. Or when I discovered Saxena has a limp.'

'Yes, it is you who did all that. That's the big reason I left the case. I can't do it without you.'

I went back to my answer-sheets.

'That jihadi put a gun to our face. That's what made me stop you,' Saurabh said.

'Yeah, I know.'

Saurabh nodded and became silent. I started checking the last few test papers. 'Why were you searching Tehreek-e-Jihad on Twitter?'

'Huh?' I said, looking up from my answer-sheets. 'Why are you talking about all that, Golu?'

'I am just curious. Why Twitter?'

'To find out about Tehreek and where Sikander might be. These organisations often have an active Twitter presence.'

'Okay, and what's the white powder? Did you find out?'

I put the cap on my pen and kept all the answer-sheets aside. I looked into Saurabh's eyes.

'Seriously, Saurabh?'

'What?'

'No, I didn't find out. You stopped me from working on the case. Remember?'

'And Sikander's cell phone records? Rana can help us get those.'

'Why are you asking, bro?'

Saurabh slammed his empty teacup down on the desk.

'I don't know what's worse. The risk of the jihadi killing us if we work on the case, or us dying a slow death here at Chandan Classes,' Saurabh said and left the room.

❖

I woke up from my regularly recurring nightmare. Almost every night, I dreamt of Zara struggling to release herself as her killer choked her with his hands.

I checked the time. It was 3 a.m.

Saurabh was awake. He was sitting next to me on my bed, working on his laptop. 'What are you doing?' I said.

'Sikander is in Srinagar. I can tell for sure,' Saurabh said.

I sat up.

'What? Who?'

'Sikander. There's a picture of him in a group. One of Tehreek's accounts posted it on Twitter. Looks authentic and recent.'

'Wow,' I said as I looked at the picture. Sikander and six other young men stood with a Tehreek-e-Jihad flag, with mountains in the background.

'How did you find this?' I said.

'I searched in Arabic, entering whatever was written on the business card we found in the safe. Took me a while using Google Translate and going through dozens of accounts. But look, they posted this picture two days ago.'

I whispered, 'Why?'

'Why did they post this picture? No idea.'

'No, Golu. Why are you doing this? Why?'

'It's the only meaningful thing I have in my life. And I think we are close. We shouldn't give up.'

'You sure?'

Saurabh tapped his hand on his heart and nodded.

Chapter 19

'Where did you get this powder again?' Rana said.

'Some kids in class. Do you know what it is?'

I had brought a spoonful of the white powder we found in Zara's safe in a matchbox. Rana, Saurabh and I had come to Moonshine, a nightclub on the second floor of a building in Hauz Khas Village. At ten in the night, the huge bar had only fifteen customers. Things pick up at midnight, the manager had assured Rana when the latter lamented the lack of girls in the establishment.

'This is cocaine. Stop acting innocent. Are you using this?' Rana said.

'No, sir. Cocaine, like drugs?' I said.

'Yes. And these rich Hauz Khas kids pay seven thousand rupees a gram for it.'

'What?' I said.

'Boys, I like you. But when it comes to drugs, I can't go easy. Tell me where the hell did you get this from?'

'I told you. Some student in class.'

'Someone preparing for IIT had cocaine? Nonsense.'

'This is south Delhi. Not everyone who comes to our coaching centre is serious about studies,' Saurabh said.

'Anyway, we will expel him from the coaching class,' I said.

Inspector Rana nodded, though he still looked unconvinced.

'You want a drink, sir?' Saurabh said as the bartender came by.

'Yeah. Rum and coke, large. For all of us. And, bloody, why aren't there any women here yet? Their dads didn't allow them tonight or what?' Rana said.

The bartender didn't answer. He prepared the three drinks and brought them to us.

'You haven't updated me on the case. That Kashmiri girl you are obsessed with,' Rana said, taking a big gulp.

'Busy with work. Haven't had the time to pursue it,' I said.

'Lost interest, eh? See how hard it is to investigate?'

'I agree,' I said.

'You met her father? The honour-killing angle? I'm pretty sure he did it. These mullahs can do anything.'

'We met him once,' I said.

'And?'

'He has an alibi. He was at home preparing for Zara's party the next day.'

'Is that so?' Rana said thoughtfully. He finished his drink, kept his glass down and let out a long, disgusting 'aahh'.

'Yeah,' I said, 'so we are at a dead end.'

My heart beat fast. I had lied to a police officer. I wondered what would happen if Rana found out that we had concealed evidence. I ordered another drink for the inspector to distract him from noticing my nervousness.

'Are you sure you didn't get this powder from Lone? How did he get so rich? That mullah could be a drug-dealer,' Rana said.

I froze.

'I'll lock him up for the rest of his life. If not for murder, then for drugs. You just tell me,' Rana said, pointing a finger at me.

'No, sir,' Saurabh said, shaking his head. 'We don't know. Actually, I told Keshav to stop working on the case.'

'Why? Scared?'

'Yeah,' Saurabh said, biting his lower lip. 'And we have to focus on our careers.'

'Good. No point screwing around,' Rana said. His phone beeped. 'I have to go. Something urgent came up.'

'Another crime, sir?' Saurabh said.

'No. It is my mother-in-law's birthday. I promised I would be home for dinner. I forgot. I didn't even buy her a gift. Bloody mother and daughter are going to nag me and chew my head all night.'

❖

The flushing sound made it impossible to talk for a few seconds.

'That's seven lakhs gone down the toilet, literally. We could have sold it,' Saurabh said.

'Things are bad career-wise, but we haven't reached the drug-dealer stage yet,' I said, washing my hands.

'Isn't the IIT dream a drug, too?'

'It is. But it is legal. Organic chemistry books at home are fine. But if anyone found hundred grams of cocaine in our house, we go in for ten years.'

We came out of the toilet.

'What next?' Saurabh said.

'Like I said. I will go to Srinagar. I won't take any risks, but will try to find out whatever I can.'

'And what do I do?'

'Stay here. Like I said, no unnecessary risks. You can help me analyse the case from here.'

'How can I let you go there alone?'

'I will be fine. We will be in constant touch on phone.'

We sat on the sofa and switched on the TV. The film *Toy Story* was playing and we began watching. In one scene, Woody and Buzz Lightyear, two toys who are best friends, have a fight. But both miss each other immensely. The song *You've Got a Friend in Me* played in the background.

You've got a friend in me
There isn't anything I wouldn't do for you
We stick together and see it through
Cause you've got a friend in me
You've got a friend in me.

Eventually, the two animated best friends make up and give each other teary bear hugs.

Saurabh wiped his eyes and turned to me.

'I am coming,' Saurabh said.

'What? But—' I said.

'No more ifs and buts. I am coming to Kashmir. I'll do all the bookings, too.'

'But Golu—'

'They say Kashmir is heaven on earth, right? Currently I am in Chandan Classes, hell on earth. Almost anything would be better. It's done, I am coming.'

'Saurabh, seriously—'

'Shh. Decided.'

I looked at Saurabh. His fat, round face made him look like a Pixar teddy bear.

'I love you,' I said.

'If someone murdered me, will you also solve my case like this?'

'I would tell the murderer to kill me instead,' I said.

Saurabh blushed. I laughed.

'You say these stupid senti lines and I agree to do stupid things like this trip to Kashmir,' Saurabh said.

❖

'Leave? What's that?' Chandan Arora said. He spat out an over-chewed slurry of paan masala and saliva into a special-purpose dustbin. We sat opposite him, across the desk in his office. His eyes oscillated between Saurabh and me in quick succession.

'Holiday, sir,' I said. 'Saurabh and I want to go on a holiday together.'

He looked at us as if we had asked him to will us his entire property.

'Why do you need a holiday?' Chandan said. 'And both of you together? What will happen to your classes?'

'It will be like an offsite for us. To figure out what we can do to build enrolment,' Saurabh said. 'And we spoke to other faculty members for substitution.'

'This is peak time,' Chandan shouted, loud enough for Sexy Sheela to look up, starry-eyed, from her keyboard.

'We will ensure there is no disruption, sir,' I said.

'I don't care. What about new students? What are your numbers?'

'Numbers?' I said.

'The students you brought in. Your referrals, Mr Maheshwari?'

'So far? Since you told me in that meeting?' Saurabh said.

Chandan nodded.

'I would say zero, more or less,' Saurabh said.

'Zero? See. And you want a holiday?'

'We will come back and meet our targets, sir,' I said.

'Where are you planning to go?'

'Srinagar.'

'Kashmir?'

'Yes, sir.'

'Why? You want to die?'

'No, sir,' I said. 'It's a full state. Millions of people live there.'

'All terrorists.'

'That's incorrect, sir,' I said.

'But why Srinagar? What are you? Some honeymooning couple?'

Saurabh and I kept quiet, unable to come up with a response. He took our silence as tacit acceptance.

'Really? Are both of you, what do they say, Section 377?'

'Sir, no,' I said, as Saurabh gaped. He had no idea what Section 377 was.

'So, why are you going to Srinagar? Where are you staying there?'

'Shelter Houseboats, sir,' Saurabh said.

'You are staying in a houseboat? Seriously? This is a honeymoon, isn't it?'

Sexy Sheela became alert at the mention of the word 'honeymoon', even though she pretended to print invoices. Perhaps she dreamt of the day Chandan would leave his wife and take her to a place far away, where nobody taught anybody to prepare for JEE.

I hadn't known about our accommodation arrangements. I turned to Saurabh.

'Why are we staying in a houseboat?'

'It is cheap. Good reviews. Well located, safe. I booked it.'

'We are going to be sharing a room in a boat?' I said.

'You told me somewhere central,' Saurabh said. 'This is right in the city, on Jhelum River.'

Chandan Arora laughed.

'This is what happens, Sheela madam, when boys can't get girls.' He winked at her. Yes, the lady-killer had spoken. His invoice-maker-plus-lover smiled coyly.

'Sir, we are not a gay couple.'

'It's okay even if you are. There are yoga exercises to cure you.'

'Cure?' I said, wondering what exactly those exercises could be.

'Sir, we are not gay,' Saurabh said.

'Even though there is nothing wrong in being gay,' I said.

'You don't need to hide your secrets from me.'

'Chandan sir, we want to go on leave for two weeks. What we do there is none of your concern,' I said.

Chandan looked somewhat upset by my defiance. He opened a file and pretended to work.

'You can't go. Peak season. I need all hands on deck,' he said, without looking up at either of us.

'Sir, we haven't taken any leave in two years,' Saurabh said.

'Neither have I. Chandan comes to Chandan. Every day,' Chandan said, speaking about himself in third person twice in the same sentence.

'That's good, sir, but we are going for two weeks. And you won't have a problem with it,' I said.

Chandan looked at me, surprised. I signalled for him to come closer. He leaned forward.

'Unless you want us to ask Mrs Chandan Arora,' I whispered.

'What?' he said, his mouth distorted.

'We know. Sheela ma'am and you. You guys don't even need a houseboat. Your office is enough,' I said.

His face turned from dark brown to apple red to dark purple in a matter of seconds.

'I … I…' Chandan was at a loss for words.

'So our leave begins Monday. Okay with you, sir?' I said.

'Yeah,' he said, mouth still not working properly. 'Sheela, please add their vacation days in the system.'

'Thank you, sir,' Saurabh said. We stood up to leave.

'Dry fruits are famous in Kashmir. You must try them,' Chandan said as we left his office.

SRINAGAR

Chapter 20

'I still can't believe you booked us into a houseboat,' I said, pulling my suitcase off the baggage belt.

Despite half a dozen extra security checks for flights to Kashmir, we had landed on time at noon. The Sheikh ul-Alam International Airport in Srinagar had more CISF and Army personnel than passengers.

'Trust me, you will love it,' Saurabh said. 'Let me call the driver.' He pulled out his phone and proceeded to stare at the screen.

'What?' I said.

'I don't have network. Can I use your phone?' Saurabh said.

I didn't have any signal either. Both of us switched off our phones and turned them back on twice. No network.

'Do you have prepaid cards?' a co-passenger at the baggage belt said to us.

'Yeah,' Saurabh said, 'I took one in Delhi when I moved. Never switched to post-paid.'

'Me neither,' I said.

'Prepaid cards from other states don't work in Jammu and Kashmir. Security reasons.'

We walked out of the modern airport. I saw a man holding a heart-shaped placard with our names on it.

'Seriously, Saurabh?' I turned to Saurabh.

'Great service, isn't it?' he said.

❖

We drove north on the Airport Road towards the city centre. As we left the white, cream roll-shaped airport building, we noticed the mountains around us. The April sun glinted off the snow-capped peaks that formed the city's backdrop. As we approached the centre, it resembled any other non-metro Indian town.

Hoardings for cold drinks, cell phones, underwear and entrance exam coaching classes dotted the landscape. I guess that is what India is about. Study hard in your comfortable underwear. Play with your phone and drink Coke. Repeat.

'It looks like any other place in India,' Saurabh said, thinking along the same lines.

'It *is* India,' I shrugged.

'Don't they have their own Constitution and flag or something?'

I pointed to the driver and placed a finger on my mouth. I had heard talking politics in Kashmir would only invite trouble. I didn't need trouble. I needed our cell phones to work.

❖

'As-salaam-alaikum, Saurabh bhai, Keshav bhai. I am Nizam,' a thirtyish, lean-bodied man with a beard and skullcap greeted us at the entrance of the houseboat.

'Come, come, follow me. I will take you to your room,' Nizam said.

Our houseboat was moored right on the Jhelum River in Srinagar city centre. It was close to Wazir Bagh, where Zara had spent her childhood. The houseboat company had half a dozen such boats, with three to four rooms each. These boats remained tied to the pier for most of the day, making the setup resemble a floating hotel. Nizam took us to our room, a wooden cabin no bigger than the size of my hostel room. It had one double bed.

'Not this,' I said. 'We want one with separate twin beds.'

'Usually couples come here, they don't want separate beds. But, come, I have another room in the next boat,' Nizam said.

'We could have booked separate rooms for each of us,' I said.

'And pay double?' Saurabh said.

I guess money trumps privacy.

'Anything you need, Nizam is here to help you,' Nizam said as we reached our room.

'My cell phone doesn't work,' I said.

'A new SIM card can take a week to get activated.'

'What?' I said.

'Indian government rules. What can we do? They do what they want,' Nizam said.

'How do I stay in touch with people?' I said.

Nizam turned to Saurabh.

'Tell your busy friend to relax. He has come to Srinagar on holiday.'

'We still need to be connected,' I said.

'There is Wi-Fi on the boat. Password is on the bedside table,' Nizam said.

'And phone calls? No way to get a SIM?' I said.

Nizam took out a phone from his pocket.

'Here, take out the SIM and use it.'

'Your SIM, Nizam bhai?' Saurabh said.

'It's my spare phone. This problem comes, so we keep a couple of extra ones.'

❖

'Zara told me about the house she grew up in. That's our first stop tomorrow to find Sikander,' I said.

We had come for an evening walk to Dal Lake, seen in countless photographs and Bollywood movies as the classic Kashmir backdrop. I tried to forget that I was in Zara's city, the place she grew up in, had been happy in. Did she feel this breeze, did she touch the water of this lake? I wondered.

'Safdar uncle gave you the exact address, right?' Saurabh said.

'He did. The one he had from long ago. My worry is if Sikander and his family have moved. Safdar only had the Wazir Bagh address.'

'We will soon find out.'

We passed a group of young Kashmiri boys in their teens. They sat on a bench playing with their phones. I went up to one of them and asked for a dinner place suggestion.

'Try Ahdoos Restaurant,' one boy with a soft stubble said. 'Good wazwan.'

'Thank you,' I said, noticing his beautiful green eyes.

As Saurabh and I turned to leave, the boy spoke again.

'Are you from India?'

I looked back at the boy, surprised by the question.

'Yes. Aren't you?' I said.

'I am Kashmiri,' he said. All his friends laughed. One of them even clapped.

Saurabh nudged me, to say we should leave.

'But Kashmir is a part of India,' I said.

'We hate India,' another boy said. He spoke in a normal tone, as if he had said 'I hate cabbage' or 'I hate radish'.

'Hate?' I said.

'Let's leave,' Saurabh said, fear visible on his face. 'Thank you for your suggestion. We have to go.'

The boys laughed at Saurabh's words.

'Don't be scared. We are not terrorists,' the first boy said.

'God-promise we are not,' the second boy said.

They spoke in a matter-of-fact tone. I could tell this had happened to them before. A bunch of Kashmiri Muslim boys sitting on a bench—obviously tourists wanted to keep their distance from them.

'I am Rajasthani, too. But also Indian,' I said and smiled. 'Don't hate your country.'

'India is not our country. India doesn't care for us.'

Saurabh rammed an elbow into my rib.

'I said let's go,' he said. He was right. I was breaking my own rule of no-politics talk in Kashmir.

'What are your names?' I asked the boys, ignoring Saurabh.

'I am Karim, and that's Saqib,' the first boy with the green eyes said, pointing to the second. The three other boys remained quiet, busy with their phones.

'What do you do?'

They looked at each other blankly.

'Studying?' I said.

They shook their heads.

'Working?' I said.

They shook their heads again.

'Nothing, we do nothing,' Karim said. 'There are no jobs.'

'No movie theatres either, for the jobless to go,' said another, and all his friends laughed.

Karim's green eyes stayed with me even as Saurabh dragged me away.

❖

'Why did you to talk to those locals yesterday?' Saurabh said. We had taken a left turn from our houseboat and were walking along Jhelum River to reach Wazir Bagh. We turned into the lane with Falak restaurant, a landmark for Zara's old address.

'I was curious. Did you see how he asked if we were from India?'

'Maybe he thought you are a foreigner.'

'I look as desi as daal-roti. And then he says, "I am not Indian. I am Kashmiri". What is with these people?'

'Now you know why there is so much Army here. Thank god for them. I feel scared here otherwise, like we are being followed or something,' Saurabh said. He pointed to the street corner. Four Army men stood there, keeping an eye on everyone walking on the road.

'It is the Indian Army people hate,' I said. 'They are the enemy. Zara used to tell me all this. It is something else though, to see it like we did yesterday.'

'Ungrateful people. If the Army wasn't here, Pakistan would turn this place into chaos.'

'It's not that simple,' I said. 'People are genuinely upset with the Army. Maybe we can do a better job listening to them. Anyway, is that Falak?'

We showed the address to a paan shopkeeper next to the restaurant.

'You want to meet Sikander? Sikander Lone?' the shopkeeper said. He took two paan leaves and smeared them with lime.

'Yeah. He still lives there?' I said.

'What work do you have with him?' the shopkeeper said. He kept a pinch of betel nut shavings, fennel seeds and cardamom on the paan leaves.

'We know him from Delhi. He is our friend,' I said. Saurabh looked at me, startled. I smiled blandly.

'Then you should know. He and his mother Farzana used to live here until two years ago. Now they only come here rarely.'

'Do you know where they stay now?' Saurabh said.

'Farzana begum moved to Raj Bagh, I heard. Near Ahdoos hotel.'

'What about her son?'

'Sikander is always on the run. Comes home briefly. Army and police are after him. You should know. Are you really his friends?'

'Yeah, we are,' I said.

'Shall I make you my special paan?'

❖

'How many Raj Bagh shopkeepers so far?' I said.

'More than fifty,' Saurabh said. 'Two days wasted.'

It was evening, and we were sitting in the common lounge of our houseboat. We were sharing it with a rather affectionate Sardar honeymooning couple, who found it too difficult to walk twenty steps to their own room and make out there instead. The Sardar man insisted on kissing his new bride while taking a selfie with the lake as a backdrop.

The woman seemed somewhat uncomfortable, still getting to know her Prince Charming. It looked like an arranged match, probably done through a matrimonial app. I looked away to give them privacy.

'What else can we do?' I said.

'Cable TV shops,' Saurabh said.

'What?'

'Newspaper vendors. Let's go after people who serve the neighbourhood.'

'Doctors and plumbers too?'

'Maybe. Let's start early tomorrow.'

'Thank you, Saurabh. I couldn't have done this without you.'

'Shut up. Senti for no reason. What are we? A honeymoon couple?' Saurabh said.

I laughed.

'Aren't you tired? Searching without success?' I said.

'Still better than seeing Chandan Arora's face. Hey, don't look now, but that Sardar is a bit too excited.'

'Should we bug him and pretend to take a selfie too? Same pose?' I said.

❖

Three more days later, a cable operator became an angel for us.

'Farzana Lone, right? She stays in that red building on Residency Road. Third floor,' he said.

'Are you sure?'

'She's always late paying the bill. I know her. Trust me.'

❖

We rang the doorbell of the said house.

A woman in her fifties in a black burqa, with only her face visible, opened the door.

'Ji, janaab?' she said.

'Farzana ma'am?'

'Yes.'

'I am Keshav. A close friend of Zara's.'

She scanned us up and down without saying a word.

'Your daughter, Zara?' I said. Stepdaughter would have been more accurate, but I didn't want to bring up technicalities.

She blocked the way into the house with her arm, as she wondered what to do next.

'Maybe you don't remember me. I used to study with her. In college,' I said.

'Zara left with her father fifteen years ago. I don't know much about her life after that.'

'I know. She used to talk about you. And Sikander.'

'What do you want? Zara's gone now.'

'Can we come in and talk to you?'

'About what?'

'About Zara and Sikander. We need to share something with you.'

She pointed a finger at Saurabh.

'Who is he?' she said.

'My best friend, Saurabh. We have come from Delhi. It took us a week to find you.'

She narrowed her eyes.

'Are you from the Army? Are you lying to me?'

'No, aunty,' I said. I took out my wallet. 'See, my student ID from IIT. The same college where Zara went. And here's my current visiting card. I teach at a coaching institute.'

She remained hesitant. I pulled out my phone and searched for pictures from five years ago.

'Here, aunty, this is Zara and me, at the college canteen.'

Zara and I were posing with our cups of Bournvita. Both of us had had individual assignment deadlines the next day. We had worked all night, finished our work and snuggled in bed until afternoon. I felt my head swim. How would I ever get over her if I couldn't forget? I swore to myself that I'd delete all her pictures. All.

'Come in. It's a small house, don't mind,' Farzana said.

Chapter 21

'Allah reham,' Farzana said, raising her open palms and offering silent prayers. Over two cups of kahwah tea, I repeated the story of Zara's death and the investigation so far.

'So that's it. We met Sikander because I found a picture of Zara with him. But he ran away,' I said.

'They used to be so close,' Farzana said. 'Before Zara's father ripped them apart.'

'She was always concerned about Sikander,' I said.

'They were step-siblings, but closer than any real ones I have seen,' she said.

I nodded and smiled.

'But this is life,' she said. 'Sometimes people become close even without a blood tie. Look at you. Zara and you separated. Yet, here you are, the only one searching for the truth.'

'Aunty, will you help us?'

'How can an old woman like me help?'

She placed the empty teacups in a tray and stood up.

'Allow me, aunty,' Saurabh said. He took the tray from her and went to the kitchen.

'Aunty, we need to talk to Sikander. I am sorry, but if he runs away, the suspicion will be on him.'

'Suspicion for what?'

'For who killed Zara,' I said.

'Are you out of your mind?' Farzana said and laughed out loud.

I looked at her, puzzled.

'And I thought you knew Zara well. Sikander would never hurt his Zara aapa.'

'He is a suspect,' I said.

'He can't be,' Farzana shook her head. 'It's like killing me, his own mother.'

'If he didn't, all he had to do was talk to us. Why did he run away?'

'He must have felt scared. He's just a little boy,' Farzana said. Her eyes began to well up. Saurabh, who had returned from the kitchen, and I looked at each other.

'He scared us, aunty. He had a gun. He's hardly a little boy,' I said.

Farzana got up and walked up to the tiny window in the room. She stared at the apartment complex outside. She spoke after she had composed herself.

'He didn't grow mentally. He quit school after class five. Low...'

'Low IQ?' I said.

'Yeah. Everyone called him stupid. He grew in height and size. Mentally, he remained a child.'

I nodded as she continued to speak, still looking out of the window.

'And then Zara's father left. He found that witch Zainab in his accounts department. She destroyed us all. Sikander lost his father and Zara aapa. It damaged him. He even tried to take his own life, twice. Allah saved him, thankfully.'

She came back to sit with us.

'I am sorry, aunty,' I said. 'I understand what you went through. But help us. Make Sikander talk to us.'

'As if he listens to me. Hangs out with those good-for-nothing fundamentalists. I told him, get a job. So what if you are not the most intelligent boy in the world, you can still open a shop. Nothing he will do.'

'Fundamentalists?' I said.

'These kattar mullah types who call for azaadi. Yes, we all hate India. But we don't go around flashing guns. Sometimes you have to accept fate.'

'Fate? Aunty, India is our country.'

'But Kashmir is our state. Our identity. Our everything.'

'Aunty, if every state talks like this, what will happen?' Saurabh said.

'Kashmir is different,' Farzana insisted. 'We are a problem nobody wants to solve. We are only useful as a political tool.'

I had to remind myself: no getting into Kashmir politics, which seemed too complicated and screwed up to understand anyway.

'Where is Sikander now, aunty?' I said.

'He was here ten days back. Then he went with his good-for-nothing Tehreek friends to Pahalgam. That's where he called me from yesterday.'

'Will you give us his number? The one we have doesn't work anymore,' I said.

'He keeps changing it. Anyway, I have nothing to hide. See my phone. The last call came from him.'

She took out her phone from her burqa pocket; I didn't know burqas had pockets.

I dialled Sikander's number.

'Salaam, Ammi-jaan,' Sikander said when he answered the call.

'Hi, Sikander,' I said. 'It is Keshav.'

Silence on the other side.

'Sikander, we need to talk.'

'Harami, how did you get Ammi's phone, now?'

'Farzana aunty is with us right now.'

'Khuda kasam, if anything happens to Ammi, I will come and kill your entire clan.'

'We just had kahwah together.'

I handed Farzana the phone.

'He says salaam to you,' I said.

'Jivo, bete,' Farzana said.

I took the phone back from Farzana.

'Nothing to worry,' I said.

'I should have killed you that day,' he said, followed by a dozen expletives.

I went out of the apartment and spoke to him in the stairwell, so I could talk in private.

'Listen, we have come all the way here to talk to you.'

'Why?'

'I have a picture of you, Zara, and a machine gun. And other things I found in her safe. Shall I tell my friends in Delhi to hand them to the police?' I said.

'What things?' he said, his voice had become normal.

'Enough proof to get you into big trouble. So meet us and never curse me again. Or you will be national news tonight, as a terrorist and as your sister's murderer.'

He remained silent.

'Sikander?' I said.

'Come to Pahalgam,' he said after a pause.

❖

'Three kahwahs. Boiling hot,' Saurabh said to the waiter. The Kashmiri drink, which consisted of green tea boiled with saffron, cinnamon and cardamom, had become Saurabh's latest obsession. He drank at least six cups a day. He liked to have it just like the Kashmiris did, piping hot with honey and crushed nuts.

'Okay, enough honey, Golu,' I said, as he poured a quarter jar of it in his kahwah.

'Honey is good for you, right?' Saurabh said, as the waiter left.

'Okay, Golu, even these "good for you" things are only good for you up to a point. In small portions.'

'Like love?' Saurabh said.

I understood what he was trying to say and became quiet. He took a sip of his kahwah and changed the topic.

'It's colder than Srinagar here,' Saurabh said. The ninety-kilometre bumpy and winding bus ride from Srinagar to Pahalgam had taken us three hours. We had come to Dana Pani, a restaurant in the Pahalgam main market. I wanted to meet Sikander in a public place, preferably with plenty of cops and

Army personnel in sight. I could count at least a dozen uniformed men outside on the road, enough for Sikander to not try the stunt of pulling out a gun again.

'Let's make this quick. I haven't told my brothers I am here,' Sikander said.

'Brothers?' I said.

'My people. None of your business. What do you want to know about aapa?'

I showed him the photographs of the contents of Zara's safe.

'Explain all this,' I said. 'Where did you take this picture? Why did Zara have Pakistani rupees and SIM card?'

'We took the picture in Delhi. At my hotel. It is a jinxed picture.'

'Why jinxed?'

'Never mind.'

'Tell us more. How did she have the Pakistani stuff?'

Sikander let out a huge breath.

'Aapa went to Pakistan. For a book fair or something.'

'The Karachi Literature Festival?' I said.

'Yes. That's why she had the Pakistani money and SIM card. What's the big deal?'

'The big deal is this,' Saurabh said. 'Why did she have a dealer-size batch of cocaine? And a bullet?'

'I don't know.' He looked sullen.

I turned to Saurabh. 'Isn't he hiding something?'

'He definitely is,' Saurabh said.

'I did not kill aapa, okay?' Sikander said and banged his fist on the table. The empty kahwah cups danced a little.

'Tantrums don't prove your innocence,' I said.

'Neither does threatening us with guns. My friends in Delhi will submit all the evidence if something happens to us,' Saurabh said, a story we had concocted to keep ourselves safe.

'You brought a weapon again?' I said. Sikander stood up and lifted his arms.

'Look if you want. I have nothing. The Army checks people at random in the main market. I am not that stupid.'

'Good. Sit down,' I said. 'And tell us why Zara had all this in her safe.'

Sikander looked around. The nearest customers were sitting two tables away. He said quickly, 'I have done wrong things. But I didn't hurt Zara aapa.'

'If you haven't, your secrets are safe with us,' I said.

'I work for Hashim Abdullah. I'm sure you know who he is,' Sikander said as if he was speaking about Bill Gates or Mukesh Ambani.

'Sorry, no. Who is he?' I said.

'He is the head of Tehreek-e Jihad. He gave me a worthy purpose in life. Taught me how to live with passion. Hashim bhai means everything to me.'

I wanted to tell him killing innocent people or hating your country did not count as a worthy purpose. However, I remembered my no-politics rule and remained quiet. Sikander was saying, 'Hashim bhai lives in Azaad Kashmir.'

'Pakistan-occupied Kashmir, you mean?' Saurabh said.

'That's what Indian propaganda calls it. In reality, where we are is India-occupied Kashmir.'

No politics, I told myself again.

'Leave that,' I said. 'Go on with your story.'

'I started as a junior soldier in Tehreek. Hashim bhai gave me a chance to do something big. That is when I made a mistake.'

He avoided our eyes.

'What mistake?' Saurabh said.

'I tricked Zara aapa.'

'Be clear,' I said. Something about Sikander annoyed me. Was he actually dumb or pretending to be?

'Hashim bhai said he knows people in Karachi who are organising a literature festival. He said they want to invite some people from India, especially bright students. To show efforts at peace. I couldn't go. Hashim bhai said my passport should have as few stamps of Pakistan as possible. He asked me if I had anyone in mind.'

'And you suggested Zara?'

'Yeah. Zara aapa loved reading books. She attended several literature festivals in India. I asked her. The organisers had offered to pay for her flight and stay, as they said they were doing for some other chosen students. Aapa jumped at the offer.'

'And that's why she went to Pakistan?'

'Yes. Hashim bhai met her in Karachi. He sent some gifts back for me. He gave her a small strolley filled with clothes and snacks.'

'And?' Saurabh said, listening to Sikander's every word.

'They switched the strolley in the drop-off car to the airport. Under a layer of clothes, they filled it with cocaine. Eight kilos of it.'

'Eight kilos of cocaine?' Saurabh whistled. 'Isn't that huge?'

'Worth around five crore rupees. It is one of the ways Tehreek funds itself. It was my first big contribution to Tehreek,' Sikander said.

I sighed. There are worse places to work, in this world, than Chandan Classes, I thought. Like organisations that fund themselves with drug money.

'You used your own sister as a drug mule?'

'I didn't know it was so wrong at that time. And Hashim bhai planned it so well. Nobody suspected her at customs. She did bring the goods home.'

'So that makes it okay? She would have spent her life in jail if customs had stopped her.'

'A young girl from IIT, coming back from a books festival, nobody would suspect her, Hashim bhai told me.'

'Are you serious? What if they did?' I said, my voice rising.

He did not respond.

I took deep breaths to suppress my anger and not slap this

overgrown, stupid oaf. Saurabh held my wrist, signalling me to calm down.

'Okay, so what happened next?' Saurabh said.

'I went to collect the bag from aapa. But before I reached, she had opened it.'

'She found out about the drugs?' I said.

'Yes. And she scolded me a lot, even slapped me. I had to tell her who I worked for. I tried to explain that Hashim bhai was doing so much good.'

'What did she say?'

'She refused to listen. She said I had to cut off from these people. She wanted me to take the bag to the police.'

'Did you go?'

'No. I couldn't let Hashim bhai down.'

'And she was fine with that?'

'Of course not. But I lied to her. I said let me deliver this one bag so they leave me alone, and then I will quit the group.'

'And you didn't?'

He gazed at the floor again.

'I couldn't quit our great cause,' he said, whatever the hell he meant by 'great cause'.

'You think it is okay to work for someone who sells drugs?'

'We have no choice. We are fighting powerful governments. To do a great good, sometimes you have to do a little bad,' he said in a rehearsed tone.

'Hashim said this?'

'Yeah. At that time, I didn't realise Zara aapa had kept a packet. Anyway, I don't do drug-related stuff at Tehreek now. I work in recruitment.'

I heard the word recruitment and my instinct was to ask if they were hiring and whether I could apply. I scolded and reminded myself that working here wasn't an option.

'Were you in touch with her just before she died?'

'Not much. Just the occasional call. She asked me to forget

all this nonsense and look for a job. In fact, she gave me your example once. Of course, she didn't know I had not left Tehreek.'

'My example?' I said, curious.

'She said, "Look at me, Sikander, I followed my passion with Keshav and never realised that practical life mattered. It led me nowhere. Finally, I had to make a practical choice in Raghu".'

'Practical?'

'I also didn't fully understand. She said she did love Raghu a lot now, but had ultimately been practical in choosing him. His family would have no issues with Zara or something.'

'Why did she tell you this?' I said.

'To tell me that sometimes our heart leads us to wrong places. Tehreek is where my heart was, she wanted me to use my head and get another job.'

'Ah,' I said. I guess I was the wrong place her heart had led her to. Yet, it felt good to hear that I was her heart's choice, and not the 'practical' one.

'Fine,' Saurabh said. 'Anything else you want to share that could be useful to us?'

'Nothing I can think of. I haven't told all this to anyone. Can I go now?'

I nodded. Sikander stood up to leave.

'Sorry, one more question,' Saurabh said.

'What?'

'The selfie with Zara. When was that taken?'

'Zara aapa came to meet me in Delhi.'

'Why do you have a machine gun?'

'I show new recruits how to use a gun.'

'Sit down, Sikander,' I said, as my mind stopped replaying the words 'sometimes our heart leads us to wrong places' and came back to the murder case.

'Why?' he said. He continued to stand with his arms crossed.

'You think we are idiots?'

'What happened?'

'You said you told Zara you had left Tehreek.'

'Yeah.'

'So why is she smiling in this picture when she comes to see you and finds you with a machine gun?' I said.

'I need to go.'

'You also said this picture is jinxed. Why?' Saurabh said.

Sikander winced. He held his head.

'I get migraines. Sorry.'

'We are not done yet,' I said. 'And trust me, you would rather we question you than the police.'

'I need to go rest. Can we talk later?'

'When? Tomorrow?'

He nodded and sniffled, like a child.

'Yes, call me tomorrow,' Sikander said and walked out of the restaurant.

❖

'We should have brought more warm clothes,' Saurabh said. He rubbed his hands. The Heevan Hotel in Pahalgam, where we were staying, had set up a campfire on its lawns. Saurabh and I sat there post-dinner.

'Something is not right about Sikander,' I said.

'Relax. Give him some time. He will open up,' Saurabh said.

'He is devious,' I said. 'He pretends to be naïve and stupid. He is not.'

'Maybe he is nervous,' Saurabh said.

'Nonsense. I think it is time we confronted the truth.'

'What truth?' Saurabh said, his round face glowing in the campfire.

'That he may be family, may say all emotional things, be a little dumb, but the little stepbrother is no innocent baby. In fact, he's the prime suspect.'

'What makes you say that?' Saurabh said. He was sitting so close to the fire, I felt he would combust any moment.

'Sit back from the flames,' I said.

'Fine,' Saurabh said, moving back three inches.

'Here is what I think happened. Sikander became a terrorist. Zara found out. Tried to stop him several times, but he didn't listen. Zara finally lost her patience. Decided to go to the police.'

'And Sikander comes and kills her before that?' Saurabh said.

'Yes.'

'Possible. Explains why she would open the window, too. It was for her stepbrother, after all.'

I snapped my fingers. 'Exactly.'

'What about the picture? Why is Zara smiling?'

'She could have felt pressured. Or wait, she could be collecting proof for the police.'

'That's why she kept the bullet and cocaine?' Saurabh said.

'Bang on. Yeah, that's it. She was collecting evidence. She wanted to go to the police because the brother wouldn't stop. Sikander found out and killed her.'

'But he loved his sister,' Saurabh said.

'If Hashim bhai told him killing her was for some "great good", what do you think this idiot would do?'

Saurabh scratched his cheek before he spoke again.

'Kill.'

We stared at each other for a few seconds. Everything added up and the theory made things fall into place. We high-fived.

'We got him. Call Inspector Rana. We will need his help,' I said. Yes, I had the killer. The glow from the fire warmed not only my face, but also my insides.

Chapter 22

'Keep him engaged,' Saurabh said. 'No more questions. Just be friendly.'

I nodded. We had come to the reception lobby of Heevan Hotel. I dialled Sikander's number from the hotel landline.

'Salaam, Sikander bhai,' I said, when I heard someone pick up the call.

'Kaun janaab?' It did not sound like Sikander.

'Is Sikander there? This is his friend, Keshav.'

'You are Sikander's friend?'

'Yes,' I said.

'Are you in Pahalgam?'

'Yeah,' I said.

'Can you come here? Moonview Resorts.'

'Where's Sikander?'

'He's here. Can you come?'

'Yeah, sure. Who are you?'

'Ahmed. Come soon, please.'

❖

Saurabh and I walked towards Moonview Resorts, which was around a kilometre away from Heevan. We had called Inspector Rana the previous night, updating him about Sikander being the prime suspect. 'You guys restarted that Zara case? And went to Kashmir? Mad aashiq you are,' is what he said first. Fortunately, he listened to our entire story and finally agreed to help us, if for nothing else but concern for our safety. 'Get the hell out of there as soon as you can. Kashmir isn't Hauz Khas. And no more meeting that Sikander alone,' he said before ending the call.

I called Rana again.

'We are on our way to meet him at Moonview Resorts,' I said, panting due to the steep climb.

'I already informed sub-inspector Saraf at the local Pahalgam police station. He's ready when you need him.'

'He should come there with us now,' I said.

'Relax. You sound tense,' Rana said, as I continued my climb.

'Of course, I am tense. Someone called Ahmed picked up his phone. He told us to come to Moonview Resorts.'

'Oh, there are other people there?'

'Yeah,' I said.

'Then definitely let Saraf reach first. Don't go in alone. You guys are such idiots. You should have told me before planning a trip to Kashmir.'

'Sorry, sir. Yes, we will wait for him,' I said.

'And listen, Keshav.'

'Yes, Inspector Rana?' I said. I expected thanks and some words of praise as we had taken huge risks but might have finally solved the case.

'Once the police get Sikander, call me first. I want to break this to the media. I don't want Saraf talking to anyone.'

❖

The grey-haired Inspector Saraf stepped out of a police jeep that seemed even older than him. Two constables accompanied him. All of them were in plain clothes, to avoid any suspicion. Saurabh and I met the three of them at an empty parking lot outside Moonview Resorts.

'Stay calm. Pretend to be normal guests at the hotel,' Inspector Saraf said.

A wiry bearded man in his thirties manned the reception desk.

'I am Keshav. Is someone called Ahmed here?'

'I am Ahmed,' the man said. 'I am the manager here. You are Sikander's friend who called?'

Then he noticed the plain-clothes cops and Saurabh. 'Who are all these people?' he said.

'My friends,' I said. 'Where is Sikander?'

'Follow me.'

Ahmed and I walked up to a room on the second floor. Saurabh, Inspector Saraf and his two men walked a few steps behind us. The corridors of Moonview Resorts did not get much sunlight and were cold. Ahmed used a master key to enter the room at the end. He switched on the yellow ceiling light.

Sikander lay on the bed, face covered in blood, his gun next to him.

'Oh,' Saurabh gasped out loud. The lower half of Sikander's face was disfigured beyond recognition. A putrid smell came from his body, which mixed with the musty smell of the hotel carpet, making it difficult to breathe. I saw his blown off face and turned numb. Everyone around me seemed to move in slow motion. A white noise in my ears blocked out all other sounds. Inspector Saraf calmly picked up Sikander's wrist, as if picking up a TV remote.

'Dead,' Inspector Saraf said. 'Shot himself in the mouth.'

'I called you here because I don't want to deal with any of this,' Ahmed said. 'This hotel is all I have to make a living. If news gets out about a suicide here—'

Inspector Saraf cut in. 'When did you find the body?'

'Housekeeping found it three hours ago. I told them to keep quiet. I kept his cell phone, hoping someone would call. You did.'

'When did he first arrive here?'

'Five days ago. Can you please take care of his body? Or inform his family? I don't want the police here. Please,' Ahmed said, his composure cracking.

'We are the police,' Inspector Saraf said. He took out his ID card.

Ahmed fell at Inspector Saraf's feet.

'I don't know anything about this. Please, sahib.'

Inspector Saraf grabbed Ahmed's shoulders and pulled him back up.

'You know who he was or what he did?'

'No, sahib,' Ahmed said.

Inspector Saraf slapped Ahmed. I don't know why the police think it is okay to go around slapping people, particularly from a lower economic or less powerful class.

'You guys know these people are terrorists, still you give them rooms. You don't inform the police,' Inspector Saraf said.

Ahmed had tears in his eyes.

'Sahib, we locals have no choice,' he said, hands folded. 'They come and leave whenever. They show us a gun if we refuse. The police and the Army show us a gun if we allow them to stay. What are we to do? I have little children.'

'Do you hate India too?' Inspector Saraf said, as if Ahmed would own up if he did.

'No, sahib. I make my living from Indian tourists. Why would I hate them?'

'What did this man do in the last few days?' Saraf said, pointing to Sikander.

'He would go out every day for a few hours. Sometimes, he would meet young boys in the lobby.'

'Recruiting new terrorists?'

'I don't know, sahib.'

'Did you find anything in the room?'

'We didn't touch anything,' Ahmed said. 'You can check whatever you want.'

'Keshav? Are you there?' Inspector Saraf said, snapping his fingers in front of my eyes. He had already said my name three times before I paid attention. My eyes went back to Sikander's mangled face. The same face I had spoken to yesterday.

'Sorry, inspector, what is it?'

'The prime suspect you wanted me to arrest is dead.'

'Ye…ah,' I said, unable to speak in a coherent manner. I saw Saurabh's face contort. He ran to the bathroom. I heard him vomit.

'Call an ambulance. Remove the body,' Inspector Saraf said to one of the constables. He turned to another one. 'And check the room for any suicide notes.'

I sat down on the study chair in the room. Saurabh's puking sounds were making me feel nauseous too. One of the constables lifted the pillows on the bed to check underneath. He also opened the desk drawers.

'If people leave the room, I can search better,' the constable said.

❖

Saurabh and I sat on a sofa in the lobby, both of us unable to talk. Inspector Saraf sat across from us and spoke to someone on the phone. Half an hour later, the constable who was searching the room came downstairs. He had an envelope in his hand.

'Found this in his pocket,' he said. 'It says, "For Hashim bhai. Please give it to any of my brothers at Tehreek. They will come looking for me".'

Inspector Saraf opened the envelope. He found a sheet of paper inside. It only had a handwritten web address on it.

www.Bit.ly/AlvidaTehreek

'What's this?' Inspector Saraf said.

'It's an abbreviated web link. Let's check,' Saurabh said, finally finding his voice.

Saurabh typed in the web address on the desktop computer at the hotel. The page redirected to a private YouTube video, which showed Sikander sitting in the same room where we had found him dead. He mumbled some prayers and then spoke into the camera.

'Hashim bhai, maafi. I let you down. Some people are after me. They will hand me over to the police for a crime I never did. Of murdering my own aapa. Allah kasam, Zara aapa was like my second mother. I didn't do anything.

'If the police catch me, they will torture me until I tell them more, not just about aapa, but also about Tehreek's activities and mission, I just cannot let myself be in that situation. I would rather give up my life than put you all in danger. I am happy to sacrifice myself for the greater good, as you taught us.

'I feel sad I won't be there to see the smile on your face when Kashmir finally becomes free. I love you, Hashim bhai, and the Tehreek family. Please take care of my Ammi. I know you will.

'Zara aapa, I will see you in jannat soon. With you gone, one less reason to be on earth for me.

'For the rest, Khuda Hafiz.'

Sikander mumbled another prayer. A few seconds later, he pulled out a gun. He placed the nozzle in his mouth. My eyes scrunched and my face stiffened in anticipation of what would happen next.

However, he simply waved and the video paused. Of course, he had to stop recording, upload the video and create the link before he shot himself.

'Wow,' Saurabh said, his mouth open, after the video ended.

'Suicide notes have become hi-tech,' Inspector Saraf said.

❖

One hour later, the constables and the hotel staff had loaded Sikander's body into an ambulance in the parking lot.

'Take him to the morgue. Keep it quiet. Just inform his mother,' Inspector Saraf said.

He turned to speak to Ahmed once the ambulance left the hotel compound.

'He was a rat who died. Nothing to investigate here. Clean up your hotel, and inform us if anyone like him ever comes to stay here.'

'I will, sahib. Thank you, sahib. Allah khair.'

Ahmed melted back into the hotel. The two constables who came with Saraf got into the jeep.

Only Saraf, Saurabh and I remained in the parking lot.

'Doesn't look like he killed his stepsister,' Saraf said, stroking his chin.

I nodded.

'They never lie at the end,' Saraf said, getting into the police jeep. He stuck his head out of the window.

'May I say one thing?' Saraf said.

'Sure, sir,' I said.

'Investigation is not everyone's cup of tea. One should stick to what one is capable of.'

❖

'Say something, bhai,' Saurabh said. 'You haven't spoken all day.'

'Did you check the flights back or not?' I said.

The bus taking us back from Pahalgam to Srinagar spiralled down the hilly roads. I closed my eyes. The view of Kashmir's blue skies and snow-capped mountains meant nothing to me anymore. I wanted to go home.

'Six flights to Delhi every day. Getting back is not an issue,' Saurabh said.

We became quiet again. I knew I sucked as an engineer and teacher. I now realised I sucked as a detective too. Maybe this was really why Zara left me. She saw the perennial loser in me. I couldn't deliver to her earlier. Now, I couldn't even deliver on one promise I had made to her—to find her killer.

'What are you thinking, bhai?' Saurabh said after half an hour.

'That I hope Chandan Classes still has a job for us.'

❖

I tossed my sweaters into the suitcase.

'Did you buy the tickets?' I said. 'I am packed.'

'Internet is not working. Neither on Nizam bhai's SIM nor the Wi-Fi.'

'Fine, we will buy them at the airport,' I said.

I noticed Saurabh's clothes still hanging in his closet.

'What is this?' I said. 'I told you to pack.'

Saurabh came to stand in front of me. In his white sweater, he looked like a polar bear. Polar bear placed his paws on my shoulders.

'First Zara. Then Sikander. It is scary. But to run away like this?' he said.

'I am not scared. I am leaving because I don't think I am capable of doing this. Or anything in life, really.'

'Nonsense. We had a setback. It doesn't mean we quit.'

I shrugged. 'Anyway, there's nothing left for us to do here.'

'Why? We still haven't found the killer.'

I walked away from him and sat on the bed. I spoke without looking at him.

'We can't. We are not smart enough.'

Saurabh came and sat next to me.

'We came so close,' he said, his voice soft.

'No, we did not. We were miserably wrong. And Sikander died because of me.'

'What?' Saurabh said, his mouth open.

'I pushed him and threatened to report him. That is why he killed himself. Even though he didn't kill Zara.'

'He was a terrorist. A rat, that's what Inspector Saraf said.'

'He was Zara's brother. Would she have ever forgiven me for this? And his mother, waiting at home for him…'

Saurabh placed his hand on mine.

'I really thought Sikander did it. I thought I had the evidence. Our theory added up,' I said to myself.

'I had zero doubt too.'

'I wanted to do this right, Golu. And not just for Zara. For once I wanted to win. I never ever fucking win.'

I kicked my suitcase in disgust. The cover of the unzipped strolley flew open. The upper flap of the suitcase had the packet with the contents of Zara's safe.

'All this,' I said, pointing to it. 'Just nonsense. Who did we think we were? Some desi Holmes and Watson jodi? A loser like me can't get a coding job at a body shop. How can I solve a complex murder case?'

'Stop calling yourself a loser, bhai. You are not.'

'Have you ever seen me achieve anything remarkable?'

'You made it to IIT.'

'A fluke. Evaluation mistakes happen. A computer error.'

'Stop it, bhai.'

'We killed an innocent man.'

'A terrorist is dead. We did the country a favour.'

I looked at Saurabh. He shrugged.

'Bastard would have only taught more people how to kill.'

'Anyway, what is there for us to do now?' I sighed.

'Let's go back to the basics. Look at Zara's digital footprints. We didn't check her Instagram posts properly.'

'There's nothing there. Her Instagram is like that of any other twenty-something girl.'

'Let's go through it again, based on what we know now. Also, we got lost in the big stuff in the safe, like the cocaine and the bullet. What about the rest of the items?'

'Like what?'

'These pregnancy kits,' Saurabh said, opening the packet that held the safe's contents.

'That bastard Raghu and Zara must have been fucking without protection. What else?'

Saurabh looked at me sternly.

'Bhai, control yourself. She's dead now. And you loved her.'

'Sorry,' I mumbled. 'I am stressed.'

'And what about these earrings?' Saurabh said. 'We never considered them so far. They look expensive.'

I held the earrings in my palm. Each of the gold earrings had a dangling pendant the size of a ten-rupee coin. The pendants had an inlay of diamonds and precious stones. Sunlight fell through the window of the houseboat's room, making the gems glisten.

Nizam knocked on our door.

'Janaab, may I disturb?'

'Huh?' I said looking up.

'Sure, Nizam bhai,' Saurabh said, quickly placing a pillow on the pregnancy kits.

'Just wanted to say the internet is working again. Government shut it down after stone-pelting yesterday. It is back now,' Nizam said.

'What? More stone-pelting?' I said.

'Don't ask, janaab. We are sick and tired. People were only protesting because two innocent boys were picked up by the Indian Army last week. News like this reduces tourist flow. I suffer,' Nizam said.

'I can understand,' I said. 'Anyway, glad the internet is back.'

Nizam noticed the earrings in my hand.

'Mashallah,' Nizam said. 'What beautiful jhumkis. You are taking them for bhabhi?'

'Bhabhi is dead,' I almost said, but tried to smile instead. 'These are typically Kashmiri, right?'

'Definitely, hundred per cent Kashmiri,' Nizam said and extended his hand. 'May I?'

Nizam sat on the bed next to me and took the earrings in his hands. He lifted them close to his eyes.

'Very fine work. Must be really expensive. Only in Kashmir will you get something like this.'

'They belong to a friend,' Saurabh said.

'We wanted to get another pair like this. Any idea where?'

'These days jewellers all over India will copy any design for you,' Nizam said. 'But if you want them to be truly authentic like these ones, they should come from one of the top shops in Srinagar.'

'Which ones?' Saurabh said.

'I can give you a list of local jewellers,' Nizam said, 'and tell them Nizam from Shelter Houseboats sent you. They will help and serve you better.'

'Thanks,' I said.

'So what happened at the protest?' Saurabh said, changing topics to take Nizam's attention away from the earrings.

'The Army retaliated, which they say they did in self-defence. Like always, they fired back with those nasty pellet guns. Some kids were hit in the ears. They may go deaf. Only made things worse. People are now even more upset with the Army. The Army cuts internet. The cycle continues.' Nizam sounded resigned. 'Ya khuda, when will this ever end?'

'What's for dinner tonight?' I said, invoking my no-politics rule before it became too late. But Nizam wouldn't stop.

'How does the rest of India live in peace? Why can't we find a way too, Keshav bhai?'

'We can, we can... By the way, will you give us the list of jewellery shops by tomorrow?'

'Oh,' Nizam said, surprised at my switching to a mundane topic. After all, we did seem awfully close to solving the Kashmir problem, which experts and world leaders hadn't been able to for the last seventy years.

'I will give it to you by dinner. Actually, I better go check things in the kitchen. We are making our special biryani tonight.'

Nizam returned the earrings to me and left the room.

Saurabh looked at me and smiled.

'What?' I said.

'The internet is back. Should I book the next flight out?'

'Wait.'

'Why?'

'I think we should visit some jewellery shops.'

'Why?' Saurabh said, with a sly smile.

'Maybe to buy a pair of earrings for my bhabhi,' I said and winked at Saurabh.

'Tinder bhabhi, you mean?'

Both of us laughed for the first time that day.

Chapter 23

'We can make this for you, no problem. And yeah, we know Nizam bhai. A lot of customers come from his houseboats.'

'Yes, he sent us. Anyway, I know you can make them. But did you make these particular set of earrings?' I said.

We had come to Akhoon Jewellers at Syed Hamir Pora, our fourth shop since we had started on our hunt that morning.

'Sir, we will make better than this. How much did you buy these for?' the salesperson said.

'You did not make these, right?' Saurabh said and turned to leave.

'Stay, sir,' he said. He signalled to one of the shop-boys, who served us two cups of hot kahwah and a plate of dates.

'Be our guest, janaab. You don't have to buy anything,' the salesperson said.

'Can you tell us if these were made in Srinagar?' I said.

The salesperson held one of the earrings.

'Definitely. Wherever it is made, the kaarigar is Kashmiri. The detail on the design tells me.'

An elderly man in a skullcap and white kurta, presumably the owner of Akhoon Jewellers, got up from his chair in a corner of the shop and shuffled up to us.

'Show me,' the owner said. He brought the earrings close to his face, narrowing his eyes. He took out a magnifying glass from his pocket.

'No, not ours. But it is from this area. I know kaarigars who make this,' he said after examining the earrings.

'Thank you,' I said.

'Give us a chance. We will make you better ones,' he said.

'His wife wants us to go to the same place,' I pointed to Saurabh. Saurabh smiled shyly. In his puffy red sweater, he did look like a henpecked husband.

'Oh, up to you,' the owner said, a tinge of disappointment in his voice.

'Uncle, can you help us find who made it?' I said.

'It's expensive, so must be a top jewellery shop. Is there a shop mark?' he turned to his salesperson. 'Get the microscope.'

The salesperson went to the back of the shop.

'How much would something like this cost?' I said to the owner.

'Three, maybe four lakh rupees,' the owner said. 'I am Hafiz, by the way.'

We shook hands.

The salesperson returned with a compound microscope. Hafiz placed an earring under the microscope and looked into the viewfinder, moving the earring up and down. He shook his head.

'Give me the other one,' Hafiz said.

He placed the second earring under the lens.

'Many jewellers put their mark, such as their initials, on expensive items,' Hafiz said, one eye peeping into the viewfinder. 'There it is. SJ.'

'What is SJ?' Saurabh said.

Hafiz returned the earrings to us.

'Let's see. SJ could be Sona Jewellers, which my friend owns. There's S. Khem Singh Jewellers opposite Hanuman Mandir. There's Salaam Jewellers on Hari Singh High Street,' Hafiz said. 'These are the shops with SJ initials that I can think of.'

Saurabh took out the list of jewellers Nizam had given us from his pocket.

'There's more. Shabnam Jewellers at Lal Chowk. Showkat Jewellers on the Srinagar–Ladakh highway,' he said, going down the list.

'Good luck in your search. If you can't find the same shop, we are always here,' Hafiz said and smiled.

'No, this is not made here at Sona Jewellers,' the shop owner said the moment he picked up the earrings.

'Not from our shop,' said the salesgirl in a hijab at Shabnam Jewellers.

Four other shops with the initials SJ turned us down that day.

'Three more SJs left,' Saurabh said.

We ate rusk and drank kahwah at a roadside teashop as we took a break between our shop visits.

'Well, last few tries. Otherwise, time to book a flight back to Delhi, I guess,' I said, dipping my rusk in the kahwah.

❖

'We just wanted to know if your shop made these earrings,' I said, passing them to the owner of Showkat Jewellers. He sat cross-legged behind the counter. The brightly lit shop dazzled with all the jewellery on the walls.

'These?' the shopkeeper said, taking the earrings in his hands. He ran a finger on top of them.

'Yes, of course,' the shopkeeper said and laughed. 'This is Showkat Jewellers' finest work.'

Hearing the word 'yes' after four days, I almost collapsed on the spot. The shopkeeper looked startled by my obvious relief.

'What happened?' He put out a hand. 'I am Showkat.'

I shook his hand. 'I can't tell you how happy we are to meet you.'

Showkat laughed.

'The pleasure is mine, actually. You want more jewellery? You have come to the right place.'

He gave us what was our sixth cup of kahwah of the day. He held the earrings up against the light.

'Look at the work. Exquisite,' Showkat said.

'Who did you make these for?' I said.

Showkat looked at me, surprised.

'I don't understand. They don't belong to you?'

'They belonged to a friend. She is no more,' I said.

Showkat touched the tips of his earlobes with his right hand and mumbled a prayer.

'I am sorry to hear. What happened to her?'

Saurabh and I looked at each other.

'Accident,' Saurabh said.

'Ya khuda. What can I do for you?'

'Her parents found the earrings in her room. But they didn't recognise them. We happened to be visiting Srinagar. They told us to check who might have given them to her,' I said.

'You know parents,' Saurabh said, though I am not sure what it meant. I guess the moment you say, 'you know parents', you are allowed to drop some logic. Showkat looked at us with some hesitation.

'The parents are quite disturbed by their daughter's death, as you can imagine. We just want to do our bit to help them,' I said.

'But looks like we found a good shop, bhai. For our family needs also, we have a good jeweller now,' Saurabh said to me.

That seemed to convince the shop-owner. He nodded and picked up a microscope from a shelf above his seat. He examined the earrings again.

'Definitely ours. Has the shop mark,' he said, head bent over the microscope.

'That's how we came here. SJ,' I said.

Showkat kept the microscope aside.

'Yes, but I don't remember selling them. Could be one of my two sons. Or my nephew, the main salesperson.'

'Do you mind asking them?' I said.

'They just stepped out for some bank work. Should be back soon. You can wait here.'

We waited at Showkat Jewellers for over two hours, before a Fortuner arrived outside the shop. Three men in their twenties, each with a French beard, stepped out of the vehicle.

'So late?' Showkat pointed at his watch.

'Army had closed the roads. Full checking. Chaos and traffic jams all over,' one of the men said.

'Screw the Indian Army,' said another man.

'Talk with some tameez. We have guests,' Showkat said, pointing to us.

'Hi, I am Mohsin, Showkat chacha's nephew,' said the man who had just cursed the Indian Army. 'Sorry, I didn't mean to…'

'It's okay. I am Keshav. This is Saurabh.'

'I am Ali, and this is my brother Salim,' said one of the other men.

'They are my sons,' Showkat said and smiled.

Showkat asked them about our earrings.

They passed the earrings to each other one by one.

'I don't remember selling this,' Ali said.

'Me neither,' Mohsin said.

'Show me,' Salim said. He took the earrings. 'When was this purchased?' he said.

'Sometime in the last few years maybe,' I said.

'It looks antique, but it is not. A good replica of an old Kashmiri design,' Mohsin said. 'Oh yes, I remember now.'

'Remember what?' Saurabh and I both spoke at the same time. Everyone looked at us, surprised by our excitement.

'Arrey, that man, he looked fauji. All tall and fit and kadak. He said he wanted to recreate his dadi's earrings,' Mohsin said.

'I remember you discussing it,' Ali said, 'but can't recollect the customer.'

'I do,' Mohsin said. 'He paid cash. Give me the cash sales book.'

Ali opened a drawer under the cash counter. He took out a carbon copy-lined notebook. It had pink and white pages filled with handwritten scribbles. He passed it to Mohsin.

'This must have cost above three lakh rupees. Let me see all high-value sales in my handwriting,' Mohsin said. He started flipping through the sheets of the notebook in a furious manner. He finished one notebook. Ali passed him another one.

Five minutes later, Mohsin paused and tapped his finger on a particular page.

'One year ago, see,' Mohsin said, and held up the notebook for Showkat to look at. The open page had an outline of the design of the same earrings.

'Correct,' Showkat said. 'Yes, see. Rs 3,80,000. Diamond, sapphire, kundan, 22 karat gold. Rs 2,00,000 advance. Delivery after a week, 28 May 2017. Paid balance. All cash.'

I looked at Showkat, somewhat confused.

'Someone bought them in May last year?'

'Yes,' Mohsin said.

'Who?'

Mohsin looked at his notebook again. He shook his head.

'He didn't leave a name,' he said.

'Any contact details?' I said.

'No. He just gave an advance for the earrings. We gave him a temporary receipt. Later, he came again to pay the balance and collect the earrings.'

'You sell such expensive items without knowing the customer's name?' Saurabh said.

'In our business, we have all kinds of customers. Some become our family friends. Others want to stay discreet. We respect that,' Showkat said, tugging at his white beard.

'Do you remember what he looked like?' I said to Mohsin.

'I do. Handsome man. He looked Kashmiri. Fair. Six feet tall at least. I told you, he looked fauji,' Mohsin said.

'Did he come in uniform?' Saurabh said.

'No. Just the gait. Faujis have an andaz,' Mohsin said. 'In fact, yes, I think he came in a military green vehicle the second time.'

Saurabh looked around the shop. He noticed cameras on the ceiling.

'Showkat bhai, will you have CCTV footage from May last year?' Saurabh said.

'No,' Salim said. 'CCTV back-up only remains for two months. Why? Is everything okay?'

'Yes, of course,' Saurabh said and stood up. 'Nothing of concern. I just thought if we could see the person…'

'I am sorry. The hard drive deletes anything older than sixty days,' Salim said.

'Thank you so much,' I said. I folded my hands. Saurabh and I stood up to leave.

'If you ever want to sell these back to us,' Showkat said, 'we can give you a good price.'

❖

The flimsy wooden bed of the houseboat creaked as Saurabh turned on his side. It was close to midnight. I placed my laptop on my stomach as I surfed random websites.

'Earrings worth Rs 3,80,000,' Saurabh said. 'Who gives such a gift?'

'Parents,' I said. 'But they didn't.'

'Or a lover,' Saurabh said.

'Raghu?' I said. 'I can check with him.'

'Yes, but Mohsin said, fair, six feet tall and fit. Nothing like Raghu.'

'He even said handsome. That's definitely not Raghu,' I said.

'Sikander?' Saurabh said.

'Nobody gives their sister earrings this costly. Also, Sikander was skinny and short. Not what Mohsin described.'

'Maybe Sikander sent someone. Or hell, Raghu is rich, he could have sent someone.'

'I can check with Raghu easily,' I said. I took out my phone and sent him a 'Hi' on WhatsApp.

'Hey, Keshav, long time. What's up?' he replied within a minute.

'Just wanted to check something with you.'

'Sure,' Raghu said.

'Where are you?'

'I am in San Francisco. Just landed.'

'Wow. That's far.'

'Yeah. I literally came down for like one investor meeting.'

'Oh. What time is it there?'

He replied after five minutes.

'Noon.'

'Sorry, you seem busy.'

'It's okay. I can chat a bit. My meeting hasn't started yet.'

'Do you recall giving any expensive gifts to Zara?'

'Not really. She never liked expensive things. I did give her an iPhone though.'

'When?'

'On her last birthday. Why, what's up? Working on the case?'

'A little bit. Not much. So no jewellery?' I said.

'No, never. I only gave her tech stuff. Bluetooth speakers. Headphones. That sort of thing.'

'Thanks,' I typed back. Loser, I thought.

'Why? What happened?' he said.

'How do I respond?' I turned to Saurabh.

'Tell him her parents asked about the earrings,' Saurabh said.

'They would have just called him directly,' I said. 'Wait, I have an idea.'

I WhatsApped Raghu again.

'Her hostel friend Sanam Razdan called me. She said Zara had kept a pair of earrings with her. Which she received as a gift.'

'Oh, really?' Raghu said.

'Yeah,' I texted back, unsure if Raghu believed me.

'I didn't give them. Maybe another girlfriend?'

'They seem expensive. More than three lakh rupees.'

I took a picture of the earrings and sent it to him. He replied after two minutes.

'These are elaborate. Can't be just a friend.'

'Exactly.'

'Maybe her parents? Or a relative?'

'Maybe,' I said. 'I will give them to her parents.'

'Can you? Please?' Raghu replied.

'Of course. Thanks, anyway. When are you back?'

'I fly back later this afternoon. It's so hectic at work back home right now.'

'Didn't you just land?'

'Yeah. I only came for six hours. Have to get back. We have a new product launch tomorrow.'

'Wow. Crazy trip! Going to the US from India for a few hours.'

'I am used to it. Do such trips all the time. Anyway, I better get ready for my meeting.'

'Sure, take care.'

'Hey, Keshav,' Raghu sent a message after a few seconds.

'Yeah?'

'Thank you. I know I have judged you harshly before. But thank you. For whatever you tried to do or are doing to help.'

'I haven't done anything. I have failed so far, actually.'

'You are still trying. To be frank, I am still scared. My parents too are paranoid and keep constant tabs on me. But you are not afraid. Thanks.'

'No issues. I judged you badly, too. You are a nice guy.'

'Thanks, buddy. Cheers.'

I didn't know how to respond. I sent back two smileys in response.

'Are you going to send him a hug and a kiss too?' Saurabh said, when he saw my message.

'What?' I said, keeping my phone away.

'What is this? Lovefest between the exes?'

'Are you getting possessive? About me talking to Raghu?'

'What nonsense.'

'You are. My Golu baby, I love you man.'

'Shut up. Come to the point. If not Raghu, who gave Zara the earrings?'

I scratched my head.

'I don't know,' I said. 'What do we do now?'

'You think Saxena gave them to her?'

'Are you kidding? No IIT prof is romantic enough or rich enough to afford these,' I said.

'So who?'

'We have to figure out who was in Zara's life. In any way.'

I opened Instagram on my phone and gave it to Saurabh.

'What?' Saurabh said.

'You said we should go through her social media again. Let's do that.'

'Look for someone tall and fit like a fauji?'

'Yes, sir.' I saluted Saurabh. 'Fair and handsome too.'

'Who is more handsome than you, Keshav bhai? Right?' Saurabh said and grinned.

'Very funny. Focus. Let's go through the posts,' I said.

Saurabh opened Zara's posts one at a time.

'Okay, the last post just before she died is a picture of Raghu in the Hyderabad hospital.'

'Read the caption,' I said.

'Birthdays are no fun when your #bae is injured far away. Miss you, my Raghu,' Saurabh said.

I shook my head.

'Actually, let's look at Zara's posts from the start. Right when she joined Instagram. Otherwise, it won't make sense,' I said.

Saurabh selected the first picture from Zara's account.

'Okay,' Saurabh said. 'First post on the day she opened her account, 12 September 2013.'

'We were together then. Is it our picture?'

'It is a picture of Ruby,' Saurabh said, 'her dog.'

'Oh. Next one, please,' I said.

'A month later, a picture of her blog on Kashmir.'

'What's the blog title?'

'*Why we can never give up on peace in Kashmir*. We will have to open the blog in a new tab though. Should I?' Saurabh said.

I shook my head.

'Next post,' I said.

'Another month later. A picture of her hostel room. The caption is "The Girl in room 105. #myspace #myworld".'

'Oh, yes, I remember. She had come back from Alwar, stressed.'

'Then on 1 January 2014. It is picture of a quote. "When you lose something, don't think of it as a loss. Accept it as a gift that gets you on the path you were meant to travel on",' Saurabh said.

'Of course. We broke up the night before, remember? On New Year's Eve.'

'The next post is in April 2014. It is a picture of her at a conference. Comment is "Amazed and inspired at the Global Artificial Intelligence Conference".'

'That's where she met the bastard Raghu, I know.'

'I thought you liked the bastard now and send him smileys,' Saurabh said.

'Shut up. What's after this?'

'The next month, a picture of her and Raghu. At another conference.'

'What does the caption say?'

'"My good friend Raghu. Started his own AI company after IIT. Fortunate to be in the same college as such inspiring people".'

'Good friend, my ass,' I said.

'Bhai, it is impressive. He started his own AI company.'

I kicked Saurabh's fat butt with my foot.

'Ouch, that hurt. Okay, the next post is a picture of two pairs of feet. On a beach. The hashtag says #journeytogether.'

'Which means this is when they started doing it. Yeah, those are Zara's and Raghu's feet, probably just after sex.'

'Bhai, focus, we are trying to find something.'

'Sorry,' I said. I let out a huge breath. 'This is tough. Go on.'

'Nothing for a while. Then pictures from the Jaipur Litfest.'

'She always liked to go there. Even we went once.'

'Next post is on 9 Feb 2015.'

'Her birthday.'

'Yeah. Says, "Birthday Special. Super busy #bae plans surprise trip to Goa". Smileys, kiss emojis, hug emojis, too many exclamation marks.'

'Fools in love. Keep going.'

'The next few posts are from a family holiday in Kerala. Then a blog on the handicrafts of Kashmir. After that, pictures from another literature festival. The Bangalore Literature Festival.'

'Then?' I said.

'Okay, see this—9 Feb 2016. A picture of a gift hamper. Chocolates, wine, cookies, Bluetooth headphones. Says, "#bae surprises and spoils me again". Bhai, why does she call Raghu bae?'

'Bae is what some people call their lover.'

'Bae? Sounds rude, no?'

'Only in Hindi. Leave that, what's next?'

'15 August 2016. Another Kashmir blog picture. Independence Day special report from an Army camp in Kashmir.'

'Wait. Open the actual blog in a new tab.'

Saurabh clicked on a blog titled 'Zara's Valley Musings'. It had a background picture of snow-capped mountains.

The blog described Zara's visit to an Army camp in Baramulla district in Kashmir. She had interviewed various servicemen with the local Army commander's permission. The servicemen spoke about their daily routine and their special projects, such as rescue work and keeping the Valley safe. One of the soldiers said, 'The job is tough. But the insults and hostility from the locals, that's the hardest part.'

The blog also had a few pictures from the camp. These included a tent with the backdrop of a spectacular sunset, one of the soldiers having tea, and another of an Army officer in uniform. The officer wore Ray-Ban sunglasses and stood proudly next to an Indian flag.

'Nice blog,' Saurabh said.

'Yeah,' I said and paused. I tapped at the officer's picture. 'Saurabh, who is that?'

'Who?'

'This dude, Ray-Ban and all. He is tall, isn't he?'

'Yes, of course. Oh, is he Mr Fair and Handsome?'

'He looks familiar. I have seen him before,' I said.

'You sure?' Saurabh said.

'Yes. A hundred per cent,' I said.

'With Zara?'

'No... Yes, I saw him at Zara's funeral. Remember when Safdar uncle insulted me? This guy was standing next to Zara's father. Uncle thanked him for leaving duty and coming all the way for the funeral.' I thought hard. 'Faiz. His name is Faiz.'

'You heard his name before?'

'Yes, Zara mentioned him once. He's Captain Faiz Khan, Zara's senior from school. They are family friends.'

Saurabh zoomed in on the Army officer's picture.

'Could he have bought them?'

'Showkat Jewellers can confirm it.'

Saurabh took a screenshot of the Army officer's picture on my phone.

He then went back to Zara's Instagram.

'After the blog there are pictures from the Karachi Literature Festival,' he said.

'We already saw those,' I said.

'Nothing after that until her birthday on 9 February 2017. A picture of an iPhone 7 plus.'

'The one Raghu said he gave her,' I said. Saurabh zoomed in on the picture.

'What are you doing?'

'Nice phone. Trying to see how many GB of storage.'

'Seriously? Focus, Golu.'

'Sorry. Okay, the next one is 3 April 2017. A photo of a sunrise, taken from the window of a houseboat. The hashtag is #goingwiththeflow.'

'Strange. After that?'

'She has posted nothing for six months after that. Finally, in

November 2017, she has a picture of a quote, "Some memories last forever."'

'Zara and her love for quotes,' I said, and sighed, as her smiling face flashed in my mind, making me miss her again. I composed myself. 'After that?'

'It's New Year's Eve, 2017. She's wearing a black sari. Oh, this is the time you called her from Chandan's terrace. Remember that night's drama?'

'I do, unfortunately. Go on,' I said.

'Nothing. After that is her final post. The picture of Raghu's plaster cast.'

Saurabh returned my phone and yawned.

'It's two in the morning.'

'We have to check with Showkat about the earrings.'

'Let's hit the bed, Sherlock janaab. We'll do it when we wake up.'

❖

'It's him,' I said. I kept the phone on the dining table so Saurabh could see.

'The Army officer in the blog? What's his name?'

'Faiz. He bought the earrings. See my chat with Mohsin. I had sent him Faiz's picture on WhatsApp.'

Saurabh looked at my phone. Mohsin had replied, 'Definitely him.'

'Wow. Why is Zara's senior from school buying her such pricey earrings?' Saurabh said.

'Also, why doesn't her fiancé have any idea about it?' I said.

Saurabh and I looked at each other, confused about what do next.

'Let's try and meet Faiz,' I said.

'How?' Saurabh said.

'I will check with Safdar uncle. He will have his contacts,' I said.

Chapter 24

'I can drive you up to the camp gate. However, I have to park half a kilometre away. Army rules,' the taxi driver said. The journey from Srinagar to Baramulla had taken us two hours. We stepped out of the hired white Innova at the Baramulla Army Camp entrance. Captain Faiz, in olive-green uniform and dark Ray-Ban aviators, waited for us at the gate.

'Welcome, Keshav,' he said. He seemed taller than I remembered him from the funeral, maybe because of his army boots. He had epaulettes and several commendation badges pinned on his shirt pocket. We shook hands, or rather he crushed my hand in his.

'He's your friend who wanted to see an Army camp?' Faiz said, looking at Saurabh.

I nodded and introduced Saurabh. I had taken Faiz's number from Safdar and asked him to arrange a meeting. I mentioned Saurabh as an Indian Army fan, who wanted to see some Army facilities during his vacation in Kashmir.

Faiz took us to the visitors' lounge tent, located a few steps away from the camp entrance. Inside the tent, we sat on cane chairs, arranged in a semi-circle around a coffee-table. A Kashmiri rug covered the muddy floor.

'This is our humble abode,' Faiz said. 'From here we try to keep our country safe.'

'Thank you for that. As Keshav must have told you, I am a big admirer of the Army,' Saurabh said.

'We are honoured.' Faiz bowed a little. A jawan came in with a tray of raisins, almonds and kahwah.

'Please don't do all this. We are already imposing on you,' I said.

'Not at all. It gets boring here. Nice to have some civilian visitors.'

I had to move the topic to Zara, so, sipping my kahwah, I said casually, 'This is the same place that Zara wrote a blog about?'

'Yeah,' Faiz said. 'God bless her soul. What a bright and positive person she was.'

'You went to school with her?' I said.

'I was her senior. The Lones are family friends.'

'I saw you at the funeral. We never spoke, but you were with Zara's father when I came to speak to him.'

'Yeah, I remember you. Such a tragic day,' Faiz said. I tried to sense fakeness in his voice, but couldn't. His sunglasses hid his eyes, making it more difficult to figure him out.

I took another sip of my kahwah. I rubbed my right cheek—our pre-decided cue—and Saurabh took the signal and excused himself to go to the toilet.

'You know Zara and I used to date, right?' I said, after Saurabh left.

'Yes,' Faiz said. 'We weren't really in touch at that time.'

'When did you last meet her?' I said, my tone as non-interrogative as possible.

'Oh, I don't even remember. Over a year ago, at her house in Delhi perhaps.'

'You didn't talk to her after that? Just heard about her death?'

'Maybe a catch-up call here and there. Nothing major. Why?'

I shook my head.

'I am still in shock. Just wondering what happened,' I said.

'The watchman, right? Awful. What kind of security is this?'

'Yeah. It's terrible.'

'The security of women has become a big issue.'

I nodded.

I felt the earrings poke my thigh from inside the pocket of my trousers. Saurabh returned from the bathroom. I switched topics.

'Doesn't it get lonely here, captain?' I said.

'It does. We aren't allowed to keep our families here.'

'Where's your family?' Saurabh said.

'My wife and kids are in Dubai right now. My brother-in-law lives there.'

'Oh,' I said and sat up straight. Saurabh and I exchanged a glance.

'What?' Faiz said.

'You look too young to be married,' Saurabh said.

Faiz smiled.

'Thank you. I am thirty-one. I have twin boys, three years old.'

'I could not have guessed either,' I said.

'The Army keeps you fit.'

'So your wife lives in Dubai?' I said.

'No, she is only there with her brother for six months. After that formal school starts for the twins. Actually, the Army has given us a home in Delhi. That's where we live.'

'That's nice. The Army takes care of its people,' I said.

'Yeah, it is a small flat in Arjun Vihar. But we have the ground floor with a small garden, which is great for the little ones.'

'A garden is a luxury in Delhi,' Saurabh said.

'It is just a small green patch. However, there's a large community of families from the Armed forces around, which helps a lot. Salma gets to meet many ladies and they complain about their absentee husbands.' Faiz laughed.

'You visit Delhi often?' I said.

'I go whenever duty allows, which isn't much,' Faiz said.

'You must miss them a lot,' Saurabh said, grabbing a large handful of almonds from the plate on the coffee table.

'I miss them every day,' Faiz said and sighed. 'Every moment.'

He removed his sunglasses. His light grey eyes looked sad. He took out his mobile phone and showed us a picture of his family. His wife and two little boys stood next to the Burj Khalifa, one of the tallest buildings in the world. Each boy had an ice cream cone in his hand.

'It's tough being in the Army,' I said.

'Yeah,' Faiz said. 'It is hard. But anything for my desh.'

'You are so inspiring,' Saurabh said, finishing the last almond in his left hand while using his right to pick up a fistful of raisins. I tried to give Saurabh a dirty look for picking up so much food, but he ignored me.

'Thank you. It's just love for desh,' Faiz said.

'We should leave. We have disturbed you enough,' I said.

All of us stood up.

'No disturbance at all,' Faiz said. 'Always nice to have visitors. Especially those who value our work. Before you go, let me show you the parts of the camp that civilians are allowed into.'

We took a walk around the soldiers' tents and a firing range. After the tour, Faiz saw us out to the camp gate. He and I walked together as Saurabh went a few steps ahead of us.

'I don't have the latest news—what is happening with Zara's case?' Faiz said to me.

'Same. Laxman is in custody. Trial yet to start,' I said.

'It is him, right?' Faiz said.

'They haven't found any other suspects. So, looks like it is Laxman,' I said. I put my hands in my pocket. My fingers touched the earrings.

'Bastard, I hope they give him the death penalty,' Faiz said.

'Did Zara ever mention anything else?' I said.

The captain stiffened. For the first time in our conversation I saw discomfort. However, he recovered in seconds.

'Mention anything else, as in?' he said.

'Like, did she tell you she had any enemies? Or felt any danger?'

'Not at all,' Faiz said, his voice calm. 'She was normal. Excited about life. Why?'

'Nothing. Like I said, I am still in shock.'

'So am I. But these watchmen, I am telling you. They come from villages and are an uneducated lot. Private security guards are no Army jawans.'

'Of course,' I said.

We reached the camp gate. The driver had arrived with the car by then and Saurabh was already sitting in it.

'Did you know Sikander well?' I said to Faiz.

He put his sunglasses on again.

'Her stepbrother? No. Zara and I became friends only after she moved to Delhi.'

'She loved him a lot,' I said.

Faiz shrugged. 'She was a loving person. Did not deserve this end. Anyway, I think your driver is waiting.'

❖

'Why don't you just sit on the coals and get cooked?' I said. We had come to Shikara restaurant, a short walk from our houseboat. The restaurant had outdoor seating on jute charpoys. Every bed had an angeethi, or a portable heater, next to it. The temperature had dropped to three degrees Celsius. Saurabh sat inches away from the smouldering coals.

He did not respond. Only his teeth chattered.

'Let's go back to the houseboat,' I said. 'Their dinner is fine.'

'No, I am okay. I heard the wazwan here is amazing,' Saurabh said, blowing on his hands.

The waiter saw Saurabh's dismal state and brought us two blankets. We wrapped one each around ourselves. Ten minutes later, Saurabh had thawed enough to talk.

'Something seemed odd about the captain,' he said.

'I agree. Maybe it is because he did not mention the earrings. Otherwise, a family man, well-mannered, hospitable, polite. All nice,' I said.

'Whenever someone is so nice, it is usually fishy.'

The waiter arrived with our food. Saurabh forgot about our conversation for the next ten minutes as he focused on ripping apart sheermal and cleaning out plates of rogan josh, meth maaz and safed kokur. Wazwan is the ultimate formal banquet in Kashmir. Elaborate wazwan meals can have up to three dozen dishes, most of them slow-cooked overnight and served communal style.

'Do you want to hear my theory?' I said.

Saurabh burped in response. I took it as a yes.

'He liked Zara,' I said.

'Romantically?'

'Yes. Zara visits Kashmir. Meets Faiz. She does a blog on the Army.'

'Fine,' Saurabh said.

'Then, one scenario is Faiz had a crush on Zara, but Zara wasn't interested.'

'More likely is that she liked him back. They had an affair,' Saurabh said.

'What? How? She was with Raghu. Faiz is married.'

'As if love, or rather lust, cares about such things. Faiz is a good-looking man, bhai.'

'Zara had an affair? With a married man?' I said.

Raw pain shot through me. I thought she hadn't come back to me because she was happy with Raghu. But she did have space for another man in her life after all—just not me.

'Yes, because I think just a crush cannot create murderous passion. An affair can.'

I didn't respond, as I was still digesting the possibility that Zara could have cheated on Raghu.

'Keshav, what happened?' Saurabh shook my leg.

'Huh? Nothing. Where were we?'

'Zara had an affair with Captain Faiz. I am quite sure of this.'

'So, during the affair Faiz gave her the earrings?'

'Exactly, before things went bad.'

'How?'

'Maybe Zara wanted more and threatened to tell his wife.'

'No. Zara had Raghu. They had gotten engaged recently.'

'Fair point. So maybe Zara wanted to end it, but Faiz didn't,' Saurabh said, his hands hovering dangerously close to the angeethi coals again.

'Zara has an affair, regrets her lapse of judgment, and goes back to Raghu. Captain can't take it. Gets jealous.'

'Yeah. He sits in his Army camp, sad, lonely and angry,' Saurabh said.

'And that's when he decides to kill her.'

'Phirni, sahib? People kill for the phirni here,' the waiter said, as he arrived with dessert.

❖

'Theory is fine. How do we prove Faiz did it?' I said.

We were eating breakfast at the houseboat dining table. Saurabh took six slices of toast on his plate and buttered them lovingly, one at a time.

'We have the earrings,' Saurabh said.

'When did it become a crime to give gifts to someone? We need proper evidence. Accusing a serving Army officer is not a joke. Rana won't even touch this until we get him solid proof.'

'What do we do, bhai?' Saurabh said. After applying butter, he proceeded to apply jam on each of his toasts.

'Can you stop eating so much? What did you weigh last time? Ninety-six kilos?'

'Ninety-five-and-a-half. Anyway, breakfast is the most important meal of the day. One should eat it well,' Saurabh said, and took a bite of his toast.

'Golu, you eat every meal too well.'

'And you hardly eat,' Saurabh said, taking a bite big enough to finish off half the toast.

'I have a plan. It may help us get real evidence. Promise you won't say no.'

'Okay, what is it?' Saurabh said, as he picked up another toast.

'We need to go back to Delhi first,' I said. 'And you need to stop eating more toast.'

❖

'It's a mad plan. I will never be a part of it,' Saurabh said. We fastened our seatbelts. The flight to Delhi began to taxi on the Srinagar Airport runway.

'It is not so crazy. We can do this. Frankly, it is the only way we can get the job done, of getting the evidence,' I said.

'Speaking of jobs, we may not have one when we arrive,' Saurabh said.

We had extended our vacation to three weeks.

'You emailed Chandan about my stomach infection?' I said.

'I did. He wanted to see a medical report from a local doctor. I'll make one on a fake letterhead. Take the logo of a Srinagar clinic. Write some gibberish. What will Chandan know?'

'That's all he asked for? To extend our leave by one week?'

'He also wanted a picture of you in the hospital bed.'

'Who is he? Our hostel warden?'

The airhostess served us sandwiches. I looked out of the window. Clouds hugged the Himalayan peaks beneath us. From this height, the valley below seemed peaceful. Of course, from here, you couldn't see human beings, the cause for most troubles on the planet.

'What do we do about the hospital picture?'

'I will say I forgot to take it. Or my phone fell into the Jhelum. Or the hospital did not allow pictures. Who cares?'

'You are right. Screw Chandan.'

'Yeah, screw him,' Saurabh said, showing his middle finger. A flight attendant noticed him.

'Sorry, ma'am,' Saurabh said and folded his finger. He turned to me.

'The idea of sitting in Chandan Classes all day after this adventure makes me want to puke.'

'The adventure has not ended. We still have to go to the captain's house and get that evidence.'

'You want to raid a fauji's home and get shot?'

'It is an empty home. Arjun Vihar is like any other apartment colony in Delhi. It is not some general's residence with fifty security guards.'

'How will we get in? Break a window?'

'We have to do a recce and see.'

'There will be some security.'

'Just at the main gate. Like campus.'

'If we get caught, we get arrested. We lose our jobs. Nobody ever hires us again.'

'You are right. Huge downside. Stupid idea. Leave it,' I said.

I looked out of the plane window again. The view below had turned into flat, dry and brown land. I closed my eyes. Half an hour later, Saurabh woke me up.

'Can you borrow a power drill from the mechanical engineering department at IIT? Will your juniors on campus help you?'

'Yeah, why?'

'I can use that to drill through the lock.'

'What happened to—"if we get caught nobody will ever give us a job later"?'

'Well, nobody is giving us a job even now.'

Chapter 25

Spit was Chandan's weapon of choice; he was like a fireman with an out-of-control fire extinguisher that day. His emotions ranged between hopping mad to completely deranged.

'Two weeks. In the middle of the peak months. I allowed you. I did,' Chandan said, with blended gutkha and saliva landing everywhere within a four-feet radius of his mouth.

'I fell sick, sir. Gastroenteritis,' I said. Saurabh and I had Googled 'stomach infections' a few minutes ago.

'What is that?' Chandan said, chewing his paan extra-hard.

'Gastroenteritis, also known as infectious diarrhoea, is inflammation of the gastrointestinal tract that involves the stomach and small intestine,' I said, repeating the first line verbatim from the Wikipedia page.

Chandan looked at me, his mouth twisted in disgust.

'Symptoms may include diarrhoea, vomiting, and abdominal pain. Fever, lack of energy, and dehydration may also occur,' Saurabh said, finishing the Wikipedia description.

'You teach JEE or medical?' Chandan said.

'JEE, sir,' I said.

'So why are you talking like medical?'

'Pardon me?' I said.

'Three weeks you disappear. I am going to cut from your salary.'

Did that mean the idiot was not going to fire us? Fine, I could live with a pay-cut.

'Of course, sir,' I said. I coughed twice. When you fake sickness, you have to cough.

'I don't care about your threats. My wife is going to leave me anyway, let me tell you.'

'Sorry to hear that, sir,' Saurabh said.

'Yes, she said I am impossible to live with. I don't care. She can go.'

'Her loss entirely, of course,' I said.

'What?'

'Nothing, sir.'

'I hope you will take extra classes for the time you were absent.'

'We will, sir. We just need a few more days off,' I said.

'More days?' Chandan said, his volume so loud the classes outside could hear him.

'Medical tests, sir,' Saurabh said. 'He has recovered, but we need to do some tests.'

'You have to go back to Srinagar?' Chandan screamed.

'No, sir,' I said. 'In Delhi only. Only for a couple of days.'

'So, you go. Why does Manish have to go?'

'My name is Saurabh, sir,' Saurabh said.

Chandan looked at him with suspicion.

'Is it?'

'Yes, sir. Anyway, I will go to help him around the hospital.'

'I am still weak, sir,' I said. I coughed five times. Chandan pushed his swivel chair back, as if a few inches further from me would make him escape my germs.

❖

'Collared sports T-shirts and white cotton shorts. That's what Army officers wear in the evening,' Saurabh said.

We stood on the road, across from the guard post at the Arjun Vihar entrance. We had scanned the entire outside perimeter of Arjun Vihar, the Army colony with twenty apartment towers located near Dhaula Kuan. We observed the security checkpost at the main gate for a couple of hours. In the evening, there was a heavy flow of pedestrians in and out of the colony. If people looked like residents, the security guards let them in without any special checks. If any officers in evening sports attire walked in with confidence, the guards did not so much as even look at them. Women and children moved in and out without any trouble. Only those men who looked somewhat lost or not fauji enough were stopped and questioned at the security gate.

'Let's come back with the right clothes,' I said.

❖

Three days later, Saurabh and I arrived at the Arjun Vihar main gate again. We came from different directions, but at the exact same time in the evening. Both of us wore the same attire as other officers, a collared white T-shirt and white shorts.

'Good evening, sir, good to see you,' I said. We had decided that since Saurabh was fatter, he had to be my senior.

'What timing, young man, good to see you,' Saurabh pronounced rather strangely, in what he thought was a colonial British accent, and patted my back hard, somewhat overdoing the Army commander bit.

'I just finished my evening walk, sir,' I said.

'Come, young man, come home for a drink,' Saurabh said.

I think we overdid the drama. The guard barely noticed us anyway.

We went inside Arjun Vihar and walked to the central garden quadrangle. The residential towers encircled this public garden.

'How do we find Faiz's place?' Saurabh said.

'He mentioned ground floor,' I said.

'There are so many ground floor flats.'

'Twenty towers. Two ground floor flats in each tower. It is one of the forty apartments.'

'It will take so long to check each one. We should just ask someone,' Saurabh said.

'Avoidable,' I said. 'Let's take a walk. Read as many nameplates as we can.'

We walked along the edge of the central quadrangle. We ignored homes that had lights on. It meant people stayed there, and Faiz had told us his family was in Dubai.

'Major Yadav. Not this one,' I said.

'Captain Ahluwalia. Not this one either,' Saurabh said.

Fifteen minutes later, we passed a ground floor home in tower eight. It had no lights switched on inside. It did not have a nameplate either. However, it had a circular sign with Arabic calligraphy.

'I know what it means. God is great. Zara had a pendant like that,' I said.

'So it is a Muslim person's house,' Saurabh said.

I looked around and saw that no one was near us. We went close to the apartment entrance. I peeped into the garden. I saw a somewhat old and neglected double stroller.

'How old did he say his twins were?' I said.

'Three years old. Oh, that's a double stroller. Meant for little twins.'

'This is the place. Let's leave. We'll come back again next Sunday, the day of the T20 finals,' I said.

❖

'When does the match start?'

'Eight o'clock.'

We had entered Arjun Vihar again using the same method, with Saurabh and me meeting at the gate in sports attire. This time we had brought a backpack with us. As we still had time before the match began, we climbed up the ten storeys of tower eight and waited near the terrace landing area. We had decided to enter Faiz's house at the time of the T20 World Cup Finals, when every family in Arjun Vihar would be busy watching TV.

'One more hour,' I said.

Saurabh played a game on his phone.

'I am on level three hundred in Candy Crush,' he said.

'Candy Crush? Why? No more Tinder?' I said.

'Screw Tinder,' Saurabh said, sliding his finger on the phone as he tried to eliminate all jellies.

'Didn't you get a Tinder match last week?'

'Turned out to be a transvestite.'

'What?'

'He said I have boobs, dick and a heart. Wanna meet?'

I burst out laughing.

'Two out of three isn't bad,' I said. 'You could have adjusted.'

'Shh. Be quiet. You want the faujis to come and clobber us?' Saurabh said, eyes still on his phone screen.

An hour later, it was time.

❖

'Careful,' I whispered.

Saurabh parted the hedge so we could get into Faiz's garden. We tiptoed over the lawn. The match had begun, and the colony looked desolate. I looked around and at the apartments above me. In the darkness, I couldn't see anyone.

Saurabh sat on the grass and opened his backpack. He took out the power drill, a battery pack and three towels. He inserted the battery pack in the drill and switched on the power. The loud whirring noise from the drill made both of us jump.

'Damn,' I whispered. 'This is too noisy.'

'Wait,' Saurabh said. He switched off the power drill and wrapped the three towels around it.

We walked up to the front door, which faced the garden, and I switched on my phone's flashlight to check the lock.

'Can you do this?' I said. 'It is a doorknob lock.'

Saurabh said, 'Yeah. But once I open this, the lock will need to be replaced. He will know someone broke in, whenever he comes.'

'As long as he doesn't know who broke in,' I said. 'And, he won't be coming anytime soon.'

Saurabh used a thin drill bit attachment on the power drill and pressed against the keyhole.

'Ready?' he said. I nodded.

He switched on the drill. It whirred into action.

'It's still noisy,' I said. The towels weren't helping much.

'Shh. Just a few seconds. Wait, I felt one lock pin go.'

Saurabh switched to a thicker drill bit. He continued to drill.

'Stop, Golu. Too loud.'

'Relax,' Saurabh said, full attention on the towel-wrapped machine. 'Done. All six pins gone.'

'What?' I whispered. He placed the drill back in the backpack.

I held the doorknob in the darkness. The drilling had made the metal warm. I turned it to the right. The door opened.

'Welcome home, honey,' Saurabh said.

❖

We stepped into a dark room. Saurabh and I flashed our phone lights around. I saw some paintings of war scenes and a sofa in the drawing room, but it was too dark to see much else.

'What to do now?' Saurabh said.

'Nothing. Find a bed and sleep. We can only search in the morning. We can't switch on the lights.'

'Are you sure we can't search using our phone torches... Oww!' Saurabh screamed in pain as I heard a loud thud.

'What happened?'

'I hit a table,' Saurabh said. He hobbled and sat down on the sofa.

'Bedroom, Golu. We do nothing until morning.'

❖

Saurabh was snoring next to me. My 5 a.m. phone alarm continued to ring. I sat up on the bed and saw twilight outside. Scared someone would find us, I had not slept a wink all night.

I saw a study table with a desktop computer in the bedroom. It had a framed picture of Faiz's family. We were in the right house.

'Rise and shine, Golu.'

Over the next three hours we learnt a lot about the Khan household. They ate two brands of breakfast cereal, Chocos and plain cornflakes. They had two crates of Milkmaid condensed milk on the upper shelves of their kitchen. They used Cinthol toilet soaps for themselves, and Johnson's baby soap for the twins.

One of the two bedrooms in the house was a kids' room. It had two cribs and two closets. We checked the closets. One of them contained clothes. The other had toys kept in steel boxes. Saurabh pulled out one of them.

'So heavy,' Saurabh said.

'What's inside?' I said.

Saurabh took a peep inside.

'Spiderman, with a broken leg. Superman with a moustache drawn on it. Works as evidence?'

'Let's check the master bedroom,' I said.

❖

'This is locked,' I said, standing next to Faiz's large bedroom closet.

'As if we haven't broken locks before,' Saurabh said.

Saurabh took out a flat-head screwdriver from the backpack and inserted it between the closet doors. A few hard twists and the door snapped open.

'You are getting good at this,' I said.

'Alternative career. Maybe I should mention this skill set in LinkedIn.'

I moved forward to open Faiz's closet.

Trrring. The ringing of the doorbell made us both jump. We checked the time. It was 8:30.

'Who is it?' Saurabh whispered.

'The hell do I know,' I whispered back.

'We are fucked.'

The bell rang again.

'Let's see who it is,' I said.

We tip-toed out of the bedroom and came to the living room. We walked to the main door, Saurabh two steps behind me.

The bell rang again.

'Bhai,' Saurabh said, his voice filled with fear.

'Shh,' I said. I looked into the peephole.

'Who is it?' Saurabh mouthed.

I kept a finger on my lips.

A minute later, the person at the door left.

'He's going to the opposite house,' I said, my eye still at the peephole. The person rang the bell of the opposite house.

'What is he going to tell them?' Saurabh said.

The door of the apartment opposite opened. A maid was standing there, holding a bundle of clothes. She gave it to the person ringing the bell. The person took the clothes and left. I removed my eye from the peephole and stood up straight.

'It was the dhobi. Came to collect clothes for ironing,' I said and smiled.

'He's ironed my heart flat. I think it will explode.'

'Let's go back to the bedroom.'

I headed to Faiz's closet and opened it. One side had his wife's clothes. I rifled through them, but found nothing of relevance. The other side had Faiz's army uniforms and civilian clothes. In the bottom shelves were multiple pairs of heavy, black boots.

I took out the shoes and kept them on the bedroom floor.

'What are you doing?' Saurabh said.

'Checking the lower shelves,' I said.

Stuffed in the back, behind where the shoes had been, I found a sports bag. I dragged it out and opened it. It had two dozen tennis balls inside. I ran my hands through the bag. I touched something cold and rectangular. I pulled it out.

'Wow,' Saurabh said out loud. I was holding a hundred-gram gold biscuit in my hand.

'Is this real?' I said.

'Yes, bhai. Are there more?'

I turned the bag upside down. The tennis balls bounced and rolled across the room. Nine more biscuits fell out.

'This is one kilo of gold,' I said. 'Worth what? Thirty lakh rupees.'

'Army guys are paid that well?' Saurabh said.

'No, Golu. This is screwed up,' I said. The gold glittered in the early morning light.

'Did you say the box of toys felt heavy?' I said.

'Yeah. Why?'

We ran across to the children's room. Under the Spiderman, Superman and other figurines, we found twenty more biscuits, neatly arranged at the bottom. Of course, the biscuits were not Parle-G.

'Everything for desh,' I said.

'This is messed up. Is he possibly doing wrong things?' Saurabh said.

'He's possibly a fucking murderer. Golu, let's check his computer.'

❖

As Saurabh switched on Faiz's PC, I noticed the four drawers of the study table.

'We need to check these too,' I said.

'He has a machine from the 1800s. Taking forever to boot up,' Saurabh said, eyes on the computer monitor. 'I am going to hack this old horse good.'

I rummaged through the drawers. The bottom three had nothing apart from stationery and other household items like measuring tapes and charging cables. The top drawer was locked.

'This needs a key,' I said.

'Key?' Saurabh smiled cockily. 'What's that?'

He pointed at the drill. Two minutes later, the top drawer was open.

'Medicines here. A bit of cash,' I said, fingering the contents. 'And these are ... wow ... so many pregnancy kits.'

'What?' Saurabh said.

I took out three packets of Prega News. Saurabh took one from me and opened it. It had a plastic strip with a clear rectangular window in the middle.

'What exactly do you do with this?' Saurabh said.

'You pee on it.'

'Faiz does?'

'Are you stupid, Golu? The woman does. If two lines appear, it means she is pregnant.'

'This could belong to Faiz's wife,' Saurabh said, pointing to the family picture. 'Maybe they want a third child?'

I examined the Prega News box. On one side, it had a small white sticker. The sticker had a barcode and text that had 'PregKit. INR 50' printed on it.

'Golu, you have pictures from Zara's safe?'

'Yeah, I do,' Saurabh said, typing on the computer keyboard. 'By the way, this idiot doesn't even have a password on his computer. No hacking required. What a let-down.'

'You could get in?'

'Here you go. This is the desktop,' Saurabh said, slapping his hand on the computer mouse.

'But can you show me the pictures from the safe first.'

Saurabh passed me his phone. I opened the pictures of the pregnancy kits in Zara's safe.

I zoomed in.

'This is the same chemist tag as the kits here,' I said.

Saurabh compared the picture with the Prega News packet.

'Oh, yes.'

'They were bought at the same place,' I said.

'Faiz bought many of them. Gave some to Zara. The affair is confirmed. Earrings explained too.'

'Zara was pregnant? With Faiz's child?' I said.

Shell-shocked, I sat on the bed, staring at the ceiling above me.

'Likely. But what happened? Did he make her abort? Was she pregnant when she died?'

I covered both my ears with my hands.

'Are you okay, bhai?'

'This is fucked up. I never imagined Zara could do this. Idiot me, thinking she's some perfect soul of this universe while she goes and fucking…'

'Shh. It happens, bhai.'

'She told me, "I am happy with Raghu. Leave me alone". I thought that is why she wasn't coming back.'

I stood up. I lifted Faiz's family picture and smashed it on the wall in front of me. The glass frame shattered in hundreds of pieces.

'Bhai, control yourself. If people hear us, we are dead.'

'I'm already dead. Let's leave.'

'Can I at least finish checking his computer?' Saurabh said.

'Whatever,' I said.

'Meanwhile, pack up the biscuits. Let's take anything that could help as evidence to nail this guy.'

'Fine,' I said. I worked on autopilot as I transferred the gold biscuits into the backpack.

I don't know what upset me more, Faiz killing Zara, or Faiz making her pregnant.

'Nothing here on the computer. I only have the captain's browser history.'

'We need evidence, Saurabh. I don't want the police saying we don't have enough.'

'He likes porn. Pornhub features a lot. I like that one too. He likes them white and young.'

'Shut up and tell me something useful.'

'Calm down, bhai. So he Google-searched "best divorce lawyers in Delhi".'

'Clearly, the perfect Khan family isn't perfect,' I said.

Saurabh continued to talk as he scrolled through the history. 'Usual online shopping sites, and damn, many searches and clicks on abortion clinics in Delhi.'

'What?'

'Yeah. In December 2017. Two months before Zara's death. The idiot never deletes his browser history.'

'Let's take his computer too.'

'No need. I took the browser history on my pen drive,' Saurabh said, showing me a memory stick.

'Good. Anything else?'

'I found some pictures on the computer. Backup from a phone,' Saurabh said.

Saurabh opened a library of photos. Most were pictures of the Baramulla camp in Kashmir. In many, Faiz posed with his Army colleagues. Thirty pictures later, we saw a selfie of Faiz and Zara. They stood in a houseboat, probably in Srinagar, his arm around her. They stared at the camera like lovers who had just woken up from a nap. The next picture showed a sunset, taken from a houseboat window.

'Need more evidence?' Saurabh said, clapping his hands.

'This sunset picture is the same one Zara posted on Insta,' I said.

'Fine then, we take the pictures too,' Saurabh said. He plugged in the pen drive into Faiz's computer and sucked out everything. Once done, Saurabh shut the computer down.

'Let's go,' I said. 'We have classes to take.'

'Wait, just one more thing, bhai.'

'What?'

'You think I can eat some of their Chocos before we leave?'

Chapter 26

Chandan met us at the entrance of Chandan Classes. Saurabh and I had reached late and missed half of our first class.

'Pneumonia today?' he said, his eyes bulging.

'No, sir,' I said. 'The alarm didn't ring. Both of us overslept.'

'What about the students waiting in class?'

'Sorry, sir. We'll fix a remedial session,' Saurabh said.

Chandan looked ready to explode.

'Should we commit a murder too?' Saurabh said, as we ran past Chandan.

'I am hoping the gutkha will do the job before us,' I said.

Later in the day, Saurabh and I met in an empty staffroom for a few minutes between classes.

'Bhai, let's give everything we found at Faiz's house to Rana soon. I don't want to keep it at home,' Saurabh said.

'We will go this evening,' I said.

My phone buzzed. I looked around to ensure Chandan wasn't lurking around.

'Oh no! Saurabh, see…'

On my phone screen was flashing: 'Capt. Faiz.'

'What the…' Saurabh said.

My hand trembled.

'What do I do?' I said.

'Did he find out about us breaking into his house?' Saurabh said.

The phone continued to vibrate in my hands.

'How do I know?' I said.

'Pick it up. Act normal,' Saurabh said.

'Good afternoon, Captain Faiz,' I said as I took the call. Saurabh kept his ear close to the phone so he could listen as well.

'Good afternoon, Keshav. What's up? How is the capital treating you?' Faiz said, his voice cheerful.

'Fine, sir. I am at work. Delhi's too hot. I miss Srinagar.'

'Oh, you must be busy. I won't take much of your time. I called because I remembered something.'

'What, sir?'

'I gave these really special Kashmiri earrings to Zara.'

Saurabh and I looked at each other, surprised.

'Oh,' I said. 'Special, as in?'

'They are traditional Kashmiri earrings. They cost a few lakhs. Zara said she would pay for them, of course.'

'She paid you?'

'I told her to pay me when she completes her PhD and starts working. She did give me fifty thousand though. The rest I said I would take when she has a proper job.'

'Oh,' I said.

'Yeah. She had always wanted these traditional earrings from an authentic Srinagar jeweller. I offered to help.'

'Sure. Thanks for calling and telling me. Don't think it is important, but still, thanks.'

'Cool. Anyway, keep in touch. Say hi to your friend Saurabh too.'

'Sure.'

'Bye then. Jai Hind.'

The call ended. I looked at Saurabh. He said, 'See, how clever he is.'

'Must have figured we had come to investigate. Or that we might find the earrings,' I said.

'Yeah, so better give an explanation beforehand.'

We sat in silence for a few seconds.

'You think he could buy Rana?' Saurabh said.

'What?' I said.

'We give all the evidence to Rana. Faiz calls him, promises more gold biscuits from wherever he gets them. Rana agrees to keep Laxman in, which he prefers anyway.'

'You think Rana can be bought?'

Saurabh looked at me like I had asked him if petrol could catch fire.

'Fine,' I said. 'Let's not go to Rana yet.'

'We can't take that chance,' Saurabh said.

I walked up and down the staffroom as I thought of what to do next.

'We need to confront Faiz in Delhi, in front of others. So he can neither bribe anyone nor escape,' I said.

'How?'

'I have an idea,' I said.

'What is it?'

'Let's discuss at home,' I said and checked the time. 'I have to teach differential equations right now.'

'Sure. By the way, bhai,' Saurabh said and paused.

'What?' I said.

'Just an idea, so be open minded. Should we sell one of the gold biscuits and buy a new air-conditioner for the house?'

❖

Safdar, deep in thought, stroked his beard. Saurabh and I sat with him in his tastefully decorated drawing room. We had just told him about the events in Srinagar.

'Sikander is dead? Really?' he said, a hand still on his freshly dyed beard.

'Yeah,' I said.

Safdar spread his palms out and said a prayer.

'Ya Allah,' Safdar said. 'Both Farzana and I have lost our children at the same time.'

Saurabh and I kept quiet.

'That boy never followed the right path. I used to tell Zara so many times. How is Farzana doing?' Safdar said.

'We are not sure. She's still in Srinagar,' I said.

'He might have been a terrorist, but Farzana's pain won't be any less.'

'Of course,' I said.

'So, Sikander didn't have anything to do with Zara's murder?' Safdar said.

'No,' I said. 'As I told you, it is Faiz.'

Safdar shook his head. 'Captain Faiz? Faiz's father Abdul Khan and I have known each other for fifteen years. They are close family friends.'

'That's how he managed to get close to Zara. But later, when Zara realised her lapse of judgment, Faiz couldn't take it,' I said.

'Faiz is married. He has kids, who I treat as my grandkids.'

'We broke into his house in Delhi, to get the evidence,' Saurabh said. 'We have pictures of them in a houseboat. Pregnancy kits from the same shop.'

'Enough,' Safdar barked. Restlessly he stood up and walked across the room to his bookshelves. His back to us, he spoke again.

'That qaatil! I treated him like a son,' Safdar said, his words throbbing with anger. 'We attended his wedding. How could he touch my little girl?'

Saurabh and I didn't know what to say.

'He's a fauji and doing this? What makes him any different from those terrorists?'

'We will get him punished, uncle,' Saurabh said.

'Will it bring my daughter back?' said Safdar in a broken voice.

A tear rolled down his cheek. He came back to sit with us again and buried his face in his hands.

'No, uncle, Zara won't come back,' I said. 'But her soul may find peace if her killer is punished. Right now he roams free, as a decorated officer.'

Safdar removed his hands from his face.

'What do you want me to do?'

'Organise a prayer meet at your house. Call everyone who was close to Zara,' I said.

'Why a prayer meet?'

'If we give the evidence to Rana now, we are afraid he could sell out. We want to confront Faiz in front of others, and then call the police,' Saurabh said.

'How do we do that?'

'After the prayer meet, invite some of us to stay for dinner. Get us in a room with Faiz,' I said.

'What do we do then?' Safdar said.

'We confront him over dinner,' Saurabh said.

'And then the police can come and serve him dessert,' I said.

❖

'Scared?' Saurabh said, looking up from his phone.

Saurabh and I were sitting on my bed. I was typing out a probability test paper on my laptop, which I had to conduct in class next week.

I folded the laptop screen shut.

'No. Just anxious.'

We had five days left for the prayer meet. Safdar had sent a sombre white invitation card. I picked it up from the bedside table.

It will soon be a hundred days since she left us.
But we miss her every day, every moment.
As someone important in our daughter Zara Lone's life,
we invite you to a hundredth-day prayer meet
at our residence:
238, Westend Greens
On 20 May 2018, 5:00 p.m.
Warm regards,
Zainab and Safdar Lone

'Faiz will buy it? Is there even something like a hundredth-day prayer meet?' I said.

'There are no rules for grieving. It's from her parents. Reads genuine. It's fine,' Saurabh said and went back to his phone. He was reading an article titled, 'How to hack Tinder for better matches'.

'You really think you can hack the matching algorithm on Tinder?'

'What if I could? Imagine. Every girl, no matter if she swiped left or right, would match with me.'

'And when they see your real picture, won't they figure out they swiped left on you earlier?'

'They may reconsider me, too. You have to get them into the shop and display the goods. Maybe they will buy.'

'You are the goods?' I said and laughed.

'When I get a hot babe in my arms, then you laugh. Okay?'

'I am teasing you,' I said and pulled both of Saurabh's cheeks. 'You are the best goods any girl can get.'

'Yeah, yeah, make fun of me. I also know I won't get any girl. Tinder or otherwise.'

'What nonsense.'

'Thank God for arranged marriages in India. If not Tinder, my parents will find someone. Indian parents have been the original left and right swipers for their kids for centuries.'

I laughed.

'Anyway, you heard the news about Mr Richie Rich? Did you call him, by the way?'

Saurabh was referring to Raghu. I had seen the news pop up on my Facebook feed: the world's biggest artificial intelligence firm had invested in Raghu's company. They had valued Raghu's company at three hundred million dollars.

'Richie Rich owns half, while his investors own the rest, so he's worth a hundred and fifty million dollars. That is a thousand crores in rupees,' Saurabh said.

'Fuck me,' I said.

'Yeah. Thousand crores. FYI, he's our age. Twenty-seven.'

'We are from the same college, same batch. He and I even dated the same girl. He's worth so much and I have nothing. Can I be a bigger loser?'

'Bhai, if he invests the thousand crores at ten per cent interest, he makes another hundred crores a year.'

'Thanks, Saurabh. That makes me feel better.'

'And that hundred crores interest alone can be invested again to make another ten. And that ten can be invested too,' Saurabh said.

'Will you stop it?'

'Bhai, we make less than the interest on the interest on the interest of what he already has.'

'Thanks for comforting me, Golu.'

'Are you going to call him? You said we need to tell him about Faiz.'

'I have to congratulate him on his company's latest valuation too?'

'Screw that. You have to call to tell him it is important for all of us to be there at the prayer meet. You know this. You said you will call him last week.'

I took out my phone.

'Yeah but, how do I say it all?' I said. 'That his fiancée had an affair, her other lover made her pregnant, etc.'

'I thought you wanted revenge. He took Zara from you. Tell him she was never really his.'

I shook my head.

'Doesn't feel right. That desire to hurt him has gone.'

'Okay, spare him the details. Tell him we found the killer. Ask him to show up at the prayer meet. We will share the rest there.'

'He'll ask who, of course.'

'Tell him it is Faiz, then. For God's sake, are you going to call or should I?'

Saurabh tried to snatch my phone. I pulled my hand away.

I put the phone on speaker mode and called Raghu.

'Hey, Keshav. Long time,' Raghu said.

'Hi, Raghu, are you in India?'

'Yeah, I am in office. What's up?'

I checked the time. It was 10:30 p.m.

'Working so late?'

'Have to. I have a new investor. We are merging some groups. So, bit of an insane month.'

Damn, should I congratulate him now, I wondered. I decided not to; I would stick to the agenda.

'We will see each other at the prayer meet, I guess,' I said.

'I am trying to come. Just that all these new investors are on my head. Oh wait, her dad invited you as well?' Raghu said, surprised. He was right to be surprised. Safdar hated me. I had no business being there.

'Yes. It's part of a plan. Raghu, we cracked the case.'

'You did?'

'Yes, we found the killer.'

'How? I mean who?'

'You have heard of Captain Faiz?'

'Yeah, the Army officer. Solid guy. Zara's family friend. He helped you?'

'No, Raghu. Captain Faiz did it. He is the killer.'

'What?' Raghu said and went silent.

'Raghu?' I said, thinking the line had got cut.

'I am here,' he said, his voice unclear. 'Are you sure? Faiz?'

'Yes.'

'Why?'

'He liked her,' I said.

'What?'

'They had an affair.'

'What are you saying? He is married. He has kids!'

'I know. They still got involved.'

I tried to be as gentle as possible, using softer words like 'involved'. But I guess any man in Raghu's situation would only hear it as 'someone else fucked your girlfriend'.

'Raghu?' I said, when I heard nothing for a while. 'You there?'

'You have evidence?'

'Solid evidence.'

'Fucking bastard.'

I think a comet must have crossed over Earth. It was the first time I had heard Raghu swear.

'Don't go to the stupid police,' Raghu said. 'I called Rana a few days ago.'

'You did?'

'To check on the case. I call him every now and then. However, he seemed to be happy pursuing the watchman theory and keeping Laxman in.'

'Yes. It suits him.'

'Rana will botch it up. And Faiz is in the Army. He will manage to slime out.'

'Thank you, that's exactly what I thought. Hence, the prayer meet,' I said.

Even though I didn't like to admit it, I felt good that someone as smart as Raghu was thinking along the same lines as me.

'Does he have any idea you know?' Raghu said.

'No.'

'Good. Now I will definitely come for the prayer meet. On the 20th, no?'

'Yeah.'

'I will be there for sure.'

'I will see you then,' I said and then took a deep breath. 'Also, Raghu.'

'Yeah?'

'Congrats. I read the news about the new investor and the latest valuation.'

'Oh, that. Thanks,' Raghu said.

'Anyway, see you in five days,' I said.

'Sure. Keshav?'

'Yes.'

'Thank you.'

'Welcome, Raghu.'

'I don't know how I will ever repay you.'

Saurabh gestured that he wanted to speak to me.

'One second, Raghu.' I muted the phone.

'What?' I said to Saurabh.

'Of course he can repay us. He's worth a thousand crores. Maybe he can give us—' Saurabh said.

'Shut up,' I said and unmuted the phone. 'Yes, Raghu. Sorry, you were saying something.'

'Nothing. Just that I can never repay you. And I hope they hang him. Or lock him up for life.'

'They will,' I said.

'I miss her every minute,' Raghu said.

Okay, I do not need to hear this, I wanted to say, but didn't.

'I had told her, let's leave India. Leave this mess behind. I just…' Raghu said and completely broke down. I could hear him sob.

'I understand how you feel, Raghu.'

Damn, was it my duty to console guys who dated my ex?

He wasn't done yet. 'I wanted to give her everything. All these achievements and congratulations. They mean nothing. Life is quite incomplete without her.'

'He can give us the money if it means nothing to him,' Saurabh whispered in my ear.

I kicked Saurabh's behind to make him shut up. I had to remain sombre when talking to a person who was in tears.

'It's nothing. All this money. Pointless,' Raghu was saying. I realised Raghu could afford a shrink if he needed a shoulder to cry on. It did not have to be me.

'I can imagine. Raghu, I have someone at the door. I will see you in Delhi?'

'Yes, sure. Sorry to take your time. Thank you so, so much again.'

I ended the call and threw a pillow at Saurabh's head.

'Fucker, is this a time to joke?' I said.

Saurabh laughed.

'You handled it well.'

'Did I?'

'Yes. You told him and yet didn't rub it in,' Saurabh said and lay down on the bed.

I kept my phone and laptop aside.

'Golu, go to your room and sleep,' I said.

'Too lazy to move, bhai. Goodnight,' Saurabh said and switched off the bedside lamp.

I lay in bed, my eyes still open. I could hear nothing but Saurabh's mild snores and the rhythmic whirr of the fan above me. I reflected on my conversation with Raghu. Had I really grown up? I didn't feel jealous of his success. Nor did I enjoy seeing him hurt about his fiancée's affair. I didn't make any taunts or jibes. He seemed to be in so much pain that a thousand crores meant nothing to him. He said he found life quite incomplete without her...

My last phone conversation with Raghu resonated in my head as I continued to stare at the ceiling fan go round and round and round above me.

Half an hour later, I switched on the bedside lamp.

'What happened?' Saurabh said in a sleepy voice.

'I can't sleep. I need to go somewhere,' I said.

'Huh?' Saurabh said, rubbing his eyes.

'You want to come on a trip?'

'What?' Saurabh said groggily.

'Let's get away until the prayer meet. It will help us deal with the anxiety.'

'What? Where? What about classes?'

'I don't care.'

'I can't travel, bhai. I am way behind on my course schedule. Chandan won't just fire me, he will kill me.'

'Fine. I am going away for a few days,' I said. I jumped out of bed and switched on the lights. I opened my cupboard and pulled out a suitcase to pack my clothes.

'Where?' Saurabh said, sitting up on the bed and scratching his head.

'I will tell you later. You sleep now. And take care of Chandan for me, please.'

Prologue continued

On board IndiGo flight 6E766 HYD–DEL

'That is some story,' I said.

Keshav grinned.

'Glad you found it interesting.'

'But you are a dude, Keshav. You actually went to Srinagar and did all this?'

'Yeah, Saurabh came with me, and that helped a lot. But not bad for two mediocre coaching-class faculty types, I guess,' Keshav said.

'It is incredible. What happened next? You went to the prayer meet?'

'It's tomorrow. I mean today, as it is past midnight already.'

'What? You just said you told Saurabh you were leaving the city for a break.'

'That was four days ago. I did go for my break. I am returning home now.'

I checked the date and time on my watch. It was 1:05 a.m. on May 20th.

'Oh. Where did you go?' I said.

'Several places. To calm my mind. Clear doubts. Figure things out.'

I took a guess since the flight was heading back from Telangana.

'Tirupati, or something?' I said.

Keshav smiled.

'I went wherever I had to,' he said.

I understood he didn't want to tell me more.

'Ladies and gentlemen, we will soon begin our descent into Delhi,' the flight attendant announced. 'Please fasten your seatbelts.'

The aircraft descended and we could see Delhi's smog-covered nightlights.

Within minutes, the plane landed with a mild thud and taxied to a halt.

'Thanks for listening to me,' he said.

'My pleasure. So, you are going to nail him today. Send Zara's killer to jail.'

'I hope so.'

'Of course you will.'

'Thank you.'

'Will you tell me what happened at the prayer meet later?' I said.

'Why?'

'Well, I want to hear the complete story.'

'The one you said, "Oh no, not again" to.'

'I already apologised for saying that,' I said sheepishly.

The moment the seatbelt sign was switched off, passengers got up and began elbowing and jostling their way down the aisle. Everyone behaved as if they all had some emergency, like their homes had caught fire, and they had to get out of the plane five seconds before the others.

'I will call you, to complete the story,' Keshav said and smiled.

We shook hands and exchanged numbers. As we left the plane, his phone rang.

'Yes, Rana sir. Okay, that footage is fine,' he said. We waved goodbye to each other while he remained busy with the call and took brisk steps to walk ahead and away from me.

❖

I reached my room at Andaz Hotel in Aerocity, less than ten minutes away from Westend Greens. I tried to sleep, but couldn't. In a few hours from now, a prayer meet would take place. Minutes away from me, a killer Army officer would be nabbed.

I tossed and turned in bed for the nth time, and then finally picked up my phone. I sent a message to Keshav.

'Best of luck for this evening, buddy.'

Chapter 27

'Dear friends, we are gathered here to find peace. Peace to accept what happened. Peace for me, despite the fact that I miss my daughter every single moment. Peace to not feel so angry and keep asking why. Peace to trust God's will,' Safdar said, addressing everyone at the prayer meet.

People were sitting in a semi-circle on the floor, men and women separately, facing a collage of black and white pictures of Zara. Around forty guests, all dressed in pastels, had come. Most of them were Zara's uncles and aunts, who sat with Zainab and Safdar's aged and ailing mother on the floor.

Raghu sat three places to my left, while Saurabh was sitting right next to me. I recognised several of Zara's hostel friends in the crowd as well.

Sanam, Zara's friend from Himadri, spoke after Safdar.

'Room 105 is still hers. It feels like Zara is going to walk out of it at any moment. I look for her in the lawns outside Himadri, where she used to sit with her books and study,' Sanam said emotionally.

I checked the time—5:30 p.m. Faiz had not arrived yet. Safdar had personally called the captain, apart from sending him the card. Faiz had confirmed his attendance as well. As per my instructions, Safdar had sent a car to pick Faiz up from the airport. We didn't want him to go to his Arjun Vihar home first and see the wreckage.

'Westend Greens is right next to the airport. You come straight to our house. Why go home when Salma and the kids are in Dubai?' Safdar had told Faiz on the phone.

I checked the Srinagar–Delhi flight status on my phone. Faiz's flight had already landed.

'What if he doesn't come?' Saurabh whispered in my ear.

I nodded at him in a pacifying manner.

After Sanam, Safdar invited Raghu to speak. As Raghu stood up to address us, I saw a Toyota Fortuner drive onto the lawns. Faiz was here.

Saurabh gave an audible sigh of relief as Faiz removed his shoes and entered the room. He folded his hands to greet Safdar and his family from a distance.

'What can I say?' Raghu said and paused. He adjusted his spectacles when he noticed Faiz enter the room. Faiz smiled at Raghu, who gave a brief nod in response. Raghu began his speech.

'I wanted to say that if there is anyone who has felt her loss the most, it is me. When you plan the rest of your life with someone, and then that someone is gone forever, what do you do with the rest of your life?'

Faiz took a seat in the corner of the men's section. As Raghu continued speaking, Faiz pulled out his phone to check messages.

'I am shattered. I try to cope. I work so much because I want no time to think. But I know I am not alone in this suffering. All of you here, Zara's parents, her grandmother, her friends... How can I say my pain is the most? All of you have endured this loss and still continue to feel the pain. We will never be the same again.'

Faiz was still glued to his phone. Raghu paused as he fought back tears. One of Zara's young cousins gave him a glass of water. Raghu took a sip and continued. 'In my whole life, I haven't met anyone as kind, as positive, as generous, as compassionate and as loving as Zara. She is the best thing that ever happened to me. It is she who encouraged me to do whatever I have done in life. I don't think I will ever feel the way I did with her again. Wherever she is, I want to tell her—I am grateful to you. For all the memories and all the positive things I learnt from you. May God bless your soul.'

Raghu finished his speech. He continued to stand, eyes closed, overcome with grief. Sanam walked up to him, placed her arm around his shoulder and walked him back slowly to his seat.

After a few more relatives had spoken, a maulvi recited a prayer, signalling the end of the prayer meet. People came forward to individually offer their condolences to Safdar before they left.

❖

At 7 p.m., a handful of people remained. Faiz came to hug Safdar.

'Uncle, I will take your leave too,' Faiz said.

'No, no, no! You have come all the way. Have dinner and go,' Safdar said.

'Uncle, I told you. Our annual military exercises are on. My senior officer gave me leave for only one day. That too on compassionate grounds.'

'Yeah, but your flight is tomorrow…'

'Yes, but I haven't even gone home and my senior officer is messaging me nonstop,' Faiz said.

Safdar looked hurt. 'Is this not home? Let me feel I can still have dinner with my children.' He turned to Raghu. 'Raghu, please, you also stay for dinner.'

'Of course, uncle,' Raghu said politely.

'Keshav, Saurabh, you too. Sanam, please ask your friends to stay and eat. You girls give Zainab company over dinner.'

Sanam nodded.

'Boys, come, we will all have a meal together,' Safdar said.

❖

Safdar Lone's dining room impressed me every time I entered it. The ornate, eighteen-seater table had only five guests tonight. Safdar sat at his usual seat at the head of the table. Raghu and Faiz sat on his left, while Saurabh and I took the chairs on his right.

I kept my phone in my lap. I typed a message to Inspector Rana.

'Are you ready?'

'Of course. Now will you tell me what this is about?' he replied. I had told Rana to be on standby for something urgent.

'How far are you from Westend Greens?' I messaged back.

'I am in Hauz Khas. Maybe forty minutes.'

'Okay. You can start now. 238 Westend Greens.'

'This is that girl Zara's parents' place?'

'Yes. Come with a few men. I will give you her killer. With evidence.'

'What? Who? How? You sure?' he replied.

'Come and get all your questions answered.'

I looked up from the phone. Safdar smiled at me.

'This generation is so addicted to their phones. Even Zara was like that.'

'Sorry, uncle,' I said. 'My mother just wanted to know if I had eaten.'

'Nobody can love you like your parents,' Safdar said.

Two servers came into the dining room, each with a tray full of food. They placed the dishes—yellow daal, phulkas, gobi aloo, chicken soup and a raita—on the table. In keeping with the sombre occasion, the Lone family had arranged a simple meal compared to the typical feasts served at their residence. The servers ladled out individual portions of the dishes on our plates.

'I too joined Facebook last year. Now they say you should be on Instantgram,' Safdar said.

'Instagram,' Saurabh said.

'Yes, that one. It is so confusing. Anything else I should be on?' Safdar said.

'Saurabh has a favourite app,' I said. 'Helps him make new friends.'

'Which one?' Safdar said.

'Nothing,' Saurabh said, kicking me under the table.

'Apps rule the world now,' Raghu said. 'By the way, Facebook owns Instagram.'

'Does it?' Safdar said, surprised.

'Yes, WhatsApp too,' Raghu said. He ate rice and daal with his hands, just as he used to in the hostel.

'I love WhatsApp,' Faiz said. 'Helps me stay in touch with people so far away.'

The domestic help had finished serving the food.

'Shut the doors when you leave,' Safdar said to them.

Faiz looked at Safdar, somewhat taken aback but still smiling.

'Sorry, I thought we might discuss Zara's case,' Safdar said. 'Didn't want anyone else to hear.'

Faiz nodded as he tore his chapati and dipped it in the daal.

'That watchman's trial will start soon?' Faiz said.

'The watchman didn't do it,' Safdar said in a cool voice.

'He didn't?' Faiz said, his chapati morsel stopped mid-way to his mouth.

'No,' I said. I kept my fork and knife on the table.

'You are sure? It isn't Laxman, the watchman? The police said he did it on TV,' Faiz said.

'I am sure,' I said. 'In fact, I even know who the killer is.'

All eyes turned to Faiz. The hand that held the chapati trembled.

'Why is everyone looking at me like this?' Faiz said.

'Gaddaar. I treated you like a son,' Safdar said.

'What are you saying, uncle?' Faiz said.

Safdar pressed his temple with his hand.

He said, 'Continue, Keshav.'

'Captain Faiz Khan,' I said. 'Please stand up.'

'Huh?' Faiz said, hesitant at first. Safdar glared at him and Faiz stood up.

'I need your help.'

'What?' Faiz said.

'I will need your strength. In case the killer tries to escape.'

Saurabh, Raghu and Safdar looked baffled.

'You said—' Safdar began, but I interrupted him.

'Uncle, I have said enough. It is time the killer tells us the truth himself.'

Everyone at the table looked at each other, confused.

'All I can say is this. 6E766. 8th February 2018,' I said.

'What are you saying, bhai? This is not what—' Saurabh said.

'One minute, Saurabh,' I said. 'I have airport CCTV footage. Own up or…'

There was a creaking sound as Raghu pushed back his chair and stood up.

'I need to use the restroom, I'll be right back,' Raghu said.

'Captain Faiz,' I said. I rolled my eyes towards Raghu. The military commando understood the message in an instant. He jumped up from his seat at lightning speed and grabbed Raghu from behind with his strong arms.

'You are not going anywhere,' Faiz said, his strong biceps bulging.

'Hey, I just want to use the toilet,' Raghu said, adjusting his spectacles with his free arm.

'No, you don't. Sit down, Raghu, and tell everyone what happened,' I said.

Faiz released Raghu. Raghu sat down again.

'What happened?' Safdar said.

'Bhai. What?' Saurabh said and looked at me.

'He was in Hyderabad!' Safdar exclaimed.

I turned to Raghu.

'Can you please end their confusion?' I said.

Chapter 28

Raghu speaks

I know this—whatever I say here, you will judge me as the bad guy. I am the villain of the story, and now you know it. I don't expect your sympathy. After all, I did kill her. A vegetarian, Tamil Brahmin boy nicknamed 'Bhondu' actually murdered someone. I almost got away with it, though. With so many Muslim suspects around, nobody even considers the Tam Brahm. Prejudices, I tell you, can be used wonderfully sometimes.

I did it with my bare hands. I still remember the night. She had fallen asleep. It is easier to do this to a person who is asleep. You get a head start in cutting off their oxygen supply. As they are asleep, they don't even realise what is happening for thirty seconds. After that, they wake up. They try to understand what is going on and panic. Panic makes it worse for them. Panic means they will thrash their hands and limbs around, wasting energy and whatever little oxygen they have. Zara panicked too. Her bird-like body fought my grip, my right hand around her neck. Her oxygen-deprived lungs became weaker by the second. Every time she tried to kick me, I gripped her neck tighter. She tried to hit my fractured left arm too. It didn't make any difference.

I remember checking the time on my watch. One minute and ten seconds had elapsed. If time flies when you are having fun, it crawls when you are strangling someone. I had read several articles on how to do this on the internet. They said it could take up to seven minutes for a person to die. Seven minutes is four hundred and twenty seconds.

'Okay, stop shaking so much, Zara, it's scaring me,' I remember telling her.

She should have conserved her energy. Instead of fighting, she should have tightened her neck muscles so her windpipe and carotid arteries wouldn't be constricted as much. Of course, she didn't know all this. My poor beautiful Zara may have been much better looking than me, but she was not as smart.

I am an introvert. I think, feel and say things in my head, even though I may not express them verbally. I remember I had a full mental conversation with her in those final minutes as she gasped for air.

Sorry, Zara, I didn't bring a cake. I just couldn't carry so much with me. I had to climb that damn tree to come into your room. You and your ex may find such Neanderthal stuff romantic. I think it is idiotic. I did it though, see. I didn't want you to feel I am any less of a man. It doesn't matter that I run my own company with a hundred people. That I can give you what almost no guy in this world can. I even gave you a stake in my company. But until I climb a tree to get into your room, I am still a scared bhondu who is not a man. But look now, not bad for a bhondu, no?

I built triceps and biceps for a month for this. I had to practice climbing a tree using just one arm, so I could do it today, with the other one broken. Maybe that is why my grip is working so well. You are protesting less now. Your lungs have realised it. No matter how hard they try, there is no oxygen to be found. Like a fish out of water. Your body trembles for a few moments, then gives up. You like eating fish, don't you, Zara? And other animals? This is how they feel before they die. This is why I am a vegetarian. Not because I am a wimp.

I didn't want to kill you. You know I am not the type. I hate arguments, let alone violence. Remember how Keshav would call? He would try to provoke me. I never took the bait. Neither am I a person who will do something on an impulse. It is not like my mind is filled with jealousy and rage. No, it is not that at all. Acting on impulse is for fools. I, Raghu Venkatesh, am not a fool. I may be ugly, nerdy, black as a tawa, a chashmish, a father to potentially ugly kids (not my words) or a scared bhondu. But I am not an idiot. I have researched and planned this for weeks. As per my plan, the police or whichever moron tries to find your killer will go around in circles forever. Oh, and I know the perfect moron who will obsess about solving this and die of frustration. Zara, you have to be proud of me for this one. I almost wish I could release you right now. I want to tell you about my brilliant plan. I want you to be impressed by my intelligence. I want to hear your praise. Okay, two minutes to go.

You've stopped moving. That's a good sign. Of course, you may not be dead yet, only unconscious. I don't know what worked first. I am pressing your carotid arteries, which will stop blood supply to the brain. However, I am also choking your windpipe. So your lungs don't have any oxygen. Maybe both these things are at play. I never took biology. Tech was always my thing. Now one more minute to go.

You wanted to get intimate tonight. I said no, even though I wanted to, one last time. You looked surprised. You see, I don't have time. Neither do I want to leave any traces. By the way, I never had a chance to ask you. How was I compared to him? I am no stud. I don't have a six-pack or a six-feet-tall body. I don't even have six inches of you-know-what. Is he big? I don't know why am I thinking about this. Okay, seven minutes done. Bye, Zara.

I remember releasing my grip. The bruises showed dark red on her neck, like a bunch of nasty, oversized hickeys. I placed her body in the centre of the bed and switched on the table lamp.

I had come to her room at 1:50 a.m. I checked the time. It was 2:45 a.m. I congratulated myself on what I had achieved in fifty-five minutes. I had chatted, pretended to fall asleep and murdered. All in under an hour. I am not only smart, I am also super-efficient.

According to my calculations, I had to leave by 3:30 a.m. But I had a few more things to do before that. First, I picked up Zara's iPhone. I placed her thumb on the touch ID. Her fingers felt like sticks of ice. The phone opened on first try, though.

I messaged the person who I knew would respond like a loyal pup. I started a chat with Keshav Rajpurohit. He had an idiotic profile picture of himself with his fat friend. I sent him a message.

'So you don't even wish me anymore?'

He did not respond. I sent another one.

'It's my birthday. I hope you remember.'

As I waited for Keshav to reply, I rearranged the bed. I shifted

Zara from side to side and changed the bed-sheet. She always kept fresh ones in her closet. I folded up the used one and tossed it into my backpack. I picked up the phone again. There were blue ticks now and I saw he was online. I knew it! I knew this lovelorn idiot wouldn't sleep on Zara's birthday. I sent him another set of messages.

'Just was surprised you didn't wish me.'

'Anyway. Don't know why I was thinking of you.'

'I guess you are busy.'

He didn't reply. I checked the time. I had to leave in twenty minutes. In desperation, I sent a few more.

'Are you there?'

'I miss you.'

A minute later, I saw him typing.

'Wow. Really?' he replied.

'Excellent. The fish is biting,' I said to myself. Ten minutes of mushy bullshit later, he was on his way to come wish Zara in her room.

With loyal pup on the way, it was time to make my exit. I picked up Zara's phone and powered it off. I switched it back on again. This time the phone insisted on a passcode. That would take care of anyone trying to open it with her thumb. I placed the phone back to charge. I wiped anything I might have touched with sanitiser and tissue, and tossed all the used tissues in my backpack. I opened the window. Delhi's cold February breeze hit my face. I checked the time—3:04 a.m. I am James Bond, I told myself, as I grabbed a branch of the mango tree and made my exit.

I walked out onto the Outer Ring Road. I was not stupid enough to take an Uber and leave a trail. I rubbed my hands in the cold as I waited for an auto. Ten minutes later, I found one.

'Airport,' I said to the auto driver.

'Not taking passengers, just going home,' he said.

I took out five purple two thousand-rupee notes and showed them to him.

'What do you think?' I said.

'Sit. What will I do at home?' the auto driver said.

Chapter 29

'Airport?' Saurabh said. He looked confused, as did Safdar and Faiz.

Raghu sat still, staring at the empty chair opposite him.

'I don't understand what is going on,' Safdar said finally. 'He was admitted in a hospital in Hyderabad. I checked with his parents too.'

'Rana obtained his phone records as well. His cell phone tower location was near Apollo Hospital that night,' Saurabh said.

Raghu laughed. He turned to me.

'See, they still don't believe it. Do you see how tight my plan was?'

'Not tight enough, obviously.'

'Bhai, I am serious. Tell us what is going on,' Saurabh wailed.

'Do you have any travel app on your phone?' I said.

'I have Cleartrip and MakeMyTrip. Why?'

'Open any one of them. Search for flights, let's say, for tomorrow night. The route is Hyderabad to Delhi and back the next morning.'

Saurabh worked on his phone for a few seconds.

'There are fifteen direct flights daily,' Saurabh said.

'When is the last flight? Hyderabad to Delhi,' I said.

'IndiGo 6E766 leaves Hyderabad at 11:30 p.m. and reaches Delhi at 1:10 a.m.,' Saurabh said.

I looked at Saurabh and smiled.

'Wow,' Saurabh said. 'I get it. He takes this flight, lands here at 1:10 a.m., goes to IIT.'

'At that time, less than half an hour from the airport.'

'Damn, he snuck away from the hospital,' Saurabh said as he understood Raghu's game plan.

'Yes. Nicely done, isn't it?'

'Oh,' Saurabh said. 'So all those chats you had with Zara that night before she died?'

'Obviously,' I said, 'Raghu.'

'Oh, no,' Saurabh said, as he gave me a concerned look.

'Never mind,' I said. 'Now check the first morning flight from Delhi to Hyderabad.'

'IndiGo 6E765. Leaves Delhi at 4:55 a.m., arrives in Hyderabad at 7:05 a.m.,' Saurabh said.

'He lands back in Hyderabad early morning, so no traffic again and he can reach Apollo in thirty minutes. Back in his bed by 7:45 for sure.'

'Oh,' Faiz said, as he also understood how Raghu had done it. Safdar sat stiffly, still in shock.

'You said his phone location…' Safdar said.

'Oh, yeah,' Saurabh said. 'Rana checked the phone tower location. In fact, he had messaged to wish her at midnight sharp. He showed you the chats when you were at Social.'

'Yeah, I know,' I said.

'Actually, bhai, how did you even suspect—' Saurabh started to ask, but I interrupted him.

'Golu, remember I told you I was going on a trip?'

'Yes, around a week ago.'

'I went to Hyderabad.'

'Why?' Saurabh said.

Chapter 30

One week ago

'You don't have to compare yourself to him. So what if he is super-rich,' I told myself again. I lay in bed but couldn't fall asleep. I had spoken to Raghu in the past as well. It had never caused insomnia before. Was it something he said? Did he make an indirect taunt or insult? I replayed our conversation in my head. I had just called him. Told him we had found out that Faiz had killed Zara. Told him about their affair. Skipped the gory bits like pregnancy kits. He had reacted as expected, cursing Faiz and becoming emotional. Later he thanked me and said everything he had seemed worthless. Life is quite incomplete without her, he had said.

Why was the phrase stuck in my head? It seemed familiar. I repeated it in my mind a few times. I picked up my phone from the bedside table.

I opened my last WhatsApp chat with Zara, one of the most precious things I had in my life. I had gone through this chat dozens of times since that day. I scrolled through it again, until I reached the end and found what I was looking for.

'Life is quite incomplete without you.'

A tremor went through me. No, this could be a coincidence, I told myself. I looked at Saurabh. He was fast asleep.

I lay down again. 'He was in Hyderabad. The hospital confirmed it. The cell phone location confirmed it,' a voice in me countered the thought that had struck me. 'It is Faiz only. Focus.'

I turned in bed, determined to fall asleep, when I had another thought.

If Faiz was looking at divorce lawyers, why would he hurt Zara? That too if he found out she was pregnant? He seemed ready to leave Salma for her.

I sat up again. I opened the Cleartrip app on my phone. I checked for all flights between Hyderabad and Delhi. I sorted the flights by time. Last flight out 11:30 p.m. First flight back 4:55 a.m. Difficult, but doable.

I remembered my earlier chat conversation with Raghu, when he was in San Francisco.

'I am used to it. Do such trips all the time,' he had said.

Maybe I should actually take the flights and check if this is doable, I thought, and switched on a light.

'What happened?' Saurabh said.

'I can't sleep. I need to go somewhere.'

'Huh?' Saurabh said.

❖

I took the same trip he did, only in reverse. I boarded 6E765, the first flight from Delhi to Hyderabad at 4:55 a.m. It landed in Hyderabad at 6:50 a.m., ahead of schedule. As I made my way out of the airport, I noticed several CCTV cameras. Hoping Rana could help me access this footage, I stepped out of the Rajiv Gandhi International Airport at 7:05 a.m. Several drivers offered me a ride to the city. They took cash and did not want any of my details. I took a taxi to Apollo Hospital. With little early morning traffic, I reached the hospital gate at 7:29 a.m. I went into the main lobby and found a common toilet. He could have changed his clothes there to switch back to the green overalls that admitted patients wore in the hospital. I checked the time; it was still 7:33 a.m. I remembered Rana had called Raghu at around 8:45 on the morning of Zara's death. Raghu would have just got back when he received the call. Rana had let me listen in. A nurse had picked up the phone before passing it to Raghu. She had a Christian name.

I took the lift and reached the private rooms on the first floor. If he wanted to leave unnoticed from the hospital, he must have taken the private rooms on the first floor itself so he could leave through a window.

'Yes, sir, how can I help you?' a nurse said to me.

'I had a friend admitted here,' I said. 'He had a nurse attend to him. I would like to meet her. To thank her.'

'What's her name, sir?'

I went blank.

'I am trying to remember. Jenny, no wait, Janie. She had a Telugu accent,' I said.

'Oh, Janie Anthony, sir,' the nurse said. 'She is around. Check the staff canteen. She must have gone for breakfast.'

❖

'Who will forget a patient who leaves a ten thousand-rupee tip, aan?' Janie said, after I showed her Raghu's picture on the phone.

The hospital staff canteen smelled of medu vadas and Dettol. The tiny room had flasks of tea and a small snack counter. All types of hospital staff, including masons, plumbers, compounders, lab attendants, accountants and nurses, occupied the various tables. I sat with Janie at a corner table, so nobody could hear us.

'So you took care of him for what? A week?'

'Five days. When he left, he still had a cast. However, once his tests came out fine, the doctor let him go home.'

'He didn't want me to get stressed, so he never told me everything properly. That's why I came to ask you.'

'Oh, it is ok, sir.'

'What exactly happened to him?'

'Left arm hairline fracture. Bruises on his arms and legs. Twisted ankle.'

'Did he say or do anything unusual during his stay?'

'As in? No, sir. He is a quiet sort of person, as you may know. His parents came to visit him. Otherwise he would rest or sometimes be on his phone.'

'Did he make any calls?'

'Just to his fiancée. I saw her picture. So nice looking. Some Muslim girl. She died, he told me. Very sad.'

'Yes. Zara.'

'It was her birthday it seems, and he was so upset he couldn't be with her. He wanted to be the first to wish her. I still remember. I helped him.'

I looked at her, surprised.

'Helped him?' I said.

'The doctor had instructed Raghu sir to sleep early, no later than 9 p.m. He wanted to wish her at midnight. So I helped him.'

'How?'

'I had night duty. He gave me his unlocked phone. He had already typed a happy birthday message. At exact midnight he told me to just press send. I did, and Zara ma'am had the first wish from Raghu sir. Wasn't he the best boyfriend in the world?'

'Yeah,' I said, letting out a huge breath. 'He definitely was.'

Chapter 31

Raghu clapped, startling everyone.

'What? Someone should appreciate Keshav's hard work,' Raghu said and laughed.

'What's so funny?' Saurabh said.

'I underestimated this idiot,' Raghu said.

'You overestimated yourself, you asshole,' Saurabh said.

'But who beat him up?' Safdar said.

'Uncle, someone who can create a thousand-crore-rupee company can't arrange some goons to do a hit job on himself?' I said.

'Thorough job, fracture and everything,' Saurabh said.

'President's Gold Medal winner, after all,' I said.

'So he gives his phone to Janie, says goodnight, slips out of the window and gets to the airport, flies to Delhi and comes back in a few hours. Air tickets?' Saurabh said.

'In cash, at the airport. Using a printout of a photoshopped Aadhaar card, with his picture and another name,' I said.

'Whoa, he really thought it through,' Saurabh said.

'Smart. Isn't it, Faiz?' I said.

Faiz was staring at Raghu with clenched fists.

'Why, Raghu? Why did you kill her?' Faiz said, his anger barely leashed. Raghu didn't answer.

Faiz stood up. He punched Raghu right in the face. Raghu's mouth began to bleed, his spectacles fell on the floor.

Raghu remained silent. Slowly, he bent to pick his spectacles. As Faiz charged to strike another blow, Raghu signalled him to stop.

'This doesn't hurt. I can take it. I hired men to give me a fracture, remember?' Raghu said.

Safdar stood up then as if coming out of a coma and said in a hushed voice, 'She loved you so much.'

Raghu did not answer.

'Why did you kill my little girl?' Safdar said in the same low voice, as if wanting only to understand.

Raghu smirked.

'Because what she did had killed me.'

Chapter 32

Raghu speaks—II

'Let's sleep, Zara.'

'Five minutes, I promise,' she said.

I turned on my side to avoid the light from her phone. I had to wake up early for a meeting in office. Zara was on a four-day trip to Hyderabad, and we had just come back from dinner at the Taj Falaknuma Palace to celebrate making her a partner in my company. I wanted her in my arms.

I turned to her after a while.

'Five minutes are up.'

'Yeah,' she said absently, eyes still on her phone. She had a smile on her face.

'So, come.'

'Coming,' she said. She stroked my hair with her left hand as she continued to type with her right.

'Who are you messaging?'

'Someone on Insta. She read my blog and doesn't agree with it. Just a bit of a debate with her.'

'Seriously, Zara.'

I wanted her. I had missed her body next to mine.

'You close your eyes,' she said, patting my head.

I turned away from her again. I stared at the wall clock. Ten minutes later, I turned my head to watch her from the corner of my eye. She grinned as she typed a message. Who grins like that when they talk to a random stranger on the internet?

Ten more minutes and she shut her phone and slid into bed. I turned away from her. She held me from behind.

'It's easier if you spoon me,' she said.

I pretended to be asleep.

'I am sorry, baby,' Zara murmured.

I turned around. She moved into position for me to spoon her.

'This is the best place in the world for me,' Zara said.

I placed my hand on her back, slowly sliding it to her chest.

She held my hand and moved it away from her breasts. I tried again. Again she removed my hand.

'Can we just hold each other tonight?' she said, turning to look at me.

Her beautiful almond eyes shone bright. How could I say no to them?

'Sure,' I said.

'Goodnight, love,' she said and pecked me on the cheek.

She fell asleep in minutes, leaving me wide awake and worried. I had found Zara's behaviour odd for weeks. When her breathing turned rhythmic, I leaned over to her bedside table and picked up her iPhone. She did not move.

I brought her phone near her hand, took her thumb, and grazed it on the iPhone's touch ID. In a flash, the phone unlocked. I climbed off the bed and went to the bathroom.

❖

I opened Zara's WhatsApp in the bathroom.

Right on top was a chat between Zara and Captain Faiz. I scrolled up to a conversation from three days ago.

'Are you tense?' Faiz said.

'Somewhat. Not in full panic mode yet.'

'Don't worry. It's nothing.'

'My periods are never this late.'

'I pulled out. You checked the calendar too.'

'I know ... but ... Worried ☹'

'My darling, you are fine.'

'Should I take a test? Prega News or something.'

'Don't overreact.'

'Why not? I am two weeks late.'

'Give it a few more days. Say a week?'

'Can we do a test when I am back from Hyderabad?'

'Sure.'

'Sorry to put you through this.'

'My fault too.'

'No, I insisted you not use protection. I wanted to feel you.'

I went weak. I clasped the phone hard to prevent it from slipping from my hand.

I scrolled down to the more recent chats. The latest one was from tonight. This was what Zara was actually doing when she said she was in a debate with some blog reader.

'How's Hyderabad?' Faiz had messaged.

'It's good. Just had a lovely dinner with Raghu at a restored palace.'

'Hmmm.'

'What?'

'Am I allowed to say I am jealous?'

'No.'

'Okay. I won't.'

'We decided, Faiz. It's over.'

'I know.'

'You have a family. Kids.'

'I know. But for you, I can change that.'

'Let's not talk like that, please.'

'I miss you, my little baby.'

'What did you do today?'

'I went to Khan Market. Bought Prega News.'

'You did?'

'Yeah. Ten packets.'

'Ten?!'

'Yeah. The chemist looked at me like I run a harem or something.'

'Lol. Can't believe you bought ten!!'

'Because I want you to double check and be calm.'

'More like a deca-check. ☺☺☺'

'Come back soon and we can test it.'

'Okay. Thanks, by the way. That's very sweet of you.'

'Just doing what I have to.'

'I am sure it is nothing.'

'Yeah. Me too. But listen…'

'Yeah, Faiz?'

'What if there is something?'

'Please don't say that.'

'Just imagine how cute our kid will be. With such beautiful parents.'

'Hahahahaha.'

Zara, good to know what you find funny these days, I thought.

'Two beautiful Kashmiris. Giving birth to a beautiful Kashmiri angel,' Faiz had said.

'Faiz!'

'Shh, Zara. Just dream with me for a moment. Can you grant me that?'

'You are crazy!'

'Yes, I am. So, say, boy or girl?'

'Girl. Of course. And my brains. Not yours.'

'Shut up.'

'Hahahaha.'

'And looks?'

'I'm okay if looks are on dad. He's mighty handsome.'

'Aww. Thank you.'

'Okay, need to go. It is late. Raghu is calling me.'

'Stay.'

'What?'

'Have my baby.'

'What?'

'Even if you are with Raghu. At least our child will be super good-looking. With him, you never know!! ;) ;)'

'What!! Faiz! Shut up!😂😂'

She had asked Faiz to shut up. She had also added tears of laughter emojis. Fuck, the emojis, man. They change everything, don't they?

'Well, you don't want Raghu's looks for your kids, do you? All black black ugly ugly.'

'Shut up, you racist captain sahib! ☺☺'

'So, at least keep a good Kashmiri gene pool.'

'How many pegs, Faiz?'

'None. Honest.'

'Goodnight. And bring those kits with you next time we meet.'

'Wait…'

'Goodnight.'

The chat had ended after that.

I looked at myself in the bathroom mirror. Sure, I am dark-skinned, or 'all black black' as Faiz calls my future kids. 'All black black ugly ugly,' he said. Funny, isn't it? I don't know, I am not finding it funny. But Zara did .

Is this what a loser looks like? Am I a classic example of what the guys back at IIT used to call me—a chutiya? My girlfriend fucks a fauji on the side, doesn't use protection, could be pregnant by him and, at least in digital emoji form, laughs hysterically when told my kids could be 'all black black, ugly ugly'.

'And what am I doing about it?' I asked the person in the mirror. Fucking nothing. In fact, I am scared. I am worried that Zara might wake up and find out I opened her phone. What will happen if I confront her about her cheating? What if she walks out? Will a loser like me ever get a girl like Zara again? More than being angry with her, I am still scared about losing her, despite what she did. Textbook definition of loser, isn't it?

❖

I went back to the bedroom. Put the phone on the bedside table on Zara's side. Zara, fast asleep, had not moved from her position.

I lay down in bed and stared at the wall clock and thought about Faiz and Zara, Zara and Faiz, the entire night.

❖

'Hot idlis and coffee,' Zara said, 'just the way you like it.'

'You didn't have to wake up,' I said. I sipped my filter coffee, something Zara had now learnt to make almost as well as my amma.

'I wanted to say sorry about last night,' Zara said. 'I was just tense.'

'Why?'

'I wanted to tell you. I am a bit late.'

Of course, honey, I already know, I wanted to say, but didn't.

'Oh,' I said. 'You think there's a chance?'

'Last month when you came to Delhi,' Zara said, 'I was mid-cycle.'

'But I used protection. I always do.'

'Then, what else? Unless it is a hormonal imbalance. No other possibility.'

How about you riding an Army man's gun, I wanted to ask. I took a bite of an idli instead.

'What do we do? Anything I can do?' I said.

'I will work it out. Just wanted you to know for now,' Zara said, refilling my coffee tumbler.

'Let me know if you need anything,' I said.

'Sure.'

I stood up to leave for office.

'Raghu,' she called from behind. Is she going to confess, I wondered, tensing up.

'Yeah?' I turned towards her.

'You know how you always talk about us taking the next step and settling down?'

'Yes.'

'Let's get engaged. I am ready,' Zara said. She smiled and hugged me.

Of course you are, honey, of course you are, I thought, and hugged her back.

❖

Safdar Lone spared no expense for his only daughter's engagement. He covered his entire house with flowers and lights. My parents had come from Hyderabad with a dozen relatives. They never said a word when I told them Zara was Muslim. How would they say no to their favourite son? Didn't I achieve whatever they wanted me to achieve? I slipped the three-carat solitaire ring onto Zara's delicate finger. She looked ethereal in a green lehenga. She placed a ring on my black black ugly ugly finger too.

'When is the nikaah?' one of Zara's aunts asked Safdar.

'It's up to them,' he said.

Zara looked into my eyes, as if trying to find an answer. She couldn't. She had no idea what was going on in my mind. Here's what I was thinking: Zara, why are you getting engaged to me? So that if you are pregnant, you can marry me and make me raise Faiz's child? Is that your plan? What would that make me? A cuckold?

'Whatever Zara says, uncle,' I said.

'Abba, not uncle,' one of Zara's aunts reminded me and laughed. I nodded and smiled. I will change my religion. I will give her half my equity stake. I will work day and night. I will call Zara's father abba. I will do all this to make Zara happy. What will she do in return? Make me raise a bastard.

'Next month?' Zara said. I looked at her, surprised.

'Really?' I said. 'So fast?'

'Or as soon as we can. I want to leave all this behind. I have had enough of India. I can't deal with Saxena, these relatives and all the noise and pollution.'

'Okay,' I said.

My mind continued to churn. If I break up with her, what if she doesn't give the stake back? I am her nominee, but if she is alive, she can hold on to it. Damn, what will I do then?

'Let's make a fresh start,' Zara was saying into my ear.

'Yes, soon all this will be over,' I said, and patted her hand.

Chapter 33

Safdar looked at Raghu and Faiz, gobsmacked. Saurabh and I waited as Raghu paused in his story to drink water. He finished the whole glass in one gulp and spoke again.

'I know all of you are emotional right now. But if you look at it logically and from my point of view, I had little choice, guys.'

Everyone looked at Raghu, shocked. He continued.

'Here were my options. Option one, I am the idiot who raises a bastard. Option two, I break up with her and bear the pain of her loss while she walks away with her lover and half my company. Both ways I am screwed for life.'

Faiz cleared his throat, as if wanting to say something at this point, but Raghu went on speaking.

'Thus, my only option was a third one. Eliminate Zara. If I did it well, I would never get caught. I would lose Zara, but I had lost her already. Zara would get her punishment. Faiz would suffer. I would get my company back. If the plan worked, this idiot Keshav would be found on the scene and create enough confusion to keep me safe. Hell, he almost ended up getting Faiz jailed. Sweet justice. It all almost did work, but...'

'But I got you,' I said. 'Last night, when I landed in Delhi, Rana told me they have the CCTV footage from Hyderabad airport. Just a matter of time before they find a person with a cast and backpack who looks like you.'

'Well done, I already told you. I clapped too. What else do you want? A Nobel Prize?' Raghu said, his voice irritated.

'She wasn't pregnant,' Faiz said in a firm voice, looking at the table.

Everyone turned to Faiz.

'What?' Raghu said.

'No. It was a real scare, but she wasn't pregnant. And she wasn't trying to marry you so soon because she wanted you to raise my child.'

Faiz covered his face with his palms and broke down then.

'You guys know why we became so close?' Faiz said, crying.

He took out his phone and showed us a selfie of Zara and Sikander with the machine gun.

'This is the same picture we found in Zara's Pak phone,' Saurabh mumbled to me.

'Zara came to me with this picture,' Faiz said.

'Why?' Safdar said.

'She had tried to get Sikander to change, leave his terrorist activities, but he wouldn't listen. Zara told me she had found out that Sikander had stockpiled guns in a hotel room in Old Delhi. For a potential terror plot in the capital.'

'How did she find out?' I said.

'She won Sikander's trust; convinced him she had changed her mind about what he was doing. He told her about the grand plan to hit the capital. She played along. He took her to the storage location. That's where she took the picture.'

'That's what I felt too about this photo, that Zara was smiling for a reason,' Saurabh said.

'What happened then?' Safdar said.

'I wanted to report it to the authorities. However, Zara had a condition. She wanted me to foil the plot but spare Sikander,' Faiz said.

'What did you do?' I said.

'My first mistake, I agreed. What else could I have done? I had fallen in love with Zara by then,' Faiz said, gaze still down to avoid any eye contact.

'Love, my foot. You didn't think of Salma? The kids?' Safdar said.

'I don't know. I had always wanted her even before Salma. But she was dating Keshav, and never gave me any attention then. It was only now, when I found her vulnerable, I was able to get her.'

'Vulnerable?' I said.

'You guys had broken up, and yet you used to get drunk

and call her, all miserable. Meanwhile, she had chosen Raghu as a stable option. Which is what she said she wanted. However, every now and then, and especially after your calls, she missed the craziness she had with you. I gave her that. And had her, at least for a while.'

'It is shameful what you did,' Safdar said.

Faiz did not answer.

'Complete what you were saying about Sikander and the guns,' I said.

'I took five men from my Army unit at night. We shot the two men who were guarding the stockpile. However, I let Sikander go,' Faiz said.

'What happened next?' I said.

'We handed the guns and ammunition to the police. They happily took credit. A small news item came on the arms haul the next day.'

'No wonder she liked you, doing these daredevil acts, even though illegal,' Raghu said, without looking at Faiz either.

'She liked me because I actually cared for her and gave her the passion and attention she missed,' Faiz said.

'While you were married,' Raghu said.

Faiz didn't respond.

'Anything else, Faiz?' I said.

'I took money too. Second mistake,' Faiz said. He closed his eyes and scrunched them hard, as if he found it difficult to make this confession.

'Sikander sent me a gift. Gold biscuits. I kept them. You don't really make much as an Army officer. I thought, if I get divorced, I might have to give a lot of what I have to Salma. The gold from Sikander would give Zara and me a good life.'

'Gaddaar. Not just to my family, but also to the country,' Safdar said.

'I am not a gaddaar!' Faiz shouted. 'I saved my country from a major terror attack. And I would have left Salma and married

Zara. Done the right thing,' Faiz said. His entire frame shook. 'I have lost everything.'

'Don't expect any sympathy,' Safdar said.

'I got tempted. I will surrender the gold biscuits to the police,' Faiz said.

Saurabh took out the plastic bag with shiny yellow biscuits from his backpack.

'You mean these?' Saurabh said.

'What the…' Faiz's pink face turned pomegranate red.

'Long story,' I said. 'And you don't have to surrender the biscuits to anyone. We will ensure they reach your Army seniors.'

'But—' Faiz began, before Raghu interrupted him.

'You used her. She was weak when it came to her stepbrother, and you used that,' Raghu said.

'No. Zara and I had something real.'

'Zara loved me,' Raghu said. 'Not you.'

'You never had time for her. You say you built the company for her, but you never gave her your time,' Faiz said.

'My company is all I have. And it was for us. She should have understood…' Raghu said, his voice trailing off.

'She did understand. And she regretted what we did,' Faiz said. 'She ended our relationship. Didn't want me to divorce my wife. She just wanted to get away. Make a fresh start with you.'

'But you had an affair!'

'It was a mistake, yes. But you don't murder people for that.'

'You have no idea how it feels—' Raghu said as the sound of a siren interrupted him.

'That should be Inspector Rana and his team,' I said.

'Are you serious?' Raghu said.

I shrugged.

'You committed the crime. You have to pay for it.'

Raghu looked at Saurabh and me.

'How about I give both of you more money than you would ever earn in your life?' Raghu said.

'What?' I said.

'All you have to do is tell the police to take Faiz. He's a crook. Let him rot in jail.'

Faiz stood up, frowning.

'Ten million dollars. Five for your friend. Deal?' Raghu said to me, his face dead serious.

I walked up to Raghu and grabbed his collar.

'She left me. For a sick person like you. Son of a bitch,' I said.

Inspector Rana entered the room just then with two cops.

'What's going on here?' Rana said.

'Inspector sahib,' I said. 'Time to replace the watchman with a millionaire.'

❖

I turned around on the backseat of the police jeep to look at the van behind us.

'Don't worry. He can't run away. That happens only in the movies,' Rana said.

Saurabh and I were in the inspector's Gypsy, driving towards Hauz Khas police station. Rana, who sat in the front, had a permanent grin on his face.

'Keshav,' Rana said.

'Yes, sir.'

'You guys are good. You never gave up. Well done.'

'Thanks, sir,' I said. Saurabh and Rana smiled.

'There's no traffic. You could drive faster,' I said to the driver, who was moving at the pace of a bullock cart.

'It's okay. I told him to go slow,' Rana said.

'Why?' I said.

Rana winked at us in the rear-view mirror.

'Gives enough time for the media to arrive,' he said.

'Of course,' Saurabh said.

Tomorrow morning, Rana would be the star cop in Delhi. Which other inspector had the guts to release a watchman and toss a multi-millionaire into jail?

'I am thinking double promotion,' Rana said, his back to us.

'Not triple?' Saurabh said.

'What?' Rana said. Before he could get the sarcasm, his phone rang. The Delhi Police PR department had called to assure him that the entire Delhi media was on its way.

As Rana spoke on the phone, I stared out of the window at the full moon.

'Bhai,' Saurabh said.

'Yeah?' I said.

'Congrats.'

'Yeah. To you too,' I said, my voice soft.

'Are you happy?'

'Yes, I am.'

'Why don't you sound happy? You found out who the killer was!'

'I also found out something else.'

'What?'

'She didn't miss me on her last day. All those chats didn't come from her. She was already dead.'

'Yeah,' Saurabh said. 'Raghu sent them.'

'I wish I hadn't found that out.'

A tear fell from my eye, even as I tried to hide it by leaning my face out of the window.

❖

Loud noise and flashing lights greeted us at the police station.

'Rana sir, look left,' said a photographer.

'Rana sir, right pose, please,' said another one.

'Rana sir, ABP news, first statement here, please,' a reporter said.

The yelling from media persons, the clicking of cameras and the hundreds of flashbulbs overwhelmed us as we stepped out of the Gypsy. I heard Inspector Rana speak to one of the reporters at the police station entrance.

'I am happy to say we have solved the Zara Lone murder case. The murderer is Raghu Venkatesh, Zara Lone's fiancé and owner of a tech company in Hyderabad. As you can see, the courageous Delhi Police is not scared of arresting rich people. Mr Raghu Venkatesh is under arrest. Watchman Laxman Reddy will be released immediately.'

❖

I had woken up at 4 a.m. to reach the cemetery at 5; early enough so nobody would see me.

I placed a white rose, Zara's favourite flower, on her tombstone.

'I don't know if I mattered as much to you, but you did mean a lot to me,' I said. I sank to my knees. I bowed and touched my forehead to the ground.

'I loved you, Zara,' I said, 'perhaps too much. Thank you. For showing me what love is all about. And thank you for also teaching me to never love someone too much.'

I stood up to leave.

'Goodbye, Zara. I unlove you.'

Chapter 34

Three months later

'A little higher,' I said.

The carpenter and his assistant raised the sign above the shop by six inches. I read it out loud.

'Z Detectives'.

Saurabh had suggested the name of our new agency. We had rented a small, hundred-square feet shop in Malviya Nagar. We had also created a webpage and social media accounts for Z Detectives.

'Tell me again the logic behind that name?' I said, sitting on one of the two wooden chairs in our agency.

'Z is the last letter of the alphabet. The ultimate one. Like Z class security given to VVIPs is the ultimate one. Sounds cool too,' Saurabh said.

'That's why you called it Z?' I said, one eyebrow up.

'You are a detective too, figure it out,' Saurabh said.

I smiled.

'I never liked her at first, for what she did to you. But I realise she was human after all. And it is she who led us to a new path in life. She deserves this little tribute,' Saurabh said.

'Thank you,' I said, and ruffled Saurabh's hair.

'Now, how can we have a shop opening without any sweets? Wait, I will call this new mithai shop. You have to try their jalebis.'

❖

'So you have a detective agency on the side?' Carl Jones, senior VP at CyberSec asked me. I sat in their office in Gurgaon, which had a pollution-tinted view of the metro track outside.

'Yes. My friend Saurabh and I started it. We had helped the police on the Zara Lone case. Just enjoy it as a hobby. He is also interviewing with you, by the way.'

'We heard about the Zara case. The IIT girl, right? Anyway, we are a cyber-security firm. Investigation skills can only help us.'

'We have no formal investigation skills as such.'

'So, what do you think helped you solve the case?'

'Just a curious and open mind, without any prejudice. And an attitude of never giving up.'

'Just those qualities can get you quite far. Not just for a case, but even in life,' Carl said.

'Thank you, sir. I am also learning that.'

'Still, I want to know your thinking. Tell me how exactly did you go about solving the case.'

❖

'Yes?' Chandan said.

Saurabh and I were in his office, facing him. He was checking the accounts sheets on his desk, and not looking up.

'We need to talk to you,' Saurabh said.

'I don't have time. And what are you doing here? Go teach.'

'We are quitting,' I said. 'We have another offer. From a leading cyber-security firm.'

'And we get to solve cases on the side too,' Saurabh said.

'What?' Chandan said, looking at us with his mouth open and gutkha quite visible.

'And you are disgusting. You suck,' Saurabh said and stood up.

'He didn't mean that,' I said and stood up as well.

'Of course I fucking did,' Saurabh said.

'Okay, maybe he did. Fuck you, Chandan. Bye,' I said.

❖

We sat in my bedroom late at night. Saurabh was on his phone. We had just finished a six-pack dinner, which contrary to its fitness-related name, involved cooking six packs of Maggi noodles.

Saurabh looked up from his phone and gave me a wide grin.

'Why so happy?' I said.

'New match on Tinder.'

'A real one?'

'Yes. Software engineer. She loves the fact that we are detectives.'

'We?'

'I told her about you too.'

'And?'

'We are meeting for drinks at Hauz Khas Village in an hour. She's bringing her best friend with her. Get ready, Mr Detective.'

***

About the Author

Chetan Bhagat is one of India's most acclaimed contemporary authors, with fourteen bestselling books to his credit. He is the author of ten blockbuster novels—*Five Point Someone, One Night @ the Call Center, The 3 Mistakes of My Life, 2 States, Revolution 2020, Half Girlfriend, One Indian Girl, The Girl in Room 105, One Arranged Murder* and *400 Days*, and most recently, *12 Years: My Messed-Up Love Story*—and four successful non-fiction titles—*What Young India Wants, Making India Awesome, India Positive* and *11 Rules for Life*. Chetan's books have remained bestsellers since their release. Many of his novels have been adapted into successful Bollywood films such as *3 Idiots, 2 States, Kai Po Che* and *Half Girlfriend*.

The New York Times called him the 'the biggest-selling English-language novelist in India's history'. *Time* magazine recognized him amongst the '100 most influential people in the world', while Fast Company, USA, listed him as one of the world's '100 most creative people in business'. Chetan writes columns for leading English and Hindi newspapers, focusing on youth and national development issues. He is also a motivational speaker, screenplay writer, YouTuber and podcaster.

Chetan quit his international investment-banking career in 2009 to dedicate his time entirely to writing and driving positive change in the country.

Chetan studied at IIT Delhi and IIM Ahmedabad. He is married to Anusha, an ex-classmate from IIMA, and they have twin boys, Shyam and Ishaan.

BESTSELLERS BY CHETAN BHAGAT

FICTION

400 Days

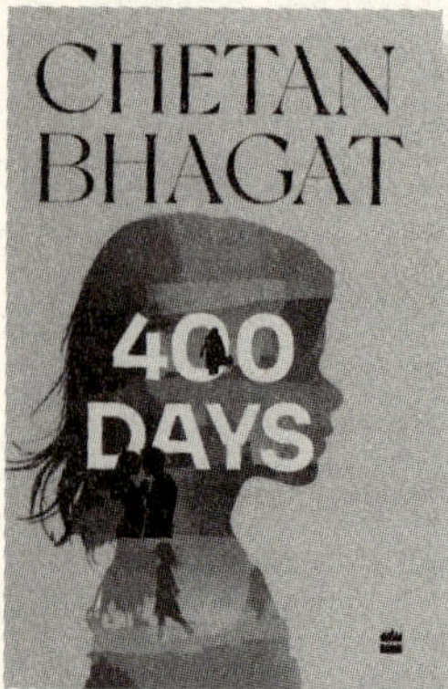

Hi, I am Keshav Raj Purohit and I am a disappointment to everyone around me.

I live with my parents, who keep telling me how I should:

a) get married,

b) focus on my IPS exams,

c) meet more people, and

d) close my detective agency.

But Alia Arora, neighbour and ex-model, wanted my help. And I couldn't take my eyes off her face ... I mean ... her case.

'My daughter Siya was kidnapped. Nine months ago,' Alia said. The police had given up. They called it a cold case. Even the rest of her family had stopped searching. Alia wouldn't stop looking, though. She wanted to know if I could help her.

Welcome to *400 Days*. A mystery and romance story like no other. An unputdownable tale of suspense, human relationships, love, friendship, the crazy world we live in and, above all, a mother's determination to never give up. From India's highest-selling author comes a page-turner that will not only keep you glued to the story but also touch you deeply.

One Arranged Murder

'Ever since you found Prerna, I lost my best friend ...'

Hi, this is Keshav, and Saurabh, my best friend, flatmate, colleague and business partner, won't talk to me. Because I made fun of him and his fiancé.

Saurabh and Prerna will be getting married soon. It is an arranged marriage. However, there is more cheesy romance between them than any love-marriage couple.

On Karva Chauth, she fasted for him. She didn't eat all day. In the evening, she called him and waited on the terrace for the moon and for Saurabh to return to break her fast. Excited, Saurabh ran up the steps of her three-storey house. But when he reached ...

Keshav has set up an investigation agency with his best friend, Saurabh. Can the two amateur detectives successfully solve another murder case that affects them personally? And where will it leave their friendship?

Welcome to *One Arranged Murder*, an unputdownable thriller from India's highest-selling author. A story about love, friendship, family and crime. It will keep you entertained and hooked right till the end.

The Girl in Room 105: An Unlove Story

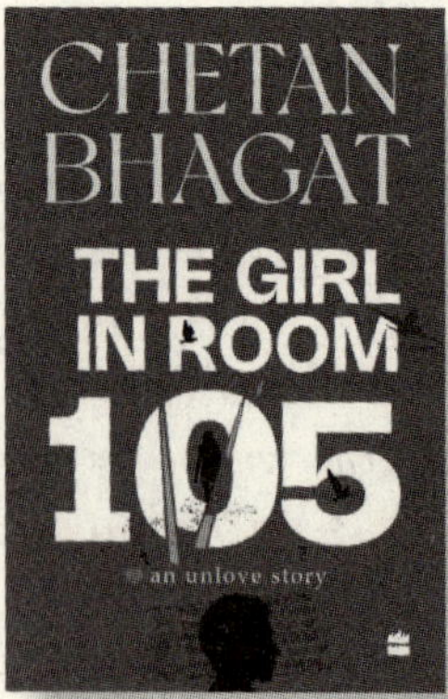

Hi, I'm Keshav, and my life is screwed.

I hate my job and my girlfriend left me. Ah, the beautiful Zara. Zara is from Kashmir. She is Muslim. And did I tell you that my family is a bit, well, traditional? Anyway, leave that aside.

Zara and I broke up four years ago. She moved on in life. I didn't. I drank every night to forget her. I called, messaged, and stalked her on social media. She just ignored me.

However, that night, on the eve of her birthday, Zara messaged me. She called me over, like old times, to her hostel room 105. I shouldn't have gone, but I did ... and my life changed forever.

This is not a love story. It is an unlove story. From the author of *Five Point Someone* and *2 States*, comes a fast-paced, funny and unputdownable thriller about obsessive love and finding purpose in life against the backdrop of contemporary India.

12 Years: My Messed-Up Love Story

He's 33. She's 21.

He's a struggling stand-up comic. She's a rising star in private equity.

He's divorced. She's never had a boyfriend.

He's Punjabi. She's from a conservative Jain family.

They shouldn't be together. But they can't stay apart.

Welcome to *12 Years: My Messed-Up Love Story.*

Saket and Payal couldn't be more different—age, background, beliefs. Yet, they're drawn to each other in ways they can't explain. Is it just chemistry, or something deeper? Is it madness and lust, or is it love?

Unputdownable and thoroughly entertaining, *12 Years* tries to answer the eternal question: How do you know if someone is *the one*—especially when everything says they're not?

From India's top-selling writer Chetan Bhagat comes a powerful new love story that will make you laugh, cry and rethink everything you know about love.

11 Rules for Life: Secrets to Level Up

MANDATORY READING FOR ALL INDIANS

One summer afternoon, Viraj, a food delivery guy, brings lunch for an author named Chetan. He is late and appears to be in distress. When Chetan asks him what the matter is, Viraj breaks down.

'I hate my life. My career is going nowhere. My girlfriend left me. I have no future,' he says.

The author offers Viraj a deal. 'I can fix this for you. Come back every day, when I order lunch. Each day, I will tell you one secret I've learnt about life.'

Welcome to *11 Rules for Life*, a no-holds-barred book that will transform your life.

In his most personal book yet, Chetan draws on his failures and triumphs, his many conversations with high achievers from all walks of life and over two decades as a celebrated motivational speaker.

Written in the inimitable style that has made Chetan one of India's top-selling writers, this inspiring, easy-to-read and straight-talking guide will help you rewire your brain for success in today's ultra-competitive and unfair world.

Ready to live your best life? If one book can change your life, this is it.

All these titles are also available in Hindi.

HarperCollins *Publishers* India

At HarperCollins India, we believe in telling the best stories and finding the widest readership for our books in every format possible. We started publishing in 1992; a great deal has changed since then, but what has remained constant is the passion with which our authors write their books, the love with which readers receive them, and the sheer joy and excitement that we as publishers feel in being a part of the publishing process.

Over the years, we've had the pleasure of publishing some of the finest writing from the subcontinent and around the world, including several award-winning titles and some of the biggest bestsellers in India's publishing history. But nothing has meant more to us than the fact that millions of people have read the books we published, and that somewhere, a book of ours might have made a difference.

As we look to the future, we go back to that one word—a word which has been a driving force for us all these years.

Read.

Harper Collins Harper Sport HARPER FICTION HARPER NON-FICTION हार्पर हिन्दी

HARPER LEARNING HARPER VANTAGE HCCB HARPERCOLLINS CHILDREN'S BOOKS 4th HARPER PERENNIAL

HARPER DESIGN BOOKTOPUS HARPER BUSINESS